The OTHER
SIDE OF
MRS. WOOD

The OTHER SIDE OF MRS. WOOD

 A NOVEL

Lucy Barker

HARPER

An Imprint of HarperCollins*Publishers*

THE OTHER SIDE OF MRS. WOOD. Copyright © 2023 by Lucy Barker. All rights reserved. Printed in the United States of America. No part of this book may be used or reproduced in any manner whatsoever without written permission except in the case of brief quotations embodied in critical articles and reviews. For information, address HarperCollins Publishers, 195 Broadway, New York, NY 10007.

HarperCollins books may be purchased for educational, business, or sales promotional use. For information, please email the Special Markets Department at SPsales@harpercollins.com.

Originally published in Great Britain in 2023 by 4th Estate, an imprint of HarperCollins Publishers.

Illustrations by Emma Pidsley

FIRST U.S. EDITION

Library of Congress Cataloging-in-Publication Data has been applied for.

ISBN 978-0-06-331731-4

23 24 25 26 27 LBC 5 4 3 2 1

For my dad

Nothing is so firmly believed as what is least known.
Michel Eyquem de Montaigne

While inspired by a true story, most of what follows is
imagined – although exactly how much, who can tell.

The OTHER SIDE OF MRS. WOOD

Excerpt from the Editor's Column
Magnus Clore
Spiritual Times, 30th January 1873

Let us begin by addressing society's recent affliction: the disgrace of Mrs Trimble.

Of all those Mediums who have been exposed as charlatans, this has been, for those who knew and loved her, perhaps the most painful to reconcile: we have believed in the power and abilities of Mrs Trimble for many, many years; we have been enchanted at her table and succoured by her readings. To determine that this woman we perceived to be wholly of truth and honesty has been hoodwinking us all the time is almost unbearable. Her ruin is one I certainly never anticipated but fully support after such disgusting revelations.

I can only hope that Mrs Trimble is the last cherished Medium proven to be false, although I fear that this shall not be the case.

Thank goodness for those Mediums who continue to evidence their gift for the greater good, the unblemished Mrs Wood remaining their standard bearer for excellence, integrity, and truth in her unparalleled work with the spirits. How fortunate we are to enjoy her glorious gift each month at her Grand Séances – those of us who are lucky enough to be offered a seat, that is!

Long may you reign, dear lady.

CHAPTER 1

Mrs Wood's séances took place in the dark, just as all interesting things should.

That evening, as the last candle wavered on the sideboard in the smart Notting Hill villa, London's most influential and affluent believers held their breath. In a few moments, the corridor to the Other Side would open and any one of their desperately missed beloveds might make their way through.

Taffeta shifted and bracelets shivered amidst a flurry of cleared throats but the Great Medium Mrs Wood was in no hurry. She sat calmly in her ornate chair before them all, her flickering shadow cast long against the closed shutters of the bay window behind. She drew in a long, slow breath, her eyes moving easily over the faces turned expectantly back. She was their sun, and they were her blooms.

There were, as usual, twenty-four guests, poised for an evening of spirit and spectacle. Most were patrons, their gems signalling to her in the gloom, but here and there were the unfamiliar faces of those grieving souls who had applied to enter the monthly ballot for one of only eight seats available to the masses at each of her monthly Grand Séances.

Tonight, Mrs Wood looked for those carefully selected eight for whom she had tailored the evening. In the front row, she noted a pocket-eyed woman clutching a *carte de visite*. Beside her sat a man of clearly moderate means, a careless nature betrayed by his unappealingly splayed knees. Behind them she took in the mother and daughter in twee matching dresses, and another man a little further along the row whose jacket was coming unstitched along the left lapel. A well-padded woman sat in the back row, fanning herself with a ringless left hand. And there, in the far corner, a young couple.

Ah.

There they were.

So easy to spot in the end: the only two people in the entire room not staring back at her. Instead, they sat pressed together staring silently into their laps, their sadness so captivating that for a moment she was snared, unable to look away. But then the faintest of coughs by her ear returned her to the room and, drawing in a long breath, she released one last enigmatic smile.

'The candle, Mr Larson,' she said, and her candle-snuffer extraordinaire leapt from his seat at the end of the front row, docking the final flame and plunging the room into a darkness as absolute as death.

Mrs Wood inhaled the collective frisson before exhaling loudly and pronouncing: 'We begin, as always, with the Lord's Prayer. Our Father . . .'

It took only a few moments from the end of the prayer for Mrs Wood to descend into the trance that would link her to the Other Side. After a little humming and a discreet moan, she was ready, opening the door to the first of an entertaining cortège of the dead through her lively spirit guide: the reformed – but still occasionally salty – pirate of the high seas, Jack Starr.

She had learned over the years to pay attention to a séance's emotional journey: too much frivolity and you became a sideshow, but wallow in too much melancholy, and you created a wake. She therefore limited herself to one tragic death per half, keeping an arsenal of livelier spirits on hand for whenever levity was needed. Useless husbands were always good value. Or a gossipy old maid.

And if she needed something quickly, she found dogs to be most reliable. Everyone loved a dog.

That night, however, the dog was not required. The séance flowed flawlessly; a carefully curated rhythm rolling from a husband with a stammer to a sister who asked why her brother had stopped leaving flowers, to touching declarations from a lover swallowed by the sea more than thirty years before, who quoted a beloved poem to a wave of delighted sighs. When the last spectral visitor – a bracing mother-in-law who elicited delighted titters from the room with an enthusiastic rendition of 'Amazing Grace' – bade farewell, Mrs Wood felt a discreet tap on her hand and, with a few delicate moans and a yawn, gathered herself from her trance.

A match was struck, the room blanching as the wick of the candle on the sideboard flared and Miss Newman, Mrs Wood's great friend and séance assistant, took her arm, explaining to the room that it was time for the Great Medium to replenish her energies.

As Mrs Wood made her way from the room, leaning gratefully on Miss Newman, she absorbed her guests' exclamations of satisfaction with a fatigued yet appreciative smile.

While her guests were given champagne and a short window to dissect what they had just seen, Mrs Wood and Miss Newman sat in the privacy of her dressing room on the floor above. Miss Newman was studying her notes in preparation for part two of the séance while Mrs Wood refreshed herself with a glass of champagne, her feet up on the lid of her séance trunk.

'Well,' said Mrs Wood, leaning back. 'I still think there's something fishy.'

Miss Newman looked up. 'Mrs Pickering was delighted to receive a late invitation,' she said patiently. 'Lady Morgan's apologies had no impact on the course of this evening.'

Mrs Wood shook her head and swallowed her champagne. 'It's not that,' she said. 'Lady Morgan seemed so keen when I saw her at the Countess's. And *healthy*.'

'It happens,' said Miss Newman. 'Now,' she said, opening her notebook. 'Mrs Kincaid is . . .'

'People have attended my séances damp with influenza, Sarah,' Mrs Wood continued, her ire brewing. 'The Colonel comes with his gout all the time. And do you remember when we had that Italian woman with the stomach disorder? If you receive an invitation, you attend, no matter what the ailment. It does not bode well for Lady Morgan to think that she's better than that.'

'Violet. Lady Morgan is unwell,' said Miss Newman firmly. 'There's nothing to be done about it.'

But Mrs Wood was not to be assuaged. 'It's this younger generation.' She thumped her glass onto the side-table. 'They're so easily felled. I bet Lady Morgan has nothing more than a sniffle.'

The final threads of Miss Newman's patience gave way and she snapped her notebook shut. 'Violet, *please*,' she said.

'But you know how influential she is amongst those young things, Sarah. The Green girls are all extremely interested in her.'

'You're making far too much of it.'

'I wish I could agree,' she said under her breath. How she envied Miss Newman for not knowing the truth of their situation. As loyal as they were, there was no ignoring the cold fact that those important patrons, her countesses and ladies, no longer drew the gaze of the society pages as they once had. When she had been starting out these were the women who were never out of view, their every move – including visits to Mrs Wood's séances – recorded for all of London to read. Now, instead of discussions around their gowns or companions, her

4

countesses and ladies were more likely to attract oblique references to ailments and hearty commendations for having braved an icy pavement. The truth was that if she wanted to continue in her position, clients like Lady Morgan were essential: young women with influence, and wealth, who could keep her séance room fresh and interesting, and soften the financial blow that the inevitable loss of those older patrons would wield.

She needed women like Lady Morgan so that she could continue to survive.

Energy hissed in her veins from the work of the séance, coddling with the nerves that curled themselves around the far more intimate second half of her Grand Séances. The chair felt suddenly too restrictive and she stood up, the speed of her movement releasing a distant chorus of clinks and rattles from her skirts that she instinctively reached down to quell.

She sighed and turned, surprising herself with her reflection in the overmantel mirror. Without thinking, she peered closer, eyes on the lines across her forehead. Was it the light? She put her fingers to her temples and pulled the skin taut. How was it possible that those lines looked even deeper than they had that morning? She tried to smooth a wayward eyebrow without effect. When had they descended into her mother's unruly briars?

In a year, she would be forty.

Forty.

She wished she could say she felt no older than twenty-one, but that would be a lie: every year lay heavy on her bones. Her knee ached and she shook her leg to ease it. She had learned to work around it as much as she could, learned to speak or cough whenever she anticipated a click or pop. But the twinging was unpredictable, and unpredictability was the enemy of everything she did.

Forty.

An old woman.

An old *widow*.

The heat from the grate was suddenly suffocating. 'I need some air!'

'Violet?'

But she was already at the window, whisking the curtains apart, releasing a sheet of frigid air into the room that took her breath away. She was about to throw up the sash when something caught her eye and she stopped short.

'Sarah!' she said, leaning into the pane. 'Sarah: that girl's back again.'

Miss Newman's skirts moved behind her. 'The same one?'

Mrs Wood squinted out into the darkness. She was nothing more than a shape in the dark no man's land between streetlamps, huddled against the Fosters' railings on the opposite side of the street. Just as she had been at last month's Grand Séance. Just as she had the month before, and the month before that. The same place. The same time.

'Should I be worried, do you think?' Mrs Wood said as Miss Newman stood alongside her.

'I'm sure it's nothing,' Miss Newman said but there was something in her voice, a curl to her tone that implied she wasn't sure either. 'Do you want me to send Mr Larson out?'

She paused. Did she?

But then, as though sensing she was being watched, the girl suddenly looked up, her face a moon in the shadows and her eyes locked onto Mrs Wood's. For a moment, they were connected: Mrs Wood and the girl who appeared, seemingly without fail, to simply stand outside her house. The girl she swore she glimpsed outside the homes of her patrons when she was visiting. The girl who always disappeared before anyone could catch her.

And then, the same girl was moving and within a minute she had been swallowed by the swirl of activity on Portobello Road.

'Well,' said Miss Newman. 'Whoever she is, that's her gone for tonight.'

Mrs Wood craned back down the street, trying to catch a final glimpse. 'She must want something. Why else would she keep coming back?'

'I'll put money on her being from your ballot,' she said. 'You know how impatient some people can get.'

'They send flowers, Sarah. Hampers of port and cheese. They don't stand out there in all weathers doing nothing.'

But Miss Newman was not to be fazed. 'You'll see. Her name will come up in the ballot, she'll have her evening with you and that'll be the last of her.'

'I hope so,' she said. 'There's something about her. Something . . . Do you feel it?'

Miss Newman gave a little laugh. 'Isn't that more your speciality?' she said with a smile and Mrs Wood felt a momentary ease in her tension. 'Come,' she said, taking her arm. 'There's work to be done.'

Mrs Wood allowed herself to be led back across the room towards the thick heat of the fireside. 'I don't know. I'm all at sixes and sevens tonight,' she said, her skirts giving off distant shimmers of metal on metal and stone on stone as she sat. 'Maybe it's the moon.'

But Miss Newman waved her hand dismissively, collecting her notebook from her seat as she settled opposite, flicking to the page marked with a ribbon. 'Now,' she said, smoothing the book open in her lap. 'First. The widow. Husband?'

'Whiskers,' Mrs Wood said with a nod. 'That recital sketch showed quite a pair.'

Miss Newman's pen hovered over the page. 'And you're certain you identified the right member of his quartet?'

Mrs Wood levelled her with a stare. 'I know the difference between a violin and a cello, dearest.' Then she waved her hand, the interrogation over. 'Right. Next. This Nicholls man,' she said. 'The brother. Fossils.' She patted the small, hidden pocket on her right hip and nodded. 'The Countess. Mrs Hart will have a go. Then . . .' She stopped. 'And then . . .' The name caught in her throat.

'William . . .' Miss Newman said quietly.

She swallowed. 'William.' It would be her least favourite moment of the séance but, and she was more than aware of this sad fact, it would be the evening's defining one. '*William*,' she whispered.

A short time later, Miss Newman rang the bell, her sign for Mrs Wood's fellow Medium and Circle Member, Mrs Hart, to chivvy the guests back into the séance room.

'The table is about to begin, ladies and gentlemen!' Mrs Hart called, but Mrs Wood's guests needed little encouragement to put down their glasses. Everyone knew that the second part of the Grand Séances was even better than the first. They spilled greedily back through the doors of the séance room to find it transformed in their absence. Whilst they had refreshed themselves on champagne and gossip, Mr Larson had been humping the furniture around, replacing the rows of chairs in the centre of the room with the Great Medium's vast round séance table. Half of the chairs had been pushed into a semicircle around the back of the room while the other half had been set at the table, ready to receive the rears of the guests who had been chosen by Jack Starr, the salty spirit guide, to join the table and receive personal messages from the spirit world.

It was Mrs Hart's job to pass on the invitation from Jack, and she carried it out with customary aplomb, announcing the names of the selected few and leading them to their seats with Barnum-level pageantry. Those who had not been called received her most *sincere* apologies and a place within the semicircle of seats, prioritising the best views of the Medium – should the candle be lit – to patrons.

That night, the allocation of seats went as smoothly as ever and, once everyone had settled, Mr Larson began arabesquing his way around the room damping the candles until only the one on the sideboard behind Mrs Wood's chair remained.

And then, Mrs Wood and Miss Newman returned, refreshed and reinvigorated in a waft of subtly applied jasmine scent. Mrs Hart guided her into her chair lit by the light of the single candle before taking her own seat beside Mrs Reynolds, another member of Mrs Wood's spiritual circle, whose gentle nature was essential for offering comfort to a sitter who might be especially upset.

'What a lovely table,' she said with a smile. 'Jack has chosen well.' And the room held a collective breath while Mrs Wood settled herself, holding her skirts carefully to avoid any tell-tale noises. She inhaled slowly, taking a moment to refamiliarise herself with the faces now surrounding her. This was her world, she thought as she felt her blood settle from the nonsense with the strange girl outside. This was *her* domain.

She exhaled and smiled at the table.

In addition to those two members from her Circle, Mrs Reynolds and Mrs Hart, the table comprised of two of her favourite patrons, the Dowager Lady Gregory and her daughter Lady Harrington, alongside the widow from the front row. She sat nervously fiddling with her *carte* while, next to her, the man with the shabby jacket skewered his ear expertly and inspected the contents with unsettling interest. He was next to a monocled man who was whispering with a thin-lipped woman. Then came the glittering Countess casting faintly appalled glances at the ear-excavating man opposite, with the young, sad couple carefully positioned between the disinterest of the Countess and the maternal warmth of Mrs Reynolds.

And then there was Mrs Hart and the Great Medium herself.

Twelve sitters.

And the girl.

What?

She shook her head, covering her confusion with a smile. Her vision penetrated the murk, and she realised that of *course* it wasn't the girl from outside sitting in her séance room. It was the girlish-looking son of Mrs Jupp sitting neatly with his hands on his knees

9

and an expression of pretty interest. She swallowed, collecting herself. The girl was not here and the girl was *not* important, she scolded herself. The séance room was.

Her *livelihood*.

She exhaled with a benevolent smile. 'Thank you, Jack,' she said to the air. 'And ah!' She gesticulated grandly at the array of instruments Mr Larson had placed, as requested, in the middle of the table. 'It looks as though we are to be treated to a musical adventure this evening.' She threw a quick glance at Miss Newman, who had taken up her usual position in the shadows beside the sideboard. Miss Newman did not sit at the table for the second half since her role now necessitated frequent movement: simple things like locking and unlocking doors, snuffing candles Mr Larson couldn't reach and helping sitters who became overwhelmed, alongside a routine of carefully curated unseen spirited mischief.

Satisfied that Miss Newman was ready, Mrs Wood exhaled and became serious. 'Now,' she said, her voice smooth and soothing. 'We begin again, as always, in the dark.'

And, thanks to Miss Newman, the final candle went out.

With the opening prayer complete, Mrs Wood instructed everyone at the table to place their hands on the tabletop, spreading them wide so that their little fingers touched the little fingers of their neighbours – as delicately as was respectable.

'We are ready!' she called, her voice bouncing off the walls. 'Spirits! *Come!*'

Anticipation sparked in the darkness as the sitters' hands grew warm and damp on the mahogany tabletop until . . .

TAP! TAP! TAP!

. . . violent rapping erupted across the table and the man with the monocle let out a shriek.

'The spirits are with us!' Mrs Wood whispered, and the room strained to breathe.

'Here comes Archangel Michael!' exclaimed Mrs Reynolds suddenly, and taffeta and silk rustled as everyone craned to see in the darkness. 'He's here to ensure the spirits' safe journey.'

'Welcome to the table, Archangel Michael,' said Mrs Wood, her voice soft and even. 'And I can see you have brought some friends.' The room shifted nervously. She inhaled, exhaled.

RATATATAT!

The face of the strange girl from outside bloomed suddenly in her mind and she hesitated for a moment; there was something in the way she had stared so boldly back . . .

BANG!

The shock made her gasp along with the rest of the room. In that moment of thinking about that damned girl rather than the work at hand, her toe had slipped on the pulley that rattled the table, causing it to fall with a force that frightened the sense back into her.

'You are so lively!' she shouted through gritted teeth, furious at herself for making such a stupid mistake. That was exactly how lesser Mediums exposed themselves. She took another breath. Forced herself to focus.

Ratatatat.

The table began to roll again, tentative, gently as she concentrated on regaining control. A moment more and her confidence began to return.

RATATATAT!

She allowed the table to speed up, and it roiled beneath their palms like a dinghy in a storm. 'Oh! Who is it?' she called. 'What do you want? Let me help you!' The table stilled suddenly, and the room was silent.

'Oh!' she said. 'I keep . . . they keep trying to turn my hand over . . . Are you trying to give me something?' And then she gave another gasp. 'Oh! They have given me something. Something small and . . . And am I to give it to . . . *Mr Nicholls*?' She paused. 'Is there a Mr Nicholls? Are you here?'

There was a clearing of a throat at the table. 'That is I,' said a gruff voice. The shabby-coated, ear-cleaning gentleman.

'Please,' said Mrs Wood. 'For some reason they want me to give you this. I think it may be a stone? You are permitted to break the circle to receive it.' The tambourine jangled on the table as the stone was passed across and Mr Nicholls cleared his throat again, his chair whispering on the rug as he resettled into his seat. 'I don't know what they were thinking,' said Mrs Wood as the room fell silent again.

'My brother,' said Mr Nicholls. 'It feels like a fossil. My brother was a great fossil hunter. Could we light a candle so I might see?'

'The spirits would prefer you did not,' said Mrs Wood. 'You may look when they have departed. They have so much to say and so little time and light drains my energy.'

A heavy pause settled and then . . .

Gasps ricocheted around the room. 'What *is* that?' wavered a thin male voice.

'Don't fret, dears. It's just the spirits!' called Mrs Hart.

A spark of light was shining above the table, quivering and then swooping up and down. 'It's difficult to read,' said Mrs Wood, and she was right: the light was tracing letters but they were disappearing as soon as they were realised. 'But this is a message from the spirits. Perhaps from your brother, Mr Nicholls? He appears to be concerned that you are overworked at the moment, sir.' She hesitated for a moment then began to read a message:

> *For our light and momentary troubles*
> *Are achieving for us*
> *an eternal glory*
> *that far outweighs them all*

'He did enjoy a good bible verse,' said Mr Nicholls.

'As did my husband!' chirruped the small widow.

'As do we *all*,' said Mrs Wood. 'Indeed, I feel it's a message for everyone – something we should remember every day. Thank you.' She bowed her head in the darkness and . . . the tambourine burst into life, shimmering and shaking with gusto, clattering overhead around the table and even towards the sitters at the back of the room. A man clapped loudly out of time while someone exclaimed, 'It was by my ear!' and then the table began to roll again and the tambourine slammed down and the violin was suddenly alive, swooping around and filling the air with 'The Last Rose of Summer'.

Mrs Wood laughed. 'We have a musician with us!' she said, as the violin finished with relish, landing back on the table with an enduring *thrum*. 'I think everyone on both sides enjoyed that!'

'My husband,' said a quiet voice from the table. The small widow. She cleared her throat. 'He played professionally.'

'*That's* who this noisy gentleman is. Bravo, sir!' she said. 'And what wonderful whiskers!'

'He . . . whiskers?' said the widow. 'He didn't have . . .'

'Oh, he would've had quite an exuberant set, he's telling me,' she replied with deceptive ease, grateful she couldn't see Miss Newman's face, even if she could feel her exasperated eye roll in the darkness. 'Should he have been permitted to let them grow. On the Other Side, they can be exactly as they always wanted to be.'

The widow said nothing as Mrs Wood moved on.

Citrus stung the air, and a short missive of love came through for the Countess, who received it with a self-satisfied sigh. She did so enjoy being the one to receive a missive of love.

The evening progressed with more rocking and knocking from the table, and a few playful souls rushed about swapping some of the ladies' hair combs in the room, even snatching the ostrich plume off the Countess and tucking it into a wildly unimpressed Mr Nicholls' parting.

And then . . .

'Oh. Oh, my darling.' The quiet of Mrs Wood's voice cut through the excitement and everything was suddenly still and silent.

'Oh, my dearest, sweetest darling,' she continued, pausing to listen. 'I understand,' she said. 'I think it's the sensible thing to do. But it will take a moment.' And then she lowered her voice to speak to the table. 'My dears, we shall be experiencing something quite special. Please. All of us. Hold hands as tightly as you can, for this little soul needs as much of our energy as we can muster.'

The room subsided into rustles.

'Oh,' she said. 'Oh, he's showing me such tiny fingers. And those eyes . . . aren't you beautiful . . .'

'*William.*' The young woman at the table whispered. 'William, is that you? Is that my son?'

'I'm afraid he cannot speak here, as he could not speak on earth,' said Mrs Wood in a distant, tired voice. 'But he's showing me the most wonderful images.'

'It's William?' she asked again.

'I think it is. Yes. William. What a beautiful little boy.'

'William!' The woman choked on a sob halfway between a cry and a laugh. 'Everyone always said so when they saw him.'

'He wants me to say thank you,' she said. 'Oh, he has such a good heart.'

'Thank you? But what can he be grateful for?' said the woman. 'I should never have taken him out. It was too cold. It was my fault. I . . .'

'He wants you to know that he was never unhappy when he was with you. All he ever knew was love. He wants you to know that he could never have wished for a better mother or father for the time he was on earth.'

'But I failed him . . .'

'What was that? Who are you showing me? Oh. Are these your grandparents?'

The husband let out a strangled cry. 'He's not alone, Cecie! He's with Mother!'

'And they tell him all the time about their wonderful son and their wonderful daughter-in-law. And when they're not doing that . . .' She paused. 'Sorry, he's showing me this with such enthusiasm it's hard to keep up.' She paused again. 'Thank you,' she said. 'Apparently, they spend time with you each day. They especially love to join you when you are out walking.' Another pause. 'Perhaps you've felt them?'

'I have!' said the woman. 'I thought I was going mad but—'

'We're so sorry, darling boy,' said the husband. 'We should have been more careful . . .'

Mrs Wood chuckled. 'He said "pish!" to that,' she said. 'He does not believe there is anything to say sorry for. He is with his beloved grandparents and the Lord.'

'Are they well?' the husband asked.

'I'm afraid his energy is fading,' and Mrs Wood's voice began to grow fragile. 'He is growing faint . . . He has one final thing . . . he wants me to tell you . . . Mother, Father. Believe me when I say that no child is luckier for love, than I . . .'

The only sounds in the room were the pitiful sobs of the bereaved mother attempting to compose herself.

'Thank you,' she said at last. 'His passing was not peaceful. The agony we have felt. But now, knowing he is safe and with my husband's parents . . . Thank . . .' Her words disappeared.

'I am merely the conduit,' Mrs Wood said softly in the darkness. 'Perhaps you might like . . .' She touched Mrs Reynolds' arm and she dutifully moved to the couple. The room waited, patiently and respectfully, as Mrs Reynolds walked them out with whispers of comfort, unlocking then carefully relocking the séance room door behind them as she went.

With the emotions managed, the room took the opportunity to gather itself and then . . .

'Well! I have a very generous soul here,' said Mrs Wood, as though nothing else had happened. 'They're saying it's time for a treat!'

At this, a wave of muted excitement rushed around the room and then, after an audible *thwock,* Lady Harrington exclaimed. 'A *banana*! It landed right in my lap!'

And then . . .

'Oh!' squeaked a woman from the back of the room and she sniffed loudly. 'An *orange*. In February!'

'. . . I think I've got . . .'

And then an *ooof*! from the Countess. 'Watermelon!' she shouted and broke into peels of uncharacteristic laughter. 'I have been yearning for watermelon since I left Naples!'

'. . . a walnut! Two of 'em!'

Citrus fizzed. 'Another orange!' said someone with a very full mouth. 'And it's *delicious*.'

The room became almost frenzied, the air thick with the smell of citrus and berries, everyone craning in the darkness, trying to make out if they too would be treated to one of the apples or damsons or sticky dates landing in laps like strange rain while Mrs Wood focused on the invisible movements around the room that only she could discern.

And then . . .

Stillness.

'The angel is leaving!' exclaimed Mrs Reynolds, who had received a kumquat on her return from seeing the young couple into a cab. 'Archangel Michael is waving goodbye.'

'And he is taking our spirits with him,' said Mrs Wood, cutting through the hubbub. 'Let us join our hands one last time to say our final prayer and thank these visitors from the Other Side for all they have given us tonight.'

She bowed her head, the Lord's Prayer falling from her mouth without her having to even think about it.

As the room prayed, sated and drowsy after all the excitement,

Mrs Wood's mind returned to that moment of potential disaster earlier in the séance, like a finger picking over a scab. She had allowed herself to be distracted by that damned girl and, as a consequence, she had made a mistake that could have cost her; if someone should have noticed how her foot had slipped, or even seen it had slipped at all, everything would have been over. She had pulled it back, surpassed herself even, but the mistake had been made.

But then she thought of the grieving parents; how she had seen the mother blossom from devastation to hope because of her work, how the father's burden became visibly lighter across his shoulders. She allowed herself to breathe. For all the fun and frivolity she was famous for, her ability to help those in emotional need was the thing that drove her. Tonight, amidst the flying damsons and dancing lights, she had done something that mattered.

The prayer was ending. She recentred herself, returning to the room and the electricity flowing around her.

She had done well. No. She had done brilliantly.

Tonight had been another success.

But then, as the collective *Amen* fluttered through the room and she lifted her head, she heard it.

It was almost imperceptible, so quiet it was possible only she had heard it.

But to Mrs Wood it was as loud as a klaxon: impossible to miss.

The sound of a poorly stifled yawn.

CHAPTER 2

Mrs Wood woke early the following morning after barely two hours of fitful, angry sleep.

That damned yawn. *Who was the culprit?*

That damned strange girl. *Who was she?*

She had never made such a mistake at a séance. Not once in the more than decade-and-a-half she had been in London, nor in her life before. She had always repressed distractions without effort, even when they had been in the very core of her, and no one had ever yawned *so publicly* during one of her séances.

Had her mistake been seen? Was that why they had yawned?

She'd sat at the top of the pile for years now. To be unimpeached in all that time was a singular rarity in her world; public Mediums simply didn't have long careers. She had lost good friends and, thankfully, irritating competitors to errors of judgement along the way while Mrs Wood remained unblemished, untouchable.

Indeed, she had even enjoyed those evenings where pious little *evidence*-obsessed scientists tried to disprove her with their ridiculous homemade machines. She had carried out séances in oversized nightgowns, been intimately frisked by the investigators' desperately awkward female assistants. She was even sewn into an all-in-one made of green cotton by some particularly overzealous psychic researcher and she'd ended up leading the table looking like an enormous runner bean. Regardless of their methods, her favourite moment during each experiment was the moment when she had to sadly report that the investigator's hostile energies had frightened off all of the spirits, especially when they were then faced by the furious host whose séance they had ruined.

Yes. She had beaten the most scrupulous testing to have her reputation confirmed again and again that she was, indeed, a Medium of integrity and unparalleled talent. But the world was changing. *Expectations* were changing. It hadn't escaped her notice that when she shared tea with friends and patrons, conversation always seemed to drift towards a young Medium starting out in some backwater or how someone in Connecticut had apported an entire family, including the dog.

Every time someone felt the need to tell her of her rising competition, the inevitability that one day her reign would be over became more real. She was acutely aware of how much people loved *new*. She had been that *new thing* once herself, usurping established Mediums with her pink cheeks and youthful exuberance.

But she wasn't pink-cheeked and exuberant anymore. Even if she chose to ignore her reflection, the pain in her joints reminded her and the unpredictable clicks and cracks from her knees had rendered some popular pieces in her repertoire necessarily redundant.

Of course, her own patrons were ageing too, and the women she sat with, her own Circle, were becoming greyer and squintier with each year. But that didn't mean that her patrons would put up with the same from their Medium. Who on earth would want to sit at their opulent séance table and see a decrepit old widow creaking back at them from a bath chair?

Perhaps that was why Lady Morgan had sent her apologies. Young, vivacious and frequently in the society columns, Lady Morgan was a newcomer to the London spiritual scene, and all the Mediums were out to snare her. Which was why Mrs Wood had been so thrilled by the introduction at the Countess's January séance. She had delivered a special, spontaneous message for her that garnered gasps and Lady Morgan had squeezed her hand when she left and whispered that she couldn't wait to see her again. So why hadn't she come? *I am unwell*, her note had said. Just that. *I am unwell*.

No one turned down an invitation from Mrs Wood.

Miss Newman may have dismissed it, but it was Mrs Wood's job to be aware of what was unspoken. And what it felt like was disinterest. Was this the beginning of her descent? She felt a thrill of panic. She still had a house to maintain, wages to pay. She wasn't ready for it all to end now. She couldn't afford for it to end.

A particularly loud clatter from Eliza in the house beyond, followed by a colourful stream of irritation, brought her back to her cold room and she began to stew that her fire was not yet lit. This was not unusual after an in-home evening séance: Mrs Wood enjoyed sleeping late, and Eliza had learned by experience she wasn't always pleasant when she was disturbed, even to light the fire. But the room had grown depressingly damp and chill and as the air slithered beneath her goose down, she was back on her pallet in Hull where the wet harbour air seeped through the patched windows and she would wake with frost in her hair.

She shook her head. Memories such as those were never helpful. She pushed herself up and shouted instead: 'Eliza! My fire, Eliza!'

An irritated sigh carried along the landing like an angry bird and then Eliza barrelled in without knocking, the basket of kindling stacked on her hip. 'You're early,' she said. 'It's not even nine.'

To the rest of the world, Mrs Wood was the Great Medium. To Eliza, who held no truck with such blandishments, she was, at best, an inconvenience.

As her maid stomped along the landing, Mrs Wood thought, not for the first time, how nice it would be to have someone in her employ who didn't mind being there. One who perhaps resented the work at hand less. But Eliza hadn't been hired for her charm; she had been hired for her obvious dislike of human company: a maid who kept herself to herself was gold dust for a Medium. And despite her heavy foot and constant state of vague irritation, Eliza's discretion and loyalty were faultless.

'The fire, Eliza.'

'Well, you can't go shouting at me when I'm only doing my job.' She dropped the basket beside the fireplace, gathering her skirts to kneel on the hearth. '"Do me last, Eliza," you say. "I cannot stand to be disturbed by you." And now you're all, "Where are you, Eliza? You're late. Eliza."'

While she quietened to focus on the task, Mrs Wood sat up, pulling her cap down to warm her ears as she watched Eliza work with expert speed. She was hungry, and she couldn't stop thinking about the cake she knew Cook had made for the previous evening: a three-layered monstrosity stuffed with coffee cream and topped by plump candied walnuts. Perhaps there would be some left over.

The fire caught and Eliza's face bloomed orange. She turned. 'Happy?' Then she squatted to pack her basket. 'Cook's got some trout in for breakfast,' she said. 'The cab for Mrs Farnham's is due for half eleven so shall I let her know you'd like it served up here?'

'I shall breakfast with Miss Newman,' she said. 'Can you let her know that I'm ready to dress?'

Eliza shrugged. 'As you like,' she said, and pulled the door firmly closed behind her.

Mrs Wood sat in the suddenly still room, listening to the fire pop and hiss to life. Even though her mind felt gauzy with tiredness, she was glad she'd woken at a reasonable hour. The power of the panic and passion that had kept her up through the night had returned and she threw her blankets back, swinging her feet onto the rug on the floor. There was too much to be done to dwell on things, she thought, shoving her feet into her slippers. There always was.

While Mrs Wood picked at her trout, Miss Newman spread marmalade an inch deep on her toast and devoured it, elaborating around mouthfuls on the content of a talk she was planning to attend at her women's society over the weekend.

'You should come,' she said. 'I'm sure you'd find it fascinating. Miss Cobbe is a brilliant speaker, and she has such a vision for the future of womankind.'

Mrs Wood gave a sigh. She had no strong opinions on the equality of the sexes – she had succeeded as a woman, after all. The idea didn't concern her one way or the other; it was the types of women that such ideas attracted that raised her eyebrows. Radicals horrified the less forward-thinking generations who made up the bulk of her more generous patrons. 'No, thank you,' she said. 'Women will do perfectly well without me on board.'

'There's talk of a rally,' said Miss Newman, finishing her coffee. 'Through Hyde Park.'

Mrs Wood stopped, her fork caught between her plate and her mouth. 'Surely you're not thinking you shall attend?' she said. 'What if someone should see you?'

'Good!' said Miss Newman. 'The more people we can get to listen to us, the better.'

But Mrs Wood shook her head. 'You'll get yourself a name,' she said, putting her fork down and pushing her plate away. 'Going about with those kinds of women. It reflects on me, Sarah.'

Miss Newman's cheeks pinked. 'What kinds of women?' she said. 'Women who think that the weaker sex deserves a voice? Gosh. How *terrible*.'

'Now there. See? You never would've spoken like that before you started going to those things.'

'If you're suggesting they've changed me, then perhaps you're right.'

Mrs Wood gave a laugh to mask a wave of concern. The last thing she would ever want was for Miss Newman to change. When she had discovered her seven years before in Sicily, Miss Newman had been a jewel dulled by the thankless job of companion to a corpulent Austrian heiress. Within a week, Mrs Wood had stolen her away and in the subsequent years she had evolved from excellent personal assistant to the closest of friends, a constant in her home and her other half in her séances. There was nothing she wanted to change about Miss Newman: her life could not continue as it did without her just the way she was.

'Change for change's sake isn't always for the best,' she said.

Miss Newman raised an eyebrow but stayed quiet. 'You're stewing,' she said suddenly.

Mrs Wood sat back in her chair. She toyed for a moment with telling Miss Newman about the yawn. Had she heard it too? She certainly hadn't said anything when they had debriefed after the séance. But she couldn't face unpicking it, not this early in the morning on so little sleep.

'Are you *still* worrying about Lady Morgan?'

She took the lifeboat from Miss Newman, returning to an area of concern that was easier, but no less pressing, to discuss. 'You know how much influence she has over young society,' she said. 'If she goes for one of the newer Mediums, then she'll certainly take Lady Cooper with her. And what of the Green sisters? They all think Lady Morgan is everything.'

'You're practically part of the Green family, Violet. You'll be with them forever.'

'Exactly! I've worked with their mother for so long those girls must think of me as some old artefact.'

Miss Newman gave a laugh. 'They love you, Violet. You know that.'

'Everyone loves an old aunt,' she said.

'Violet. You're being ridiculous. You're the best Medium working . . .'

'I know, I know.' She forced a smile, the weight of the

conversation suddenly unbearable. 'You're right,' she said with a forced smile. 'I've just been disappointed. I'm sure everything is fine.' And she laughed as brightly as she could in the hope that it would convince her that her words were true.

❧

Mr Larson cleared his throat on the threshold of the back parlour.

'It's all right, dearest,' said Mrs Wood from her seat beside the fire. 'You can come in.'

He leaned forward, his long legs taking a single, loping step. 'I don't mean to interrupt . . .' He cleared his throat again and looked at Miss Newman, who blinked back. 'I wondered if you might have . . .'

Mrs Wood looked at Miss Newman. 'I think he would like a moment,' she said, and they both turned back to Mr Larson, who was rocking on his heels in a manner that suggested he was either about to begin a sermon or propose, although the ledger tucked beneath his arm was a firm indicator that his actual purpose was even drier.

It had been Mr Wood who introduced her to Mr Larson. Back then she had been Miss Bell and Mr Wood had had a whole other wife. When that wife died suddenly in late 1863, Mr Wood's private consultations had swiftly evolved into social occasions which, in turn, evolved into an association that was, if not love, most certainly *very fond*. Mr Larson had appeared shortly before Mr Wood's offer of marriage: a tall, spindly accountant who managed Mr Wood's investments. He had never been to a séance before and was intrigued. That intrigue turned to conviction in a single moment, when Mrs Wood reached his long-dead twin on the Other Side, delivering a choking confession of enduring love into the dark room that changed his life.

For Mrs Wood, it had been easy: the moment she saw him she

had read the weight of his loss, seen how his shoulders wilted beneath it. He was a man desperate to be healed. And so that's what she did: she put him back together, piece by piece, until he was able to forgive himself for what he had always considered his part in the accident that had taken his twin brother. This act of attention and redemption had secured his loyalty to Mrs Wood for life.

When Mr Wood died in the summer heat of 1870, Mr Larson assumed not only an all-encompassing sense of responsibility for the preservation of his friend's widow, but also for his investments. Mrs Wood was maintaining her own day-to-day income through her patrons' stipends and gifts, and it seemed logical to them both that he should continue in his role with his knowledge of the complex labyrinth of accounts that Mr Wood had tied his money into.

When she'd made that decision, however, she hadn't anticipated quite how often Mr Larson would want to talk about those investments until even the sight of the ledger filled her with despair.

And there it was again, tucked neatly beneath Mr Larson's arm like a pet, indicating only one eventuality: another impromptu meeting about finances.

Excellent.

'Don't keep her too long,' Miss Newman was saying as she gathered her notebook and pen and stood. 'We have a very busy day ahead and she had a late night.'

'Wonderful work!' he said abruptly. 'Last night, I mean. Simply splendid.'

Mrs Wood smiled. 'Thank you,' she said, and then she stopped. 'Mr Larson. Did you see a girl across the road when you arrived last night?'

Mr Larson paused, and Miss Newman laughed. 'Mrs Wood has a little ghost.'

'She's not a ghost, Sarah,' Mrs Wood said, and Miss Newman

held her hands up in submission. She looked back at Mr Larson. 'Did you see anyone out there?'

'I . . . I don't think so,' he said. 'No one of note.'

'Are you sure?'

'Not even a tiny spirit?' Miss Newman teased as she came alongside him in the doorway.

'I . . . I . . . ahhh . . .' Mr Larson stammered, but Mrs Wood shook her head.

'Ignore her,' she said pointedly. 'It's nothing.' She smoothed her skirt. 'What did you want to discuss?'

Mr Larson waited until Miss Newman had left and then closed the door quietly behind him. But he didn't come into the room as Mrs Wood expected.

'Mr Larson?'

He cleared his throat again.

'Mr Larson. I am due at Mrs Farnham's before lunch. I don't have much time.'

He turned briefly, as though checking that the door was quite closed, and then took a breath. 'Mrs Wood,' he said, his eyes on the floor at her feet. 'I am not the bearer of good news.'

Mrs Wood slumped back in her chair. 'All of it?'

'I fear so.' Mr Larson turned his hands, staring at them as though he had answers written across his fingers.

She sat blindly, still absorbing what he had just told her: how the diamond mine riots in New Rush towards the end of last year had wiped out their investment.

'You're remaining remarkably calm,' he said, his jaw flexing. 'Although I would always expect a sensible response from you.'

'Investments fail, Mr Larson,' she said, her mind whirling behind her facade. 'We weren't wholly reliant on New Rush were we?'

'No, of course not. Mr Wood was a clever investor.'

'I know.' She looked at him and he gave a strangled smile. 'But?' she said.

He exhaled. 'The New Rush mine was a substantial part.'

Her stomach clenched. 'I see.'

'The rest of his investments remain healthy. There is . . .' his cheeks pinked a little as he braced himself for the word. '. . . *money*.'

'Just not as much as before.'

His embarrassment deepened and he shifted awkwardly from one foot to the other, patches of red appearing on his neck. He cleared his throat. 'Not quite.'

Her mind instinctively ran through the séances she had planned for the next few weeks, calculating the expenditure, where costs might be cut. Her Circles didn't need much, a cake and some tea, but her patrons and the sitters at her Grand Séances expected the glitter and gleam that was usual for a woman of her class – or, more to the point, the class of her patrons. She couldn't possibly be seen to cut any corners when her patrons were present: they gifted her each month to ensure they were prioritised. Being served anything other than the finest tea and exquisite patisserie would raise eyebrows. And her Grand Séances required champagne plus a hot meat buffet at a minimum.

'How long have you known?' she said.

She heard him sigh. 'The news came on Monday.'

She looked up. *Monday*?! 'You should've told me,' she said.

'I didn't want to upset you ahead of Tuesday's séance. I never would've forgiven myself if—'

'You should have told me.'

He winced at each syllable. 'I was protecting you.' But he looked away. 'I blame myself,' he said. 'I should have kept myself abreast of the political situation, reacted sooner. I . . .'

'It's not your fault,' she said, but it lacked the conviction she knew he wanted to hear.

'I'm the one responsible for your investments, Mrs Wood. I'm the one who manages them. The blame sits squarely with me.'

She gave a quick inhale and shook her head. 'And you're also a friend who I know will always do his best by me.'

He stopped, his face set. 'Mrs Wood,' he said. 'I am sure that this is something that you will come to in your own time, and it is the most delicate of suggestions for me to extend but . . . while I am resolving this . . . situation, might I suggest that you . . . if at all possible . . .'

'I will see what adjustments can be made,' she said, becoming increasingly desperate to end the discussion. 'I am sure there are areas where I may make some quiet reductions without causing any alarm.'

He sagged with relief and wrung his hands. 'I promise, just as I did to your late husband, that I will always protect you, Mrs Wood.'

She smiled briskly. 'Thank you,' she said, gathering her skirts. 'But now, Mr Larson, *dearest*. I must really be getting on. Mrs Farnham is expecting me.' She gave the politest of nods and hurried to the door so that he wouldn't see quite how furious she was with him for placing her in this predicament.

CHAPTER 3

'At last! My reason for living is here!'

One of Mrs Wood's wealthier patrons, Mrs Farnham had sprained her ankle in the early January blizzards and had been trapped in her vast villa at the top of Cricklewood ever since. For someone who liked to keep a finger in most pies, this isolation was Mrs Farnham's purgatory and so she had increased her regular sessions with Mrs Wood, summoning her every Wednesday lunchtime for company in both flesh and spirit form.

That particular Wednesday, as the butler showed them into the morning room, she sat up eagerly from the crumb-strewn sofa, her bound ankle raised on a velvet pillow and a teacup and saucer somehow remaining balanced on her luxurious bosom in her excitement. 'What do you think about Mrs Trimble! I've been desperate to talk to someone about it!'

'It's very sad,' said Miss Newman, kissing Mrs Farnham on the cheek and glancing at Mrs Wood. 'She was a good friend.'

Mrs Trimble had been more than a good friend to Mrs Wood. She had been a part of the Circle Mrs Wood had joined when she arrived in London almost fifteen years before and had watched her youthful sessions with careful eyes, giving gentle, cloaked suggestions for improvement. Mrs Trimble was beloved, respected. Talented but never showy. She didn't take risks, which affected her popularity, but meant that she had endured all of these years. And she'd been popular enough to be able to keep herself and her daughter in good order with her own rooms and a maid.

The news of her exposure had felt like a death.

'Did you know?' continued Mrs Farnham obliviously.

'We did not,' said Mrs Wood with a silent apology to her old friend. 'It came as a complete surprise to both of us, didn't it, Miss Newman?'

Mrs Farnham gave an extravagant sigh. 'She'll be missed in society. She made a lovely lemon drizzle. But one cannot have these frauds sullying the good name of Spiritualism, can we dear. We must chase them from our doors.'

But Mrs Wood's mind had slid to Miss Trimble's daughter – a round, happy thing who had only recently debuted herself as a Medium in her own right at her mother's table. 'What will become of her girl?' she said, starting when she realised she had said it out loud.

'Oh, there's no hope for her after all this,' said Mrs Farnham. 'A cheat is a cheat, don't you agree? And we all know that the apple never falls far from the tree.'

Mrs Wood gave a non-committal smile and dropped her cloak over the back of the armchair with an ease she didn't feel.

'Shall we discuss happier things, dearest?' she said, swallowing down the unsettling idea of ruin by association. 'We were greeted by some wonderful smells from the kitchen . . .'

'Oh yes!' Mrs Farnham was always happy to talk about food. 'The lamb came from Wales yesterday. I'm treating you to some of my finest cutlets!'

After a luncheon of mutton chops eaten from lap trays so that Mrs Farnham could remain recumbent, accompanied by a sweet muscadet wine and one of their host's more meandering monologues, the room was darkened, and the reading began.

Today, Mrs Wood received a message from Mrs Farnham's beloved great-uncle from whom she had inherited a small Welsh hill farm. He reminded her that the rates were due and that the tenant farmer should check the catches on the lambing pens. He was also worried about thieves, both in Wales and at Mrs Farnham's

30

home in Cricklewood, and encouraged Mrs Farnham to ensure that her butler kept everything locked. Mrs Farnham enjoyed reminders about such things: it allowed her to segue into a titbit of gossip she might have picked up or wanted to recycle from a while ago, about so-and-so being burgled or pickpocketed *right there in the street*.

At the sound of the two o'clock chimes, Miss Newman discreetly tucked Mrs Wood's gift from Mrs Farnham into her pocket, and they bade farewell with promises to return the following week without fail.

They stepped onto the Edgware Road just in time to catch a passing cab, and then they were off again, heading towards Kensington and the red-brick townhouse of Miss Cram, spinster heiress to the Cram & Isles Matches fortune, and her platoon of indulged Jack Russells.

As they settled into the worn seats of the cab, Miss Newman turned to Mrs Wood. 'What did Mr Larson want?' They had talked only of the upcoming séances during the ride to Mrs Farnham's, a welcome distraction for Mrs Wood, but now she could feel her friend's eyes on her, trying to read her face in the quiet.

'Nothing of any importance,' she said, and passed over the gold bracelet Miss Farnham had slipped into her hand as she left. 'She bought it for her niece, apparently,' she said, nodding at the carefully crafted loops and links. 'But changed her mind after our séance last week.'

Miss Newman gave the piece a respectful glance before sliding it into her pocket alongside the more formal stipend Mrs Farnham had given her. 'She's very sweet,' she said.

'Isn't she. Now,' she continued. 'Miss Cram . . .'

'Whatever he said, it's bothered you. That much is obvious.'

Mrs Wood shook her head. 'It was nothing. There's nothing for you to worry about.'

Miss Newman was about to say something more but then she

stopped suddenly and smiled. 'He asked you to marry him again, didn't he!'

Mrs Wood gave a dismissive laugh. 'No. Really. We talked over a few financial things, that's all.'

'It's rather amusing, don't you think?' Miss Newman continued, oblivious. 'How everyone else sees you as a woman of means and ability while he can't see beyond his assumption that you're desperate for another husband.'

'It's not like that,' she said, feeling strangely defensive. 'Mr Larson is simply worried about me.'

'How romantic.'

She gave a weak smile and returned to the window and the turned fields stretching away towards the chaos of the distant Kensal Green rooftops.

But Miss Newman was right. She was distracted, and she was worried.

No one understood what it cost to be Mrs Wood. The actual economics of it.

As a Medium she was in the unusual position of being a woman and also able to generate her own income, made up of monthly stipends from her patrons, tokens from those who came for private consultations and gifts for seats at her Grand Séances.

The amounts weren't commensurate with those accrued by a man, necessarily, but the monthly totals gave her the reassurance that, no matter what, her household would remain afloat on the simplest level: there would always be bread in the pantry and coal in the grate. It covered the laundry, the cabs and the grocer and kept Miss Newman comfortable and Eliza and Cook paid.

But she could not be Mrs Wood without Mr Wood's money. She could live on her own income, but she couldn't feather herself in the way that her patrons expected. His money provided the gilding that maintained the all-important signifier of propriety: polished respectability.

The patrons she cultivated were men and women who had never known anything but splendour. As such, they didn't notice how much she gave to maintaining her reputation. None of them cared that her gowns were made of paramatta silk, but if she were to come out in bombazine, eyebrows would go up across town. The same went for a fire being too small, or not lighting enough gas jets; if the linens weren't Irish or if there was only – God forbid – one side of salmon in the buffet. Those were the details people of their station noticed, and any slip risked embarrassment and descent out of favour.

Mr Wood's investments ensured she could maintain her most important illusion of all: that she was one of them.

Still, she thought, glancing up and recognising Paddington Cemetery beyond the window, things could be a lot worse. A widow's life was always precarious, but she was fortunate. The loss of Mr Wood's income was a blow, but it was not insurmountable. Not in the short term, at least, and she would focus on what she could do to keep the loss invisible to her patrons until everything was back to normal. Since she'd been presenting a story her whole life, this was nothing new for her.

All she had to do was keep her patrons' stipends and gifts coming in.

This was a bump. A blip. It was not the end. She could hold the fort until Mr Larson resolved the investment. He was a good money manager. Surely it wouldn't take long.

As usual, Miss Cram had set her séance table in the back parlour overlooking her snaggled garden, and they all settled in together along with Miss Cram's cousin, Sybil, six of the fleet of Jack Russells and, shortly after Mrs Wood's arrival, Miss Cram's long-deceased mother.

Mother Cram returned to the Other Side just after four, which was later than planned, but Mrs Wood had been forced to discreetly remove an attentive dog from her ankle in the dark more than once, which had delayed things a little. There was to be no rushing off, however: Miss Cram was always very generous with her tokens of gratitude at the end of each séance and so, in return, they would always stay for small talk over cups of tea replete with dog hairs bobbing across the surface like drowning spiders.

'I saw in the *Spiritual Times* that you're visiting with the Rosebournes at Mrs Hart's this evening,' Mrs Cram said as a dog licked a crumb of seedcake from her chin.

Cousin Sybil gave a gasp. 'The Americans!' she said. 'I hear they've been doing the rounds of all the tables in town.' She turned to Mrs Wood. 'Of course, I'm sure they've been at yours a dozen times already, Mrs Wood.'

Mrs Wood smiled and Miss Newman leaned forward. 'They've been saving the best until last,' she said, patting Sybil's knee. 'We tried to fit them in sooner, but as you know Mrs Wood is so busy.'

'Oh, I *do* know,' said Miss Cram, the licking dog's tongue flapped excitedly into her open mouth as she spoke and she squealed and pushed the dog's muzzle down. 'Mumu's such a naughty girl. Aren't you!' Mumu stared at Mrs Wood with eyes like beads, challenging her to disagree.

'I wonder if they've seen any of those materialisations we've been hearing about,' Miss Cram continued. She gave a wistful sigh. 'Boston's so advanced compared to us little bumpkins here in London. I read that they've had full spirits materialised. *Full spirits, Cousin!*'

'Oh, I would so love to see your mother again,' interrupted Sybil. 'Wouldn't you, dearest?'

'Cousin! You're so thoughtful,' said Miss Cram. 'And there's only one Medium in London we would expect to achieve something so new.'

They turned as one to Mrs Wood, who smiled again and drained her tea without thinking, gagging discreetly on the clutch of fur that went down with it.

As they rode back to Chepstow Villas to prepare for the evening's séance at Mrs Hart's, Miss Newman gave a snort.

'A full spirit,' she said and shook her head. 'Whatever next.'

Mrs Wood snorted in agreement. She'd always found the idea of materialising a full spirit abhorrent. The whole circus of the thing – the use of the cabinet, the equipment required and the management of the lighting – not to mention the bone-chilling level of risk for what amounted to nothing more than spectacle. It felt to her not the pinnacle but the lowest depths of Spiritualism. Mrs Wood was dedicated to the people who sat at her table, the ones who sought her out for what only she could do. Yes, there was fun and surprises and a level of skilled performance that only a Medium of her standard could present. Yes, she often bobbed around the ceiling or dangled in trees and had once flown from Notting Hill over the rooftops to land in the middle of a séance room in High Holborn. But performance wasn't the thing that drove her. The japes were necessary: they validated her as a Medium by affirming her reputation. They allowed her space for the quieter moments where she did the thing that mattered: brought comfort and solace to those lost in grief. If she could apport an afternoon tea, complete with milk and sugar, she could channel a message of love.

Which was why she had so little regard for those who talked about materialising spirits. Such a stunt was nothing to do with the sitter but everything to do with the Medium. When others had begun producing spirit hands and faces in the mid-sixties, a fear of being left behind had caused her to join in for a brief spell, long enough to see what dangerous work it was, but also to see how, for a sitter, a spirit in the flesh offered something so different to a spirit in mind. A Medium was the focus of a séance, of course, but Mrs Wood believed wholeheartedly that when it mattered, a

Medium must disappear and become only the conduit between the sitter and their loved one, not gadding about in gauze singing songs about pixies. What good did that do anyone?

No. No matter how dire her financial situation, she would never forget who she was. She would never allow spectacle to overtake duty.

'Those Americans,' Mrs Wood said eventually. 'They're all about the show.'

They were due at Mrs Hart's for an early supper at seven, but with the delay at Miss Cram's, they didn't arrive back at Chepstow Villas until almost half past five, rushing in to find Eliza steaming Mrs Wood's séance silk and complaining that her fingers were red raw.

Mrs Hart had arranged for her carriage to collect them at a quarter past six, so Mrs Wood had no choice but to take a slice of banana bread and a large glass of sherry for refreshment, while Miss Newman buttoned her into her séance dress and ran through the notes she'd made on the Rosebournes.

She was clipping diamonds onto her lobes when the driver rang the doorbell, and they were back out again, the shrill night air giving her the only moment's pause she'd felt all day before they were off towards the Uxbridge Road and a glittering supper and séance which would, no doubt, be reported on both sides of the Atlantic.

Excerpt from the Editor's Column
Magnus Clore
Spiritual Times, 13th February 1873

This week we bade farewell to Mr and Mrs Rosebourne, who are returning to Boston. We saw them off in style at Mrs Hart's elegant home with a table hosted by Mrs Wood, whose old rascal Jack Starr presented the Rosebournes with a pair of china dogs that matched entirely their own dear pets, who had remained at home for health reasons. Mrs Rosebourne said that they were the perfect complement to the set she had also received from a spirit in Mrs Addison's séance room.

Elsewhere, I was delighted on Saturday evening by an introduction to a new lady Medium operating in Balham. A blue-eyed, yellow-haired girl by the name of Miss Jane Hooper. Hailing from a respectable Bristolian family, she is in possession of a guide with the most delectable singing voice. According to her sponsor, Mr Jeffries, she is growing in demand, so I would recommend making an appointment now to avoid any disappointment!

CHAPTER 4

Westbourne Grove thrummed with life beneath the crisp, white sky.

Everywhere skirts and cloaks bustled, colourful silks and crêpe brushing alongside dull serge and cotton, hems dragging through grit and mud and the occasional grey slick of slush clinging on from January's blizzards. Gentlemen tipped their hats, and ladies gave polite nods as they passed, everyone commenting on just how cold it was.

'It's almost *March*,' said Mrs Foster, who lived directly opposite Mrs Wood and was on her way back from the chemist's, her round face peeking pinkly out of a swaddle of hat and shawl.

'So true,' said Mrs Wood with a commiserating shake of her head. 'But dearest, how are you? I feel as though I've barely seen you this winter.'

'Well, we were away over January of course, but Mr Foster has forced us into isolation this week with his wisdom teeth.' She raised the little paper bag she was carrying and gave it an angry shake. 'Apparently, I'm the only one who's capable of purchasing the correct clove oil. We couldn't possibly send the girl out for it, not even in this weather.' Disdain sparked around her in sharp, frozen crystals.

'Will he not see a dentist?'

'I tell you, Mrs Wood, he'd rather let every single tooth rot in his head than allow an implement near one.'

'But wisdoms are the easiest to pull!' Mrs Wood said, before remembering herself with a wince.

Mrs Foster stopped and squinted at her, then laughed. 'Oh, of *course*! Your grandfather was a dentist, wasn't he? I always forget about that!'

Mrs Wood fumbled with her shawl, furious for not having more control over herself. 'Only a provincial one . . .'

'Did he have any fellow dentists that you might recommend? Perhaps if it came from you, Mr Foster might be tempted to change his policy.'

'He didn't practise in London, I'm afraid,' she said quickly.

But Mrs Foster wasn't listening. 'I didn't see you at Miss Hooper's the other day,' she was saying.

'Miss Hooper?'

'Yes, you know. That young singing Medium from Balham. A crowd of us went down after we read about her in the *Spiritual Times*. I thought you'd be there – some of your people were.'

'We've been so busy . . .' Miss Newman said.

'Was she any good?' she asked lightly.

But Mrs Foster had stopped listening again. This time the woman's eyes had slipped beyond Mrs Wood's shoulder and she gave a shout. 'Oh, for goodness' sake,' she said. 'Again?'

'What is it?' asked Miss Newman, while Mrs Wood turned but all she could see was a laden omnibus, its wheels throwing out great ropes of filth in its wake as it barrelled on up towards the Gate.

'You!' Mrs Foster shouted, and then to Mrs Wood: 'It's that damned young urchin,' she said. 'She's there every time you have one of your parties. Standing outside our home like she owns the place. Mr Foster thought she was one of yours, but I couldn't imagine that she was . . .' Mrs Foster's words drifted into noise as Mrs Wood stared into the chaos.

Through a gap in the traffic she could see who Mrs Foster was shouting to.

The girl!

That same girl she'd been seeing.

In the daylight. In the *flesh*.

She was on the other side of the road, her back to them as she studied the window of Carmichael's tobacconists. Even without seeing her face, she was sure: the line of her shoulders – narrow and straight – felt as familiar as if they belonged to a family member.

It was her, all right.

She didn't need all those years of experience reading people in an instant to know: this girl was a runner. She had to get to her before the girl saw her. And so, without even thinking, she was moving across the road, feeling rather than seeing vehicles swerve and honk around her as she closed in on the girl, her eyes fixed on her in case she should disappear.

But as Mrs Wood reached the kerb a gig sounded its horn at her and the girl turned at the sound. As their eyes met, a flash of horror crossed the girl's face.

'Please,' she said, smiling as reassuringly as possible. 'I just . . .'

The girl's mouth opened and Mrs Wood thought she was going to speak, but instead she abruptly gathered her skirts and took off.

No!

She could not let this opportunity pass by. She could not afford to miss this chance to find out who that girl was and what she wanted. And so, in a split second decision borne of utter desperation, she went after her, her knee screaming and her delicate boots slipping beneath her on the grit. 'Wait!' she shouted as she dashed on, somehow still upright, the girl's filthy shawl a flag in the distance. 'Please!' she called again. 'Wait!'

Through the wall of pedestrians, she saw the shawl turn onto Hereford Road, the gap between them extending further, but she ploughed on, hustling through the crowds with as much dignity as possible until she finally reached the corner, cresting around, expecting to see the girl as a dot in the distance, not paying attention until she crashed into something.

A body. Small. Hard.

They tumbled to the ground, Mrs Wood landing on top.

The world had ceased to exist; all she could hear was her raging breath and her heart thumping. She hauled herself onto all fours, waiting a moment until decency prevailed and her ability to breathe without needing to vomit forced her to clamber to her feet where she gripped a nearby railing, holding her side as she glanced at the person she had sent flying.

The girl was sitting up on the pavement, staring forlornly at the palms of her hands.

'Are you all right?' she asked, through gasps.

The girl nodded as she gingerly wiped her hands on her skirt. 'Are you?'

She started at the familiarity of the question. She hadn't just humiliated herself on Westbourne Grove for pleasantries. She released her grip on the railings, inhaling slowly to regain herself just as she did in seances, and when she looked at the girl again it was as Mrs Wood restored to all her glory. 'Who are you?' she asked, her voice clean and level.

The girl tried to turn and scrabble to her feet but Mrs Wood was ready. 'No you don't, she said grabbing her arm and pulling her up. 'I've seen you out there,' she continued, holding tight. 'I know you've been watching me. What do you want?'

This close, she could see that she had been wrong when she had assumed the girl was an urchin. She wasn't someone of means, that was certain: not with the shabby skirts or the shawl that looked like it had been rescued from a sewer. But her face was clean, and she'd clearly taken time over her hair, and when she reached out a hand to fix her tatty little hat, the nails were clipped and cared for.

The girl had gone limp in her grasp. 'I . . .' she began, her voice childlike, and Mrs Wood found herself straining to hear her, to understand how this enigma sounded. 'I didn't mean . . .' But then she cringed into herself as Miss Newman came suddenly around the corner, calling for Mrs Wood.

'Violet,' cried Miss Newman. 'Violet, what are you *doing*?' Then she stopped as she saw the girl. 'What happened? Did she assault you?'

'No. Of course not,' Mrs Wood said with a snort.

'Then . . . Then what is it?' Miss Newman asked.

'This is the girl,' said Mrs Wood. 'The one we've been seeing.'

Miss Newman's eyes darted between them in confusion until the truth suddenly dawned. 'Oh! *You!*' she said, rounding on the girl. 'What are you up to? What do you want?'

The girl shrank back again. 'Nothing! I promise!' she said, Mrs Wood recognising the estuary she was trying to hide in her words. 'It's not how it looks.'

'Come,' said Mrs Wood finally, and she let the girl go. 'We can't have this conversation here on the street.'

'Violet?' Miss Newman said, turning her back slightly towards the girl, trying to catch Mrs Wood's eyes. 'What are you doing?'

'This child clearly wants something,' said Mrs Wood. 'Shouldn't we at least find out what?'

They sat in Tilly's Coffee House, a quiet establishment of doilies and elderly ladies on the corner of Ledbury Road. The waitress seated them near the glass display cabinet of oozing cakes and pastries, but for once, Mrs Wood found herself too distracted to covet one.

'So,' she said, folding her hands in her lap as the girl fidgeted with the napkin and silverware. 'Shall we discuss what's been going on?'

The girl cleared her throat, but before she could speak, they all had to sit back as cups of hot chocolate were slid onto the table and when the waitress left, the girl seemed to have been bolstered by the interruption. She took a mouthful of her hot chocolate and replaced the cup into its saucer, turning it slightly by the handle as she stared thoughtfully at it.

'I'm sorry,' she said. 'What I've been doing. I can see how you might think it was odd.' Her voice was light and Mrs Wood placed her as not much older than sixteen. 'I just . . .' she tailed off, and took another mouthful of chocolate as she considered her next words.

Mrs Wood shared a glance with Miss Newman.

'Would you like a bun to go with that?' she asked.

The girl shook her head. 'You've been more than generous with the chocolate – I couldn't hope to pay you back for a bun . . .'

Miss Newman gave a sigh of submission. 'They're very good in here,' she said to the girl. 'You must try one.' And she leaned back in her chair and called the waitress, ordering three buns.

'Shall we start from the beginning?' Mrs Wood said after the waitress had slid their order onto the table with too much fanfare. 'What's your name?'

The girl looked up from her plate with a coy smile. 'Emmeline,' she said. 'Emmeline Finch, but my friends call me Emmie.'

Mrs Wood nodded. 'Well, we're not friends yet, so I shall hold with Miss Finch for now.'

The girl – Miss Finch – flushed and looked away. 'I'm sorry if I scared you,' she said. 'I really didn't mean to. I was. . . I was getting up the courage to speak to you. The *Spiritual Times* is always saying where you're off to and whose table you're supposed to be sitting at, and I thought that I might be able to catch your attention. But . . . you always looked so busy.'

'So, you *were* following me, then.'

And the girl dropped her face into her hands and groaned. 'I'm such a fool!' she said. 'Every time I knew where you'd be, I told myself that I would be brave enough to speak with you.'

'Could you not have simply written, like everyone else?'

She blushed again and looked down. 'I thought I might get lost in all the letters you must get sent. I really was going to speak to you I . . . I suppose I hoped this might happen one day.'

'You took some serious risks just for a conversation,' said Mrs Wood with a frown. 'What if I should have called the police?'

'I didn't know what else to do,' the girl said earnestly. 'I only wanted to talk to you.'

'But what is it that you've been so desperate to talk to me about?'

The girl took a breath. 'I want to learn,' she said.

'Learn what?'

There was a pause as the girl collected herself and, when she finally spoke, there was a noticeable shift in her tone and her eyes met Mrs Wood's with an unnerving certainty. 'I've been told I have the gift,' she said.

'Well, that's very nice for you,' she said, but the girl shook her head.

'I don't want to be one of many,' she continued. 'I want to be like you.' Her eyes were unyielding now. 'I want to be the best.'

Miss Newman gave the tiniest laugh, but Mrs Wood remained still. 'You want me to teach you,' she said. 'That's what this is about. You want me to teach you to become a Medium.'

Now Miss Newman snorted. 'Mrs Wood doesn't take on . . .' she began, but Mrs Wood placed a halting hand on her arm and she stopped.

'Why should I do that?' she said. 'You've seen yourself how busy I am. Even if I had the inclination, why on earth would you think I had the *time* to do such a thing?'

'Because I'm different,' she said, and Mrs Wood felt Miss Newman move to interject and she squeezed her arm to hold her steady.

The girl's audacity was oddly charming, and she couldn't help smiling. 'You are?' she said, and the girl nodded.

'I am,' she said. 'And if you give me the chance, I know you'll see it too.'

Mrs Wood released Miss Newman's arm and clasped her hands

together, resting her chin on her thumbs. She took in the girl across the table, saw how young she was, how bright her cheeks and fresh her eyes. And then, beyond that childishly flustered facade, she could see her core and it was cool, composed and startlingly familiar.

Something stirred and began to gather weight.

Hadn't she been worried about keeping her patrons' interest? Hadn't she been concerned about becoming old-fashioned and dull? What would happen if, instead of everyone reading about a brand-new Medium with pink cheeks and pretty eyes breaking into the London spiritual community, they read that Mrs Wood was the one responsible for introducing her? Lady Morgan would surely be intrigued to discover this young, exciting talent at Mrs Wood's table. And once Lady Morgan was on board, there would be no limit to how much the rest of young society might pay for the same privilege too. Perhaps this way she might even be able to work her way out of the investment hole without having to rely on Mr Larson.

'Come to the house,' she said suddenly, and she felt Miss Newman start beside her.

'Violet?' she said, her voice laced with caution.

But she ignored her. Of course, the girl could have been lied to by some well-meaning soul. Or, worse, she could be lying full stop. There was every chance that, despite what she said, the girl would have no more gift than one of Miss Cram's disgusting dogs. But she had seen too many girls being lauded with mediocre talents to not understand the power of a handsome countenance. And Mrs Wood knew that when it came to Mediums, the right table made all the difference, with even the most hopeless capable of presenting a modicum of interest beneath a more understanding tutelage. Some of her own Circle were testimony to that. She set her jaw and smiled. 'Monday morning at ten o'clock. Come to the house and I shall tell you my decision.'

The girl's face flushed. 'Really?' she said, breathless, childlike again.

'Violet? Should we not consult the appointment book first?'

But she continued, steadfast. 'Come to the house on Monday and I shall tell you what I have decided.'

'Of . . . of course,' stammered the girl half-rising, looking about, appearing suddenly unsure of what to do with herself.

'Now,' Mrs Wood said and, ignoring the consternation radiating from Miss Newman, she collected her gloves from the table and stood. 'We must be getting on. I have a lot to do.'

CHAPTER 5

The girl arrived the following Monday morning at the stroke of ten. Eliza showed her in, making no effort at all to hide her contempt for waiting on a girl who was clearly of her own station.

She stood in the hallway, blinking and pale, clutching that filthy shawl in shivering hands, wearing a cream cotton dress sprinkled all over with fading pink rosebuds that was far too thin for winter and stiff with filth around the hem. Her hair was a dull yellow, coiled into a bun at the nape of her neck, the parting severe and the fringe stringy against her forehead. As Mrs Wood approached, she caught the smell of clove oil and railways over something faintly animal that spoke of cheap lodgings.

'Come,' she said. 'Eliza has set out hot tea in the parlour.' And she led her towards the room where she held her private consultations. 'A sacred space to some,' she said with the sweep of the door, immediately regretting the joke as the colour drained entirely from the girl's face. 'You remember Miss Newman,' she said quickly, and propelled her gently into the room. Miss Newman's caution had remained. *You have no need to worry about your audience*, she had insisted, of course, but she had to admit that she too was rather intrigued to know what the girl's young blood could bring to their table. She greeted Miss Finch warmly, stepping forward with her society badge on prominent display on the lapel of her jacket. 'How was your journey?' she asked, taking her hand.

'Oh.' The girl allowed herself to be ushered into the room. 'It's really easy,' she said awkwardly. 'I'm only over near the Rec.'

Mrs Wood hesitated. 'Towards St James's church?' she said, and glanced at Miss Newman. 'On your own?'

'I share a room with another girl. She's at the abattoir, but she's nice enough. And there are other people in the house. They're all decent sorts.'

Mrs Wood nodded and turned to straighten the cushion on her chair, grimly curious as to what the girl's understanding of 'decent' might be in the context of the dwellings she knew to exist around the recreation ground.

'Have some tea,' said Miss Newman, and she settled the girl into the green wingback chair on one side of the fire and handed her a cup.

'Thank you,' said the girl as it rattled nervously in her hands, but Mrs Wood was cheered to see the roses returning to her cheeks.

She settled herself opposite, positioning and repositioning the cushion until she was comfortable.

'Now then,' she said without ceremony as Miss Newman moved to the chair in the corner to observe. 'Why Mediumship?'

The girl hesitated, resting the cup and saucer in her lap as she considered her words. 'Because,' she said, 'there is nothing else that I care about or can do so well.' She looked up and there was that fight Mrs Wood had seen in the café the previous Thursday. 'I feel the Spirit world around me all the time. I hear them. And I want to see them, help them transform into this world. I want to bring them to the people they want to speak with. I want to be that channel for them. I want that more than anything in the world.'

The words seemed to have emptied the girl, and she sat back, suddenly self-conscious. 'Or maybe that's too much,' she said quickly. 'Maybe that's just a silly dream.'

'Not at all,' said Mrs Wood. 'Everything you said . . . it's *all* the right reasons.'

The girl looked fully at ease for the first time since they'd met and Mrs Wood was struck again by how pretty she was – her eyes were spring-sky blue, her smile luminous. Good, she thought, noting her delicate fingers and small ears. After a bath and a new dress there would be much to say about this girl, even if very little of it were about her skills as a Medium.

'All right,' said Mrs Wood. 'There's no need for suspense. I have decided that I shall offer you the opportunity of learning with me. You have yet to show me this gift you've alluded to, but I will assume it exists until proven otherwise. If it transpires the gift is remarkable only by its absence, then we will stop immediately. Do you understand?'

The girl blinked. 'Are you saying I can learn? Are you saying you're going to teach me?'

Mrs Wood offered one of her most benevolent of nods. 'I will give you my time and my experience for free. In return, as you become more confident and capable, I will permit you to join my table where you will learn how to present your work in a public arena and meet people you would never have access to in any other position.'

The girl's teacup rattled and splashed as she sat forward, her whole body braced in excitement. She shoved the cup onto the side table without looking, her eyes on Mrs Wood, her face everything Mrs Wood had hoped it would be: lit up with delight. 'You're saying you will?'

'She is,' said Miss Newman, with a laugh. 'She's saying yes.'

'Oh, Mrs Wood! Mrs *Wood*!' the girl exclaimed, jumping to her feet, her hands pressed to her cheeks as her words tripped over themselves. 'Are you sure? I mean . . . do you mean it? You're really going to . . . ?' Her eyes glittered and tears spilled from the corners like diamonds. 'I can't believe it. I didn't ever think you would. After what you said . . . I thought a policeman might be waiting for me rather than . . . *this*.'

'Miss Finch,' said Mrs Wood, but she couldn't hold the smile in; the girl's pleasure was intoxicating. 'Please, let's remain calm,' she said. 'We have things to discuss. Sit. Please.'

The girl sat immediately, attempting to restrain herself, turning in her chair and looking at Miss Newman and then back to Mrs Wood. 'I'm sorry,' she said. 'I'm sorry, I . . . I can't believe it. I really can't.' She took several ragged breaths until she could finally take one long, deep inhale. Then she exhaled and looked back at Mrs Wood. Her cheeks were red, her fringe askew and her eyes still damp, but she had subdued the energy and, with another breath, she spoke in a voice that was almost calm. 'Thank you,' she said. 'You will not regret this opportunity.'

'I do understand that you're pleased, Miss Finch,' said Mrs Wood. 'But this is not a prize. You are to work and work hard when you are with me. This is the beginning of something I believe will be very special, but it is also the beginning of a journey for you that will only end with your passing.'

The girl swallowed.

'We will discuss the process, but the thing I insist upon is that while you are my pupil you are loyal only to me. You must not host your own tables or consultations without my permission. And you never speak of what we do. Discretion is key, Miss Finch. I have a reputation and I cannot have my name associated with anything but excellence.'

'Yes ma'am.'

'I have decided too that as you will be known as my pupil, you will receive a stipend. It's important that you look as though you belong in the society you will perhaps soon be moving amongst, after all.'

'Illusion is everything,' the girl said.

Mrs Wood's eyes widened in surprise at the girl's turn of phrase. 'Well,' she said, wondering for a moment if perhaps she might have said it herself earlier. 'Well, yes,' she fumbled. 'Illusion is important.' Then she cleared her throat. 'But it's talent we shall be working on,' she said, recovering. '*Talent* is everything.'

The girl nodded. 'Of course, ma'am.'

'Now,' Mrs Wood said, with forced change of tone. 'Why don't we confirm our arrangement with a nice little séance, just the three of us.'

As arranged, Miss Newman kept an eye on the girl while Mrs Wood slid into her trance, noting how she responded throughout the short session. Over the ten minutes, Miss Finch was treated to a welcome from Jack Starr and one of her distant relatives also stopped by before the candles were relit.

In the half-light, the girl's eyes shone like moons and when Mrs Wood glanced over towards Miss Newman, she felt a silent wave of relief when she responded with a smiling nod of approval.

CHAPTER 6

It was a Monday morning.

A Miss Finch morning.

A Miss Finch morning with a very special event!

Mrs Wood bounced from bed not caring about the cold, empty grate, throwing open her own curtains to allow the watery morning light to wash across the room while she waited for Miss Newman to arrive with coffee and her séance silk.

How quickly she had come to look forward to a Miss Finch morning, she thought, sitting on the edge of the bed. How quickly the girl had knitted her way into her life.

Mrs Wood had surprised herself with how well she had taken to the role of tutor. While the decision to do so had been easy, the actual content and method in which she would deliver her lessons had loomed as a great unknown. She could hardly call on her own training – she didn't know enough public houses around which to drag the girl for a start, and she wasn't about to start hiding her beneath tables at Tilly's while charging punters a penny a spirit.

She quickly realised that the challenge was this: how did one impart the skills of a Medium without giving *away* the skills of a Medium? And so, as they progressed, every word she spoke was double-checked to ensure its safety: there existed a very fine line between teaching skills that may enhance one's gift and declaring oneself a fraud before one's own pupil. It was a high-wire act of grand proportions.

After much discussion with Miss Newman, she settled on a programme that would introduce the girl to the world of spirits through trance work. Explaining breathing methods seemed a benign enough place to start – creating the right rhythm to loosen the tendons and sinews of her mind. Then she introduced listening, combined with visual cues to fill in the blanks when the spirits were a little quieter. There was nothing untoward in any of those skills, after all.

Whoever had told the girl that she had the gift had been right, though. She most certainly had something. She was naturally attentive, one of the foundation stones of Mediumship which relied on a honed ability to listen to both what was and was not said. That this appeared to be second nature to the girl spoke to her exciting potential.

And so, the girl slowly blossomed in her care.

That morning marked their fifth week of lessons and Mrs Wood trotted down the stairs, heading straight to the back parlour where the girl was waiting.

She stood at the window, staring out towards the budding garden, so transfixed that she didn't notice that Mrs Wood had entered. Her distraction gave Mrs Wood a moment to peruse her pupil without embarrassment. She wondered when she might be able to offer to purchase a new gown for her. She had managed to launder the cream cotton thing a few weeks ago – it had got to the point where she had needed to open a window after the girl left, and while it looked better and was becoming more suitable with the improving weather, she had noticed a button missing from the left wrist last week.

She calculated the cost of a dress. Mid-grade cotton, or even bombazine, with decent petticoats – nothing too showy but of a quality that suited her Circle. That couldn't be more than five pounds. Six at the most.

Mr Larson had promised an update on a potential new investment later that week in a tone that was certainly more optimistic than when they last had spoken, giving her hope that her period of austerity was coming to an end.

And she had been austere. There had been no fires lit on the first floor since that day in February when she'd heard about the mine; they'd been eating meat the texture of shoe leather every day, and the industrial cleaner had loosened a seam on her newest silk which she had had to fix herself. These measures meant that she was quite confident she could spare a few pounds to invest in a dress for the girl. Especially as she intended for her to attract the eyes of both Mrs Wood's existing and, more importantly, potential patrons. No matter how well she was learning, the very thought of introducing her to someone of such status as the Dowager in her present state made Mrs Wood feel quite sick.

No. The plan was set, and so was Mrs Wood's mind. Investing in the girl's improvement, inside and out, was a clever diversion of her remaining funds. Talent dressed in tatt would never do the trick.

Would green be the best choice for a spring gown? Was that what girls Miss Finch's age wore? Or would she prefer a pale blue like a duck's egg? *She needs gloves too*, she thought, taking in the pinkness of the girl's hands, still raw from the walk. And those boots, although clean and buffed, had obviously belonged to at least one previous wearer; they would give her origins away immediately. If the girl were to showcase Mrs Wood's skills, she needed to mirror her, and Mrs Wood would not wear someone else's boots. Something smarter. Something new. And slippers for the evening events. Silk. No more than eight pounds on the whole wardrobe, ten at the absolute limit. She would put an order in that afternoon and present them to the girl as a surprise. A reward for her hard work.

The floorboard creaked beneath Mrs Wood, and the girl jumped, whirling around.

'Oh!' she said, her hand at her throat and she laughed when she saw Mrs Wood. 'Oh, you gave me a fright!'

'I apologise,' she said. 'You looked so peaceful standing there.'

'It's such a nice view,' said the girl, turning back. 'I could look out at all that green forever.'

Mrs Wood came alongside her, took in the girl's scent of woodsmoke and damp beneath the more pungent smell of clove oil that she'd grown to associate with her, even grown to like. In a way. *She'll need a posy,* she thought. If the girl were to stay in the room she was renting over by the recreation ground, she would need a posy for visiting. She'd already been thinking about raising her stipend, but perhaps she could invest it into somewhere better for the girl to live. Somewhere more fitting for someone of her elevating status.

'There wasn't much like this where I grew up,' the girl was saying, pointing out of the window. She sighed. 'Not unless you count the weeds coming through the slabs. There was plenty of them.'

'But you had the sea,' said Mrs Wood, suddenly reminded of her own childhood framed by the whipping wind and angry waves of the North Sea.

The girl shrugged. 'There's so many boats in Chatham, you don't get to see much more'n a sliver of the thing.'

'Well.' Mrs Wood patted the girl's thin arm. 'That's all in the past now. So,' she said, taking the girl's elbow and steering her towards the chair beside the fire. 'Big day.'

'Yes,' said the girl, and her face became suddenly anxious. 'I can't wait to meet the Circle. I can't believe you think I'm already good enough.'

'You're coming along well, dear. And you're only there as an observer, so that you can get an understanding of how Circles work. There's no need for you to say or do anything other than watch those with experience at work.' She patted the girl's hand again. 'It's simply a wonderful opportunity to meet some ladies who can teach you almost as much as me.'

While they sat in the drawing room waiting for the women to arrive, Miss Newman explained to Miss Finch everything she should and shouldn't do when she met the Circle – *do* compliment either one of the Adams sisters on their hair/dress/complexion, *do not* ask Miss Brigham about her eyepatch.

And then, with a light tinkle of the doorbell, the first member arrived in the form of gentle, powder-soft Mrs Reynolds, entering like a whisper.

Then the kerfuffle of the Adams sisters, Hyacinth and Laetitia, gushing about the power of a séance they'd taken part in the night before as they unwrapped themselves to reveal startling orange dresses. They had been coddled and closeted children, doted upon by a widowed father and devoted to one another. On his premature death ten years prior, when Laetitia had only just come of age, they had moved into rooms on Bayswater Road that had, over the years, grown chaotic with the fabric remnants they used to make their own, giddy gowns.

Behind the sisters, briskly removing her gloves to fan her pink cheeks, came Miss Brigham, a woman who lost her eye and any sense of decorum in a riding incident when she was fifteen. She, like the rest of the group, had a soft spot for the sisters and always called on them ahead of Circles even though the Bayswater Road added an extra half an hour to the walk from her home by Westbourne Park station where she lived in relative ease with her invalid mother.

There was no Mr Larson, nor Mrs Reynolds' husband, as it was a Wednesday afternoon, and they would be ensconced in Important Work in town. The group was completed that afternoon, then, by the arrival of Mrs Hart a few moments later, frantic and flapping.

One of the more well-known members of Mrs Wood's Circle, Mrs Hart was the only member, besides herself, who hosted her own tables and séances within the community. She'd honed her gift while living with her diplomat husband in Philadelphia and found Mrs Wood on her return to London. Mrs Wood still remembered the first words Mrs Hart had said to her after sitting at one of Mrs Wood's tables. 'I've been searching for someone with commensurate talent. And now I have found her.'

While she was good, Mrs Hart's star had never ascended to the height of Mrs Wood's and it was only through sheer luck of the draw that Mrs Hart's self-absorption prevented her from realising: she didn't need to prove she was as good as Mrs Wood because Mrs Hart simply believed that she was. And they worked well together, which meant that Mrs Wood was able to forgive her more irritating idiosyncrasies – the way she talked to the frayed edges of her breath and how often she rearranged her corsetry when she thought no one was looking. She would endure all of that because, when the candles went out, their séances were the stuff of wonder that regularly delighted readers of the *Spiritual Times*.

'Leopold's nurse stopped me as my hand was on the door handle!' she complained, flooding the room with noise as she tugged at her hat, which had caught on one of her many elaborate curls. 'I told her I simply had to leave for my Circle, but she was very insistent. You know how *dramatic* that woman can be.' She finally freed her hair with a flourish and tossed the hat into Eliza's waiting hands. 'But, of course, it wasn't important in the slightest,' she continued. 'He had simply put something disgusting in her shoe which I told her is what little boys are supposed to do. As a nurse of her years, you would think she would already know that.' She gave a sigh as only one who has really had quite enough can give. 'You are all so lucky to be childless,' she said. 'It is *nothing* like the stories.'

Mrs Reynolds placed a comforting hand on her arm. 'It sounds as though you have had a vexing morning,' she said. 'Come,' she gestured towards the sideboard where a cluttered tray of tea-things sat. 'Let me pour you something.'

Mrs Hart sighed again. 'Do you have anything stronger, dear?' she asked Mrs Wood. 'I'm not sure tea is sufficient today.'

'You should dismiss that nurse if she's bothering you so much,' said Miss Newman, whose archness was lost on Mrs Hart.

'Oh no,' she said. 'I couldn't possibly. You know she was Mr Hart's nursemaid. She's been with his family forever. I'm stuck with the old baggage.'

'Perhaps you could get someone in to help her, instead?' said Laetitia Adams. 'If I were a child's nurse, I would play with my charge all the time and never grow bored or tired. I have plenty of books I could share with them. And we could draw all day. And go for walks.' She sighed. 'It would be a dream.'

Mrs Hart gave a snort. 'Mr Hart would never agree,' she said. 'And besides, Leopold will begin his schooling soon.'

'As long as she's *compos mentis*, she's fit for work,' Miss Brigham said, her good eye pinning Mrs Hart. 'I told Mother I can manage with the invalid chair, but if she begins to lose her marbles I shall take her out into the garden with Father's shotgun.'

'You have a shotgun?' asked Hyacinth Adams with a gasp.

'No,' said Miss Newman. 'She doesn't.'

'I have two,' said Miss Brigham.

Hyacinth exchanged an excited look with her sister. 'And you'd really shoot her?'

Mrs Wood placed a calming hand upon her arm. 'Of course she wouldn't. She's playing with us.'

'I would,' said Miss Brigham.

'You wouldn't,' said Miss Newman.

'There shall be no more talking of shooting, thank you,' said Mrs Wood.

In the hubbub, no one seemed to have noticed the girl standing quietly at the foot of the stairs. But now, as Mrs Wood moved beside her, they saw her and the noise fell to a sudden silence.

'Before we start,' she said, 'I have someone I would like to introduce you to.' She looked at her pupil and couldn't help the pride billowing in her chest. 'Everyone: this is the girl I have been telling you about. *This* is Miss Emmie Finch.'

CHAPTER 7

Mrs Wood had only officially joined a spirit circle when she came to London. Before that, she'd been too busy with the actual work to dedicate herself to any one particular Circle, but London had been different. In Hull, Circles were the domain of old ladies who valued a good seedcake above anything else. The first Circle she joined when she had arrived in the capital was initially for appearances, but it quickly became clear that Miss Quinn, while a cliché with her white hair and abundance of long-tailed cats, had a more interesting approach. She and her small collection of spinsters and widows sat together in a bold sisterliness that taught her more about real, rooted Mediumship than she ever knew she needed: she and her Mediums, including the now ruined Mrs Trimble, came together in a way that relied more on trust than trickery.

The idea of this shrouded approach had felt alien to Mrs Wood as a newcomer to the Circle. She had grown up with Thirza and nothing had gone unexplained between them, but it was apparent from the day she joined Miss Quinn's Circle that such candour was not only unexpected, it was unwelcome. Her table was a place of earnest spiritualism, where the women brought only their dedication to hearing and seeing spirits with them into the darkness.

She worried during those early tables that she would find this approach stymying; that it would be too hard to deliver anything of interest without investment from others. But, actually, it taught her discipline and after years of conditional demands from Thirza and then the Dentist, the fact that the Circle wanted nothing from her but her company at the table filled her with a sense of security she hadn't realised she had been missing.

By the mid-sixties most of the Circle, including dear Miss Quinn, were dead or had moved to further parts of London, and so Mrs Wood had used all she had learned to launch her own Circle in Notting Hill. She purposefully sought out women who mirrored Miss Quinn's tribe, surrounding herself with the soft, sherberty soul of Mrs Reynolds, the relentlessly sunny Adams sisters, fuss-free Miss Brigham, the talent of Mrs Hart, and the marvellous logistical skills of Mr Larson and Mr Reynolds.

But she still missed having someone in whom to confide. Mr Wood believed too much to ever be that person, and the Circle deserved their innocence. So when Miss Newman agreed to become her assistant after that chance encounter in Sicily, Mrs Wood's world was finally complete. Miss Newman: far more interested in the manufacture of the spectacle than in hopeful calls to the beyond. Miss Newman, the genius planner with a focus on the technique; ready to listen, ready to help, ready to elevate Mrs Wood's séances to the next level. Miss Newman: who gave her an outlet to discuss the glorious *art* of it all without fear of ruin.

How wonderful to be fully, entirely, *truthfully* herself.

And so she had offloaded every single secret onto Miss Newman with all the joy and energy of a suddenly unburdened pack horse.

Well.

Almost every single one.

The girl took in the interest and intrigue from the Circle with sweet patience.

'I've heard so much about you,' she said to Mrs Reynolds, who pinked brightly.

'I've never known anyone who has two guns,' she said to Miss Brigham, who looked slightly less irritated.

'Your hair is every bit as wonderful as the papers say,' she told Mrs Hart.

And she purposefully mixed the Adams sisters up – 'I could've sworn you were the younger one' – which gave Laetitia the giggles while Hyacinth made a show of being wounded.

Mrs Wood looked on with maternal pride when she saw Miss Newman rub the girl's arm.

With a clap of her hands, she regained authority. 'Come,' she called over the noise. 'We shall run out of time with all this chatter! To the séance room, please!'

The women swarmed around Miss Finch, but as they neared the threshold of the already darkened room, the girl hung back, reaching out for Mrs Wood's arm.

'Miss Finch?'

'What if I let you down?' the girl said suddenly.

Mrs Wood give a laugh. 'Don't be silly!' She smiled and leaned towards her. 'You're only watching, remember. You have nothing to worry about.' She held her eyes for a moment longer until the girl's face softened, and then she led the way inside. 'Just sit and watch,' she whispered. 'That's all you need to do.'

She stepped back, letting the girl see the room for the first time. All their sessions had taken place in the back parlour and now she saw that the girl's hesitation had been more than a lack of confidence: this was one of the most famous rooms in all of spiritual London. This was where some of the most exciting things in spiritual lore had happened.

She steered her in, directed her to the table, where she stood amidst the bustle of the Circle as they settled themselves in their seats, fussing with bags and wraps, fetching glasses and cups, re-arranging corsetry and hair, everyone still on the topic of both Miss Brigham's guns and Mrs Hart's inept staff.

But the girl stood motionless, her eyes wide as she drank in the room. She placed a hand on the tabletop, a pillar in the sea of activity, looking wide-eyed around the room. Mrs Wood watched her take in the forest-green damask wallpaper and burgundy velvet drapes drawn tight across the shuttered window; the fat silver candlesticks on the mantel glimmering in the light from the subdued fire. And suddenly, she too was experiencing the room for the first time and was startled. This was hers. *This* was hers. Those silver candlesticks. The drapes and wallpaper. The bowls of hothouse roses on the sideboard giving off the tantalising smell of spring. Crystal glasses and a decanter glittering on the sideboard beside the bone china cups and laden cake-stand, mostly obscured by Mrs Hart, who couldn't decide if she wanted an éclair or Viennese slice to take to the table.

'Ladies, shall we?' Miss Newman called, and Mrs Hart slid both the éclair and Viennese slice onto her plate and settled finally beside Miss Brigham.

'Good,' Mrs Wood said, and pulled back her chair, which had a broader seat to allow for her skirts, pointing across the table at the chair she had chosen to be the girl's. 'Miss Finch. Please sit,' she said, and the girl sat.

Now that the table was complete, a calm settled across the room like a gauze.

Mrs Wood smiled around at these faces – so familiar, so dear – and then the girl. How quickly she had found her place in her world. 'It's lovely to see you all,' she said. 'And to welcome Miss Finch.' She inhaled deeply. 'Now. Shall we begin?'

Then the women reached for one another's hands and Mrs Wood began the opening prayer.

It was a perfectly serviceable séance. An afternoon that might have been considered rather good, she thought, had it been held in a lesser Medium's home. But as the proceedings drew to a close she felt a strange itch, as though everything was over before it had really begun.

There was nothing wildly wrong. She herself was, of course, flawless but here was Mrs Reynolds' angel, and there was Miss Brigham's highwayman and Hyacinth's glowing forehead. She worked to keep a sparkle going – Jack Starr delivering messages from the Adams sisters' lost mother and a salty sea-shanty which made Miss Brigham slap her knee in time – but as the Circle progressed with a series of intense rapping and spinning acorns, she couldn't help but see the whole thing through the eyes of a stranger and find it all a bit . . . pedestrian.

Perhaps it was the recent, seemingly incessant, talk about advancements and the whole damned full spirit nonsense that had put her on edge, but with the pat of Miss Newman's hand indicating that it was time to close the Circle, she had been nothing but despondent. Had no one anything new to bring? Had no one anything more exciting to do? She began to kick herself for not having an apport in her back pocket, something which would have given the girl a hint as to her main work, but she hadn't wanted the afternoon to be about her. She had wanted to show off the power of a united Circle, as Miss Quinn had shown off hers all those years ago.

The power was there, but that afternoon it felt buried beneath complacency and cake crumbs.

As the candles were relit, she found herself anxiously seeking out the girl's face, racked with a sudden fear that she should see confirmation of her own doubts. But as the shadows withdrew, the girl was revealed, her cheeks bright and her eyes looming with tears.

Perhaps all was not lost.

Mrs Wood was about to ask if she had enjoyed herself when the girl suddenly gripped Miss Brigham's hand and said in a quivering voice, 'That was tremendous, just *tremendous*.'

Miss Brigham, unaccustomed to being touched, yelped as though she had been burned.

'I'm so glad you enjoyed it,' said Mrs Reynolds, reaching in to replace Miss Brigham's hand with her own. 'You will come again, won't you?'

The girl looked across at Mrs Wood. 'I do hope so,' she said.

'Of *course*, you will,' she replied, trying to keep the relieved smile from giving everything away.

'And you must participate next time.' said Laetitia Adams.

'Oh,' said the girl, folding in on herself. 'Oh, I don't think so. I'm not ready in the least.'

'We all have to start somewhere,' said Miss Brigham, raising a questioning eyebrow at Mrs Wood.

'I'd ruin it for you all,' the girl protested. 'I'm nowhere near good enough. You are all exceptional. I've never . . .'

'Ladies,' Mrs Wood said, calling the room to order. 'Miss Finch will make her debut when I believe she is ready, and not a moment before.'

'Hear, hear,' said Mrs Hart. 'If I were you, Miss Finch, I would feel blessed simply being in the presence of some of the Mediums in this room.'

'Indeed, Mrs Hart,' said Mrs Wood, sharing a glance with Miss Newman. 'Now. After all that, I'm sure we've built up a thirst. Who would like some tea?'

After the bell had been rung, the Adams sisters drew the girl into a corner while Mrs Wood watched from the fireplace mantel, her mind playing over what they could've done differently. She barely registered Mrs Hart beside her until she spoke.

'I wonder if we shall ever have a séance without Miss Brigham's dreadful highwayman,' she murmured, wincing as her fingers wrangled with an element of her bodice.

Mrs Wood raised a warning eyebrow. 'Miss Brigham's heart is in the right place.' And Mrs Hart gave a dramatic gasp.

'Are you suggesting that ours are not?' she said.

'Fenella. I am suggesting that you would do well to remember that the Circle belongs to us all.'

'I know, I know,' she grumbled with one final poke at her bodice. 'But sometimes it would be nice if one of them did something vaguely fun, don't you think?'

'How do you like Miss Finch?'

Mrs Hart stopped and blinked. 'She's . . . Young.' She peered towards the girl, appraising her as though selecting a cut of meat. 'Well mannered. Pretty, if you like that sort of thing.'

'*Yes, yes.* But what of her as a member of our Circle?'

Mrs Hart's eyes turned sharp. 'What're you planning?'

'Planning? Why on earth would you think I was planning anything?'

'Because when have you ever shown the slightest interest in an inexperienced Medium,' she said.

She gave a withering sigh. 'Must you always be such a cynic? The only plan I have is to help Miss Finch become a capable Medium.'

Mrs Hart nodded slowly. 'Of course,' she said and patted Mrs Wood's arm. 'You are a true philanthropist.' Before Mrs Wood could reply, Eliza clomped in with a heaped tea tray, and Mrs Hart clapped her hands. 'Wonderful,' she said. 'I'm hoping there's more of those Viennese slices.'

Excerpt from the Editor's Column
Magnus Clore
Spiritual Times, 13th March 1873

How delightful: last Monday, I was treated to a little séance from young Miss Hooper – the singing Medium of Balham, of whom I have already 'sung' the praises in this column. Oh, what a voice! And what an unforgettable evening as Miss Hooper was joined by *another* Miss Hooper, the girl's cousin, who is just as pretty and in possession of a spirit who sings just as beautifully. Indeed we were treated to a veritable choral concert between them! Miss Hooper is becoming rather booked up, and even more so while the cousin is visiting. Make haste to Balham, I urge you!

CHAPTER 8

March picked up speed into spring, the endless wash of winter clouds now broken every so often by tantalising fragments of sunshine that teased of warm spells and parasols.

And yet, even with the girl's attention and flourishing talent, Mrs Wood found it difficult to match her spirits to the rising temperatures.

That month's Grand Séance had been and gone without note. Lady Morgan sent another message of apologies, although this time she was polite enough to note that she wasn't ill, simply that she had another engagement. It stung, however, when Mrs Wood read in the following week's *Spiritual Times* that Lady Morgan had been at Mrs Addison's niece's séance over in Mayfair.

And then, a week later, Lady Morgan and Lady Cooper had both been in Dalston, according to the *Spiritual Times*, at the table of an upstart who practised from a poky terrace. In the company of *clerks*!

When Miss Newman had read that out across the breakfast table she hadn't seemed anywhere near as concerned as she should have been. But Miss Newman didn't have to worry about making ends meet. She didn't have to worry about mines that went bankrupt or ageing patrons. No matter what happened, Miss Newman always had a hot meal on the table before her and clothes in her wardrobe. But the Dowager had scared them all with pneumonia the previous autumn and, while she'd made a full recovery, the incident had instigated a nagging reality around how much longer she would be able to rely on her monthly stipend. And hadn't Miss Newman even considered what would happen if Mrs Pepperdine or Mrs Farnham or the Countess had their heads turned by the upstart in Dalston or that dreadful singing Miss Hooper in Balham Mr Clore was so excited about. She thought of those stipends – the ones that kept them warm and fed – and she felt sick and furious at the same time.

But all was not bleak, no matter how frustrating the *Spiritual Times* or the fickle affections of youth became. Because here was the girl: something to invest in. A reason to contain her fears and believe she had a future. Besides giving her plenty of distraction, the girl was proving to be something of a talent.

So, when Mrs Wood woke on the morning of a Miss Finch day in late March, the sun was so glorious, the sky almost too painfully blue, she decided that, instead of spending the afternoon cloistered in the back parlour, they would take a stroll around the neighbour-hood. They had been all work since that very first session six weeks before – it was time that they took some time off and got to know one another and perhaps show off the little something Mrs Wood had picked up for her that week.

The girl hadn't even rung the bell when Mrs Wood threw open the door.

'You gave me the shock of my life!' the girl laughed, her hand pressed to her chest.

Mrs Wood took the girl's arm. 'Come!' she said, shutting the door behind them. 'I have a present for you.' She unlooped the old green shawl with the filthy embroidered fruit on it as she talked, dropping it into a puddled heap beside the umbrella vase as though it were toxic. Then she placed the brown paper parcel tied with a maroon silk ribbon into her hands.

'Here,' she said, and the girl's eyes opened as wide as a doll's.

'Another present?' she said with a gasp.

'Shush now,' said Mrs Wood. 'Open it.'

'Really, Mrs Wood. The dress and boots; the *gloves* were enough—'

'Just open it,' she said, peering keenly alongside.

The girl looked back at the package, a smile fighting at the corners of her mouth as she slid her fingers free of her new pale kid gloves, placing them delicately on the console. Then she took it with both hands, turning it in wonder before picking at the knot of the maroon ribbon. 'You really don't have to . . .'

'I know, I know,' said Mrs Wood. 'But I *want* to.'

The ribbon came free and the package sprung open and the girl let out a gasp as the paper fell to the floor. 'Mrs Wood!' she said, whipping out a short brown mantle made of velvet as lush as a camomile lawn, matching silk ribbons unspooled from the high, fluted neck as she lifted it up.

'It's beautiful, isn't it?' said Mrs Wood. 'Look at the back!' She spun the mantle in the girl's hands, fluffing the smart ruffled bustle that would sit over the girl's own. Now that the girl had a bustle, of course.

'I've never seen anything so lovely,' whispered the girl. Then she looked up. 'But I already have a wrap . . .' She glanced absently towards the corner where the shawl had been tossed.

'You can't possibly wear that old thing with your nice new dress,' said Mrs Wood with a laugh. 'They don't go at all. They're two different greens entirely.'

The girl shied away. 'I won't ever be able to repay you,' she said, pushing the mantle back to Mrs Wood. 'I'll never make enough money, no matter how good I am.'

But Mrs Wood held her hands up. 'I didn't buy any of these things because I expected you to pay me back.' She guided the girl towards the mirror. 'Let's try it on.'

'I can't accept it,' said the girl, but Mrs Wood draped it over her shoulders, the silk lining sliding easily over her arms, and when the girl looked at herself in the mirror, her chin rose.

Mrs Wood took a step back. 'The picture of elegance,' she said.

'I can't . . .' The girl began, but she turned her shoulders, her eyes drinking in the details. It fell perfectly to her hips, as Mrs

Wood had hoped it would, and her dainty hands and wrists peeped elegantly from the little openings.

'It's exactly how a girl like you should look,' she said. 'Polished, refined and sweet.'

'But it's practically summer,' she said. 'I shall get hardly any wear from it.'

'It's not even warm yet,' she said. 'And autumn will be here before you know it.'

The girl laughed. 'You're wishing away the best part of the year!' she said, and Mrs Wood gave a shake of her head.

'When you get to my age, dearest, heat is even less attractive than the cold.' She smiled. 'You must keep it, and you must wear it. Today. Now!'

'Aren't we supposed to have a séance?'

'We are,' said Mrs Wood. 'But your new mantle is far too becoming to be kept inside. Let's go for a walk along Westbourne Grove. Perhaps the confectioners will be open . . .'

The girl turned again, peering coquettishly over her shoulder and smiling at the ruffle. 'I never thought I'd look so smart.' Then she frowned suddenly and touched the nondescript felt hat that sat on top of her braided hair. 'Does it work with the hat, do you suppose? I worry it makes it look a bit . . . poor.'

Mrs Wood considered her. 'Perhaps we can look in at Madame Forlione's.'

'Oh no,' she said. 'She's far too expensive.'

'I have an account there,' she said. 'If we don't find a design you like today, we could always see if there's anything in Mr Whiteley's. A hat is as important as the coat.'

'And it will be summer soon . . .' said the girl. 'I always dreamed of having a summer hat and a winter hat.'

Mrs Wood smiled. How smart the girl looked as she secured the fat brown ribbons at her throat with a rabbit-eared bow. How different. She had started plaiting her hair into a neat roll since

Mrs Wood had suggested it might make her look more genteel. And now that that awful shawl was gone, the green silk dress she'd given her a few weeks ago was as vibrant as a spring day against the new earth-brown mantle. The girl was transforming, a swan shaking off the vestiges of her former gosling life.

It had been unfortunate that she and Mr Wood hadn't had their own child. His previous marriage had been barren too, and she had sometimes wondered in those early years of their marriage if he had chosen her, a much younger wife, to be surer of issue. He would never have told her even if he had been disappointed, of course, remaining silent when she had eventually converted the empty nursery into a dressing room. Instead, his gentle knocks on her bedroom door simply diminished until they stopped altogether, and she had been relieved that, finally, the endless failing was over and they could settle into comfortable proximity.

Still, she was luckier than other unfortunates who filled their empty arms with the comfort of small dogs; she had her work. Without the hindrance of a confinement, she was a constant presence at London's tables during the ribald days of the mid-sixties, the years when she established herself over all other Mediums through fearless persistence.

She had been too busy to regret what was obviously not supposed to be.

And then along came the girl. She'd been wondering recently: that profound surge of warmth she felt when she was around her – was that what a mother felt when they looked at their child?

The girl sighed. 'It's so lovely,' she said.

'Good,' said Mrs Wood. 'You've been learning well. You deserve it.'

'I was never good at school before,' she said. 'All I wanted was to get out and earn.'

How familiar that felt. Thirza had wanted her to learn to read and write so that she could improve her hidden value in séances, to know her numbers so she could keep track of the pennies and shillings. She had hated the forced nature of it all though, much preferred the real work of life: rapping beneath tables or snatching hair combs in the dark. But words needed scratching onto slates, and when you lived beneath the threat of poverty, knowing the difference between a ha'penny and a crown was essential.

'What was your family like when you was growing up?' the girl asked suddenly. 'I imagine you in this big house with a garden and a view and a *governess* and a pretty mama in fancy dresses. And a papa. With a monocle.'

Mrs Wood forced a laugh as she gathered the fallen wrapping paper. 'Oh, it wasn't so grand.'

'I heard your father was a doctor.'

'Mm,' she said, bending to fetch the ribbon.

'And your mother?' the girl continued lightly. 'You've got such lovely taste. I bet you get that from her.'

'Yes, she was very nice.' She busied herself scrunching the rubbish into the wastepaper basket beside the console, hoping that Mr Larson wouldn't visit and see that she'd bought the girl more things and not understand. She turned to the cloak stand to pull her bonnet from the top hook. 'Now. We should be quick if we're going for that walk. I have a consultation at five and I need to prepare.'

'Of course,' said the girl, then she hesitated. 'Do you mind me asking who your consultation is with? Only I was wondering if I could . . .'

'You know I can't tell you that,' said Mrs Wood briskly, knotting her bonnet in place. 'Private means private.' She pulled on a smile before she turned back to the girl. 'Come. Let's go show your new mantle off to everyone.' She placed her hand on the girl's back, ushering her towards the door. 'You really do look quite splendid.'

CHAPTER 9

Mrs Wood held her private consultations in the back parlour rather than the large séance room. Its size and position in the house offered an intimate sanctuary and, when clients were expected, she kept it dimly lit and comfortably heated, lightly furnished with two deep velvet wingback chairs placed before the fireplace, a gleaming walnut occasional table set between them topped by a round glass ashtray, the floor crossed with Turkish rugs. A glass-fronted display case against the far wall contained neat rows of red and green leather-bound books that, as far as Mrs Wood knew, had never been read, and a rubber plant collapsed in the opposite corner like a wounded actress. There were no photographs on the mantel here, only a simple painting of a calm seascape hanging above the casement clock.

She had always liked being in this space, more so than the séance room. It felt safe, like a cocoon, especially with the thick plum drapes pulled tightly shut. She liked to think that it offered the same to her clients, that they saw these four walls as a place of hope and discretion where they could unburden and reveal without fear of judgement or exposure.

That afternoon, her heart was still racing from the exertion of rushing back from successful hat-shopping with the girl, where both a spring and a summer selection had been purchased. She had devoured two hot cheese scones while listening to Miss Newman running through her preparation, impressed with the detail she'd managed to glean from her own carefully curated network that spread like invisible tentacles through society's kitchens. And then she was alone, finishing off a small bowl of orange segments that filled the room with the smell of continental trips, something she now understood Lady Frances to enjoy.

She lit the final candle in the back parlour and the room settled into a soothing flicker. She sat with a sigh, the vestiges of the day rising from her like ashes from the comfort of her chair. The orange finished, she slid the empty bowl beneath her chair and sat back, closing her eyes and allowing her breath to become long and deep; her heart growing steadier and stronger in the warm and quiet room.

The clock in the hallway tinged.

With one final exhale, she opened her eyes.

The front doorbell rang.

Lady Frances. Childhood playmate of a lady-in-waiting meant connections into the royal household. At any time, this would be a woman worth cultivating. With her current situation, however, she was now a woman Mrs Wood very much needed.

Lady Frances marched into the parlour with a countenance that spoke of saddles and hunts and plenty of older brothers, her skirt whipping about her manly strides.

'Lady Frances,' she said, shoving her hand at Mrs Wood.

'Welcome,' said Mrs Wood, wincing at the crush of the woman's grasp. 'I am delighted to have you in my home.'

'Heard a lot about you,' Lady Frances continued, and she hitched her skirts before sitting, as though forgetting that they weren't a pair of riding breeches. She shifted in the chair, attempting to cross her legs but finding the dress and chair too restrictive. Instead, she sat forward, her elbows on her knees as she watched Mrs Wood sit opposite her.

'Before we do anything,' she said, serious, brown eyes holding

Mrs Wood's. 'I want you to know that I don't believe any of this.'

Mrs Wood smiled instinctively. 'Oh?' she said.

'No,' she said. 'Ghosts and all that nonsense.'

'Ah,' said Mrs Wood. 'I'm glad you've told me. I tend to call them spirits, but . . .'

'After I . . .' she paused and glared before remembering herself. 'Lady Harrington told me I had to come and so . . .' She slapped her hands on the arms of the chair. 'Here I am.' She looked about the room, clicking her tongue before turning her stare back to Mrs Wood. 'Don't tell her I said that, will you? She can be sensitive about trifles.'

'Everything that's said between us is treated with the utmost of discretion. I think my reputation speaks to that.'

Lady Frances nodded and then sat back. 'So. What is it you do, then?'

'Do?'

'Yes,' she said. 'Do we sit here and then some *ghost* comes in and we . . .' She shrugged. 'I mean, what do you do?'

'As a Medium, I am a bridge to the Other Side.'

'So, if I fancied a chat with my mother . . . ?'

'It's not always as straightforward as that. I can't see who's coming, or even necessarily *hear* a spirit . . .'

'. . . then how do you know they're anything to do with me then, these *spirits*?'

'It's a sense,' she said. 'They show me images and I translate from that.'

Lady Frances levelled those penetrating brown eyes at her again. 'Images? That's it? You see stuff?'

'Yes. They'll often progress to voices, but firstly, when I'm new with a sitter, it starts with images.' If Lady Frances wanted to challenge her, she was more than happy to rise to it. Her connections were certainly worth the fight. 'And if you don't mind me saying, I'm already getting a very strong image here.'

Lady Frances's eyebrow went up, cynicism writ large across her face. 'You do,' she said.

'Oh yes,' she said. 'Usually I have to go into a trance to reach my spirit guide, but he's bashing me on the head with this one. That can happen if the mood is right.'

Lady Frances smiled, clearly not buying a word of it. 'Tell me.'

Mrs Wood closed her eyes and inhaled. She took a moment then opened her eyes again, relieved to see that Lady Frances was still there, albeit with an amused rather than awestruck gaze. 'I see a woman,' she said. 'He – my spirit guide is a man, Lady Frances – he's showing me a woman. Young. Very young. Barely a woman.'

Lady Frances rolled her eyes. 'Well, that could be anyone.'

'Of course,' she said, squinting. Breathing deeply. 'Would you mind if I . . .' She reached forward and grasped one of Lady Frances's hands. It was dry and awkward in hers, but she didn't pull away. 'Ah yes,' she said. 'It's much clearer now.'

'I suppose it's my mother.' Lady Frances's voice, for all its brusque bravado, was beginning to present as less sure. Yes. She was almost there.

'No,' said Mrs Wood, closing her eyes again. 'She's young. Very young. She's . . . she's showing me a . . . oh.' She stopped and looked at Lady Frances. 'I feel we have moved into this very quickly. Perhaps you would like some tea before we continue?'

'No,' said Lady Frances firmly, then cleared her throat. 'Continue if you must.'

Mrs Wood gave a clipped nod and closed her eyes again. Lady Frances's hand lay heavy in her own. 'She's showing me a . . . a rabbit.'

Lady Frances snatched her hand away and Mrs Wood opened her eyes to see a flurry of skirts. 'Lady Frances?'

'I don't know what you think you're doing, but I am *disgusted*,' she said, already at the door. She stopped, her hand on the handle, her face in disarray as she spat across the room: 'Disgusted!' And she heaved the door open, slamming it behind her so hard that the sashes rattled and one of the candles went out.

Mrs Wood sat in the suddenly empty room, her head reeling, listening to the disappearing footsteps of Lady Frances, a woman whose wealth and patronage could've made all the difference to her current financial precariousness. She had been too desperate and she had pushed her too far, overstepping the social boundaries between them before she had established the all-important emotional connection.

But then she realised, beneath the thudding of the blood in her ears, that the steps had stopped but the door had not slammed. And then, the footsteps began again. They were returning. Lady Frances was coming back. She prepared herself, straightened her skirt, took a mouthful of cordial, cleared her throat. She stood as the door opened.

'Lady Frances, I can only . . .' she said, fighting to keep the desperation from her voice.

But Lady Frances stood in the doorway, staring. 'What did she say?' she said. 'The girl with the rabbit, what did she want?'

Mrs Wood gathered herself quickly. 'I . . .' she began.

'What did she want?' Lady Frances said again.

'She showed me the horse,' Mrs Wood said. 'She showed me that . . . that it was her choice.'

Lady Frances staggered a little. She pushed the door shut behind her, reaching forward for the chair as Mrs Wood jumped to take her arm and helped her to sit. Then she bobbed down beside her. 'She keeps telling me that it was her choice. She wanted to see the river.'

'Who told you?' Lady Frances said, her voice a hoarse whisper.

Her mind snagged involuntarily for a moment on the hidden layers of work Miss Newman had put into this moment, those hard-won friendships through the understairs world. 'Your dear cousin has shown me,' she said, her voice matching her client's own.

'Clemmie,' the woman whispered.

'Such a sweet name for a girl.' Lady Frances gave a sad snort in agreement before Mrs Wood continued. 'Clemmie has shown herself to me because she worries. You cannot continue to carry this with you. It wasn't your fault.'

'The rabbit scared the bloody horse,' Lady Frances said. 'But I was the one who'd told Clemmie to go away in the first place. I didn't want her around, not with Ferdy there. She was always such a bloody limpet . . .'

'And if only you hadn't . . .'

The mask finally fell, and Lady Frances crumpled into her arms.

As Mrs Wood held her, the woman's sobs shaking both of their bodies, she felt a sense of completion: she had done her job.

Eventually, Lady Frances sat back, wiping her face on her sleeves. 'You must think me grotesque,' she said. 'It wasn't as if anything came of that idiot Ferdy after everything. Especially once . . .' Her words disappeared but her eyes, now small and pink, held Mrs Wood's. 'Did she really come to you?'

She smiled and squeezed her arm. 'I couldn't keep her away. She's been waiting to tell you for a while.'

Lady Frances sat back and wiped her face again. 'My word,' she said after a while. 'I'm not sure what to believe now.'

Mrs Wood laughed and returned to her chair, her knees clicking irritably after being bent for so long. 'Do you still think it's nonsense?'

'I don't know what it is,' she said, then she paused. 'You won't tell anyone, will you? That I came here today. That I . . . that this happened.'

Mrs Wood sat back, offended. 'I've already explained, Lady Frances. Everything you say in here is only between us. I have never and would never tell a soul about what happens in my private consultations.'

'Good,' said Lady Frances. She cleared her throat, settling finally.

'In which case, can I come and see you again?' she said, and she tried to laugh. 'There're loads I should probably apologise to over there.'

'I'm sure that's not the case,' said Mrs Wood, patting her hand. 'But I should like that very much.'

'And I will ensure you are compensated,' she said. 'Double for today, of course. As a gesture of my gratitude.'

'There's really no need,' said Mrs Wood lightly. 'But that's very kind of you, nonetheless. So now,' She pulled out a pencil and the thick datebook from the drawer in her side table. 'Why don't we make another appointment for you next week?' And she flicked the book open to the appropriate page, her pencil poised. 'How does the same time on Thursday sound?'

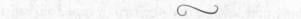

CHAPTER 10

When Mr Larson called on Mrs Wood later that week, he was, as usual, accompanied by Fox, his squat little sausage dog. She watched him from the drawing-room window, loping slowly along from Westbourne Grove, eyes set on the ground before him as though he were responsible for everything wrong in the world.

Ever since that awful day in February when he had told her that the investment had failed, she had dreaded seeing his dreary figure approaching, dreaded the updates that revealed no relief and the borderline patronising reminders to let him do his job; this was his area of expertise after all. Above all, however, she dreaded the look in his eyes when he questioned her increasing expenses around the girl when she should, didn't she think, be in reduction.

But the dread had become tiresome, and so, today, she had decided that instead of worrying about his judgement she would use the two things she had available to her to bring him around to her way of thinking: her effortless charm and the truth. By investing in the girl, she was securing her own future. After the whole mine debacle, she had come to think that a young, talented Medium might be a wiser investment than something so easily lost at the whim of men. Embarrassment would surely make it difficult for him to argue with that. She had a new client in Lady Frances, which would cover the outlay for the girl's hats, and once Lady Frances secured her with a stipend, she would have access to a whole new tranche of possibilities. Perhaps even a royal tranche with Lady Frances's connection to Princess Louise: hadn't there been loud whispers that the Queen herself was looking for an authentic connection with Prince Albert?

She watched him trot up the front steps, Fox pausing to sniff around a crack at the top, and then Mr Larson was coming through the door in a bluster of irritation and scarves. She went out to greet him.

'Mr Reynolds told me that you've let that girl join the Circle,' he said, unwinding the woollen muffler from his neck to reveal his whiskerless chin. The tip of his long nose shone, and he wiped it briskly with his handkerchief. 'Was there no consideration of a consultation on an addition?'

'Oh, pish, Mr Larson,' she said, leaning down to turn Fox's velvety ears between her fingers. 'How are you, little man?' she asked, and the dog strained to lick her face.

'I mean,' Mr Larson was continuing to unravel himself. 'Do we even know where she comes from? Are we opening our door to all kinds of riff-raff now? Is there no concern for respectability anymore?' Then he stopped and noticed Mrs Wood collecting her thick blue shawl from her cloak stand. 'Mrs Wood?'

'She comes from Chatham,' she said. 'Is the sun warm? You never know in March, do you.'

Mr Larson's hands had frozen at his neck, the robin red scarf she had bought him for Christmas dangling between his fingers. 'Warm?'

'Yes,' she said. 'Do you think I shall need to wear my coat and my shawl, or will just one of them suffice?'

He blinked back at her. 'But . . . Where are you going?'

'For a walk,' Mrs Wood said and looked at the dog, who gave an anxious yawn. 'With you two.'

'Mrs Wood . . .' He looked at the ledger he had placed on the console. 'We have *business* to discuss.'

'Could we perhaps discuss such matters with some fresh air?' she asked. 'Fox looks like he could do with a run and . . .' She wrapped herself in the shawl, leaning in to nudge Mr Larson's arm as though she had not a care in the world. '. . . So could I.' She smiled, and Mr Larson returned a faltering version back.

'Are you sure?' he said. 'It's still quite brisk and . . .'

'I'm sure,' she said, whipping the ribbons of her hat into a bow and straightening her shoulders. 'I would much prefer to talk with you whilst we walk.' She looked around her at the house, and experienced a sharp stab of horror at where she might end up should she lose it. She forced another smile. 'The sun will do me good.'

The gardens were busy with nannies and their noisy charges, so they turned up Ladbroke Grove towards Holland Park instead, Fox trotting obediently between them.

'You can almost smell summer in the air, can't you,' she said, as he pulled Fox away from a heap of dung in the gutter.

'You can.' He cleared his throat. 'I don't suppose . . .' he paused. 'I'm aware I haven't been at your table for a while now, what with the time this investment work is taking from me, but . . . Have you heard from Leon?'

Mrs Wood put her hand on his forearm, sensing him start and then relax into her. 'He's been chiding you,' she said. 'For being so absent.'

Mr Larson stopped, his face open like a boy's. 'He has?'

But Mrs Wood laughed. 'He's teasing,' she said. 'Just as he did when you were boys together.'

He cleared his throat and gave a short laugh. 'He always was a boy for japes. Mother said I was made in Father's likeness while he, being the younger, received hers.' His jaw flexed and Mrs Wood squeezed his arm.

'He always seems to show you two being quite playful as children,' she said. 'I think your mother isn't entirely correct.' A flicker caught at the corner of his mouth, and she captured the opportunity, leaning in. 'When you're together again, I can only imagine the trouble you'll get up to.'

And he laughed suddenly, genuinely, before remembering himself. 'To lose a brother must be difficult,' he said, serious once more. 'But I wonder if a fellow ever recovers from losing a twin.'

'I don't know how one ever could,' she said.

He paused for a moment and then cleared his throat. When he spoke again, suddenly and out of the blue, the mood had changed entirely. 'She's very young,' he said, and Mrs Wood took a moment to realise who he was referring to.

'Oh,' she said. 'The girl?'

'Who did you think I was talking about?'

'Yes,' she said lightly. 'She's young. But she's committed. She works hard.'

'I've heard she lives in some room near the recreation ground.'

'Not all of us were born into comfort,' she said.

'I also notice that there have been a few . . . ah . . . additional expenses since she arrived?'

Here it was. 'Well, as you say, Mr Larson, one cannot have riff-raff at one's table.' But the sideways smile she gave him was rather wasted as he continued staring straight ahead, his own mouth set in a line of grim reality.

'Is now the time to be frittering money on an ingenue?'

'It's an investment,' she said with rehearsed patience.

He gave one of his sighs. 'Well,' he said, and her heart sank. 'I suppose . . .'

'Is there any news of our own investments?' She kept her eyes on Fox's rump as he darted around the pavement before them.

'I don't understand why you want to discuss such private matters like this in public. I would find it easier sitting across a table with you in the privacy of four walls so that I might show you the numbers rather than hold them in our heads.'

'I'm capable of—'

'There are a lot of numbers, Mrs Wood,' he said firmly. 'Even I find it difficult to hold them in my head.'

She bit her lip before continuing. 'Then give me an overview. One a woman of my limited intellect can understand.' But the joke was lost on him. He frowned as he skirted around another pile of mess, his hand escorting Mrs Wood through the small of her back.

'I hope to hear back from the contact within the next few weeks.'

She stopped. 'I had thought you might have something more certain than that. You said you had news.'

He took the opportunity to catch his breath. 'I did. I *do*,' he said. 'It's moving forward.'

She tutted and started off again. 'As long as it's not mines. Not like last time. We need an investment with less risk.'

'All investments are a risk,' he said grimly. 'But I've investigated the possibility of a ship. Two, actually.'

She stopped again. 'Boats? You're turning to boats?'

'*Ships*, Violet. And these are proven vessels,' he said.

'Then why are they available?'

He looked taken aback at her directness. 'Their previous investor died.'

She flushed. 'Ah,' she said.

'But they have been very profitable.'

She looked away. 'One can only hope.'

'I understand I must earn your trust once more, Violet,' he said, quickly. 'Of course I do. And I appreciate how hard you are working to keep your expenditure down. Aside from the . . .'

'She's as much an investment as those boats,' she said.

'Ships,' he said, and she raised an eyebrow at him. 'Please,' he said. 'I will make it up to you.' He cleared his throat suddenly and shifted, and Mrs Wood winced, acutely aware of what was about to come. 'I am sure you will be returned to comfort soon enough. And you know that if you should not, I am always . . .'

'Is that rain?' she asked brightly.

But he was not so easily deterred. 'I will always protect you, dear Mrs Wood,' he said, his cheeks reddening with urgency. 'I will never let anything happen to you as long as we are friends. Or . . .' He cleared his throat again, running his finger inside the loop of his scarf as if it were strangling him. 'Perhaps as something . . . more?'

He waited for her to complete his sentence.

The air had become brittle. She felt suddenly old and tired, too old and too tired for such a demonstration. She had been fortunate to find Mr Wood, and his gentle nature had made her almost forget everything from before. But now, three years since his death, widowhood had settled comfortably on her bones. She neither needed nor wanted to open her life back up to a husband. At her age, what would be the point? 'It's . . .' she began.

'. . . too much,' he finished for her and then their words tumbled over one another. 'Of course. Think nothing of it . . .'

'I am flattered . . . I . . .'

He withdrew his hand and held it up in submission. 'There's no need, Mrs Wood. I understand completely.'

'I'm sorry,' she said.

'My promise remains: I will always look after you.' He turned and tugged on Fox's lead. 'You're cold,' he said. 'We should return to the house.'

They retraced their steps back down the hill on the crisp, white paving slabs, leaving the tumult of Uxbridge Road behind them. Her mind turned in the awkward silence between them.

She wasn't afraid of the idea of another husband. They were a comfort when the plumbing made odd noises, and helpful retrieving things from high shelves. And Mr Larson wasn't terrible to look at. Indeed, she had enjoyed a flush of *something* Tuesday last on finding him hammering out a dent from her back parlour fire screen. But everything she wanted from him she was able to achieve from his friendship alone. Did she need Mr Larson's financial security more than she needed her own peace of mind?

She gave a dismissive laugh which she covered with a cough.

Absolutely not. Failed investment or no failed investment, she had earned the right to call herself a respectable widow, and a respectable widow she would remain. After everything, she had earned the right to choose.

CHAPTER 11

At seven o'clock the following Monday evening, Miss Newman knocked softly on Mrs Wood's bedroom door, waking her from the nap she was taking in preparation for her monthly séance at Mrs Green's spectacular home in Orme Square.

As Miss Newman let herself in, Mrs Wood pushed herself up from the pillows, shaking the fog from her head.

'What time is it?' she asked.

'Seven, as agreed,' Miss Newman said, carefully placing a handful of pussy willow branches and a small saucer of water on the floor beside the trunk that lived at the end of Mrs Wood's bed. 'Did you sleep?' She turned to collect Mrs Wood's black séance silk from the front of the armoire where Eliza had hung it earlier, still wrapped in the cheap industrial cleaner's cover.

Mrs Wood sat watching Miss Newman creating a deep puddle of the dress around the dressing stool while she came to her senses, giving a final stretch before she slid off the bed, collecting her froth of petticoats from where she had left them on her chair and crossing the room.

'Thank you,' Miss Newman said as she received them over one arm, using her other hand to help Mrs Wood step up onto the stool before briskly brushing down her drawers with the back of her hand.

Miss Newman was the first person since Thirza to treat Mrs Wood's body as invisible. At first she was startled when Miss Newman started talking as she pressed her knee into her back to close her corset. As her clothing had grown richer in those early years, she had been forced to employ people to dress her, but if any of those had said even a word, she would've dispatched them. Even in her marriage, anything but awkward small talk while in a state of undress would have been unthinkable. Mr Wood became easily overwhelmed by ladies' accoutrements; buttons and ties could only be tackled when they were both firmly beneath the blankets in a blind fumbling that took far longer than anything else that followed. And before him . . . before, she could only remember the weight of her skirts over her face in the dark.

Miss Newman, on the other hand, appeared to have become immune to squeamishness after forcing fleshy parts into small openings in her four years with the corpulent Austrian heiress. From the moment she began working with Mrs Wood, it was as though modesty had never existed. She strode into the room, approaching the whole process like a Smithfield porter, poking and pushing, squashing and squeezing as nimbly yet dispassionately as if she were trussing a joint for Sunday lunch.

It had taken Mrs Wood a while to be able to converse about an evening's plans while the errant flesh of her bosom was being prodded unceremoniously back into the top of a half-closed corset, but eventually she had followed Miss Newman's professional lead and now she enjoyed these times. Almost.

Which was fortunate because dressing for a séance was an art. Beyond the simple act of putting on the gown came the far more complicated act of filling it. A séance dress contained a myriad of secrets that Miss Newman had quickly committed to memory so that each hidden pocket and crevice could be accessed without any unintending goosing. What a relief it was! Before, without a trusted soul, she had had no choice but to do it herself, it either took forever to find each well-hidden pocket, or she had to contort herself for so long to achieve the correct position to slide an object home that she'd see stars.

That evening, once she'd tied off Mrs Wood's corset, Miss

Newman began the arduous routine of dropping the petticoats over her head. 'Has Mr Larson recovered yet?' she asked, as she piled on yet another layer.

'I hope so,' she said, trying not to panic beneath the weight of the latest addition. 'Dearest,' she said from within the deluge of skirts. 'Dearest . . . I think I'm . . .' Ever the expert, Miss Newman gave a gentle pull on the errant petticoat, then it popped free and Mrs Wood re-emerged with a sudden, grateful intake of air.

'Thank you. Anyway,' she continued, returning to the topic of Mr Larson as she smoothed her hair. 'I hope this is the last time. His proposals always put me on edge.'

'I don't blame you,' Miss Newman replied, completing the last in a series of loops with the petticoat waist-ribbons before bracing to bring the black silk up from the floor. 'It's becoming quite a thing,' she said as she hauled the dress to Mrs Wood's waist, securing it with a single hook.

'I always end up feeling as though I've done something wrong, though,' Mrs Wood said. 'It makes me feel so cruel.' She stopped. 'Do you think I was cruel?'

'Of course not,' said Miss Newman, and she circled to her front, collecting the pussy willow branches from the floor. She took each branch in her right hand as she talked and then returned to stand behind Mrs Wood, placing her other hand on Mrs Wood's shoulder and sliding each branch, one by one, along the channel of loops sewn diagonally across the front of Mrs Wood's corset from right shoulder to left hip. 'What else are you supposed to do. Say "yes" just because you're uncomfortable?'

'I suppose others have married for lesser reasons.'

With all the branches in, Miss Newman returned to her front, her fingers checking how tight each loop was against the bundle. 'Do they feel secure?' she asked, and Mrs Wood pressed her hand against them, nodding.

'What would you do?' Mrs Wood continued as Miss Newman

gathered the bodice of the black silk dress, sliding first one of Mrs Wood's arms then the other inside the sleeves before disappearing to the back, her fingers working quickly over the line of tiny silk-covered buttons that ran from Mrs Wood's nape to her tail-bone. 'Would you marry someone to stop them asking?' She looked over her shoulder at Miss Newman, who was focusing on pairing the buttons with their loops.

'Yes,' she said, still concentrating. 'Because that's exactly how I dreamed romance to be.'

'Let's just stay here in Chepstow Villas the two of us until we die,' said Mrs Wood with a laugh, closing her cuffs at her wrists.

'Don't forget Eliza,' said Miss Newman, and Mrs Wood gave a snort.

'Who could forget Eliza.'

Miss Newman slid the last button home and smoothed her hands across the back of the dress. 'There,' she said. 'Is that comfortable?' Her head appeared over Mrs Wood's shoulder as she peered down the front of the dress to make sure no tell-tale ridge could be seen from any angle. She checked the hidden opening between the lace yolk and silk shoulder seam of the dress and fiddled with the tips of the pussy willow branches inside to line them up. 'They seem secure. Do they feel it?'

Mrs Wood shifted her hips, jiggling her body a little before patting her front. 'Perfect,' she said. 'Thank you for fetching them, dearest,' she said. 'Mrs Green will love them.'

'They weren't easy to find,' Miss Newman said, fiddling with the bustle. 'They're still a bit damp.'

'You don't need to tell me that.' She tugged on the seams of her bodice again. She most certainly wasn't going to forget that they were there.

Miss Newman gave her work one final flourish. 'There!' she said, and then made one last circuit of her handiwork for a full appraisal before stopping in front of her. 'You'll do.'

'The mend is barely noticeable,' Mrs Wood said, squinting at the repair along the bodice she had made the previous evening. 'Even if I do say so myself.' Miss Newman raised an approving eyebrow before turning towards the trunk.

'Now then,' she said, setting the trunk beside them. 'I've been told it's the usual sitters,' she said. 'No surprises.' She pulled on the silver chain about her neck until the key appeared from inside her bodice, leaning to slide it easily into the trunk's lock. The lid popped open with a satisfying clunk and Miss Newman reached inside to gather the usual séance instruments, placing them on the floor at their feet: the long, thin spirit trumpet, a roll of gauze and a switch of hazel.

'You know Mrs Green's cousin's boy turned up,' Miss Newman said as she crouched at her side.

'I gather from your tone it's not good news.'

'Found amidst flotsam on some beach in Rio de Janeiro.'

Mrs Wood felt a genuine tug of sadness at the thought. 'He was so young.'

'Awful,' said Miss Newman, peering into the layers of Mrs Wood's skirts until she found the small loop sewn beneath a double layer of the black silk and hooked the long hazel switch inside. She swivelled Mrs Wood a half-turn on the stool. 'Was he a Yorkshireman? Have I got that right?'

'Lancashire,' said Mrs Wood.

'Oh, well done,' said Miss Newman. 'People can take exception to mixing those two up.' Then she stopped, her hand hovering over the trunk. 'What order?'

'Stones,' said Mrs Wood without hesitation. 'Then the rose petals, please.' But her mind wouldn't leave the question unanswered. She looked down at Miss Newman, willing her to say what she wanted to hear. 'Am I being foolish. Should I attach myself to someone now before it's too late?' Miss Newman looked up, confused. 'Mr Larson,' she said, and Miss Newman rolled her eyes, sitting back on her heels. 'He's a gentleman,' she continued. 'And he's wealthy. And kind.' She paused. 'And he likes dogs.'

Miss Newman laughed. 'Well, there you go then.' She returned to her work, reaching into the trunk, pulling out two large pickling jars, tugging out the stopper from the nearest one and carefully removing six smooth pebbles. Then she took a safety pin from her pocket to scratch a letter into each one before returning to Mrs Wood's skirts and dropping them into the small left-hand pouch hidden amongst the copious folds.

'I don't know,' she said, taking up a jar stuffed with rose petals. 'It would be so different if he were in the house all the time. I don't know how he'd take to all the closed doors.' She unscrewed the lid and released a puff of powdery scent redolent of Mrs Reynolds and reached in to take a good handful of pink and yellow petals, passing them to Miss Newman, who dropped them into the strip of muslin Miss Newman had placed on the floor.

'It would complicate things,' Miss Newman said, sprinkling water from the saucer over the petals before wrapping the muslin around them loosely so as not to dent or dry the petals out, and placing the little package into another pocket amidst the right-hand folds of the skirt. 'Even an overnight guest has demanded more restraint around what we can deliver on a séance night.'

'Exactly,' Mrs Wood said, dropping the petal jar back into the trunk. 'Imagine what it would be like if that overnight guest never left.' She sighed. 'It's not as though I'm lonely—'

'Why would you be,' said Miss Newman. 'You've got me.'

'Indeed,' she said.

'And Eliza, of course.' She let the smile slide playfully to one side.

'Of course.' Mrs Wood took up her trumpet, a permitted tool of the séance used to amplify voices from the Other Side, hanging it from the hook at her right hip, well away from the switch and pocket of pebbles to avoid the chance of any revealing clinks or clanks, then obediently bent so that Miss Newman could slide a stick of white chalk into its home at her waist.

'Right,' Miss Newman said, running her hand through Mrs Wood's skirts. 'Are we missing anything?'

She looked at herself in the long mirror of her armoire. From this distance her face looked less terrifyingly old, the lines blurred and her cheeks pink from the exertion of getting ready. Perhaps things weren't as bad as she thought. Perhaps this was the woman the world saw, rather than the other one with the ridiculous eyebrows and deep grooves and impending irrelevance. 'That's all,' she said. 'I don't want to do anything too complicated tonight.'

'Then you're complete. Does everything feel secure?'

Mrs Wood shook her body, patting and poking for tell-tale rattles or clinks or the peep of a rogue petal, and Miss Newman nodded approvingly. She found the key again, locked the trunk and then pushed it back to its innocuous home.

She stood, brushing the knees of her skirt. 'I'll go and check on the cab.'

Mrs Wood reached out suddenly and caught her arm. 'What would you do?' she said. 'Would you marry if you needed to?'

Miss Newman looked back at her. 'Who knows,' she said after a moment. 'If it were the right man asking. Perhaps the wisest thing to do as a woman is to keep our options open.'

She watched her go and then forced herself to meet her own eyes. The lines were back.

Options. Did Miss Newman really believe that a woman really had any of those?

The Dentist had another name, but over the years her mind had stopped remembering it. To Mrs Wood, he was simply the Dentist: the man who had taken her away from Hull, away from

Thirza and into that patchy, shadowed period that swallowed her youth.

Thirza had found him in London. Forever the magpie, his glinting crowns and fat purse had proved irresistible, and she had brought him with her on a visit back to Hull. The moment he stepped over the threshold, his eyes had pinned her as though she were a butterfly, and she understood immediately what the introduction was about – she'd been working the tables for too long by then to miss something so obvious.

At first, he struck her as an odd choice, not showing even the slightest bit of interest in her work with the Other Side. But then, he opened his mouth, and the picture was complete: the Dentist had *connections*. He had been in Crimea, fixing teeth and dandling in the black market, and cultivated an enviable contact book of wealthy families that he was offering to open up to Thirza in exchange for something that would be just as useful to him.

'She's better looking than you told me,' he'd said, prowling around her as though he were appraising at a cattle auction. 'I'll give her a month on the Yorkshire circuit. Introduce her around. If she's as good as you say, we can share what she makes. Sixty-forty.'

Thirza had looked scandalised. 'We agreed on half. And the rest to make sure she's turned out right for the nice houses.' They'd haggled for a while, the Dentist trying his luck, unaware that, when it came to money, Thirza was a terrier.

Half or nothing.

He took half and, just like that, she stopped being Vi Thwaite and became Miss Violet Bell, daughter of a late doctor, granddaughter of a dentist.

'Make sure you keep her dressed nice,' Thirza had said, three bottles later, slinging a salty arm over Vi's shoulders. 'Got to keep up the illusion, eh!'

'As long as you pay attention and do as I say, I will always be kind to you,' the Dentist told her three days later as their train rattled towards Ilkley, cutting through steep, alien landscapes. And without warning he moved seats in a single fluid motion, his leg suddenly pressed against hers, and she stared even harder at the sheep clinging to hillsides and lonely, distant farmhouses so that she could avoid his sagging cheeks and watery eyes and the back of his hand, almost translucent with fat, raised veins as grey as coal dust, sitting proprietorially upon her skirt.

Later, when he closed the door of their rooms on the high street, his proximity was unavoidable, and she flinched when she remembered the way his skin gave beneath her pushing fingers and how his body shone as white as milk in the darkness.

He had paraded her around all the great northern estates, performing to some of the country's most notable families, whilst visiting London every so often to pay homage to Thirza's ascending star. But then, after Vi had spent almost three years beneath the Dentist, Thirza suffered an irredeemable exposure at a table in Mayfair and found herself chased out of town with ruin on her tail. Sensing a lucrative opening in Thirza's sudden departure, the Dentist hastily packed Vi up and rode them into London using the names of the families they had met during those years in the north to place their feet on the ladder that would, within a few short months, take them to a level of society that eclipsed any they had met before.

Her money furnished their rooms, it kept them well dressed and well fed. But it was always the Dentist her patrons spoke to first. It was because of him that she met Mrs Bartlett, who offered them an apartment near South Kensington station, where Colonel Phillips lived with his spirit-mad wife who knew Mr Wood, who was, then, still very much married.

The Dentist had died two years after they had arrived in town – from an infected gum abscess, of all things. But his mark remained and, despite everything, she was never free of him, no matter how financially independent she would become. He had given her a respectability and reputation that made her an appealing proposition, not just to spiritualist society, but to a man like Mr Wood: a man who offered the financial stability and social status she needed to reach the wealthiest of patrons unavailable to a single young woman.

That the Mrs Wood society knew and loved would not exist without the Dentist was one of the greatest injustices, and a truth she kept buried deeper than anything else.

ARE ENGLISH SPIRITS REALLY SO SHY?

Magnus Clore
Spiritual Times, 3rd April 1873

When will we be able to show the Americans that our
English spirits are as forthright, if not more so, than any
they may see in their gaudy little parlours? We're hearing
more and more from the East Coast that a spirit will
materialise in full to a Medium soon. Surely, with the
dazzling talents working today in our fair city, one of them
will rise to the challenge and show these Yanks that they
are no match to our superior talent.

CHAPTER 12

The next *Spiritual Times* edition following Mr Clore's call to arms featured a letters page stuffed with commentary on the topic of full spirits. There were those who dismissed the idea as vulgar, and those suggesting that perhaps it would be an opportunity for a younger Medium, one less trammelled by vestiges of experience. And then there was a letter from Mr Larson suggesting that Mrs Wood held no truck with such novelties and that people should continue to support her work rather than be drawn to sensation.

She understood what he had intended when he rose to champion her, but no matter his intentions, his old-fashioned assertions only made her look even more old-fashioned. And instead of shutting down the conversation, he only succeeded in inflaming it so that in the week that followed, full spirit materialisations were all her patrons and clients wanted to talk about. 'Do you really believe it can't be done, Mrs Wood? *Really*?'

Once again, she was grateful for her foresight with the girl: what better way to change the conversation than to *change the conversation*!

It was now only a matter of time before she could finally introduce her and set in motion the purpose of her plan.

The first few months teaching the girl, they had focused on trancework. At first her pupil had been tentative and tremulous. 'Is someone with you, dear?' Mrs Wood would ask, and the girl would respond awkwardly, voices emerging for her pretty lips that were too like her own to carry authenticity. And the things the girl would talk about were juvenile and ubiquitous: the weather, what it was like on the Other Side. Or else she'd ask closed questions with no point, or have her spirit proclaim an ache or pain of the kind everyone over the age of thirty-five complained about. Afterwards, Mrs Wood would gently suggest that she listen harder to the voices coming to her, allow them to come through in their own way. Encouraging her to pick out the things that might be more interesting or relevant to a listener.

'It's not necessary to get everything right,' she said. 'Indeed, in my experience those who are too accurate are often those found later to be fraudulent.'

And so, gradually, the girl's voices grew more distinct: a man with a round face she felt connected with Miss Newman, an elderly woman who didn't know where she was. Someone singing. A riddle? Yes. A saucy one at that!

In the shadows of the parlour, the girl unfurled into her Mediumship like a flower: petal upon petal falling open to reveal a rich, multi-hued centre that no one could have imagined was hidden inside. Not even Mrs Wood.

Now, with all this nonsense of full spirit materialisations banging on around her, the girl was more indispensable than ever. It was time to move onto the next phase of her education. Thirza had always said that the best way to learn the art was from real, unsus-pecting subjects. For Mrs Wood, this had meant rare, magical moments when Thirza would steal her into the Hamburgh Tavern on the Hull dockside, settling her beside its dimpled bay window, sipping small beer together as the seasoned public Medium taught her how to read.

Not books, of course. There was no money in that.

People.

'Everyone has a tell, Vi,' Thirza would say as they watched the chaos of the harbour through the window. 'No matter how hard they try and hide it, it's there.'

Those moments where she had Thirza's full attention glittered in her memory. Under her experienced eye, she was taught to notice the way a shellfish seller tucked her hair, or how a coalman tied his scarf or the wear on the soles of a supervisor's boots. And then she was taught how to translate this information into rich and, more importantly, accurate identities for these strangers. During those afternoons there was no audience, no client, no drunken paramour. It was the two of them, nestled together, without labour or toil. Just them. And every time she did something right, the rare smile of Thirza's approval sustained her through the darker days that were far more typical of their lives.

Notting Hill Gate was no Hull harbour, but the parade before the tea rooms was equally as rich in learning opportunities. She scheduled a weekly meeting there for Thursday mornings, ordering hot chocolate and pastries from their table in the wide, curved window as they worked.

They would sit in relative silence. Watching.

A gentleman with a smudge of rough dust along the rear of his coat had come from the building site at Holland Park.

Another, squinting around a monocle with a narrow paper package poking from his pocket, was going to have his spectacles repaired.

A slim young woman with her hat on backwards and a sour flush to her cheeks was early with child.

A cross-looking maid rubbing the backs of her red-raw hands against the sides of her dress and grey stains on her skirts worked for an invalid who required harsh detergents to clean up all the accidents.

A plump woman obscured her pink cheeks beneath an enormous, plumed hat and voluminous cloak to hide the fact that she had recently fallen in love.

As Mrs Wood spoke quietly over her cup, it was Thirza explaining to the girl how to read each stranger who walked by, telling her how she must look beyond the obvious – a black dress or a poor shave – to the details others would not see: a tiny black button missed in a row of fifty, or a red earlobe.

The sessions were more relaxing than the four walls of the séance room and, just as she had in Hull, Mrs Wood would feel herself lighten as she watched the girl read the street.

Always an excellent pupil, the girl quickly gathered confidence in the tearoom, and within a few weeks, as April crept into May, Mrs Wood made her decision.

They sat together at their usual table that Thursday morning, staring comfortably through the great curved window.

'She's been baking,' the girl said suddenly, nodding towards a woman in a purple coat with street-dust staining the hem and large, sad eyes beneath a plain hat. 'She has flour on her neck behind her ear. A fingertip's worth.'

'Excellent,' said Mrs Wood, replacing her cup. 'But who's she baking for? Why is she baking?'

The woman hesitated to glance at her reflection, absently dusting the front of her coat with her grey-gloved fingers.

'Someone's going away,' said the girl as the woman's gaze dropped and she walked on. 'Someone she cares for but isn't close family or a beloved.'

'Why would you say that?'

'She's sad, but she's not been crying. She's not wearing black, so no one has died. She's going to miss them though, so she's made them something nice. Not something bought in and not made by her cook.'

'Wonderful,' said Mrs Wood.

The girl picked up her iced finger and took an enthusiastic bite. 'I'm getting there,' she said.

Mrs Wood looked politely away. 'Not with your mouth full, dear,' she said. 'But yes. Yes, you are.' She waited an appropriate amount of time before speaking again. 'Miss Finch,' she began. 'You know we have a Circle scheduled for this afternoon . . .'

'Has it been cancelled? I really wanted to show Laetitia my new dress.' She brushed her hand over the skirts of the pale blue cotton dress that Mrs Wood had arranged to be delivered the day before, crumbs of white icing scattering carelessly from her fingers.

'No, not at all,' she said. 'In fact . . .' She paused again; a woman always aware of the importance of delivery. 'I think this afternoon is your time, Miss Finch.'

The girl stopped, swallowing the rest of the bun as quickly as she could. '*My time?*'

'Yes. You're ready.'

'You mean . . . ?'

'I do. Today I want you to take part in the Circle. Properly.'

'As a Medium?'

'As a Medium.'

The girl dropped back in her seat with delight. 'I can't believe you think I'm ready.'

She took a moment to observe the girl's delight. 'You are,' she said, eventually. 'I'm sure of it.'

Would an old-fashioned or desperate Medium devote herself to new talent? Would an old-fashioned or desperate Medium be quite so magnanimous, or bold?

Miss Newman was late back from her meeting with her society, arriving into the settling Circle with garbled apologies.

She need not have worried too much, however: the Adams sisters were still telling the girl about a séance they'd attended in Clapham with all the drama of a trip to deepest Borneo.

'When we came down the road afterwards, it was almost dark,' said Laetitia. 'We didn't know which would be safer: the omnibus or the train, and we asked the spirits, as we always do: *should we go left to the omnibus stop or right to the train station?* But for once, we received nothing in reply, which left us quite confused. But then—'

'An omnibus arrived as we came to the corner!' Hyacinth interjected with a thrill. 'You see! The spirits weren't ignoring us: we had neither to go left or right!'

'I wanted to tell that part,' grumbled Laetitia, but the girl gave an incredulous laugh and said: 'Well, you can always trust the spirits!' And they both beamed.

On the other side of the table, Miss Brigham was going into detail about how she'd turned the dead partridge found on the track near Notting Barns into a hearty supper. '*It could've been diseased,*' Mrs Reynolds said, but Miss Brigham bit back that she was *absolutely fine*, wasn't she?

And Mrs Hart continued to work her way through her plate of cake.

Mrs Wood caught the girl's eye as she settled into her chair and they shared an excited, secret smile. She had given the girl her instructions: simple, clean. Nothing fussy. This wasn't about spectacle, this was about letting the Circle know why Mrs Wood had invested so much time in her. She felt a sudden thrill as she watched the girl laugh at something Miss Brigham said, the same kind she'd felt as a child when she knew Thirza needed her for a séance.

'Everything all right?' Miss Newman asked in a low voice, settling herself beside Mrs Wood.

'Perfectly,' she replied. 'It's a simple session today.' And she tapped the right side of her skirt where the deepest pocket had been sewn.

Miss Newman squinted at her. 'You look suspiciously happy. What's happening?'

'You'll see,' said Mrs Wood.

As the whispered *Amens* faded into the darkness, raps snapped across the table and the Adams sisters gave giddy gasps and whispered, '*They're here.*'

Suddenly Mrs Reynolds sat up. 'Oh!' she exclaimed. 'Oh! I've been given a message!'

'What is it, dearest?' said Mrs Wood.

'I hear a voice. As clear as day,' she continued. 'It's saying . . . it's saying that they're very glad to see our new friend again.'

Mrs Wood felt Mrs Hart's judging eyebrow in the gloom as the girl gave an audible intake of breath. 'Thank you,' she said with a quiver, her chin tipped upwards as she spoke out to the room.

'The spirits are asking for the candle to be extinguished,' said Mrs Wood, and Miss Brigham jumped up, damping the flame on each candle between her fingers.

'Why you insist on doing that . . .' Mrs Hart grumbled. 'There's a snuffer right there.'

In the darkness the huge table burst into life, rocking and rolling violently beneath the women's hands, its feet thumping on the floor. And then, as quickly as it began, it stopped, and the room was thrown into another silence before the raps started again.

'They have gifts,' interpreted Mrs Wood.

'Oh good,' said Miss Brigham. 'I'm peckish.' Just as something small and sticky thudded onto the table.

'I think that must be for you,' Mrs Wood said, to the sound of Miss Brigham's hand thumping around on the table to find the treasure.

'Oh,' she said with an uncharacteristic sigh of satisfaction. 'Dates! They always know what I want.'

Mrs Reynolds, who never liked to spoil her appetite, received the gentlest wisp of an object. 'Spearmint! I shall enjoy this on my journey home!' Then, with a series of clomps, Miss Newman was gifted a handful of carrot tops, which Mrs Wood told her was obviously punishment for her complaints about a bruised apple she received at the last séance.

Then, after Mrs Wood caught a half-full teacup as it came sloshing across the tabletop, Laetitia Adams exclaimed as something round rolled so quickly in the dark that it flew off the table's edge and landed with a thump on the floor.

'Fiddlesticks!' she said, but as she reached to retrieve it her head caught on the edge of the table and she let out a yelp of pain.

The Circle asked if she was all right, and Mrs Wood was about to launch into another round of raps when, as the Circle quietened, she heard a voice she couldn't place.

Small.

Distant.

Accented.

'*Poor Miss,*' the voice said, louder this time, and everyone stopped.

Who was that? Mrs Wood's mind raced around the Circle, trying to find the tell, a thread of familiarity, but she couldn't.

'There is a new spirit at our table,' she said, slightly disarmed by the intrusion. 'Who's there?'

'It's me,' said the voice. And giggled.

Mrs Wood felt a jolt of surprise. *The girl?*

'Miss Finch?' said Mrs Reynolds.

'Is that you?' Mrs Hart asked.

'Do you have a name?' asked Mrs Wood above the restlessness, ignoring the swift jab from Miss Newman's passing elbow. She was dealing with this.

'Of course. I apologise for arriving uninvited, but I could wait no longer!'

'You are welcome,' said Mrs Wood, squinting in the darkness towards the girl. She was unmoving, her hands settled on the table, her chin on her chest. 'Please. Introduce yourself.'

'I am Mona,' said the voice. 'I . . . I am Miss Finch's guide.'

The ladies all clamoured with unrestrained excitement, while Mrs Wood tried to make out the shape of the girl in the dark.

'Are you hurt, dear lady?' Mona continued. 'You bumped your head.'

'Oh!' said Laetitia, remembering. 'Oh, the bump. It was quite a bonk.'

'Let me,' Mona began, and Mrs Wood could fathom the movement as Miss Finch moved towards the other Adams sister.

Laetitia gasped. 'Is that you, Mona?'

'What?' said her sister, Hyacinth. 'What's going on? Can we have a candle?'

'She's stroking my head!' Her voice was no more than a whisper, as though terrified of scaring her away. 'Her fingers are so tender and gentle.'

'I bring all of my spirit energy to heal you,' said Mona. 'You shall feel no more pain.'

'That's very kind of you, Mona,' said Mrs Wood, with a lightness she did not feel. *What was the girl thinking?* Introducing a spirit guide without consultation at her table. *Her* table. Treating Mrs Wood as though she were a mere spectator just like the others . . .

'I am growing weaker, Miss Finch is tired . . .' The girl's gown rustled and her chair creaked. 'I must . . . bid you . . . farewell . . .' Her voice was so faint it was as though she were speaking from another room. 'I hope I shall see you all again soon.'

'Oh, Mona,' said Laetitia. 'Thank you. I will never forget your magical fingers. Never!'

The room ached in silence.

'Has she gone?' asked Miss Brigham, eventually, still chewing on a date.

But no one said anything, and the room grew heavy until Hyacinth could hold herself in no longer.

'I'm so jealous!' she exclaimed. 'What did the spirit feel like?'

'So gentle,' sighed Laetitia. 'As though the angels themselves were touching me with the very tips of their wings.'

'Perhaps they were,' said Mrs Reynolds, her voice full of dreams.

'Do you think?' asked Laetitia.

'We should check on Miss Finch,' Mrs Hart said. 'Will someone light the candle?' Mrs Reynolds knocked her knee in her haste to get to the mantel, the match flaring and dazzling the room as she touched the wick.

'Miss Finch?' Mrs Wood's voice cut through the excitement. As her eyes grew accustomed to the feeble candlelight, she could see Miss Finch slumped in her chair, her breathing laboured. 'Miss Finch!'

The girl started before giving a loud, unseemly yawn. She raised her face, blinking in the shadows. 'Is . . . is everything all right? What happened?'

The Adams sisters practically tumbled over one another to fill Miss Finch in. 'Your spirit guide helped me!' exclaimed Laetitia.

'She touched her!' said Hyacinth.

'A spirit guide?' Miss Finch's voice was fragile, confused. 'What do you mean?'

'You don't remember any of it?' asked Mrs Reynolds.

'Any of what?' There were tears around the edge of her words. 'What happened?'

'We met your spirit guide, Miss Finch,' said Mrs Wood. 'Mona.' Her eyes were level, but the girl simply laughed.

'Mona?' she said. 'She was here? I thought she was just in my head!'

'She was. And she was wonderful!' said Laetitia, but Miss Finch carried on blinking back at Mrs Wood.

'She was wonderful!' said Laetitia.

'She was an angel!' said Mrs Reynolds.

'She healed my sister!' said Hyacinth.

'I don't . . .' whispered the girl, her eyes large in the candlelight. 'I don't know how it happened.'

'That's often how it goes the first time,' said Mrs Wood. 'They arrive without warning. *But not at her table,* she wanted to say. Not when a Medium was as inexperienced as the girl. What a *risk!* Hadn't she told her to stay simple? Anything could have happened!

'It must be all the work we've done,' the girl was saying. 'Mrs Wood must have opened something inside.'

'Mrs Wood has more experience in all of this than any Medium I know,' said Mrs Reynolds, but Mrs Wood bristled beneath her smile.

'I assure you that your guide is the result of your own hard work,' she said. 'How very exciting – discovering one's spirit guide is such an important moment for a Medium.'

'Oh, it is,' the Adams sisters said and catapulted themselves off into a wistful duologue about how they found their own.

As she listened to her Circle enthuse around the table, Mrs Wood's smile remained fixed while her mind whirled.

No one had ever been so audacious at her table. Not even Mrs Hart, who never shied away from the limelight.

She was young, she reminded herself. Young. *Ambitious.* All the things that had drawn her to the girl in the first place. Of course, she wouldn't understand the etiquette of tables yet. Or the risks that such manifestations presented.

She rolled her shoulders and Miss Newman, who had been silent throughout the excitement, leaned into the table. 'Now may be a good time for us all to have a short break,' she said. 'Let us light the other candle and I shall organise some refreshments.'

As their eyes adjusted to the light and Miss Brigham excused herself, the rest of the table observed the red mark clearly visible across Laetitia Adams' forehead as she repeated several times how delicate Mona's touch had been and how the injury no longer hurt at all.

Mrs Wood remained in her seat, hardly noticing when Miss Newman approached with two cups of tea shivering in their saucers. 'Here,' she said, passing one to her. 'You look like you need it.'

'Nonsense,' she said briskly as she took her cup. 'I was just thinking how lucky we are. To be present for such a momentous occasion in Miss Finch's life.'

'*Very* lucky,' said Miss Newman.

'You're not happy,' she said.

Miss Newman opened her mouth before hesitating. Then she turned, closing off the room to their conversation with her back. 'You could've warned me, that's all,' she said, 'I wasn't prepared. I almost forgot myself when she started speaking and I was right beside Mrs Reynolds.' She ducked her head closer. 'Nothing like that has ever happened before, Violet.'

But Mrs Wood couldn't tell her that she hadn't known. That would raise Miss Newman's hackles even more, and it would've shown Mrs Wood for being something they swore they would never be: unprepared. 'You were so late returning from your *work* today, when would I have been able to talk to you?'

'I have other commitments, yes,' Miss Newman replied with an exasperated sigh. 'Nevertheless, I assumed you would include me in big decisions like this. I am part of this too.'

Mrs Wood drank some of her tea and replaced the cup and saucer on the table.

'The girl has barely any experience and suddenly she's trying to conjure up things like a spirit guide,' Miss Newman continued. 'She's very lucky she hasn't ruined herself already.'

They drank their tea in an unusually stiff silence, both watching the girl as she laughed with the Adams sisters, her confidence an almost visible entity, growing around her with each moment like a cloud.

CHAPTER 13

Mrs Wood asked the cab to idle outside 36 Tavistock Crescent.

The yellow-brick houses on this street were narrow with dark-painted window frames, thrown up as part of the thousands that lined the cuttings and embankments of London's new railway lines. At one end was a public house, at the other Westbourne Park underground station. She had chosen this street because it was home, in the main, to respectable working men and women who had jobs that required them to remain sober most of the time. It was also near Miss Brigham's rickety villa, which meant that the girl would have someone to walk with to Circles.

She stepped down onto the pavement with faint uncertainty at being in an unknown, lower-class area without a companion. She had hoped that Miss Newman would have accompanied her, but when Mrs Wood had come down for breakfast, she had already left. For her society, Eliza had said with one of her looks. But the conversation with the girl was important and so she had no choice but to rely on the chivalry of the yawning cabbie who tipped his hat over his eyes and settled into his scarf as soon as she turned her back.

Miss Finch's room was a palace compared to the squalid box she had left behind, a good size on the ground floor with indoor shared facilities and a neat bay window looking out over the area steps. From the street, she was satisfied to see the white Venetian blinds she had ordered for her from Whiteley's, and that the girl had turned them for modesty. She also noticed several terracotta pots planted with jolly red geraniums on the windowsill, which warmed her. She was well aware that philanthropists and critics of the poorer classes made assumptions about their interest in beautifying their environments. What those entitled fools who had never experienced a moment of want didn't understand was that, while poverty ruled out a pretty home, it didn't stop the poor from dreaming of having one.

She felt a swell of pride that she was giving the girl the opportunity to experience a life beyond patched calico. She knew how much it would have meant to her when she was young.

With one last glance along the street, she climbed the steps towards the door.

She wasn't looking forward to this conversation, but it must be done. What if Miss Finch took to going off plan regularly? She couldn't manage having someone unreliable at the table. Not now.

She knocked on the communal front door, leaving smudges in the grime with her gloves.

There was no sound from within.

She brushed the dirt from her knuckles and knocked again.

She was about to knock for a third time when she heard the click and squeak of a latch turning deep inside. And then, a moment later, the door was opened an inch or so by a squat woman with hair like a nest and a bright orange brooch at the throat of her mustard dress.

'I'm sorry,' Mrs Wood said, stepping back and casting a quick glance at the number on the bell: 36b. It was right. 'I'm looking for Miss Finch.'

The woman pressed a stubby finger to her lips with a scowl.

'Miss Finch is indisposed,' she hissed, the words coming out in careful syllables. And then she cocked her head toward her. 'Are you a believer?' she asked.

The woman was so close that she could see each individual hair that ran over the line of her top lip. She took a polite step back, smiling tightly. 'A believer?'

'In the Other Side.'

'Oh,' she said with relief. 'Well. Yes. I am.'

'Well. Me and Emmie was having a séance,' she said. 'So, it's not a good time.'

'A séance?'

'Yes. She's in a trance so she can't speak to you. Now, if you don't mind . . .' The woman started to push the door closed.

'Mrs Wood?'

The woman jumped and turned at the girl's voice.

She was standing in the door to her rooms, her face pale in the shadows, her eyes surprised. 'Oh! Emmie!' the woman continued, clutching her chest. 'You scared me half to death! I heard the front door and didn't want to disturb you whilst you was communing.' She nodded towards Mrs Wood. 'This lady was asking after you.'

The girl's eyes were on Mrs Wood and then, as quick as if a match had been struck her face filled with a smile and she strode happily forward. 'What a treat!' she said. 'Mrs Busby, this is Mrs Wood!'

The woman swooped her hands to her mouth, her eyes like planets. 'Mrs Wood?' she said around her fingers.

Mrs Wood smiled her steeliest smile. 'It's a pleasure to meet you, Mrs Busby.'

'Well, I almost made a fool out of myself then,' she said, pressing her hands to her face. 'What a pleasure. My days. Mrs Wood. Right here! Can you believe it, Emmie?'

Mrs Wood smiled and then looked beyond the woman to the girl. 'I wondered, Miss Finch,' she said. 'Might you be available for a little chat?'

Mrs Busby was a woman who had a lot to say about nothing and took her time in saying it. Eventually, after she'd promised to leave them to it for what felt like the hundredth time, the girl managed to close the door of her room on her broad back, and they listened in welcome silence as her boots clomped slowly up the stairs to her own rooms on the first floor.

The girl stood at the window, turning the blinds, filling the room window by window with cool morning light. The air smelled of hot wax and sage.

'Well,' said Mrs Wood, sitting on the edge of the blue upholstered chair, one of a pair she had arranged to have sent over from Whiteley's. 'She seems friendly.' The table she had bought the girl was covered with a white cotton tablecloth, a single brass candlestick at its centre, its candle still warm. She noticed there was a new ornament on the windowsill – a china cat dandling a ball of wool.

'Mrs Busby's been keeping an eye on me,' said the girl.

Mrs Wood's shoulders tightened. 'I was careful to choose a respectable area for you,' she said.

'And it *is*,' the girl replied quickly. 'Very respectable. But . . . sometimes I get a bit worried at night.'

'If you had said, I would have found you a companion. Someone trustworthy.'

'I wouldn't trouble you for such a thing,' said the girl with a smile. 'And I think Mrs Busby likes it. Having someone to fuss over.'

'How serendipitous.' There were peacock feathers, new ones, in a brass vase on a sideboard.

'Did Mrs Busby say anything about séances?' the girl asked. 'Only once she knew what I do, she insisted I show her some of the things I've been learning,' she said. 'I don't do it for anyone else, honest. I know what you said about not doing anything public.'

Mrs Wood calmly smoothed her skirt. 'I'm glad to hear it.'

'But when I mentioned to her that I'd been learning with one of the best in London. Well, she insisted.' She fiddled with her skirts before suddenly reaching for the candlestick on the table and putting it up on the cluttered mantel, trailing hot wax across the cloth as she went. 'There,' she said, pulling the tablecloth free and balling it in her hands. 'Mrs Busby's a bit of a Medium herself,' she continued. 'I was hardly doing anything at all.'

Mrs Wood shifted in her seat and cleared her throat. 'I wanted to talk about the séance last Thursday. With the Circle.'

The girl dropped into the matching blue chair holding the table-cloth on her lap like a baby. 'Is everything all right?'

'I was very proud of your performance,' she said. '*Very*. And proud to be there at the birth of your new spirit guide. You have come so far from the novice who appeared before me only a few months ago.'

The girl's eyes sparked. 'Thank you,' she said, but Mrs Wood held her hand up.

'But . . .' she said, and the girl sat back again. 'While it was an extraordinary display, and an extraordinary honour, there is, in the spiritual world an etiquette that I have been remiss in underlining with you.'

'Etiquette?'

'Behaviours,' she said. 'Things that are appropriate and things that are . . . not.'

'And my spirit guide wasn't appropriate?'

She thought for a moment. 'It wasn't the spirit guide. It's . . . Miss Finch: a host plans her séance with care. Who's invited, who speaks. Everything. And throughout, it's the host who must take responsibility for the manifestations or messaging that come through, no matter which Medium is sharing them. It's the only way balance and order can be maintained and the host can ensure that the séance is as rewarding as it can possibly be.' She levelled her eyes. 'Do you understand what I'm saying?'

The girl stared at the floor before her feet. 'I'm sorry,' she whispered, eventually. 'I didn't think . . . It just happened. The spirits . . .'

'Indeed,' she said. 'And everyone enjoyed it, and everyone was most impressed. But it took me by surprise, and surprises make my role as host of the table very challenging.' She took a breath. The misery settling across the girl's face was making the conversation even harder. 'Miss Finch. I am telling you this for your own good. If I didn't speak with you and explain for the future, you can only imagine how difficult things might become.'

The girl was ashen. 'You must think me unspeakable.'

'I think no such thing,' she said, her edges unconsciously softening. 'You're ambitious. That's *good*. You've only recently come to this world, no one would expect you to know such things without being told. We will be more prepared next time.' She paused. 'I am not angry, Miss Finch. You understand that, don't you?'

She waited for the girl to compose herself, taking the opportunity to drink in a little more of the room: in addition to the ornamental cat, there was a print of the Queen on one wall and she had tied jaunty yellow ribbons around the curtain tie-backs.

'Thank you for being so kind to me,' the girl said, eventually, with a final sniff. 'But I am sorry.'

'Then we shall speak no more of it,' she said, and reached for her bag. 'Now. We shall use our Monday morning session to talk through everything so that we don't have any more repeats of things.' She stood. 'I'm sorry I interrupted your séance with Mrs Busby.'

'It wasn't really a séance,' said the girl quickly, following her to the door. Then she hesitated. 'Mrs Busby mentioned something which I . . .' The girl stopped, chewing her cheek.

'What did she say?'

'Well. There's so much talk about these full spirits these days. She wondered if . . .'

Mrs Wood narrowed her eyes. 'Was Mrs Busby suggesting that I should materialise a spirit?'

The girl laughed. 'Oh no,' she said. 'I don't think anyone's thinking that you might do such a thing.' The words stung like a whip. 'No, she was asking if I thought *I* might be able to do it.'

'They're a parlour trick,' Mrs Wood said airily. 'The Americans are obsessed with them, which says as much as we need to know.'

'You're right,' she said. 'That's why I told her not to be stupid. I mean, if it were a respectable thing, you'd be doing it already, wouldn't you?'

She left her cab at Ledbury Road to save on the fare and proceeded to stamp her way home along the busy streets of Westbourne Grove, seeing nothing and hearing only Miss Finch's last words.

Those damned full spirits! When were people going to stop talking about them? Or at least stop talking about them in the same breath as her name. She was not a sideshow. She was not a performing seal.

She was Mrs Wood.

There was no time to wait. She needed to introduce the girl to her patrons.

It was time for Miss Finch to take her first steps into society.

Excerpt from the Editor's Column
Magnus Clore
Spiritual Times, 24th April 1873

Word has reached my ears of a skilled young Medium who's been taken under the wing of none other than Mrs Wood. I hear that she is blossoming into quite the talent – a fact I consider an inevitability under such experienced tutelage. The only question I have, however, is when I will be lucky enough to meet Mrs Wood's ingenue. You can be sure that when it happens, I will tell all here first!

The Dowager Lady Gregory
8 Cromwell Gardens, South Kensington

24th April 1873

Dearest Mrs Wood,
Regarding our séance planned for this Saturday coming. Might I
request that you bring your young pupil with you? Lady Harrington
extended an invitation to Mr Clore when she saw him at Lady
Frances's luncheon last Sunday and I know that he is rather
desperate to meet her.
    Do let me know if this would be convenient for all.
    Delphine, Dowager Lady Gregory

CHAPTER 14

Mrs Wood set the Dowager's letter neatly upon that morning's *Spiritual Times* beside her untouched soup and sat back with a satisfied smile.

That carefully placed crumb of gossip had worked. The Dowager had clearly put pen to paper as soon as she'd read her morning's *Spiritual Times* so that it would make the afternoon post.

That said, she was surprised that it had been the Dowager; she had always seemed so unimpressed with the young Mediums Mr Clore discussed. She had expected something from Mrs Green, whose expensive home shone with the gloss of new money, or the Countess, who enjoyed a pretty face.

But the Dowager was her most important patron and so her interest was gladdening, as was the Dowager's plan to include Mr Clore on the list.

A favourable evening indeed! Exactly how she would have wanted to introduce the girl, if she had been able to engineer it herself.

'Why are you looking so pleased with yourself?' Mrs Wood looked up to find Miss Newman staring curiously over the table.

She gave her an enigmatic smile and picked up her soup spoon, dandling it absently amidst the carrots and shredded chicken that bobbed in the broth, allowing herself to wonder if making her Sunday joints last a week might soon be another unnecessary budget constraint.

'Violet? What've you been up to?'

'Securing our future,' she said. She let the confusion cross Miss Newman's face, but felt too pleased with herself to go into the details of Mr Larson's ledger. He had told her about the ships he was interested in, but he hadn't been able to confirm how quickly they might see a return or if he even thought he might invest at all. He was a steady man, but he seemed to be being particularly cautious following the mine fiasco. Infuriatingly so. She shouldn't have told him that she was able to support herself in the interim. She should have made it clear that she needed that money: she had a whole household dependent upon it.

But now, finally, she was about to see the investment in the girl pay off. On Saturday, she would present Miss Finch as her loyal pupil to her most important patron in the company of the voice who could reignite the passion for Mrs Wood to people who mattered.

When she looked up again, she noticed that Miss Newman was in the hall buttoning her mackintosh.

'I said I'd help put the chairs away at the society tonight,' she said. 'You don't mind, do you?'

'It's filthy out there,' said Mrs Wood. 'Is it really that important?'

Miss Newman gave a helpless shrug. 'I'm sorry,' she said. 'But I promised. They're always short of help with the dull chores. I wonder why!' She smiled playfully and Mrs Wood gave a flat stare in return.

'I'd hoped we could talk about the Dowager's séance for Saturday,' she said.

'Hadn't we agreed to do that tomorrow?' Miss Newman pushed her notebook into her pocket and pulled up the hood. 'I shan't be late.'

'Of course,' she said. And then, quickly, hoping to entice her. 'You know the girl is now invited?'

Miss Newman hesitated. 'It was you, wasn't it,' she said.

'Me?'

'Who told the *Spiritual Times*. About the girl.'

She felt her cheeks pink. 'I don't know what you mean.'

But instead of smiling ruefully as she ordinarily would, Miss

Newman frowned, and Mrs Wood felt a sudden clang of realisation: this was something they would usually have connived together.

'You've been busy,' she said defensively. 'With all your work outside of the house these days, I find it hard to know when I'm going to be able to discuss anything beyond a rushed overview of a séance.'

'That's not fair,' she said. 'I'm always here for you, you know that. I'm away for a few hours at most . . .'

She was about to return a swift reply, but she started, suddenly aware: she had never argued with Miss Newman. So instead, she swallowed the words and nodded sagely. 'I should have told you,' she said. 'We can talk more tomorrow. As planned.'

Miss Newman gave a stiff nod. 'Yes,' she said. 'And if there's anything more going on behind the scenes of your mind, be sure to share lest I happen to stumble across it. We're still friends at the very least, aren't we?'

'Oh no, you can't mean for me to come,' the girl stammered. 'No. You're teasing, surely . . .'

'The Dowager asked for you herself,' Mrs Wood replied with a reassuring smile.

'But I'm not ready!' the girl continued, her eyes wide. 'Where would she get the idea that I was ready?'

'From me.' Mrs Wood sat back with a steady smile. 'You performed beautifully at our last Circle. You listened, respected, paid attention to cues. You are progressing swiftly, dear girl, and I am happy to take you with me.'

The girl looked away. 'Someone like me,' she said, her voice a whisper. 'In a *lady's* home.'

'Obviously, you will continue to follow my lead. These are people who may well support your career as a Medium in the future.'

The girl nodded and swallowed. 'If you're sure?'

'Dear thing,' Mrs Wood said. 'I would not have suggested it if I weren't. Besides, there won't be much for you to do beyond employ your charm and present a few simple events.'

'I can do that,' she said.

'Wear the green dress and slippers, and make sure it's clean. I noticed a mark on it last week that has now been there some time.' She ran her eyes over the girl, squinting when she hit the fat sausage-like coils she'd taken to wearing around her ears. 'Eliza will pin your hair. Those silly things do you no justice.'

The girl tugged shyly on one of the coils. 'All the girls in the fashion plates are wearing their hair like this,' she said.

'You are not a fashion plate,' Mrs Wood replied. 'You're a Medium. Or you will be one day, at least. You must dress accordingly.'

The girl nodded demurely. 'Illusion is everything,' she said, and Mrs Wood hesitated.

'Yes,' she said. 'You've said that before.'

The girl blinked. 'Have I?'

Mrs Wood watched her for a moment more before standing abruptly. 'Shall we get on with today's session?' She stepped up to the candelabra on the mantelpiece and picked up the snuffer. 'Let's lead with some trance work.'

The Dowager Lady Gregory was a renowned host.

Her home was an unfathomably large house near the South Kensington Museum, with so many floors that the uppermost windows were often shrouded in smog. Fires blazed all year round to counter draughts, and gaslights chased the shadows from even the furthest corners throughout. She had created a dedicated séance room on the first floor, with rugs criss-crossing the floor and thick drapes that damped unwanted sounds and kept the room dark and warm, no matter the time of year. The table was large, with lightweight spindle legs, and the chairs were solid, giving off barely a creak in even the most excitable of moments.

And with the Dowager came more of Mrs Wood's patrons.

The Dowager's daughter, Lady Harrington, had private appointments with Mrs Wood every other week. Her marriage to the MP for North Wealden had grown bleak, his neglect forcing her to rekindle, with Mrs Wood's assistance, her love of a long-dead suitor. Their consultations involved Lady Harrington whispering wistfully with him through Mrs Wood, going over their shared memories and lost future.

Then there was the Dowager's sister, a wonderfully eccentric spinster. She wore ropes of pearls entwined with American Indian necklaces and strings of tiny bells around her hidden ankles. She encouraged everyone to call her Solange, even though it was nothing remotely close to her given name (which no one could remember anymore), and lived in rooms decorated by giant tribal masks, Chinese cabinets, Indian rugs and seven Bengal cats.

While Mrs Wood would never be invited to one of their parties or where a séance was not needed, when she was in their home, the Dowager always behaved as though Mrs Wood were no different from any one of her society friends. They always began the evening with champagne and platters of exotic canapés and rich conversation revealing scintillating (and valuable) insights into a life spent on the edge of the Queen's court, as though Mrs Wood were one of them.

Was she ready for that access to be diluted with the inclusion of the girl?

If it meant she could continue to work, then yes: she was.

As agreed, Miss Finch arrived half an hour before they were due to leave for the Dowager's.

'We're in here,' Mrs Wood called from the back parlour where she and Miss Newman had been working through some last-minute choices for that evening, but she stopped when the girl entered. 'Is that a new dress?'

'Do you like it?' the girl asked, holding in a smile. She picked up the skirt of a teal taffeta dress as though she were about to curtsey and turned. 'It was a present.'

'From whom?' asked Mrs Wood, standing so she could get a better view. It was a rather extravagant thing with puffed sleeves and a small bustle topped with a rose in a dark blue velvet. The same velvet had been threaded through the modest, frilled neckline, and she had tied a length of it into her hair – the fat sausage coils now dangling sweetly from the back of her head. 'What's happened to you?'

The girl stopped. 'What's wrong with me?'

'You look very nice,' said Miss Newman, casting a glance at Mrs Wood. 'I think that's what Mrs Wood meant to say.'

'Yes. Of course,' said Mrs Wood, distracted. The dress was modest and befitting to the evening, and the girlish coils actually looked quite fetching clutched together rather than dangling like spaniel's ears. It was just that she looked so . . . expensive. The cost of the silk alone was well beyond the girl's stipend. 'Where did you get it?'

The girl blushed. 'The dress? It was a present,' she said. 'From an admirer.'

Mrs Wood turned sharply. 'Which admirer?'

'Haven't I told you?' Miss Finch replied with a lightness that was suddenly irritating. 'I met him with Mrs Busby when we went over to Dalston Spiritualist Church the other day. He said he knew you. A Mr Humboldt?'

Ugh. Mrs Wood couldn't help the wince at the man's name. Oh yes, she knew Garrison Humboldt. A man of long limbs and brown teeth, and hands that liked to roam in the dark. 'You shouldn't be taking gifts from someone you do not know, Miss Finch. Especially a man,' she said. 'If it should get out—'

'It's not new,' she said, turning again and admiring the bustle. 'Mr Humboldt's granddaughter grew out of it, apparently.'

'Why were you there?' she asked. 'Dalston. I wasn't aware you were planning a visit.'

'I hadn't planned anything. Mrs Busby suggested we go the other day, out of the blue. Her cousin is a member of the church there, and she thought it might be nice for me to meet her. She's not much older than me, and . . .' She glanced between the two older women. 'Did I make a mistake?'

Mrs Wood hesitated, but the clock tinged on the mantel. If they didn't leave soon, they would be late. As much as she would like to, she couldn't afford to get drawn on this when they needed to prepare.

The girl's eyes had filled. 'I only . . . I wanted to make a good impression, and I didn't think the green dress was very . . .' Then she reached forward, urgently. 'It's lovely, you know I love the dress, Mrs Wood. It's just . . . isn't it more of a day dress?'

The girl looked down. A tear dropped onto the bodice, leaving a spreading stain on the silk.

'Here,' she said, pushing a handkerchief into her hand. 'You don't want to ruin it before we've even left the house.' She moved closer, her voice softening. 'You look very nice.'

'Thank you,' the girl sniffed, still not looking up.

'But you must be careful,' she said. 'Trust me, you may think he's old and therefore respectable, but men are always men. You don't want to owe him anything.'

'I won't,' she rushed. 'I didn't ask for it, I promise. I doubt I'll see him ever again, anyway. Dalston is a long way away. And I'm learning everything I need here. In West London. With you.'

'Yes,' said Mrs Wood, finally. 'That's absolutely right.'

One of the Dowager's disappointed footmen ushered them into the drawing room, where the family were scattered in various chairs beneath raging gaslights, fanning themselves in the almost obscene heat from the fire.

At the announcement of Mrs Wood, Lady Harrington and Solange were on their feet, rushing towards her in a chaos of hair ornaments and feathers, pressing kisses onto her cheeks and squeezing her hand and clamouring suddenly over the girl. The Dowager waited more sedately, taking the girl's hand calmly on introduction, smiling and glancing approvingly at Mrs Wood as the girl gushed about how lovely the house was and how lucky she was to be there. Solange, coiled in furs, returned to pumping the girl's hand and congratulating her on her beautiful hair. 'I can't get mine to do anything more than this,' she said, pointing to the whip of grey froth that topped her head like a decoration.

'I think it's beautiful,' said the girl, and Solange looped her arm into Mrs Wood's.

'Excellent specimen,' she whispered, as though appraising a horse. 'You'll be pleased to hear that I have been developing my gift since we last met,' Solange continued, leading Mrs Wood across the room. 'I have discovered Buddhist meditation and chanting. Do you know of it? Oh, it's marvellous. It's as though I've accessed another channel in my mind altogether. I think you shall be most impressed.' She laughed brightly.

'What a pretty dress,' said Lady Harrington, and as the girl took the opportunity to show it off, Mrs Wood looked across the room. There he was: Magnus Clore, editor of the city's most influential spiritualist newspaper, the *Spiritual Times*. He stood quietly, leaning against the mantel, clearly biding his time before making his own introduction.

Magnus Clore had taken on the editorship of the *Spiritual Times* eighteen months before, transforming what had essentially been a weekly list of Mediums' contact details into the leading spiritualist publication in London. While he enjoyed a séance as much as the next man, he made no bones of his interest in exposing those who risked tarnishing spiritualism's good name. Since Clore's appearance, several less-than-sincere Mediums had either disappeared themselves or been forcefully disappeared through gleeful unmasking in his weekly column, which quickly established itself as essential reading for the community. It was his duty, he liked to remind people, to winkle out the charlatans on behalf of those Mediums with only honest intentions. For that reason, he was greeted everywhere with enthusiastic delight that wasn't entirely commensurate with his rather oily personality.

But still, he was a great fan of Mrs Wood's and that meant one less thing to worry about.

'My dear Mrs Wood,' he said with outstretched hands. 'It's been too long.' She kept the smile firm on her face as he leaned in, his smooth cheek against her ear and whispered, 'Is this her?' before stepping back as though nothing had happened.

'How lovely to see you, too,' she replied, giving him a quick nod of confirmation, and she watched his eyes flicker over the girl with increasing interest. 'Miss Finch,' she said, disengaging from Mr Clore's damp grasp. 'Please allow me to introduce you to Mr Clore. Editor of—'

'—The *Spiritual Times*!' said the girl, her hands over her mouth. 'Oh, my days. I had no idea you'd be here, Mr Clore. Oh, I've been dying to meet you!' Mrs Wood's fingers pressed into the flesh of the girl's arm and she finally remembered herself. 'Mr Clore,' she said, dipping her chin politely. 'It's a pleasure to meet you.'

He took her hand, pressing it between both of his. 'Please, dear girl. Call me *Magnus*.'

The girl giggled and Mrs Wood closed quickly around her. 'Mr Clore,' she said, sliding her hand into the crook of the girl's arm to subtly disentangle her. 'You're being greedy,' she chided, and then turned back to the room. 'What a wonderful welcome,' she said. 'But perhaps we should begin?'

Miss Newman hurried up behind Mrs Wood as Solange swept Miss Finch ahead.

'He practically inhaled her,' Miss Newman said, steering them both after the Dowager.

'She took it all in her stride,' she replied, as though she were simply commenting on the weather.

'I ran through everything with her one last time,' Miss Newman continued. 'I'm confident she'll stay on track.'

Mrs Wood laughed as though Miss Newman had made a joke. 'Why on earth wouldn't she!'

And suddenly, Lady Harrington was beside her. 'We are still confirmed for next Tuesday's consultation?' she whispered. 'I have much to discuss with . . .' She lowered her eyes and Mrs Wood patted her hand where it rested on her arm.

'Absolutely,' she whispered back. 'I am sure he's looking forward to it just as much as you.'

Miss Finch won everyone over during the séance, exactly as Mrs Wood had planned.

She was sweetly charming, commenting only when something was apported onto the table or when Solange proclaimed she'd received a vision. And, as agreed, Mona's visit was short and non-revelatory. Of course, there had been a few heart-stopping moments: the girl had given off a firework of a laugh at one point, and when the Dowager's brother had sent a message through Jack Starr, she had clutched at the Dowager's hand with no regard for etiquette. But overall, Mrs Wood sensed nothing but goodwill around the table and, as the candles were relit and the room bloomed back into light, she felt a flood of pride when she caught the Dowager and Solange sharing a favourable glance with one another.

Yes, the girl had been a dream in the dark.

She followed the Dowager from the room with a light heart, watching Mr Clore descend on the girl as she chatted easily with Lady Harrington. He would have nothing but praise for her pupil in his next column; his approval was most certainly secure.

As usual, a lavish buffet had been laid in the second drawing room, and they all trooped downstairs to avail themselves of the Dowager's imported treats, everyone energised and excited by all that had happened.

While they chose from seeded crackers and caviar and roast beef and cold tongue and figs and watermelon and syllabub, the Dowager's family talked candidly about mutual acquaintances, Mrs Wood listening discreetly as titbits on health and romances were shared for Miss Newman to add to her notebook later, and Miss Finch piling her plate with grapes.

She gathered herself as the girl approached. 'You did very well,' she said quietly.

The grapes wobbled on the plate in the girl's hand as she gave a nervous shrug. 'Are you sure?' she said. 'I know I'm prone to completely forgetting myself at times.'

Mrs Wood gave a quick nod. 'I've heard no complaint yet,' she said. 'But it would be wise to get into the habit of restraint. Some families are more formal than this household.'

The girl nodded, biting her lip. 'You were wonderful, of course,' she said. 'No, really. You were so . . . easy. The way you moved between things . . .' Miss Finch gave a sigh, and Mrs Wood realised that the girl had only ever seen her work at a Circle table. She hadn't been to a Grand Séance, and this was the first time they had gone out in public together. 'If I could ever gather a smidge of your skill, I would die happy.'

'Let's hope that's not necessary,' said Mrs Wood, feeling touched, nonetheless.

The huddle had dissipated from the sideboard, the family finding seats across the room while Mr Clore had settled himself back at the mantel. He caught her eye, moving his chin as though summoning her, and she collected her glass. 'Excuse me, dear,' she said to the girl, but then she realised that he hadn't been looking at her at all. He raised his glass, and the girl giggled back at him.

'Excuse me,' the girl said. 'I think Mr Clore might . . .' And, choosing to ignore Mrs Wood's fixed expression, she tripped sweetly away.

Miss Newman appeared at her shoulder. 'I see his net has been cast,' she said beneath her breath.

'It's in our interest that he likes her,' she said, bristling, but Miss Newman raised a playful eyebrow and moved on.

She turned back to the girl, watching as she stopped before Clore. He nodded at her dress, and she looked down, pulling out the skirt and giving a series of half-turns with yet another giggle.

Solange loomed suddenly in Mrs Wood's periphery, and she collected herself, tearing her eyes from the girl and Clore with a broad smile. 'Dearest,' she said. 'The chanting is clearly working. You did some splendid work tonight.'

'Do you really think so?' Solange said, her necklaces rattling as she tugged them. She continued to talk but Mrs Wood couldn't keep track of what she was saying; Clore was whispering in the girl's ear. Mrs Wood bit the inside of her lip, switching glances between what was playing out at the fireplace and Solange until she couldn't keep up.

'Please do excuse me,' she said abruptly, and Solange stopped talking immediately.

'Is everything all right?'

'I'm just . . . I'm suddenly greatly fatigued. And cold.' She pulled her shawl closer and gave a little shiver.

'Of course, you are!' And she ushered her towards the fire. 'Here,' she said, placing her on the sofa. 'I'll get you one of your sherries.'

The girl was now only an arm's length away, Mr Clore's head close to hers as he whispered into her ear and the girl fluttered. As she laughed, she turned and started on seeing Mrs Wood looking back at her. Straightening, she said quickly, 'Mrs Wood.' Then smiled brightly. 'I didn't see you there.'

'That's all right,' she said. 'Mr Clore's keeping you busy.' She fixed him with a knowing eye.

'Mr Clore is very charming,' she said.

'That's not been said enough times,' said Mr Clore. Mrs Wood bit her lip again. 'I was explaining to Miss Finch that I've been waiting far too long for us to be formally introduced.'

'And I was reminding him that I'm not anyone important.'

'Come and sit with me, Miss Finch,' said Mrs Wood, indicating the cushion beside her. 'Keep me company.'

'Of course.' The girl hesitated for a moment, Mrs Wood clearly the less attractive prospect, before smiling stiffly and sitting crisply beside her. 'Do you need anything?' she asked.

'Not at all,' she said, patting the girl's hand. 'Solange is bringing me a sherry.'

'How nice!' said the girl. 'I've only got cordial.' She lifted her glass and pulled a face.

'You're much too young and pretty for such poison,' said Mr Clore, absently swirling his own glass. 'Don't you think, Mrs Wood?'

Solange arrived with the sherry, and Mrs Wood took it with a forced smile. It felt like a chalice in her hands, and she placed it, untouched, on the side table.

'Mr Clore was asking about the things we've been doing together,' she said. 'I told him how wonderful and generous you've been. How everything I'm doing is thanks to you.'

'You are a lucky girl,' he said. 'Mrs Wood has never before taken on a pupil.' He gave her a smile. 'It speaks to your talent, Miss

Finch.' Then he turned to Mrs Wood. 'Next time, I'd like to see exactly what she can do.'

'I think it's marvellous,' said Solange loudly. 'Mrs Wood has so much experience: I learn from her every time she visits. You are very fortunate, Miss Finch.'

'Oh, I am,' said Miss Finch. 'Very fortunate. A girl from where I come from, sitting in a room like this: it's like a dream.'

Solange hesitated and excused herself, and Miss Finch looked confused. 'Did I say something wrong?'

'Don't mention position, dear,' whispered Mrs Wood. 'It's vulgar.'

'Of course,' she said, her eyes dropping to her hands in her lap. 'I'm always making mistakes like that. I don't blame you for not introducing me to any of your private clients. I'm bound to embarrass you then too.'

Mr Clore's eyebrow snapped up, a crocodile in the shallows suddenly alerted to fresh meat. 'Private clients?'

Mrs Wood put her hand quietly on Miss Finch's wrist. 'Dearest—'

'Oh yes,' the girl continued blithely. 'Mrs Wood sees some of the finest people in town. Don't you, Mrs Wood.'

Blood rushed to Mrs Wood's ears. 'Are you going away at all this summer, Mr Clore?'

But it was too late. He had bitten. 'She does, Miss Finch?' he said. 'Anyone I know?'

'Why, only the other day I was passing and saw Lady Frances's carriage leaving.'

Mrs Wood started as though she'd been shot. 'Dear thing. You must've been mistaken,' she said, sure her voice was far too loud. 'These carriages all look the same.' She gave a laugh, looking up at Mr Clore, trying to smile and cover her panic. 'Miss Newman: look at the time! We have overstayed our welcome.' She collected the girl up, holding her arm firmly as she began the circle of farewells, and Miss Newman went to arrange the cab.

It wasn't until she had slammed the cab door shut behind them and they were rushing away from the Dowager's house that she finally turned to Miss Finch.

'You *never* speak of who we see behind closed doors, do you understand?'

The girl opened her mouth. If Mrs Wood had struck her, she would have appeared less stunned.

'What happened?' said Miss Newman. 'What's going on?'

'If there's *one* thing I have tried to teach you – *one thing!* – it's that discretion is *everything!*'

'I know! I'm sorry! It just came out . . .'

'A lot of things *just come out*,' she snapped back. 'Perhaps you should take time to think before you open that silly little mouth of yours.'

Her words bounced around the carriage, and she was shocked at how much of Hull had escaped in that moment of lost control.

'I'm sorry,' said Miss Finch eventually.

Mrs Wood clenched her jaw. 'I know.' And she turned to glare at the streetlamps sweeping slowly by in the wet world beyond.

CHAPTER 15

The next morning, Miss Newman made it absolutely clear that she thought Mrs Wood was overreacting.

'She's going to make mistakes, Violet,' she said. 'She's still learning.'

'That's not what you said when she introduced Mona,' she said, using every ounce of control to manage her growing frustration.

'Mona was different. That was overstepping the mark in a séance – that's dangerous. This was—'

'Worse!' said Mrs Wood. 'This is my reputation. What if this should get out? That my pupil is so loose-lipped that their identities are no longer secure?'

'You're overreacting now just as you overreacted last night. It was a slip. That was all. And no one would've noticed if you hadn't rushed her out of the house.'

'Clore noticed.'

'It could've been anything,' she said. 'Instead of whisking her away, you could've simply countered it. That's what you do at the table all the time, isn't it?'

Mrs Wood glared at her across the room. The weather had not improved overnight and outside the parlour window budding trees were whipped wild in the roiling rain. She wished they could have lit the fire, but instead she wrapped her hands around her teacup and made do.

How could Miss Newman, who had been so concerned by the girl introducing Mona without notice or permission, not understand the risk that this indiscretion posed to them?

'This is my reputation, Sarah. If my clients think that I give up their names to someone like *Clore*, they will not come.'

'It's *our* reputation, Violet. And they won't.' Miss Newman sat forward in her chair. 'Look,' she said. 'I understand why you're feeling sensitive. Lady Frances is a good client to have – she would make a wonderful patron.' Mrs Wood looked away, the truth of everything on the tip of her tongue. She clenched her jaw as Miss Newman continued: 'But the girl made a mistake. That's all. Some sensitive countering is what's needed now.'

'What do you suggest? I take out an advertisement in the *Spiritual Times*? *Mrs Wood is not seeing Lady Frances for private consultations!*'

Miss Newman gave an exasperated sigh and sat back. 'You chose to take the girl on,' she said. 'You chose to bring her into your life knowing nothing about her. You took that risk.'

She blinked. 'Are you saying it's my fault?'

'You're taking her into a society she's never moved in before,' Miss Newman continued. 'You need to be fair to her.'

Did she? Why did the girl deserve to be treated with kid gloves? No one had been fair to her. She had been thrown into grand drawing rooms and fancy back parlours without any such care. The difference between them, perhaps, was that she had been smart enough to pay attention to the Dentist. She had listened to him as a good pupil should, fear of his stinging reprimands keeping her Hull vowels at bay, the correct fork in her hand and her skirts arranged with perfect decorum.

She would never have made such a mistake. *Never.*

She sat up resolutely. 'No,' she said. 'I will not tolerate anything that risks our reputation.' And she picked up a small book that was on the side table and flicked it open to a page – *any page* – pulling her pince-nez up on its chain and placing them pointedly on the end of her nose. 'Now,' she said. 'If you don't mind. I have an hour before Mr Yurick is due for his consultation and I would like to catch up on my reading.'

She could feel Miss Newman's eyes on her as she went over the same random sentence over and over until she heard the rustle of her dress.

'You're too stubborn for your own good,' Miss Newman said as she stood, and Mrs Wood ignored her. 'Enjoy your guide to pickles and preserves.' Mrs Wood looked up and Miss Newman pointed at the book. 'Mrs Reynolds dropped it off for Cook,' she said. 'You'll no doubt enjoy the chapter on sour fruits.'

Fortunately, the girl settled the debate by making a surprise visit that afternoon.

After Eliza had shown a satisfied Mr Yurick, sniffing and dabbing his eyes, from the house, Mrs Wood came stretching into the hall.

'Did I hear the door while I was engaged?' she asked as Eliza returned for the used cups.

'She's in there,' she said, jerking her head to the drawing room.

'Who is?'

'The girl,' she said.

Mrs Wood started. 'Miss Finch?'

'Who'd you think?'

'Eliza.'

'Yes,' she said. 'Miss Finch.'

'Thank you,' she said, stretching out her hips and knees. 'Could I have some tea. And perhaps a crumpet, please? In the drawing room.'

The girl was perched on the edge of Miss Newman's chair, her back to the door, fingers fiddling with her skirts.

'Miss Finch,' she said, closing the door behind her, and the girl jumped up. 'I wasn't expecting you.'

'I know,' she said, rounding the chair. She looked wrung out. The shoulders of the familiar green dress were damp, and her coils had slumped, curls of wet hair sticking to her forehead from her walk. She smiled, but her eyes were diminished and small. 'I had to come,' she said. 'I haven't slept for fear of the position I put you in last night.'

A smile threatened at the corner of Mrs Wood's mouth. If Miss Newman could see them now. But, of course, she was out pamphleting with her society. 'I'm glad you understand the gravity of your behaviour,' she said, and the girl nodded quickly.

'I don't know what came over me,' she said. 'I don't want to blame anyone else, but Mr Clore . . . he has a way of making you forget where you are.'

'He's a newspaperman. That's his job.' She steadied her gaze. 'And it's your job, Miss Finch, to make sure that you don't.'

'I know. It was out before I could even realise it was wrong.'

'You know what you did, don't you? Discretion is critical to a Medium's reputation.'

'I know.' A fat tear slid down her cheek.

'Especially amongst those who are as influential as Lady Frances.'

'It was out before I realised,' she whispered. 'I wanted you to be proud of me. To feel like you could take me to another séance and trust that I would do everything right.' She looked at her feet. 'But I let you down.'

Mrs Wood inhaled slowly. No matter how steeled she made herself, the girl affected her. It was part of her talent, the empathy. A benefit but also, in situations like this, a hindrance. She looked at the girl, forlorn and childlike sitting hunched in her wet dress. Miss Newman was right; she had brought her into a life that may as well be a foreign land. 'You didn't,' she said.

'I shall write to Mr Clore,' the girl said, desperately. 'Explain that I made a mistake. That I didn't see Lady Frances. That it was someone else entirely.'

'No,' she said with a sigh. 'This is my responsibility, dear. Chepstow Villas is often used as a cut-through. You could easily have seen Lady Frances's carriage and it have nothing to do with me.'

The girl looked up. 'But he knew what I meant. I must write and say that I was wrong.'

'There's no need, Miss Finch.' Miss Newman was right. She had to take control, deflate the gossip. 'The more we draw attention to the gaffe, the more we'll stoke his curiosity. It will be best if you leave any reparations to me. I'm used to gentlemen like our Mr Clore.'

Miss Finch sensed the shifting mood and her shoulders lifted. 'He's so easy to talk to.'

'Let's just call this a mistake,' Mrs Wood continued, glossing over the girl's almost mooning sentiment. 'But it's the last predicament of yours that I shall clean up,' she said, regretting it immediately. That was something the Dentist would say while swiping the back of the head or pinching her leg. She drew on a broader smile to cover herself. 'Besides,' she said. 'I'm sure what I offer Mr Clore is far more valuable than the name of someone who may, or may not, be a private client of mine.'

'Thank you,' the girl said. 'I promise I'll never do anything like that again.'

'I know you won't,' she said.

Eliza's heavy footsteps announced the arrival of Mrs Wood's tea and crumpets. She turned, reaching out for them. 'Thank you, dear,' she said, taking first the tea, then the plate with a pair of hot buttered crumpets in its middle like buttons. 'Would you like to join me?' she asked the girl, but she shook her head.

'They do look especially delicious but I'm afraid I can't.' She stood to collect her belongings, sliding her arms into the dainty brown mantel which looked as sweet as ever over the green dress. 'I have an appointment today that I must not be late for.' She pressed a kiss into Mrs Wood's cheek. 'Thank you,' she said as she turned to leave. 'For everything. I'm so glad that you agreed to take me in.'

And Mrs Wood watched her go, a bead of butter from the crumpet she'd absently bitten into escaping down her chin.

Mrs Violet Wood
27 Chepstow Villas, Notting Hill

3rd May 1873

My dear Mr Clore,
What a treat to see you at the Dowager Lady Gregory's home
yesterday evening. How well you look, dearest: your tailor is doing a
wonderful job. I was also glad to see how well you took to my pupil,
Miss Finch. She is still very new: this was her first foray into society
and I fear she was a touch overwhelmed by the occasion, hence our
rather swift departure. By the end, she was so overwrought from her
work at the table that I'm afraid she was saying things that were
simply figments of her own imagination. Poor dear.

She is fully recovered now – while their stamina is no match to
one more experienced, the young are able to bounce back so quickly!
I shall keep you at the top of my list for her next society
appearance, dear friend, and hope you will be able to join us for
more fun.

With all best wishes,
Violet Wood

Excerpt from the Editor's Column
Magnus Clore
Spiritual Times, 8th May 1873

One is proud to announce that this week, your humble editor was among the first in London to finally meet London's finest new Medium, Miss Emmeline Finch. She is, as you already should be aware, the pupil of our dear old friend, Mrs Wood, and I can reveal that she is every bit as delightful and talented as we have been led to believe.

Sitting with the Dowager Lady Gregory, she introduced her spirit guide, a girl named Mona who is as sweet as her Medium and charmed us all in every way.

It is no wonder that Mrs Wood has kept her so jealously guarded these past few months, but now we must implore the Great Medium herself to make more space at her table for Miss Emmeline Finch.

After the appalling exposure of that devious strumpet Miss Hooper of Balham, who was revealed by the actions of a brave sitter to be no more a singing Medium than I, London is crying out for a pretty face with a true gift. Ladies and gentlemen, I suspect you would be well satisfied on both counts should you be lucky enough to spend an evening with Miss Finch.

CHAPTER 16

Miss Finch's next social appearance came around the following week at Miss Cram's monthly séance. Mrs Wood, with her hostess's permission, invited Mr Clore, but it transpired that he was travelling with Mrs Addison to a gathering in Brighton that he, according to his letter, really could have done without and would have much preferred to have sat with the girl once more.

She had smiled when she read this. Mrs Addison was an old hand and a good Medium, but the woman's competitiveness had precluded any kind of friendship. By chance, they'd both been at drinks in a Mayfair townhouse shortly before Christmas the previous year and Mrs Wood had taken a dark pleasure when she noticed how dependent the woman had become on her walking stick. The woman's portfolio of capabilities would no doubt begin to diminish with her mobility over the next few years. How different Mrs Addison's future might have been, she thought, if she too had realised the power of a pupil.

The girl arrived early, dressed modestly in the green spring dress, her velvet hat smart on her coils. When Mrs Wood had shown her Mr Clore's piece in the *Spiritual Times*, she had flushed with relief.

'I don't know what I'd do without you,' she said, clinging to Mrs Wood's hand.

'You are my responsibility,' Mrs Wood said, extricating herself delicately. 'But remember this so that you never forget the importance of your words. As a Medium, Miss Finch, everything you say matters.'

Miss Cram sent her carriage to collect them after lunch, Miss Newman arriving almost late from her society work, collecting bread and butter and her notebook in a flurry while Mrs Wood and the girl waited for her to join them. And then they were off, almost immediately snarled in the traffic on the Uxbridge Road, progressing at tortoise speed, which made Miss Newman grumble that it would've been easier to walk.

Mrs Wood pointedly took the notebook from her hands and flicked it open to the page Miss Newman had marked with a ribbon. They had discussed the plan for the séance over breakfast and Miss Cram generally required little preparation, the profusion of dogs that came into her séance room with them did a fair-share of the heavy lifting with all their unexpected bumps and smells, but there was no such thing as being overprepared. Of course, she could not discuss the details with the girl present, and so she spoke in a shorthand which Miss Newman – between complaints about slow-moving carts or meandering costermongers – understood effortlessly.

The girl, meanwhile, seemed perfectly content to sit within the velvet cocoon of the carriage, her fingers working on the upholstered walls, toying with the gold blind-pull, peering beyond the silk curtains onto the riotous street beyond.

'I wonder who Miss Cram's surprise will be,' Miss Newman said, and Mrs Wood looked up.

'Surprise?'

'Yes. Didn't you see? I left the letter on the console.'

Mrs Wood took a patient breath. 'No,' she said, aware that the girl's attention had shifted to her.

'I'm sorry, dearest,' Miss Newman replied, having the good sense to look sheepish. 'I was in such a rush this morning and . . .' She stopped; even if Mrs Wood's irritation was well hidden, Miss Newman knew her well enough to sense it. 'She said that she had a surprise guest. Something to do with her niece.'

'A friend?'

'She didn't say. I'm sure it won't affect anything,' Miss Newman said. 'Surprise guests never do.'

She looked at her for a moment longer then forced a smile. 'You're absolutely right,' she said. 'Perhaps next time, however . . .'

'Of course, dearest,' said Miss Newman, her smile equally as artificial and they both turned to the girl, who was watching them with interest.

'A surprise?' she said. 'What fun!'

After being introduced to Miss Cram, the girl immediately squatted to engage in enthusiastic hellos with the boiling ball of Jack Russells while Mrs Wood cast an inquisitive glance around the house.

'It looks brighter in here,' she said. 'Something has changed.'

'Father's portrait is being cleaned,' said Miss Cram, and she looked wistfully up at the huge rectangular void on the staircase wall where the bulbous face of Mr Cram usually kept disapproving watch. 'I have never felt more of an orphan.' She gave a sad laugh. 'I know it's only a picture. But seeing his face each day always made me feel as though he were still taking care of me.' There was a tremble in her voice and Mrs Wood reached for her hand.

'You mustn't worry, Miss Cram,' she said. 'He's very much here. In fact, I'd say his energy is perhaps even stronger today.' She closed her eyes and took a deep breath. 'Gosh,' she said, opening her eyes with a laugh. 'You should have his portrait cleaned more often – he wants me to assure you that the house needs nothing more than your own pretty face.'

Miss Cram lifted like a flower in the sun. 'He always knows when I'm missing him,' she said with a satisfied smile. 'And I am so lucky that you are always here to find him.' She bent to pick up a dog. 'Come . . .' Then she stopped, remembering. 'Did you receive my note about my guest? I'm so sorry about the short notice, but I knew you wouldn't mind. She's a friend of my niece's and when they came for tea yesterday, I told her that Miss Finch was coming today and . . .'

'It's perfectly all right,' said Mrs Wood, glancing at Miss Finch, but the girl was on her haunches scratching a dog as though she had heard nothing. She turned back to Miss Cram. 'I'm always happy to meet new people.'

'She said you've met before,' Miss Cram said. 'At the Countess's?'

Mrs Wood hesitated. 'I have?' she said.

'Apparently. Shall we?' And as she walked towards the garden room where she kept her séance table, the dogs skittering around her ankles, their nails clicking on the marble tiles, she called out. 'Lady Morgan! Mrs Wood and Miss Finch are here!'

Mrs Wood grabbed Miss Newman's hand and they flashed a glance at one another.

'You're forgiven,' she whispered.

'I told you she'd come to you.'

'And I told you the girl was the right investment.'

She turned to Miss Finch, who had stood and was brushing hairs from her skirts with the same demure countenance as though nothing had happened. 'Miss Finch,' she said, her voice low. 'Nothing changes for the séance.' A faint flicker crossed the girl's face. 'But Lady Morgan could be a very good patron for me, so feel free to charm her as much as you like.' She smiled. 'I know how good you are at such things.'

It could not have gone better if Mrs Wood had curated the whole afternoon herself. Lady Morgan, with her thick, brown hair loose and coiled, cheeks as pink as a summer sunset, bobbed up immediately, embracing them, talking about how excited she was to finally meet Miss Finch and to be at Mrs Wood's table once more.

She said everything Mrs Wood had been hoping for: that she had been so sad to have missed the Grand Séances of the past few months, how it had been through no fault of Mrs Wood's and that she would absolutely be there at the next one. And that she might bring her good friend Lady Cooper with her too – Lady Cooper was as keen as anyone to meet new Mediums.

'She's so pretty!' Lady Morgan said, her teeth glinting in the candlelight. 'Aren't you a pretty thing.' She turned to Mrs Wood. 'How old is she? She looks very young.'

'She's sixteen,' said Mrs Wood, and Lady Morgan exclaimed: 'A baby!' and Miss Finch bloomed.

'She is still a pupil.' Mrs Wood's hand instinctively went to the girl's arm to silently reassure and restrain. 'But she is learning well.'

'Will we see her work today?'

Miss Finch's mouth opened, but Mrs Wood interrupted before she could continue, her fingers a little tighter on the girl's arm.

'I'm careful not to put too much pressure on Miss Finch at this stage,' she said with an easy smile, 'while the girl's gift is slowly emerging.'

Lady Morgan pressed her hands to her cheeks with a gasp. 'How exciting!' she said. 'To be here at the birth of a new Medium!'

'Indeed,' said Mrs Wood. 'One can only imagine how she may blossom. You must join us more so that you may watch her gift grow with your own eyes. We could perhaps do something more private, if you would like?'

'If she's anything like you, dear woman,' Lady Morgan said, her eyes on the girl as she squeezed Mrs Wood's arm with a familiarity that made her start. 'One can only dream of how far she will go.'

Lady Octavia Morgan
The Langham Hotel, Portland Place, London

14th May 1873

My dear Mrs Wood,
What a splendid afternoon at Miss Cram's. Miss Finch was utterly
charming. You do yourself a disservice as her teacher: her gift is
very clearly advanced already – what a delight to meet Mona!

You're no doubt aware that I am living at The Langham while
an issue is resolved at the Grosvenor Square house. As such, I do
not have a table I can invite you both to and I am finding this a
daily distress! Perhaps, providing the girl is also sitting for your next
Grand Séance, you wouldn't mind setting some seats aside for me? I
am sure Lady Cooper would love to join me too. She's dying to meet
Miss Finch after I had such a wonderful time with her. She's
obscenely jealous.

With best wishes,
Lady Octavia Morgan

From the desk of celebrated English Medium
Mrs Florence Addison
24 Stockwell Park Road

Dear Violet,
I have been reliably informed that you are still at this address,
although I'm surprised you've not yet outgrown that little place. I
can vouch for the comfort a larger home affords. Mr Addison
recently acquired a substantial villa off Clapham Road for me
which offers two dedicated séance rooms, as well as an entire floor
for staff.

As interesting as houses are, however, I write after reading much
about your new young pupil. I believe that she would benefit from
spending time with another experienced Medium, for the sake of
balance. I have availability for tea Saturday week at three o'clock,
prompt. There's no need to accompany, dear. As you know, I prefer
to keep our work separate. Also, I don't know if she has any pets,
but I'm sure you remember that Marshall does not like other cats,
so tell her not to bring anything with her.

With all my very, very best wishes,
Mrs Florence Addison, Celebrated Medium

CHAPTER 17

In the weeks that followed Mr Clore's gushing review of the séance at the Dowager's in the *Spiritual Times*, Mrs Wood experienced a deluge of requests from patrons and acquaintances, and queries from fellow Mediums keen to get in on the action. Mrs Addison had even made an impromptu visit to Chepstow Villas after Mrs Wood had written to apologise that there was no time for Miss Finch to travel all the way south of the river with their pressing schedule. It had been an awkward half an hour, dominated by the pain of Mrs Addison attempting to woo Miss Finch with stories about her grand new home and the parade of unnamed dignitaries who populated her two séance rooms. She had noticed the girl's eyes widening and braced for an unfortunate comment; instead, as Mrs Addison wound down, Miss Finch had simply smiled and said that it all sounded wonderful but she was probably a bit too busy at the moment to divide her time between two tables.

It took all Mrs Wood had not to leap up and crush her with pride.

The requests for tables. The piqued Mediums.

Everything was coming together to prove to her that her investment in the girl was moments from paying off.

Which was helpful because what Mr Larson had omitted to say when he informed her that two boats – *ships* – had become part of their investment portfolio, was that their returns would not be realised until they completed their journeys safely with their cargo intact and that these journeys often took months.

Months!

She had never needed her own income more.

Each morning became exciting, letters arriving with invitations and queries about her new young pupil; interest was at an all-time high. To ensure that the fever brewing among the public remained stoked, she only agreed to tables with those who were already her patrons – Mrs Pepperdine, Colonel and Mrs Phillips, Mrs Farnham, with her repaired ankle, and the Countess. The rest, she would keep dangling, suggesting dates that were several months away; there was nothing more alluring than the unattainable, after all.

The mistakes had all been part of the process. How would she know how to school the girl in public if the girl hadn't made them? How would she know that the girl could only be presented in environments where she had complete control and could not be left alone for a single second? With those precautions in place, the girl was ready to make her mark and cement Mrs Wood as the purveyor of Mediumship's past, present and future.

She sent out her proposed dates to her patrons with a delighted sweep to her penmanship, her mood bolstered by the weather, which had cheered itself into blue skies populated by clouds like meringues. She even sent Lady Frances an unsolicited invitation to a private table with the girl – her burgeoning patron-to-be was away and had missed the excitement, and Mrs Wood felt sure that when she returned home to find that Mrs Wood had prioritised her, she would feel both delighted and touched by her thoughtfulness.

Then, as she strode towards the postbox on Westbourne Grove, she had another thought: if she received eight requests following the small sitting with the Dowager, imagine how many she might receive if she were to show the girl off to a much larger group. It wouldn't detract from the intimate tables, patrons always enjoyed those private moments, and she would keep the girl from performing so as to keep her skills tantalisingly unknown. But what if she threw a party that drew all eyes, that happened to include one of Mrs Wood's world-famous stunts? She would be killing two birds with one stone: establishing herself as the future while reminding them of her own brilliance.

Mrs Wood had performed her most famous apport in the spring of 1869, a feat that had never yet been replicated. And for good reason: the Flight had been astonishing, a testimony to Mrs Wood's parity with the spirits, enormous in both distance and accomplishment. She had, according to the sitters, been transported from her parlour in Notting Hill, where she had been looking at her household accounts, over the rooftops of London for six miles until she landed in the centre of a séance in High Holborn simply because someone at that table had suggested it wasn't the same without Mrs Wood. She had appeared before them in her housedress with stockinged feet, a detail that shocked and titillated.

The table's host had been Mr Farmer, a man who had disappeared to America a few months later, but was, at that time, a Medium she had worked with occasionally with great success in the late sixties. It had taken Miss Newman and herself working with Mr Farmer three weeks to even choose the right location for the landing séance, and then the sitters had to be carefully curated to ensure maximum gossip. The stunt itself had required second-by-second logistics, everything moving from start to finish with the tick of the clock.

It had paid off, though. The Flight of Mrs Wood remained her masterpiece, and no one had ever replicated it, or even come close.

Still. It didn't feel right to do another one. Her Flight had been so special, so audacious that attempting to revive it would feel . . . cheap.

But she had talent, skill. That skin of audacity. It could be something just as wild, just as unique.

Miss Newman was out for the evening at a lecture, so after Eliza had helped her to prepare for bed with all the care of a sheepshearer, she sat alone at the dressing table, cold creaming her face. The lamp beside her cast a greenish light across her cheeks. As she squinted closer to the mirror to wipe off some cream that had adhered to the fuzzy curls at her temples, she noticed something caught in her hair above her ear. Something white. Fluffy. She reached up and pulled it free.

A tiny feather, no more than down.

An escapee from a pillow, or perhaps even her puff.

It was so soft, so delicate between her fingers that it was almost as though it didn't exist.

As inconsequential as a snowflake.

She stopped.

A snowflake.

She started as though she'd received a physical poke.

It had been late spring of 1869, Mr Wood and she were making their first visit back to Siena since Miss Newman had joined them. In that moment of recollection, she was hit by the heady aromas of citrus and woodsmoke that had filled the blue room painted with angels and cupids, and her ears rang with the memories of her hosts' delighted whoops and hollers.

This was it!

She was about to call out to Miss Newman when she remembered that, of course, she was out with her band of worthy spinsters. The bedside clock showed that it was almost ten. She would surely be home soon. How much did anyone really have to say on emancipation? She reached for her house wrap, tying it tightly around her nightgown and tugged her nightcap over her ears. The days might be warming, but the night-time draughts that haunted 27 Chepstow Villas were stubborn.

Sliding her fur slippers on, she descended the back stairs to her parlour carrying a lamp and determinedly ignoring the leering shadows it threw up about her. She hated being around the house when it had been shut up for the night. It reminded her of how vulnerable she was, here in the middle of town without a male protector, although she had once seen Eliza beat a rug with such violent enthusiasm that perhaps all would not be lost should a burglar appear with her around.

The parlour was cold as she settled herself into her chair to wait, tugging the blankets from the seat back and swaddling herself as she ran through that night in 1868 over and over and over in her head remembering each, important step so . . . that . . .

. . . there were voices in the hall.

'Thank you,' Miss Newman was saying. 'You didn't have to walk me all the way.'

Blinking, she sat up. The clock read close to midnight. Midnight? She must've fallen asleep.

She hauled herself up from the chair, discarding the blankets, pulling her house wrap tighter, and was about to go into the hall and tell Miss Newman what she'd decided when she heard a voice respond.

A man's voice.

Mrs Wood froze.

'It has been a pleasure, Miss Newman,' the man said, his voice rich with kindness. 'Thank you for allowing me.'

They shared an awkward laugh and then there was a pause and Mrs Wood instinctively rushed from the parlour but by the time she had bustled noisily into view, Miss Newman was closing the door and whoever had been speaking had gone.

'You made me jump!' she said, clasping her chest and laughing awkwardly as a very un-Miss Newman flush appeared in her cheeks. 'Is everything all right? It's late, Violet.'

'I'm . . .' She craned to look beyond the door. 'Who was that?'

Miss Newman gave a dismissive shrug. 'A colleague from the society.'

'Men go to your society?' she asked in genuine surprise.

Miss Newman's smile faltered. 'The cause attracts many different kinds of people, Violet. Including men.'

'What kind of men?' Mrs Wood began, but Miss Newman's stifled yawn stopped her from continuing.

'It's been a long evening, dearest. Do you need something?'

She looked at her for a moment, trying to pick out any tells. But Miss Newman was closed. There would be nothing more from her tonight. 'It can wait until breakfast,' she said.

'Good,' Miss Newman said. 'I am shattered.' She stretched and began to climb the stairs, unbuttoning her jacket as she went, as though nothing of interest had happened.

Questions bubbled away in Mrs Wood's head as she watched Miss Newman eat her toast the following morning: who was that man? Who were his family? What kind of a man goes to meetings about women? But there was something about the way she had shut herself away last night that made her hesitant to ask a single one.

'Why are you staring at me?' Miss Newman asked without looking up from the pamphlet she was reading.

Mrs Wood laughed. 'You're wasted not applying yourself to Mediumship.'

Miss Newman stopped reading. 'There's nothing to say about my friend,' she said pointedly, and Mrs Wood feigned innocence. 'You forget I know everything about you, Violet.'

'Not everything,' she muttered, and Miss Newman gave her a look.

'What was this thing you wanted to talk about that kept you up last night?'

She sat up and smiled. She wanted them to be friends again. She placed her hands on the white tablecloth. 'Do you remember Siena?' she said, a little thrill of vindication sparking when Miss Newman's face turned in interest.

She smiled. 'That was one of our best,' she said. 'If I may say so myself.'

'Oh, you may!' said Mrs Wood with a laugh. 'Do you remember their faces?'

'I do,' she said, the smile deepening. 'It was so . . . unexpected.'

Mrs Wood waited a beat. 'Sarah,' she said. 'How about we do it here? For a séance.'

Miss Newman sat back. 'Really?' she said. 'We haven't done it before in England, have we.'

'No. We haven't . . .' She leaned forward. 'And it's got me thinking. The girl's generating so much interest. You've seen that, haven't you. Instead of us drawing out her introduction, why don't we throw a large reception with our favourites – imagine how much conversation it will start . . .'

'But what has that to do with Siena?'

'While we introduce Miss Finch, we perform an event that captures society's attention. Introduce the inexperienced girl whilst reminding them all what experience actually means.'

Miss Newman took a final bite of her toast and dropped the remaining crust onto her plate, brushing the crumbs from her fingers as she thought.

'I was thinking we could throw a party for Mrs Hart's birthday,' Mrs Wood continued.

Miss Newman gave a laugh. 'You know that Mrs Hart's birthday is in three weeks, don't you?'

'Interest in the girl is growing, Sarah. People will move their diaries. They'll come,' she said. *And I need to secure our income for the next few months.* 'And when it comes to the work, this is us! We can achieve more in a week than anyone else could deliver in a month.'

'I suppose we have done it before. I'll need to refresh my memory. See if it's even possible . . .'

'Of course,' she said, turning the coffee cup in her saucer nonchalantly. 'Have you any time this morning?'

Miss Newman was a prolific note-taker; it was essential in her role or there was always the risk of presenting the same thing more than once to a patron or forgetting how the complex steps of a successful act had been performed. She filled notebook after notebook with her own unique form of shorthand and sketches, keeping them locked in a trunk in her bedroom.

Mrs Wood stood on the threshold as Miss Newman opened it, and began rooting through piles of notebooks inside, bright orange, purple, green linens and silks passing through her hands. Then she sat back on her haunches, turning as she brandished a turquoise-bound book.

'Ta-da!' she said. 'Come!' She pushed herself up, brushing her skirts off as she walked towards the window. She leaned, turning the blind to draw in more light before pointing with the book to the chair. 'Sit,' she said, pulling over her dressing table stool and settling herself onto it.

Mrs Wood stood hesitantly on the threshold. She never felt comfortable coming into Miss Newman's space. While this was a room in her home, everything inside felt alien. The mahogany wardrobe with the hint of the marine silk's skirt caught in the door; the sleigh bed that had belonged to her mother-in-law now topped by Miss Newman's sampler pillow. The oval mirror and the picture of Blenheim Palace beside a miniature of an elderly woman that Mrs Wood had always guessed at being Miss Newman's grandmother. The leafy green plant standing like a soldier before the heavy drapes, the wooden vanity set on the dresser. The pile of books and pamphlets teetering on the nightstand.

'You can come in,' Miss Newman said, pointing at the chair. 'I've nothing to hide.'

With an awkward smile she stepped inside, following Miss Newman's instructions and sitting. Miss Newman held the notebook on her lap and turned slightly so that she could see.

There was the date and location on the front in Miss Newman's spiky script: *Spring 1868 - Italy*.

She flicked through page after page of memories, stopping every so often to reminisce wistfully about a balmy night in Naples or that especially dreadful journey up to Montepulciano.

And then.

There it was.

The Siena séance.

Scribbles and scrawls filling almost a third of the book.

As she turned the pages she came to a spread of hand-drawn footprints – hers in blue, Miss Newman's in red – as though a pair of mice had enjoyed a waltz, while a chaos of measurements and numbers sprawled across another.

Miss Newman slid the book onto Mrs Wood's lap and leaned over to her nightstand, pulling another notebook from the stack sitting there, an ochre silk with a tasselled magenta ribbon, collecting a pencil from the drawer. This was her current book with *Spring 1873* written across the front page and she leafed through the pages, pressing it flat across her knees when she came to a blank page.

'We'll do it in the séance room, of course,' she said, as she began to fill the page with notes like scattered crumbs. 'That makes it so much more straightforward . . .'

It was like old times, the two of them sitting together as Miss Newman sketched and noted Mrs Wood's tumbling thoughts and descriptions; working through every possible tangent, every possible fail. In the early days of their working relationship, they would do this at least once a week, plotting out the careful steps and machinations behind dazzling ideas that had now become commonplace in her séances: from the knee-knocker to the dancing lights to the disappearing hair combs.

As the first fragments of light began to leech from the day, they closed the notebook, their minds exhausted but whirling, the floor at their feet littered with gravy-smeared plates and scribbled-out pages. Over the next few days, they spent what spare time they had in conference, picking and poking every single element – the size of the room, the increased number of sitters, the basic logistical challenges – unknotting complexities on long walks and over late-night sherries.

The last time they had committed this much effort to an idea had been for her famous Flight, the one that had catapulted her to the top of the pile. Which, now she thought of it, underlined quite how sedentary she had become. How complacent.

As preparations for Mrs Hart's party progressed, she tapped into that almost forgotten joy of doing something big. As they moved around the séance room, first in daylight then candle by candle, day by day, into darkness, she felt her body begin to loosen with the careful choreography as she swirled and swerved around Miss Newman without so much as a whisk of a skirt or tap of a toe.

She was revived, ready. Alive.

CHAPTER 18

In order for the party to be a success, Mrs Hart needed to agree to be the reason – which she did wholeheartedly, implying that it was about time someone celebrated her – and Miss Finch informed that she would be introduced.

'How long will I have at the table?' she had asked Mrs Wood at the end of one of their sessions, her eyes sparking with excitement.

Mrs Wood had placed her cup and saucer on the side table. 'Now Miss Finch. Dear. You shall be introduced as my pupil rather than take a seat at the table. There will be a lot of important people there and I would like for you to complete more private tables before you represent me on such a grand scale.'

Miss Finch sat back, chewing her cheek.

'Then why introduce me at all if you don't think I'm ready?'

'People are interested,' she said. 'They would like to see who I have been tutoring. It's the perfect opportunity to stir up their curiosity for the future. You see that, don't you?'

'But they'll expect me to be at the table, won't they?' she said, her disappointment clearly not assuaged. 'After I'm introduced won't they expect me to be part of it?'

'They expect only me, dear girl. It is my home, after all. My table.

I understand you're disappointed,' Mrs Wood continued gently. 'But we wouldn't want your first public table to be at a séance being held for someone else, would we? Surely you would want such an important occasion to be only about you.'

The girl had given such a frustrated sigh that an unsettled sensation stirred in Mrs Wood's stomach. She had never seen the girl in this light – her bright optimism, all of the bubbling energy had been replaced by a petulance that was most unbecoming. 'Miss Finch. Please. Have faith. I know what I'm doing.'

The girl started, suddenly aware that she was being read. Her face closed then opened again, bright, bubbling. 'Oh, I'm just being silly,' she said. 'I know you're only thinking of me. As always. To be introduced to all of your patrons at the same time will be honour enough!' she said and then she had smiled a smile that hadn't quite reached her eyes.

With the increasing excitement brewing towards the upcoming séance, Mrs Wood looked for a way to still her mind during quieter moments, when there were no consultations and Miss Newman was busy with her other work. During those pockets of time, she took to walking, the rhythm of her feet on the pavement delivering a soporific effect. She strode along street after street, her age for once standing her in good stead by rendering her essentially invisible to the kind of trouble that may have approached her in her younger years.

One Monday afternoon, ten days or so into this new habit, after a productive morning with the girl in the back parlour, she had eaten bread and broth for lunch and then, with no consultations until four, collected her spring cloak from the stand and headed out.

It certainly hadn't been her intention to cut so close to the girl's street in her route, but it began to make a good loop: along Westbourne Grove, up towards Westbourne Park Station and then along to Portobello Road, skirting Tavistock Crescent quite by coincidence. She had no intention of turning into it, she had a reputation to maintain and what if the girl should see her? But as she walked along Tavistock Road, she felt her pace slow when the station on the corner of her street came into view.

The forecourt was always busy with cabs and tradesmen, and it was no different that afternoon. She hesitated, as usual, in front of the flower seller on the opposite corner, peering into buckets of fat peonies and rhododendron heads as big as a baby's, throwing casual glances up towards the steps of Miss Finch's house. It was easy to spot from that position – ten houses up, its windowsill ablaze with the girl's geraniums.

Was it intuition? Was that why she felt compelled to come back and watch the girl's house? Had she known something was afoot?

That afternoon, she was waiting for the flower seller to wrap up a ha'penny's' worth of random stems when she saw a figure appear from Miss Finch's front door. It turned, stooped, gave a wave and loped towards the pavement and was most certainly *not* Mrs Busby.

As the figure ambled along the pavement towards her, she raised the bunch of flowers to obscure her face, craning around the leaves and the shoulder of a newspaper boy to get a better view.

Her stomach sank.

Oh, Miss Finch.

It was, of course, Mr Humboldt.

The brown-toothed leader of the Dalston spiritual circle. Giver of pretty velvet dresses to girls forty years his junior.

Despite his assertion to the girl, Mrs Wood had only met him a handful of times before, but she would know that long-faced drear in a heartbeat. She gave an involuntary flinch at the memory of his papery handshake as he passed by on the other side of the road, settling and resettling his hat, stuffing the end of his scarf inside the buttons of his jacket and tugging every now and again on his trouser leg.

Oh, Miss Finch.

What a dreadful choice.

She looked back up at the girl's house. The door was closed.

160

There was the part of her which understood. A side which would most certainly not judge.

But then there was the side of her that was indignant precisely *because* of that. She had given the girl everything that she herself would have wanted when she had been starting out: unconditional attention, stability, a safe place to grow away from the predatory, quaking hands of deviant old men.

And yet she had turned to one anyway.

She heard his braying voice as he slapped the side of a pony, pointing at its driver and braying again before striding inside the station. She recognised the buoyant step, the sense of victory that trailed behind him like a banner.

She steadied herself on the wall, her fingernails digging into the greasy, yellow bricks as the Dentist reared again in her mind and she realised suddenly that perhaps she and the girl were very different after all.

'Are you sure?' Miss Finch settled herself beside Mrs Wood at the table while the rest of the Circle milled about ahead of the séance. She had not been at the house for a few days, it being the weekend, and besides, how could she broach the topic of Humboldt without giving away that she had been there.

She was, therefore, somewhat surprised when Miss Finch leaned in with her own question.

'Quite sure,' Mrs Wood said, folding the corner of her napkin.

'By the flower seller at the station. The one with all the peonies.' The girl peered at her with a smile. 'I could've sworn it was you.'

'No,' said Mrs Wood. 'I do walk that way sometimes, but I haven't for a week or so.' She smiled easily at her, ever the professional.

'Ah well,' said the girl raising her hands. 'You must have a *twin*!' The word carried and the room tightened suddenly as Mr

Larson's head turned in an instant from the sideboard. She shushed Miss Finch with her eyes and then threw a placatory smile to Mr Larson. 'Perhaps Leon will come today,' she said across the room.

'That would be nice,' he said sadly, and turned back to the plate of cheese scones – simpler treats for everyone today, seeing as he, with his economical eyes, was present.

Then she cleared her throat and called the room to order. 'Now,' she said once the Circle was settled, Miss Newman to one side, the girl to the other, the rest licking crumbs from fingers and finishing off their teas. 'As you know, we're getting closer to Mrs Hart's birthday party.'

Mrs Hart gave a self-satisfied bustle.

'Everyone seems to be as excited as you, dear,' Mrs Wood said. 'We've not had a single apology yet. It's set to be a very happy birthday celebration indeed!'

'I love birthdays,' said the girl.

'Of course you do.'

'I'm the sixth of October,' she said, levelling her eyes playfully at the rest of the table. 'Now you know, I don't expect you to forget!' And the Circle all laughed.

'Have we finished talking about birthdays?'

'Any excuse to have cake,' the girl continued blithely.

'Me too,' said Mrs Hart. 'I make sure that there's a cake for each member of my family and for the staff, but obviously to maintain this figure I can't be—'

'Could we continue—'

'My mother always made such a fuss on my birthday,' Miss Finch was saying and then she looked at Mrs Wood. 'Did yours?'

She felt a sudden chill in her chest and pressed her lips together. 'Of course.'

'Oh, I love the fuss,' said Laetitia. 'Hyacinth always decorates the whole place.'

'I do,' said Hyacinth.

'I'd rather shoot myself in the good eye,' said Miss Brigham.

'Can we *please* not talk about guns again?' Mrs Wood said, her voice shifting in pitch as she struggled to regain authority. An awkward silence settled across the table. 'Thank you,' she said. 'Now. What I intended to say was that, as much as we're excited about Mrs Hart's birthday, it will also be a big occasion for Miss Finch.'

'I'm sure all the guests will be as excited to be introduced to Miss Finch too!' Hyacinth said, and a fat cloud passed Mrs Hart's face while the girl made humble noises.

'Indeed,' said Mrs Wood. 'But Miss Finch's introduction will only be part of the evening,' she said. 'It will be Mrs Hart's night and we shan't forget that.'

'Thank you,' said Mrs Hart. She glanced at Hyacinth. 'Some people aren't always as thoughtful as they should be.'

But Laetitia and Hyacinth weren't listening. 'Will there be any bachelors coming?' asked Hyacinth. 'Young ones!' said Laetitia.

'And I am planning something extra special for Mrs Hart in the second half,' Mrs Wood continued as though the sisters hadn't said a word. 'So please bear that in mind.'

'It's so exciting,' said the girl. 'My first big séance!'

'But you've been to the Dowager's, haven't you?' said Laetitia Adams.

'That wasn't a party,' she said.

'Miss Finch is right,' said Mrs Wood. 'She won't have seen anything quite like this before.'

'Nothing too extravagant, I hope,' said Mr Larson, and she deepened her smile.

'It's a party, Mr Larson. Let's just see.'

The sense of chaos she had felt at the beginning of the séance seemed to set the tone of the Circle that afternoon.

Within a few moments of the candle going out, Hyacinth Adams had made Laetitia cry with a message from their father while Mrs Reynolds desperately tried to placate them with her angel.

It took all of Mrs Wood's strength to wrestle the proceedings from maudlin, sending Miss Newman into the darkness to deliver Jack Starr's dog, who sniffed and fussed his way around the table, fluffing at the women's skirts and hats and eliciting squeals of delight.

'What a terror!' cried Laetitia.

'His nose is very wet,' said Miss Brigham.

The table was resettling, Jack having called his mutt to heel, and Mrs Wood was about to move seamlessly onto one of her favourite old curmudgeons when there was a low moan from across the table.

'Miss Finch?' said Mrs Reynolds.

'Is she all right?' Miss Brigham called out as the girl moaned again. 'Give her a shake.'

'No . . . I can't . . . She's very deep,' whispered Mrs Reynolds. 'Do you think it's—'

'*Hello* . . . Hello?'

'Is that you, Mona?' said Laetitia.

'Can you hear me?'

'Yes!' cried the Adams sisters as one.

'Is that you, Mona?' asked Mr Larson. 'I don't believe we have met.'

'It is,' said the girl. 'I . . . it feels so long since I came to you last.'

'We've missed you!' said Mrs Reynolds.

'And I . . . you,' she said, her voice, soft and girlish, became slightly strained as she continued to talk. 'It is very busy in here today. Lots of people. They all have so much to say.'

'Can you hear anyone in particular?' asked Mrs Reynolds.

'No . . . I . . .' She paused. 'There is a big event coming up?'

'My birthday,' said Mrs Hart. 'We're holding a séance.' Mrs Wood sensed her leaning towards the girl. 'All of society are coming,' she said.

'Of course they are,' said Mona. 'Who would miss such a thing?'

'Do you have someone with you?' said Mrs Wood, keen to move things along. She could hear the girl take a few quick breaths, followed by the sound of fabric moving, and she assumed that Miss Finch was moving further into her trance.

'It is so busy,' the voice of Mona continued. 'So busy . . .' And then there was an abrupt movement in the dark, as though the girl had been given a shock.

Silence.

'There is someone here,' Mona said and, almost as one, the Circle drew in closer. 'Someone . . .' she said. 'They are . . .' Another swift movement. 'Very . . . insistent,' she said. 'I would not ordinarily allow such a person to . . .' Another shift. 'I cannot . . .'

'Miss Finch? Miss Finch, please,' said Mrs Hart. 'What's happening? I can't see – can we light a candle?'

'No. Please,' she said. 'They—'

Mrs Wood stepped in. They had agreed that Miss Finch should have a role as it would be the first Circle that Mr Larson had attended with the girl, but this was becoming unbearably dramatic. 'Who is with you, Mona?'

'They are too loud. They are . . . shouting . . . I . . .'

'Who is *there*, Mona?' said Mrs Wood, wanting this over.

The girl stilled. 'They are speaking to me. I can hear one voice now,' Mona said. 'It is a woman. She is old. She smells of . . . brandy? Her face though . . . I – I cannot see her face.' And she issued a sudden, long moan, her dress rustling frantically.

'Mona?' said Mrs Wood.

'*Who's Mona?*' A voice like grit cut through the room.

Mrs Wood jumped at the violence of the voice beneath the cover of darkness. 'Who are we speaking with?' she asked.

'Who'd yer think?' the voice growled, and the Circle shifted awkwardly.

'We don't know,' Mrs Wood said, trying to remain light. 'Perhaps you could—'

'Stop your messin',' the voice said, and Mrs Wood's blood froze, because there was something sickeningly familiar in that voice. 'Don't you know who I am?' it continued. 'None o'yer?'

'That's enough now,' she said firmly. 'I don't think you're welcome—'

'You want to know who I am?' The voice was grating, nightmarish. If she didn't know the girl, she would never have dreamed it could've come from her.

'I . . .' Mrs Wood began, the panic swelling.

'Don't you know me?'

'Stop it, Miss Finch,' Mrs Wood said.

'She's in a trance,' whispered Mrs Reynolds. 'She can't—'

'Miss Finch. Send this spirit back!'

'Course you know me, dear. Tell 'em who I am. *Tell 'em*—'

'Spirit, be gone!' shouted Mrs Hart.

'I'll tell 'em then!' the voice said, heavy with menace.

'Be gone!' shouted Miss Brigham.

'It's me, child! It's *Thirza*!'

Mrs Wood slammed her hand on the table. 'That's *enough*!' she said as the Circle reeled. 'Spirit! Leave this Medium! I command you!'

The girl gave a sudden cough which turned into sobs and the Circle, stunned and frightened, jumped up to comfort her, except Mr Larson, who rounded the table to stand beside Mrs Wood, his hand protectively upon her shoulder while she sat like an obelisk.

Miss Newman rushed to throw open the curtains and fetch some sherry from the decanter on the sideboard. 'Here,' she said, and the girl took the glass, blinking in the bright afternoon light. Her head was still rolling a little, her cheeks glowing white.

Mrs Wood watched her from across the table, her mind whirling so wildly she couldn't hold onto a single thought.

What had just happened?

How had it happened?

'Mrs Wood, why would such a dreadful spirit come through to

poor Miss Finch?' Mr Larson asked, but she could barely understand him; everything beyond the girl felt muffled and insignificant.

She stared at her, trying to quell the unnamed fear rising in her throat.

'Does anyone know a Thirza?' she heard Laetitia ask.

'I know a *Teresa*,' said Miss Brigham.

Her scalp prickled and her mouth was dry.

There was no possible way that the girl had discovered her connection to Thirza. None.

No one knew about Thirza.

No one.

Not even Miss Newman.

Her breath caught in her throat as a single, horrifying thought spun through her mind.

She had always assumed that Thirza had died years before; death would've been the only reason why that woman would ever have left her alone when there was money to be had.

Was this then confirmation? Did this mean that Thirza was dead and that . . .

Had she just witnessed the impossible?

The Circle chittered mindlessly around her. 'Wasn't there a Medium way back called Thirza? Mrs Wood? Mrs Reynolds? Back in the early fifties?' Mrs Hart was saying. 'Hold on. Wasn't Thirza that Medium who ruined herself at a Duke's table?'

'If it's the Thirza I'm thinking of, she liked a brandy,' said Miss Brigham.

She wanted to tell them all that no, they were wrong. The name Thirza meant nothing. But she couldn't move.

In all this time, had she been wrong?

Mrs Hart was still wittering on. 'You know who I'm talking about, don't you, Violet. The one in Mayfair. You know. Don't you, Violet. *Violet.*'

The shout of her name was as sharp as a slap and she found

herself back in the room in an instant, blinking the fog away, trying to reclaim herself and her position in the room. 'Miss Finch,' Mrs Wood said, clearing her throat and smoothing her skirts. 'Are you recovered?' The girl looked back helplessly but nodded.

'Thirza *Thwaite*!' Mrs Hart cried suddenly, slapping her knee in delight, and it was all Mrs Wood could do to stop herself from launching across the table to shut the damned woman up. 'That was it, wasn't it. Thirza Thwaite! Remember? Oh! That was such a *scandal*, wasn't it, Violet.'

Mrs Wood tried to cover her panic with a smile. 'I have no idea,' she said with an authority she didn't come close to feeling. 'Now,' she continued, unclenching her fists, smiling harder. 'After such an event, I must share with Miss Finch the ways in which a Medium can recover from an unwanted spirit.' She exhaled a benevolent smile. 'In private, if you don't mind, friends.'

'Will you be all right without me?' asked Mr Larson, and she nodded sternly, and he joined the rest of the Circle as they left the room like a gaggle of geese, craning their necks as he pushed them along the corridor to see if they might hear anything more.

Miss Newman stood at the sideboard.

'Dear?' said Mrs Wood, and Miss Newman started.

'Oh,' she said. 'Sorry. I didn't realise . . .'

She sat as calmly as possible, watching the girl until Miss Newman had closed the door behind her.

'That was excellent work,' said Mrs Wood in the sudden silence of the room, using the words to bolster herself.

Miss Finch nervously swallowed another sip of sherry. A pin had fallen out of her coils with all the activity and a handful of hair was hanging loose. 'I don't know what came over me,' she said. 'It sounded like everyone was quite afraid.'

'Oh, don't worry about them,' she said. 'They're unsettled by a sea-shanty.'

Miss Finch smiled gratefully.

'You don't remember anything, then?' she said, and the girl shook her head, staring into the glass in her hands. 'Nothing about the spirit who took you over.'

'Was it that bad?' she said, eyes wide.

Mrs Wood watched her for a moment. 'It was a rather forthright old woman, that's all.'

'Oh dear,' said the girl and covered her mouth. 'Was she rude?'

'Not really,' she said. 'Merely unpleasant. You don't know who she was, then?'

The girl blinked.

'I'm sorry,' she said. 'I feel terrible because she's obviously upset you.'

Mrs Wood waved her hand dismissively. 'It happens,' she said. 'Sometimes unpleasant spirits come through. It's one of those things.' She cleared her throat. 'In the early days, anyway. When you're less experienced.'

The girl stared, despondent.

She hesitated, judging how she should ask the next question. 'Does the name Thirza mean anything to you?'

The girl stared back blankly.

'The old woman. You called her *Thirza*.'

'Thirza,' said the girl, as though trying the name out for the first time. 'No. I've no idea where that came from.' She blinked again and the corner of her mouth had tipped up. 'I suppose it goes to show how good your teaching is. You told me to keep my eyes and ears open at all times so who knows what's going in!'

Relief flushed through her. Of course there was no magic! Of *course* there was no mystery. She gave an involuntary laugh at her own silliness. The girl had only been doing what she had been told.

But the relief was brief, replaced by the humiliation that after all these years, Thirza remained the one person who could still upend her. She had allowed the horror of hearing that woman's name in her own Circle to overtake her common-sense, to reduce her to a fool who thought that this child might have a gift that even the greatest Mediums could not truly possess.

The girl had simply been doing what she had been told, she repeated to herself. What did it matter that Mrs Wood hadn't heard the name Thirza outside of Hull. The girl lived in another social world. There were probably half a dozen Thirzas in the pub down the road from the girl's rooms right at that moment.

And then, as her mind cleared and reason returned, she felt her chin rising.

The girl hadn't just been doing what she had instructed her to do. The girl had gone far beyond. Her work during the Circle had transcended into brilliance. Because this sixteen-year-old slip of a thing – fresh, raw, untested – had succeeded in creating in the Great Mrs Wood a moment of *doubt*.

She gave another laugh. Wasn't that what she wanted? *Brilliance*? Hadn't she taken the girl on to be an impressive presence at her table?

'Your hard work is paying off,' she said, returning gladly to the role of teacher. 'But I would prefer that you focus on the softer spirits for now. Aside from how they may be received, you're far too young to be presenting anything so ugly in public.'

'Of course,' said the girl with a satisfied flush. 'And I hope . . . I hope I didn't upset you.' She held Mrs Wood's eyes so tightly that she felt suddenly uncomfortable and looked away with a laugh.

'Why on earth would you think that?' she said. 'I'm only thinking of my more sensitive patrons. They find comfort in the lighter souls.'

'I'll do my best,' said the girl, smiling sweetly before stifling a yawn. 'They do take it out of you, don't they,' she said. 'Spirits, I mean.'

Mrs Wood nodded. 'Oh, they do,' she said as she took up her

glass of sherry, swallowing down that strange, unsettled sensation she still couldn't quite shake. It was the shock of the séance, that was all. Because how could she not be delighted at this moment? How could she not be absolutely thrilled that her pupil could already perform at such an extraordinary level?

Really, she told herself with firm resolution: she could not have planned the whole thing more perfectly.

28th May 1873

Mrs Wood,

Word has reached me of news circulating amongst the most
sensitive of circles that I have been visiting your home for private
spiritual consultations. And that this was shared at a party held by
our mutual friend, the Dowager Lady Gregory!

Naturally, I have denied that this has ever happened, but the
embarrassment I am enduring, having to even acknowledge
something so deeply personal, has been unprecedented.

Lady Harrington assured me that I would find a confidante in
you. You yourself promised me your discretion. But now not only do
I discover that that has been dashed, but that it was done so as the
subject of gossip! It is too much to bear, Mrs Wood. Too much.

It goes without saying that I no longer require your services. I
have no wish to ever be reminded of your duplicitousness. I hope
that you will take this as the warning you clearly need. I don't
suppose a woman such as you can afford to lose many more like me.

It goes without saying that I have not the slightest interest in a
private table with this young girl you're toting around town, nor
attending a party for this woman, Mrs Hart. Please explain to her,
clearly, why, and refrain from issuing unsolicited invitations to
events – our connection and any future that may have come from it
is over.

I remain,

Henrietta, Lady Frances

CHAPTER 19

The world shook as she read Lady Frances's words.

She had hoped that, as Lady Frances had been out of the country when the girl made her mistake that the whisper would've died before it had the opportunity to land in her ear. That her hope had been dashed was both infuriating – she had *told* Mr Clore that it had been a mistake – and heart-crushingly disappointing: the kind that eked into her gut and ruined her appetite.

All the possibilities of Lady Frances. The relief of her future stipend, the links into the palace.

Gone.

Miss Newman lowered the letter when it came to her turn to read it and levelled a steady, I-told-you-so stare at Mrs Wood, her opinion that Mrs Wood's overreaction had caused the news to spread writ large: *if you hadn't made a fuss, no one would've noticed.*

'You're wrong,' Mrs Wood snapped. 'I told you that this would happen, regardless. With a man like Clore present, how would such an indiscretion *not* have leaked?'

She hadn't intended it to come out as sharply, but Miss Newman's insistence on being right was irritating. After all, what did it matter? Lady Frances was gone. Her instinct had been right. Of course. All she could do now was count her blessings that she wasn't taking the rest of society with her.

Miss Newman put the letter on the table with a sigh. 'What's done is done,' she said.

'Precisely,' Mrs Wood replied tightly.

'We can't change the past.'

'We cannot.'

'There's no use crying over spilt milk.'

Mrs Wood looked up and was startled by the smile playing across Miss Newman's face. 'This isn't a joking matter,' she said.

'If one does not laugh, one might cry . . .'

'Sarah.'

Miss Newman paused. 'They say it's darkest before the dawn.'

Perhaps it was the relief borne of Lady Frances finally making her move, no matter how painful, or some strange neurological response to the dreadful news, but she couldn't ignore the bubble of mirth that was rising in her own throat. 'Without rain there would be no sunshine,' she said.

Miss Newman slapped her knee with a laugh. 'I knew I'd get you,' she said.

But Mrs Wood collected herself. 'Sarah, I mean it. We shouldn't be making light of this. Lady Frances was worth a lot to us.' *More than you know.*

'We can't do anything about it now, though,' Miss Newman said. 'What's done is done.'

'Don't start again.'

'But it is,' said Miss Newman. 'Yes, your reputation has been brushed by Lady Frances's response, but she has simply withdrawn her patronage. A letter of apology will calm her and her obvious embarrassment at even being seen near your home means that it's unlikely she'll tell anyone else her thoughts. Which means you are intact, dearest. We live to fight another day!'

She tried to join Miss Newman's optimism, but her mind was hooked onto the truth. Was *intact* enough? Yes, the girl had infinite possibilities for the future, but what about now? She had needed Lady Frances to keep her replete, and to cover her investments: her biggest expenses were no longer food and fuel in the house, they were Miss Finch's lodgings and last month's hat bill.

'Now. Enough self-pity. We still have work to do,' Miss Newman

174

was saying, and she forced herself to pay attention. 'Come. Why don't we treat ourselves with a run-through of Mrs Hart's party. I know how happy minutiae makes you, Violet.'

Planning for Mrs Hart's party and the spectacle had been continuing apace. At every opportunity they went through the steps, refining and reworking, so that on the night of Mrs Hart's party everything was perfect. It had to be. When had she last had all of her patrons and followers in the same room at the same time? When had she last held a séance where *no one* sent an apology? The temptation of the girl was clearly far more powerful than anything else they perceived Mrs Wood to deliver anymore, and so she needed to capitalise on their gaze: she must dazzle so that, while they may have come to meet the girl, they would leave thinking only of how they must sit at Mrs Wood's table as soon as could be rearranged.

They would all be there.

And they would all be reminded.

The plan was moving forward as it should.

All would be well.

But even that wasn't enough to entirely reassure Mrs Wood, and in quieter moments when Miss Newman wasn't available for distraction, doubt crept through her like bindweed, strangling her optimism and belief. And that doubt sprang from the unsettled feeling that she hadn't been able to quell since the Thirza incident.

Despite being certain that it had all been a coincidence, she found herself paying more attention to how she acted around the girl; measuring each word and movement, studying herself for tells in a way she hadn't for years. Of course, the whole thing would have been resolved in a moment if she had been able to simply turn to the girl and ask: 'Where did you hear the name Thirza, Miss Finch?' And the girl could reply with equally easy candour: 'Oh it's just the apple seller on the Harrow Road Mrs Wood.' But of course she could not. To ask would break the rules of belief and put herself at too great a risk.

Her only recourse, therefore, was to focus on the upcoming spectacle of Mrs Hart's birthday. At least that wouldn't be *all* about Miss Finch.

CHAPTER 20

Fortunately, by the time Mrs Hart's birthday séance arrived, Mrs Wood was too wrapped up in what lay ahead to think of anything else.

Oh, how she had missed this feeling: the electric fear laced with fizzing anticipation.

It had been too long since she had done this. Too long since her house had shone with the glitter of a real reception.

There was a stillness in the air as she came down the stairs that evening. After months of austerity, the house was suddenly resplendent, as though a maiden aunt had acquired an inheritance and discovered couture. Every gaslight was blaring on the ground floor, including the enormous chandelier that blazed triumphantly from the skylight, and her diamonds flashed and her best séance silk slipped from step to step behind her with a satisfying whisper.

It was hers, she reminded herself, the walnut banister that was cool and smooth beneath her fingers, the silver bowls heaped with dew-damp roses that filled the house with the smell of summer. It all belonged to her. The girl from the patched curtains and pallet bed owned not just one canteen of silver cutlery, but three. She owned piped gas, layers of rugs, stacks of mattresses and more bedframes than she needed.

For now.

Miss Newman appeared on the landing above and peered over the balustrade. She had turned her hair into a braided knot, and the pearls Mrs Wood had bought her for her birthday hung neatly at her throat.

'Is everything out?' she called, fastening the wrists of her marine silk dress. She shook her arms out and then smoothed the bodice of her dress and presented herself for Mrs Wood's approval, who smiled up at her.

'Very nice,' she said. 'That's such a lovely colour on you.'

Miss Newman gave a dismissive snort at the compliment and started down the stairs, screwing her pearl-drop earrings onto first one lobe, then the other. 'What's happening with the food?'

'It's all arranged,' Mrs Wood said, nodding towards the dining room where they could make out the edge of the buffet which, as they descended, opened out into an almost obscene cornucopia of epicurean delights set around three tall silver flower bowls filled and festooned with so many flowers and fruit that they were all but obscured. There was Mrs Hart's favourite whole salmon, a cold rib of beef, two baked hams studded with cloves, several ducks decorated with candied orange slices, six brown-skinned pheasants and four glossy pies topped with berries and capers. Placed between everything were bowls of pickled cucumbers, devilled eggs and hot housed tomatoes, platters of Italian meats and French cheeses, and no less than seven shimmering blancmanges and jellies, including a green octopus and a smooth-backed bunny.

Miss Newman pulled a face from the door. 'It makes me yearn for a nice piece of toast,' she said.

Mrs Wood circled the table, turning a pie slightly so that its more perfect edge was facing forward, swapping a platter of crab vol-au-vents with a dish of oranges in brandy before stepping back, squinting. She nipped a loose raisin from a heap of scones and put it in her mouth. 'We'll have leftovers for weeks,' she said. Which would be helpful considering the wreckage of her budget.

Eliza appeared alongside Miss Newman, a trail of awkward girls hired to assist Eliza from Mrs Kitt's agency hovering behind her in the hallway.

'Everything to your liking, ma'am?' she said, enunciating pointedly.

'I think so,' she said.

'Very good, ma'am,' Eliza said. 'The girls are ready for your inspection.'

'Excellent,' she said, dusting her hands together. 'Line them up, please.'

There were five girls, their cheeks pink from scrubbing, their hair scraped from their faces and hidden beneath neat little mop caps that she had hired along with the black dresses and white aprons the girls fidgeted in. They held their hands out and she turned each one over to ensure that her hygiene standards had been met.

'Very good, Eliza,' she said, giving a restrained nod of approval, and Eliza clapped her hands, leading the girls back to the kitchen for Cook to load them up with serving trays.

In the silence left behind, Mrs Wood heard the anticipation that was already building on the street beyond: scraping hooves, the creak of a carriage, a snort.

She waited for the flutter of nerves to settle before moving purposefully towards the back of the house.

'Miss Newman?' she called.

'In here,' she replied, her voice carrying from the séance room.

The shutters on the deep bay window were already latched shut, the room looking strangely embarrassed in the bright gaslight.

Here were the machinations of the evening's event: Mrs Wood's round table, gleaming quietly beneath a slender three-armed candelabra and set with its full complement of twelve chairs, one with a gold paper crown hanging from a finial. A further horseshoe of chairs curved around them to cater for the non-table guests, of which there would be twenty-four.

Miss Newman stood up from behind the table. 'Just checking a few bits,' she said, and then pressed on the far right-hand side door of the sideboard before which Mrs Wood's larger, more ornate chair had been placed. The door swung noiselessly open, an arm's reach away. They looked inside and smiled at one another.

'Clore won't know what to write about first,' said Miss Newman as she closed the door, careful not to dislodge anything. 'That you're finally introducing the girl. Or quite how brilliant you are.'

'It's cold in here,' Mrs Wood said, rubbing her nose. The weather had sunk into an unseasonably low temperature the previous night which hadn't been improved by the sun, and this room with its huge bay window and French doors was always difficult to keep warm without bodies, especially as a séance ruled out the light from the fire.

'They'll soon warm up,' said Miss Newman. 'It was colder in March.'

'True,' she said, then she gathered herself. 'Let's do one last run-through.' And Miss Newman went to the door and pulled it closed.

For one final time, they moved through their opening overture turning with the rhythms towards the crescendo, weaving and leaning around each other, every placement of a foot, every raise of a hand, every imaginary toss following the same shared beat. In the bright glare of the gas lamps Mrs Wood delighted in how bizarre it looked, knowing that in the darkness it would be invisibly beautiful.

'Stay steady between the first pass and the next,' said Miss Newman. 'Wait until you feel me.'

Mrs Wood nodded, smoothing her bodice as she caught her breath.

A clutch of feathers had escaped from the sideboard and she opened its door, one hand around the mouth of the bursting sack to prevent the whole lot from spilling out as she shoved the escapees back inside.

'Mrs Wood?' Mr Larson's voice came from down the hall and they started. She closed the cabinet swiftly with her hip, blew some down from her face and brushed her dress as she headed for the door, taking a moment to collect herself before stepping out to almost be floored by him rushing along. He stopped, peering into the room beyond before returning to his quarry. 'There you are.'

'Is everything all right?' she asked, smoothing her hair discreetly.

His face looked pinched. He held up a bottle of champagne. 'Is this necessary?' he said.

'It's a birthday party,' she said.

He put his hand on her elbow and steered her towards the back parlour, away from Miss Newman. 'Dearest,' he whispered into her ear. 'This is very expensive.'

She tried to tug her arm from his grasp, but he held tight. 'I have all of my patrons coming, Mr Larson,' she whispered back. 'You expect me to serve them . . . what? Gin?'

'You didn't have to order such . . .'

'I have a reputation, Mr Larson.'

'For excess?'

She stared at him. 'You understand what I'm doing, don't you?' she said, but he shook his head.

'Need I even mention that buffet. Things are not as they have been, Mrs Wood.'

'No,' she said, removing her elbow and glaring at him. 'They are not.'

'I just wished that you'd waited until the investments were more—'

'But it wouldn't be Mrs Hart's birthday then,' she said. 'Would it.'

'The guest of honour is here,' Miss Newman called, and Mrs Wood gave Mr Larson one more stubborn stare.

'I don't interfere in how you do your job, Mr Larson. Don't interfere in how I do mine.'

She could feel his eyes on her back as she walked towards Miss Newman, smiling to hide the burning irritation she felt at Mr Larson's unwanted advice. He would not ruin this for her. Not tonight.

Two figures shimmered in the glass of the window beside the front door and she felt a hard thrill of nerves: after all this preparation it would only be a matter of hours now until she changed the conversation for a second time.

First the Flight, and now ... Let's see how much people wanted to talk about spirit materialisations after tonight's exhibition.

She looked at Miss Newman, squeezed her arm. 'Are we ready?' And Miss Newman gave a laugh.

'Of course we are!' she said.

And together they went to open the door, moving as one without a word.

An hour later, the house gleamed with money: throats radiant with three-deep jewelled chokers, hair dramatic with rare feathers, and wrists wrapped with twinkling strings. The hired girls darted around collecting emptied glasses and discarded plates, marshalled by Eliza, who stood beside the stack of plates in the dining room, her fingers tugging at the neck of her best uniform.

Mrs Wood settled Mrs and Mr Hart, she resplendent in a beaded silver gown that frothed at the low neck and shoulders like an ocean, he in tails and a trail of disinterest, into the window seat of the drawing room with a bottle of champagne, so that they were the first to see each new guest, and each new guest could directly congratulate Mrs Hart.

At the chime of eight, just before the door was opened to the increasingly impatient carriages beyond, she made her way discreetly upstairs so that she could watch the arrivals from a seat in the shadows of the landing and spend some time cramming in secret. Parties always made any last-minute preparation with Miss Newman difficult: if she was present, she was gobbled up into conversation; and if she was not, Miss Newman was required to circulate and keep everyone happy in her absence. There was no real opportunity for them to review what information they had acquired during the usual social rounds in the first fifteen minutes, not as they would with her Grand Séances. Instead, on a party night, she settled herself into a comfortable chair on the landing that was unseen from below but with a perfect view over the hall and into the drawing room. She was cheered that Miss Newman had placed a flagon of cordial on the side table beside a glass of champagne, along with a plate of bread and dripping, and a small dish of red jelly and cream that throbbed lightly in time with the footsteps of the hired help as they ran hats and cloaks from one end of the house to the other.

The air was heady with cigars and the delicate notes of lavender water and lily-of-the-valley powders. Roars of manly laughter erupted through the rumble of conversation, and every so often someone loudly wished Mrs Hart all the very, *very* best.

Mrs Wood sat in the shadows and watched, looking for those she expected messages for: The Dowager and Solange hovering around the drinks; Miss Cram beside the raging fireplace (a risky move for one so coated in dog hair); Mrs Pickering and Mrs Preston, heads together in conversation as always, their dull husbands quietly picking their teeth by the door. Lady Morgan laughing with abandon at something Lady Cooper was saying. One of the young Miss Greens making light work of her plate in the corner while Mr Clore – all primped and greased – helped another Miss Green find some more champagne.

Directly below, she saw the top of Mr Lawson's head, a glint of pink hinting at a thinning pate that she had never noticed before. His nose was regal from this angle and gave off a soft sheen in the light. His hands were behind his back, and it took her a moment to realise to whom he was talking: Mrs Jupp – recently widowed with a fine fortune behind her. She was a pleasant enough woman, a little sharp-tongued at times, which had kept them from being true friends but since the passing of her husband just after

Christmas, her private consultations had become regular and reliable.

Mr Larson seemed interested enough in Mrs Jupp's conversation – her hands danced before her as she told a tale that he had to cock his head towards her to hear. She wondered if Mrs Jupp, with her fat forearms and unruly grey hair, would ever overtake her in Mr Larson's esteem, and was surprised when she felt a pang of jealousy at the thought. She had no interest in Mr Larson's offers of marriage, but she was still a woman after all: no one liked the thought of being replaced.

She moved on.

Everyone was here.

Everyone apart from the girl.

She craned to see the grandfather clock.

It was almost nine! Had something happened?

Guests had made swift work of the champagne and buffet and the atmosphere was beginning to shift from anticipation to restlessness.

'Violet?' Miss Newman had crept up the back stairs without her noticing and she jumped at her voice. 'Sorry,' she said, laughing. 'Are you ready?'

'Do you think something's happened to the girl?'

'I was thinking the same thing,' she said, suddenly serious.

'She knew the time we were due to start, didn't she?' She craned over the banister. 'This is not like her.'

Miss Newman came up beside her. 'I'm sure she'll have a reason,' she said.

'What shall we do? Shall we start without her?'

'I suppose we could begin and then introduce her if she arrives in the interval . . .'

'You don't think—'

The bell clattered and Mrs Wood's heart gave a jolt as Miss Newman's face softened into a smile. 'See. That will be her now.'

Mrs Wood smiled tightly. She felt discombobulated by the tardiness. If it had been her, she would have been the first to arrive. The girl had offered to help prepare but she had, of course, told her that it was unnecessary. But that hadn't meant that she should arrive late. It hadn't even really meant that the girl shouldn't have arrived early to lend a hand anyway.

She watched Miss Newman bob down the stairs and through the crowd who were peering around her towards the door; their interest piqued.

'Oh gosh,' came the girl's voice as Miss Newman pulled open the door, a wave of chill air bracing the hall. 'Are we too late? Supper took forever and then the carriage—'

'Come in, dear,' said Miss Newman and then Mrs Wood heard her say, 'oh,' and she craned over the banister to see first the girl and then a man enter behind her.

People shouted *hellos* and the Colonel boomed 'What time do you call this!' as the girl stepped into the hall, the square form of Humboldt easing himself in behind her wearing a dramatic cloak and white tie.

What on earth did the girl think she was doing? There had been nothing about a guest on her invitation. She began down the stairs, eschewing her tradition of not being seen directly before a séance, the girl's arrival drawing everyone's attention, making it far easier.

'Miss Finch!' she called as she reached the middle step, casting a smile across the gathering as her guests realised that she was making an unprecedented pre-séance appearance 'Miss Finch, please,' she said as she continued her way down and wove her way through the crowd. 'You must not apologise. These things happen.' Now before the girl, she reached for her arm, perhaps a little too firmly because the girl looked startled, the enormous purple feather in her hair giving a sharp quiver. 'Come,' she said, guiding her back through the crowd towards the stairs, where she led her up a few steps so that they stood together above the heads of the party.

She looked at the girl, who looked steadily back, then she turned to the crowd. 'Everyone, please!' she called, but her voice was swallowed by the excitement of all the unusual activity. 'Everyone. Please! Can I have your . . .' Someone began tinging a glass and the Colonel shouted: 'Quiet in the back!' and finally the house settled.

'Dear things. It's so lovely to have you all here. You know that I wouldn't usually do such a thing ahead of one of my séances, but I have two important announcements to make before the main event begins.' Her eyes swept across a sea of expectant smiles. 'Firstly: we must wish a very happy birthday to our dearest Mrs Hart.'

The house filled with the cheers of best wishes, a wave of raised glasses glinting in the gaslight, Mrs Wood laughing when she realised that her hand was empty. Then she turned to the girl.

'And now, I also wanted to introduce you all to someone you may have been hearing about – I know our dear Mr Clore has had a few words already to say about her.' Mr Clore raised his glass from the drawing-room doorway where he stood on tiptoes to see over the crowd. 'All of you are here because you are special to Mrs Hart, and to me. And so, I thought that this would be the perfect moment to introduce the newest member of our Circle.'

She stepped back, her arm outstretched towards the girl like a ringmaster. 'All, please meet London's newest Medium of note, my pupil, Miss Emmie Finch.'

'Emmeline,' said Miss Finch with a laugh and Mrs Wood looked at her in confusion. The girl lowered her chin and whispered. 'Mr Humboldt thinks Emmeline is more elegant.'

She blinked at her once more then turned back to the crowd. 'My apologies,' she said, covering her surprise with a laugh. 'Please. All. I introduce my pupil, Miss *Emmeline Finch*.'

More cheers, more glinting glasses.

The girl shone with delight like one of Mrs Reynolds' angels.

'Shall we be seeing something from Miss Finch this evening?' called Mr Clore.

'Sadly, no,' said Mrs Wood. 'Tonight is about Mrs Hart, but I am already introducing Miss Finch at private tables where she is proving to be a growing talent.'

'She is indeed!' called Lady Harrington, followed by a flood of whispers and the flutter of a myriad of hair ornaments all turning in her direction.

'If you should want to meet Miss Finch yourself, do please let dear Miss Newman know. We will do all we can to accommodate your request.'

The whispers grew louder, the hair ornaments friskier.

'Now,' she called over the rising tide of noise. 'If you will excuse me, I must prepare for the séance to come. I shall see you all again within the half-hour.'

And she waved, still holding onto the girl. 'A word, please,' she whispered into the girl's ear as the room began to turn back to one another. She took her through the fringe of the crowd towards the back parlour.

'I'm so sorry,' the girl was saying, the purple feather bouncing in the pile of golden curls at the back of her head. 'We only meant to have a quick something to eat, but the restaurant took ages and—'

Mr Humboldt appeared suddenly, making her jump. 'It was my fault,' he said, loosening his silk scarf and tipping his hat into his hand as though he were remotely welcome. 'I insisted that she joined me at Claridge's, seeing as we were in town anyway.'

Mrs Wood looked at him coolly. 'I wasn't expecting you.'

'She was beside herself all the way here,' he said.

'I felt awful at the thought of letting you down; tonight of all nights.'

It was then that Mrs Wood noticed the lace froth of a mauve dress spilling out beneath a new spring shawl that she was unravelling.

'What a dress,' said Laetitia Adams, who was eating a peach by the console. The girl stopped and turned to her.

'Do you think?' she said coyly, turning to show off a large bustle crowned with a pink flower, smoothing her hands over its ribboned corset, pulling at the multi-layered skirt. Her bare shoulders were creamy, contrasting beautifully with the black ribbon tied at her throat.

'Don't just stand there,' said Miss Brigham, marching through the crowd like a general. 'Come and get a drink,' she said to Miss Finch, then she turned to Humboldt. 'Brigham,' she said, putting her hand out.

'Humboldt,' he said, and gave a bow.

And then the girl was lost to Mrs Wood, absorbed by her Circle and the clamouring crowd and she stood helplessly beside Humboldt, watching her go.

CHAPTER 21

The girl's arrival had ruffled her, but she was far too experienced to permit it to undermine all her hard work.

Closing herself into the back parlour, she forced the irritation from her bones, lighting a candle and sitting in the half-light, her hands gradually relaxing on the armrests of her chair as she breathed in and breathed out, focusing only on the sensation of the smooth wood beneath her fingers.

What could've been a few moments or a few hours later, Miss Newman let herself in with a whisper and Mrs Wood returned to the room, watching her gathering her accoutrements.

After a moment, she pulled over the footstool and Miss Newman took her hand. 'I stayed by her side the whole time,' she said. 'She didn't put a foot wrong.'

Mrs Wood's relief surprised her, but she covered it with a smile as she stood. 'Good,' she said. 'And Mr Humboldt?' She stepped up onto the stool. 'What was he up to?'

'Miss Brigham took him on.' She gave a laugh as she began fussing with Mrs Wood's skirts. 'He didn't look especially pleased.'

'I bet he wasn't,' said Mrs Wood.

The hallway beyond bustled to life under the exacting guidance of Mr Larson. She allowed herself to imagine the house's rapturous faces when the evening's finale had been revealed to them, but a sudden rush of nerves startled her and she returned quickly back to the steps that lay ahead.

Just before half past nine, Mrs Wood heard Mrs Hart's voice

strident over the settling guests as she asked if someone wouldn't mind fetching her fur, she was going to catch a chill.

Miss Newman opened the door another crack and then turned back. 'Ready?'

She nodded and took Miss Newman's arm and, together, they walked across the hall and into the séance.

The excited sighs subsided and Mrs Wood released an enigmatic smile.

'Welcome,' she said as Miss Newman settled beside her. 'We're so glad that you could come for such a special occasion.' She turned to Mrs Hart, who was wearing a gold paper crown. 'Dearest,' she said. 'Happy *birthday*!'

The room cheered and she took the opportunity to shift her skirts quickly beneath the noise.

The single candle that Mr Larson had left lit wavered on the sideboard, casting just enough light for her to see the faces staring back at her. The guests curved in two rows beyond the table, the girl – unmissable anyway in the frothy concoction – had been seated in her eyeline, as instructed, on the far left of the front row, Colonel Phillips craning dramatically from his seat behind to see around that alarming feather. There was Mr Clore beside the Dowager and Solange. Here was the Countess and her cousin, Miss Cram and *her* cousin. The Medium Mrs Addison sat eyeing her intensely from her seat, which gave Mrs Wood a momentary twinge because dear Mrs Trimble would have been sitting in that chair if she hadn't been ruined. Then the Pickerings and Prestons. Mrs Green with her daughters and Mr Yurick looking a touch too glad to be sitting beside the youngest.

She rode a happy wave of satisfaction. This was her table. This was her room. This was her audience.

The last ripple of nerves dissipated.

'Let us begin, as we always do, in the dark.' And Mr Larson

turned and snuffed the final candle, plunging the room into a charged darkness.

'Our Father, who art in Heaven . . .'

$\sim$

At first, it was a fun if ordinary séance, the underlying excitement rising in waves as cotton reels skittered across the table and words were scratched onto a slate . . .

Fondest birthday wishes

. . . the letters formed in trembling white chalk.

For a while, the air was filled with the smell of the sea and a clutch of whelks clattered onto the hearth. Then it was teaspoons – not her best set – scattered across sitters' laps, followed by some saucers and then teacups.

She gave over an interlude to Mrs Hart, who sang an off-key song from a well-wisher and tossed in some sugar cubes.

'I think the spirits are telling us something!' said Mrs Wood when a warmed teapot, complete with tea leaves, landed in her lap. 'Later, dear things,' she said. 'We're rather busy at the moment.'

She had messages for the Dowager and for Mrs Green. She sensed Mrs Jupp's hopeful eyes on her, but for some reason they made her bristle, so she moved on.

A mischievous spirit played behind the back row, stealing hair ornaments that, when the candles were lit on request, were discovered glinting in hidey-holes around the room: on the mantel, tucked into the curtain, and one sapphire beauty slid neatly into the back of Mr Pickering's thinning curls.

They *loved* it.

All of them.

She stole glances across the shadows to Miss Finch, who watched with her chin resting in her palm, Mr Humboldt whispering every now and again in her ear. And Mr Clore, nodding along, even laughing when an acorn bounced off his knee.

Just you wait, she thought as Lady Morgan reached to retrieve her hair comb from inside an empty decanter on the sideboard, laughing gaily with the rest of the room. *The best is yet to come!*

The nerves were a memory, replaced only by the rush of holding the room in her thrall: eyes glinted in the dark.

She felt the faintest whisper of a skirt behind her and then a hard rap on the floor at her feet. She gripped the table between her hands. 'Oh me, oh my! This is a lively one! And not just one. Oh, they really are. It's not just one. It's a . . . a whole clutch of them. Oh, they're running around you all like merry little sprites.'

Just you wait.

With a nonchalant stamp on the rug she signalled to Miss Newman to be ready, before slipping the toe of her slipper into the loop of string beneath the table, releasing a volley of cracks across the table.

'They're saying how cold it is tonight. *Yes, it is, we were all saying so* . . . They're saying how much they prefer the cold . . . *well, I'm not so sure we entirely feel the same way!* . . . They're asking if we can . . . if we can rub our feet on the floor? *Are you sure? That sounds so* . . . yes. They're asking if we can all rub our feet on the floor. They need energy, ladies and gentlemen.'

There was a tentative whisking sound as a few leather soles began to rub on the Persian rug, accompanied by the odd titter.

'Rub your feet as hard as you can,' she shouted. 'We need to charge this room!' The rubbing intensified to a low roar as slippers and boots ravaged the rug. 'That's marvellous!' she called over the cacophony. 'They're saying thank you and . . . and how much they love it when it . . . when it . . . when it *snows*? Oh, for goodness' sake. *We* don't enjoy snow! Not in *May!*' She paused. 'Can you feel them? Oh! They're so lively!'

Just you wait.

Miss Newman's hand gave a gentle touch to her shoulder to let her know that she was there, and she stood to join her, bumping her hip against the sideboard and calling 'They're so lively!' again to cover the click as its door popped open, although the noise of the scrubbing shoes would've been enough to drown out a string quartet.

And then, in the darkness, the finale began.

At first, it was simply the gentlest of touches.

'I can feel them!' shouted Solange.

'I felt a spirit!" shouted Mrs Green.

'There's something else!' said Mr Yurick.

The sisters exclaimed that they thought they might be angels touching them, which was of course not unusual for them, but the proclamations began to spread through the room as more and more felt the tickling flutters on their faces, their hands, down their necks. And then someone sneezed and another coughed and said, 'It's real!'

With one final toss, Mrs Wood's sack was empty, and she spun around Miss Newman and back to the sideboard, shoving it inside and leaving the door open for Miss Newman to do the same in a few moments.

'The candle, Mr Larson!' she called, sliding back into her seat with a laugh to hide her breathlessness.

In the moment before she sensed Mr Larson was to strike his match, she grasped two final handfuls of down and dashed them up so that as Mr Larson struck his match once, twice, three times and it flared and eyes adjusted to the single light, they saw flurries of white against the pitch darkness.

'More!' she called. 'We need more light!' And he struck more matches, lit more candles.

And then it all came into focus: the entire room was filled with the stuff, twirling and whirling in the air, falling over on the sitters as soft and white as snow.

'It's a snowstorm!' exclaimed Mrs Wood. 'Those naughty spirits have given us a *snowstorm!*'

And the room broke into tentative whispers as the realisation of what was happening increased. A few of the husbands jumped up, grabbing at the feathers in the air and tossing them at each other. Some of the ladies held their hands out, patiently collecting the down as it fell gently into their palms.

'They know how much I love the snow!' Mrs Hart shouted. 'It's a gift for me!'

'But this isn't *snow*, dear thing,' continued Mrs Wood. 'These are feathers! Oh, they're so naughty! They're laughing. *I'm not!* I'm wondering who's going to clear this up?' And when Mrs Wood laughed, the room suddenly burst into life and everyone broke into wild thunderous applause.

'How clever!' Mrs Hart said, her hand darting quickly across the table to touch Mrs Wood's. 'How very, very clever.'

Mrs Wood met her with an even quicker smile before returning to the room. 'Shush,' shouted Mrs Wood. 'Please! We shall scare them.' But the excitement was too real and no one could be quite quiet enough as they took in the wonderland vision of the room, and themselves, coated in feathers.

'I think we shall have to call a close to Mrs Hart's birthday party,' she called over the giddy noise, the success of the finale almost bringing her to tears. 'The spirits have exhausted me. So please!' she shouted above the unrelenting hubbub. '*Please!* Join with me to say our farewell prayer.'

They took a while to resettle, but finally they coughed and giggled their way into silence and when all of the heads had bowed, she allowed herself to take a moment, looking around the white-layered room, her eyes catching deliberately on Miss Finch, who was picking at the frilled layers of her dress. Even *she* had behaved.

She exhaled, reached for Miss Newman's hand and began the prayer so quietly that everyone in the room had to strain to hear.

Eliza and the hired help were waiting outside the séance room, as planned, spreading sheets across the floor ready to receive the feather-covered guests. They tumbled out from the gloom, as excited and giddy as foals, blinking in the bright light of the hallway while Eliza steered them into a space, ready for plucking.

Guests called to one another as the help set about plucking the feathers from their clothes, taking champagne from a circulating tray and sharing delighted thoughts on how much fun it had been.

But then . . . it was taking too long.

'Are you not finished yet?' asked the Dowager as two girls worked together on her woollen shawl. 'I need to sit.'

'I can't go home like this!' said Colonel Phillips, his seat almost entirely coated in down but refusing any help in brushing himself off.

Frustration prickled through the hallway, the excited laughter and chatter quietening as the clock ticked on and dresses and trousers and jackets and shawls remained covered in stubborn white fluff.

'I can only apologise for my naughty spirits,' said Mrs Wood as brightly as possible, taking over the circulation of the champagne and truffles on a large silver tray. 'Send us any cleaning bills you may encounter. I shall ensure I cash them in when I see those mischievous souls in Heaven!'

'I'm not sure you're going to Heaven,' said Colonel Phillips, furiously picking at his hair before the mirror.

'Oh pish, Colonel.' She raised a saucer of champagne towards him which he took with a growl of thanks. 'Imagine the story you can tell in the club tomorrow!' He shook his head but drank anyway.

'I most certainly *will* be sending you a bill,' said an irritated voice and Mrs Wood turned to see Mr Clore, fluff in his pomade and a thorough coating of feathers along his left leg. 'This is new and I have no idea if I shall ever get all this nonsense off.'

'I shall take it up with the sprites,' she said, laughing as she passed the tray to Miss Newman, who was going around stuffing loose feathers into a cotton bag, so much fluff caught in her hair she looked as though she'd been plucking geese for Christmas. 'Those spirits don't know what they're doing!'

'No, they don't,' Clore said. 'What possessed them? Look!' He spread his arm wide to the rest of the house and Mrs Wood began to take in the whole, awful show before her. 'It's as though we've been tarred and feathered!'

'You're exaggerating,' she said, forcing her smile to stay put.

What was happening?

Here was Lady Harrington, her beautiful peach velvet gown speckled with tufts of white; here was one of the Miss Greens with a fox fur stole now almost entirely goose; Mr Humboldt pointing out each tiny piece of down on his trousers and insisting that the girl assigned to him pick each one out; Mrs Preston wheezing in a chair.

They had loved the feathers in Siena, hadn't they? So much so that when she got to Florence, they had called her *Señora Piume* and toasted her with tall fizzing glasses.

Had she used the wrong type of feathers?

Was there something different about English geese?

Mr Clore was still grumbling but she ignored him, focusing on her facade while she realised that something had gone terribly, terribly wrong.

She watched the poor help's fingers pick fruitlessly while the feathers clung like molluscs to all those wool trousers and velvet brocades.

Wool.

Velvet.

How had she not *realised*?

It had been spring when she had delivered the feathers in Italy, but the evening had been as hot as an English summer's day and the women had been wearing light cotton dresses, their consorts in pale linens. The feathers had drifted as though in a dream, dusting the sitters like kisses before fluttering harmlessly to the floor.

There had been no wool jackets.

No velvet dresses.

No brocades or fringing.

In all their planning, why had this not occurred to her? That an English spring did not call for anything close to the smooth, light materials necessary in Italy.

She almost laughed when she thought back to the time when her greatest concern had centred around how she might get them out of her rug. She hadn't given a second thought to how they might be removed from a rich couture gown that had been handmade in Paris.

The hall felt suddenly overwhelming – the complaints whirling like a storm about her ears.

This had never happened before.

She had never made a bad call; never misjudged a situation.

Never.

'I'm so very sorry, everyone,' she said, moving as calmly as she could from guest to guest. 'I cannot be held accountable for my silly spirits, but I shall pay for all of your cleaning. Just send me the bill! I know! They're *very* bad!'

They should have thought it through harder; she should've known better.

'Mrs Wood,' Miss Newman said, appearing at her shoulder, her voice intended for the room, and Mrs Wood fell against her with relief. 'You must be exhausted after such a wonderful séance. You need to rest, I insist. Ladies and gentlemen, this is unprecedented, Mrs Wood amongst you following a séance. We all know how much they take from her.'

'Thank you, dearest,' she said, gathering herself into an air of benevolent exhaustion as she leaned on Miss Newman. 'I am feeling quite . . .'

Mrs Hart met her at the foot of the stairs. 'Well,' she whispered, glancing pointedly at her ruined fur stole. 'I could've told you that would be a dreadful idea.'

197

Her smile was beginning to hurt. 'I am at the mercy of my spirits,' she said. 'You of all people understand that.' And Mrs Hart opened her mouth to reply but Miss Newman came between them with a light and easy smile.

'Mrs Hart. Dearest,' she said. 'Have you had a lovely birthday?' She clapped her hands. 'Happy birthday to Mrs Hart!' she said, and a few voices gave her a half-hearted cheer while Mrs Hart smiled, benevolently and, with a final flicker of a glare, moved on.

'Make sure the Dowager gets a chair,' she whispered to Miss Newman before turning back to the room. 'Thank you all for coming, I do hope that you'll find it in your heart to forgive those naughty spirits. I'll be sure to speak with them very sternly.'

There was a smattering of laughter, which gave Mrs Wood hope that they weren't all furious, and then Mrs Reynolds and the sisters began a round of applause and Lady Morgan led a three cheers, but it was limp in comparison to the reception she had received only a few hours earlier.

Nonetheless, she bowed her head, humbly. 'Thank you,' she said. 'Thank you very much.' She made as though she was suddenly overtaken with tiredness, reaching out for the end of the banister. 'Now, I must rest.'

She allowed Miss Newman to 'help' her up the stairs, turning at the top to cast a final glance across her guests: some had given up being brushed down and were waiting for their cloaks in resigned irritation. Others were enjoying the attention and finishing off what remained of the champagne.

And there, on the window seat of the drawing room, sat Miss Finch, plucking at her skirt while engaged in deep conversation with the Dowager's daughter, Lady Harrington.

As if sensing she was being watched, Miss Finch looked up and caught Mrs Wood's eyes, holding them for a moment while a slow, curling smile tipped the pretty corners of her mouth.

5th June 1873

Dear Mrs Wood,

Thank you for your wonderful séance in honour of our dear Mrs Hart's birthday. It really was a spirited evening (!), and the snowstorm was so exciting.

I wonder, however, if I might trouble you to cover the enclosed note I received this morning from my service. I feel just awful asking, but you did say and it's a large expenditure I wasn't expecting and since becoming a widow, I must look after every penny.

I look forward to seeing you on another occasion soon,

Augusta

From A Birthday Celebration at Mrs Wood's
Spiritual Times, 5th June 1873

What an evening of night and day we experienced on
Saturday eve for Mrs Hart's birthday. Hosted with her usual
aplomb by the old hand Medium Mrs Wood, the reception
was also an opportunity for her young pupil, Miss
Emmeline Finch, to be introduced to some of London's
most important believers.

While Mrs Wood dominated at the table, I was not alone
in finding the spirits a little dry while the enormous flurry
of feathers that engulfed us and ruined many suits and
gowns (cleaning bills have been issued) smacked of a
Medium not in control of her spirits.

All this while the talented young Medium, Miss Finch,
sat with the guests and was prohibited from contributing,
despite many of us desperate to see the girl in action.

By the end, Mrs Wood appeared tired. I don't think I
was alone in thinking that her tables would benefit from a
more balanced approach. She would do well to, rather than
show off how pretty her pupil is, set her to work and bring
some youthful delights to her table. At her age, I am sure
she'll welcome the reduction in demand and her spirits may
find themselves refreshed too.

CHAPTER 22

She wrote to Mr Clore on Monday after receiving his cleaning bill; her words full of teasing remorse, remaining as playful with him as ever. But his response was unusually brief, only a single line, and it had contained not even a hint of the warmth he usually bestowed upon her.

It was so hard to face the fact that her great séance had failed. She couldn't remember a time when one of her exhibitions hadn't been received with awe. But now. Here she was, desperately in need of attention, and she had not only disappointed her guests for the first time in her professional life, she'd also alienated one of her most important followers. The single blessing was that it had not been an exposure, but Clore's faltering support and the lukewarm letters of thanks received from her guests only served to remind her that all the things that had driven her towards the girl were coming dangerously close.

The way forward was clear: if she were to redeem herself, she would need the attraction of the girl. Gift or no gift.

She had to rise above the humiliation she had endured in the girl's presence – of all things! – but the girl needed to believe that this was all par for the course, that mixed reviews happened all the time and the sign of a great Medium was her ability to accept such things in good humour and move on.

The plan must continue, it had never been more necessary.

Mrs Green's house was the grandest on Orme Square, which was no mean feat. A gleaming Italianate mansion, wide and white with glossy black railings, smooth stone steps and a huge gilt knocker in the shape of a stag's head hung upon one of the double front doors. Mr Green was a grotesquely proud huntsman and the knocker had been cast from his first blood, the poor beast's final humiliation a gleaming ring hanging from its mournful mouth.

Each time she saw it, rather than being reminded of quite how manly Mr Green was – which had surely been his intention – Mrs Wood was simply reaffirmed of the inherent difference between those who were born into their wealth, and those who had made it for themselves.

Still, she always thought as she swung the ring of the stag's head door knocker, money was money. And, really, who was she to judge?

Fortunately, Mr Green was at his club – or perhaps out murdering more defenceless animals – and Mrs Green greeted her with her usual enthusiasm, dismissing the staff as soon as they had opened the door, and pulling her and Miss Newman inside.

'Wonderful, wonderful!' she said. But then, unusually, she was almost pushing Mrs Wood out of the way. 'And there she is,' she said with a gasp. 'Our *dear* Miss Finch.'

Mrs Wood stepped forward. 'Miss Finch,' she said, attempting to reassert herself. 'May I introduce Mrs Bertrand Green.'

Mrs Green's smile deepened as she pulled the girl over the threshold. 'At last!' she said, reaching out to take the girl's hands in hers. 'I know that I saw you at Mrs Hart's party, but it's so much better to meet you in person. And you must call me Eileen. Please. I insist.' She pulled the girl into the hall. 'Now, come, *come*! We have so much to do tonight!'

Then, as usual, the woman held out her elbow but when Mrs Wood took a step forward, she realised that it hadn't been directed towards her at all. Instead, Miss Finch, with carefully curated shyness, looped her hand tentatively inside.

'Your house is . . .' the girl began, her eyes wide as Mrs Wood watched her devour the sweeping staircase and the glittering chandelier and the gilt-framed portraits of Mrs Green and her husband, and their myriad of daughters and dogs.

'Yes, yes,' said Mrs Green, flapping her free hand dismissively. 'It's all very nice. But *you*, dear girl,' she said. '*You* are what we've been waiting to see.'

The girl had chosen to wear the spring green dress she had bought her. 'I didn't want Mrs Green to think I was trying too hard,' she had said when they had collected her. 'I thought she would prefer a plain look.' Now her coils bounced as she trotted innocently along, gleaming in the blazing light of the hall.

She felt a sense of dread settle in the pit of her stomach, and when Mrs Green nudged the girl into the drawing room, Miss Finch threw a glance of excitement over her shoulder towards Mrs Wood that landed on her like acid.

'Are you coming, Violet?' Miss Newman asked before she followed the girl inside, not waiting to hear Mrs Wood's response, so that when she said, 'Of course!' her voice echoed around the vast empty hall, and she found herself rushing to avoid the drawing-room door shutting her out.

Miss Newman had waited for her inside the door and as Mrs Wood closed it behind herself, she leaned in. 'Someone's making an impression,' she said.

Miss Finch stood engulfed in a crowd of the five rambunctious Green daughters, their chittering rising like a dawn chorus as five pairs of alabaster arms reached out to squeeze, prod and poke the girl, taffeta silk whispering as they hopped from foot to foot, excited hands patting together in wrist-length laced gloves.

'Miss Finch?' Mrs Wood said, walking towards the chaos. 'Miss

Finch, are you in there?' She gave a laugh but realised that no one had heard. She reached the girl's elbow, raised her voice a little louder. 'Are you all right, dear?'

The girl turned, her cheeks very pink, her eyes very wide. 'I am,' she said, breathless. 'It's so very nice to meet you all,' she said.

'Girls!' Mrs Green said, clapping her hands as though they were nuisance dogs. 'Enough! Let poor Miss Finch be.' The five daughters gave way, talking loudly to one another as they settled themselves back on the arms of various sofas and chairs, and as they moved that gave Mrs Wood a view to the other end of the long, densely furnished room.

And there, leaning, customarily, against the fireplace, was Mr Clore. Was there ever going to be a time now when she looked across a room and *didn't* see that man eyeing her from the mantel?

'Why,' she called, forcing a smile to meet her eyes. 'Mr Clore! How lovely to see you!'

'Did I not mention Mr Clore would be coming?' Mrs Green said, carefully enunciating each word for fear of losing a vital consonant. 'You don't mind, do you? I was fortunate enough to enjoy Mr Clore's company with Mrs Hart the other day and he happened to say that he wished to see Miss Finch again and I said she was my special guest today and—'

She smiled brightly. 'Of course I don't,' she said. 'Are you recovered from Saturday night?'

'Quite,' he said. 'More importantly, are you?'

'Of course she is,' twittered Mrs Green. 'Why would you say such a thing. It was wonderful, Violet. It really was. We all loved the feathers, didn't we, girls.' Her daughters giggled and agreed. 'Some people have no sense of fun.' She gave a playful twinkle at Clore, who responded with a raised eyebrow.

'Some people's trousers were all but ruined,' he replied, but Mrs Wood felt a thawing in the smile that caught at the edge of his mouth. If she made him feel special and the girl performed well, he would be back on her side.

'It's ever so nice to see you again, sir,' said the girl, suddenly by her shoulder as if on cue.

'You see,' Mrs Wood said. 'We're always happy to see Mr Clore.'

The girl proved irresistible and he slid his glass onto the mantel and was across the room within a few heartbeats. 'Well,' he said, taking her hand. 'I didn't get much of a chance to see you at the party, but you looked as charming as ever.'

The girl flushed furiously. 'Don't,' she said. 'You're too much.'

'And how are the Green girls?' Mrs Wood said pointedly. She took Miss Finch's arm with a polite nod to Clore, and turned them both to one of the girls: 'Miss Sheba, you've become quite the young lady in but a few weeks.'

The youngest daughter, seventeen-year-old Bathsheba with her father's big, boisterous cheeks and a shock of orange hair, bounced to her feet, ironed curls spilling around her cheeks from a red ribbon at her crown. 'Mama said it was time I looked more grown up. I'm to be presented soon, you know.'

'Oh, I do,' said Mrs Wood. 'Though I find it hard to believe that it's your turn already.'

'Don't,' said Mrs Green. 'Where has my littlest darling gone?'

'I remember yours, Mrs Logan,' she said, turning to the eldest sister, round and dark like her mother, wearing a purple velvet gown that failed to hide the signs of yet another impending confinement. 'And yours too, Miss Hepzhi. Which was surely only last week.'

The penultimate daughter giggled behind her fingers. 'It's been a whole year,' she said.

'What about mine?' whined Cressida, the tallest girl.

'How could I forget,' she said, patting her arm. 'You showed me your beautiful yellow gown every time I came for months!'

Cressida gave a sigh. 'I loved that dress,' she said.

'Shame you couldn't fit into it now,' said Sheba. 'It'd come to your knees!'

'Bath*sheba*!' snapped Mrs Green, but Alexandra, the middle daughter and family diplomat, placed a calming hand on Cressida's arm and Sheba rolled her eyes.

'Well, now,' said Mrs Wood, taking advantage of the sudden lull. 'It's very lovely to see you all.'

'Let's have a little refreshment before we begin,' said Mrs Green, tugging on the bell-pull. 'We don't want to have to finish early due to thirst!'

'I want ginger!' shouted Sheba.

'Can I have champagne tonight?' said Hepzhi.

'You're such a pig,' said Cressida.

'And you're a giraffe,' said Sheba.

And they descended into their usual squabbles and snipes as Mrs Green raised her voice over the rabble, explaining to Miss Finch where the séances were usually held – in a small back room crammed with taxidermied animals and silent clocks – and told her how charming her hair was as though nothing unusual was happening at all.

With the exception of Mr Green, she had always found the Greens endearing. Their home was warm, their relaxed manner refreshing. From her first visit to their home with Mr Wood all those years ago, she had felt welcome. The girls had been very small then and it had been a few years before Sophia, now Mrs Logan, had come to the table, the rest following one by one as they came of age. They were loud and unreserved in the privacy of their home, and she had always felt that their lack of inhibitions when she was with them spoke volumes about how they saw her. That she was almost one of them.

But here they were, acting like barbarians before Miss Finch. Mr Clore she could understand, Mrs Green was far too rich to receive anything arch from him in his columns, but the girl was a complete unknown. She felt the scene shift before her like a kaleidoscope, the family sliding from a place of warm inclusion to something other, something colder. She had thought that they had behaved so wildly because they loved her.

Had the reality been, all that time, that they simply didn't care?

Even the sisters calmed when they stepped into the dim séance room, set for the evening's event with two candles on the mantel glinting darkly off the glass cases and unseeing eyes of taxidermied creatures covering every scrap of wall. Mr Clore, the first in, sat quickly below the polar bear's head, whose inclusion in this gallery of death always made Mrs Wood smile with *schadenfreude* that Mr Green, who'd never set foot on a boat larger than a punt, thought he was fooling guests into believing he'd had anything to do with the slaughter of that majestic beast.

Mrs Wood took her usual seat below the stuffed owl, wings spread wide within its glass dome, extended claws inches from collecting her scalp. Miss Newman sat to her right; Miss Finch she pointed purposefully into the chair across the wide, round table, where she could keep an eye on her beneath the one-eared antelope.

Mrs Green wedged herself into her seat below a stack of three stag heads, the girls twittering like birds onto perches, overseen by muntjacs and badgers and foxes and minks and two beagles with high, pointed tails. With the final settle of Alexandra beneath a mallard, Mrs Wood called the séance to order.

'Now,' she said, her eyes slowly sweeping the sitters as she breathed deeply and slowly. 'Welcome to you all,' she said. 'And welcome to my newest friend, Miss Emmie, I'm sorry dear, *Emmeline Finch*.' She smiled benevolently towards the girl who bobbed her head as the girls all whispered hellos and giggled. 'Miss Finch and I have been working together to develop her gift since February and I can say that she is doing exceptionally well for a novice, as you will discover for yourself this evening.'

The girls bubbled.

'Now,' she said again, and the room fell silent. 'Let us snuff the candles . . .' Mr Clore craned to see who was going to do it, so Alexandra stood and picked up the snuffer from the mantel and things unfurled in the dark within Mrs Wood's steady grasp. The girl knew what was expected of her. She knew that she was permitted a small interlude with Mona, a charming little read of her chosen sitter. And that was it. It may have been Miss Finch's entry into Mrs Green's orbit, but it was still Mrs Wood's room.

Beneath the glint of a hundred glass eyes that pricked the darkness like stars, the spirits announced themselves through enthusiastic raps and table heaves.

Mrs Green, another burgeoning Medium herself, suddenly exclaimed that she saw Miss Newman's forehead glowing, as though alight. 'It's a message,' she said. 'It's a message of enlightenment!'

'How nice,' said Miss Newman.

Mrs Wood then moved into her trance to open the channel to the Other Side, quickly receiving a message from Mrs Green's beloved grandfather, whispering John 15:9 in a fragile, breaking voice: *'As the Father has loved me, so have I loved you . . .'* and the whole table sighed. An unnamed relative came for Mr Clore and advised him to have his liver checked. And Mrs Green's mother stroked Sheba's curls, stating them very pretty, patted Sophia's growing bump, wishing her luck, and finally tucked a loose strand of Mrs Green's hair behind her ear. *'Do not forget yourself in your duty to others,'* she said, an assured burr to her words that would have been familiar to those from Rochdale, a place that Mrs Green had never told anyone she had been raised in.

And then *poor* Mr Clore was the reluctant victim of a playful soul who picked his pockets, ruffled what remained of his hair and dropped his tobacco pouch into Alexandra's skirt before a single, bright light began dancing overhead, bouncing from point to point, drawing gasps from the table until it disappeared in a blink (back into Mrs Wood's skirt).

There were some songs, a couple of visions. Some more rapping and another table heave.

And then.

Mrs Wood gave a groan, an indication that she was rising from her trance and Miss Finch gasped. It was her turn now.

'Your mother!' she said.

'She's back?' said Mrs Green.

'No,' she said. 'No, it's not your mother, Mrs Green. Mr Clore, I believe . . .' the girl coughed, moved in her seat. 'I believe she belongs to you.'

'Me?' said Mr Clore, and Mrs Wood could hear him stretching about in the dark. 'Where? Where is she?'

Miss Finch made a low moaning noise. 'She's a very strong woman,' she said. 'Can I help you, dear?'

An electric whisper ran between the sisters.

'She has a message,' the girl said. 'She's saying . . .'

'Yes?' said Mr Clore. 'What does she want?'

'She's saying . . .' The girl gave a chirrup of a laugh. 'Oh, she is a funny thing, isn't she.'

'Not to me,' said Mr Clore.

'The Other Side changes them,' said Mrs Wood quickly. 'We often find levity in those who have spent their earthly lives bound by solemnity.'

'She's telling me that you need to be kinder,' Miss Finch continued.

Mr Clore gave a laugh like a gunshot. 'Ha!' he said. 'That's rich.'

'She's saying words matter. She should know, she's saying. She wasn't careful with hers. She said too many cruel things. She wasn't the mother she wanted to be.'

Mr Clore was silent.

'She's saying you shouldn't be like her. That you should be more thoughtful with your pen. That your words carry weight.' The girl paused. The room held its breath. 'She's saying that she's . . . she's sorry.'

'Oh, Mrs Wood,' whispered Mrs Green. 'She's *very* good.'

Mr Clore cleared his throat. 'Thank you,' he said. 'I'll take my business advice from my accountant, if you don't mind.' But the laugh he gave sounded strangled and he didn't say anything more.

She heard the girl give another groan and, as agreed, took the reins back once more.

'Thank you, Miss Finch. You have surpassed yourself. Now,' Her voice was bright and light. 'We have another of those playful spirits here.'

'Let's hope it's not Pater,' Mr Clore said, with only a hint of humour.

Miss Newman broke into a coughing fit and Mrs Wood said: 'When you're finished, Miss Newman. The spirits prefer when things are silent.'

The cough subsided and then: 'An angel!' Mrs Green shouted. 'An angel stroked my cheek!'

'Oh! Mine too!' cried a sister. And then another and there were calls for a light to be struck as the room filled with the delicate scent of flowers.

'Mr Clore! Mr Clore: the candle!' shouted Mrs Wood over the clamouring.

After a moment, he struck once, twice, three times before the match flared, temporarily blinding the table before he lit the candle, and there were sudden gales of gasps and laughter across the room because the table and floor was littered with creamy, pungent petals in pinks and reds and yellows.

'Where did they come from?'

'What are they?'

'They're petals, you dolt.'

'Oh, they smell glorious!'

'Thank you, dear things,' said Mrs Wood, her eyes raised to the spirits. '*Thank you!* What a wonderful treat to close this evening.'

She smiled at the table, the sisters pushing their hands into the petals and laughing, Mrs Green crushing one between her fingers and inhaling its scent with a smile, Mr Clore brushing them pointedly from his trousers. And then she stopped. Across the table in the bare, flickering light, Miss Finch remained statue-still, her eyes closed.

What was she doing?

She had had her turn. The roses were the finale.

She glanced quickly at Miss Newman, who gave a discreet shake of her head.

The girl's face was as empty as though she were dead, and a shot of irritation fired through Mrs Wood. Hadn't she been very clear about the danger she posed going off plan? She would most certainly be having words with the girl in the cab home.

'Miss Finch, are we not finished?' Mrs Wood said lightly. But the girl didn't move.

Instead she gave a tiny gasp and opened her mouth. 'Hello?' Her face remained immobile in the light of the single candle, her eyes closed, but the voice was loud and clear. 'Hello?'

The sisters descended into a flurry of excitement.

'I think something's happening!' said Sheba. 'Mrs Wood, what's happening?'

Mrs Wood smiled sweetly. If the girl wanted to play on, then she would have to go with it on this occasion. What choice did she have? Oh, but the girl would hear about this later. She cleared her throat. 'Is someone there, Miss Finch?' she asked.

'Goodness!' said the voice from the girl, slow and soft. 'There are so many people here.' She coughed.

'Who's there?' asked Mrs Green.

'Oh,' said the girl. 'H-hello. This is my first time . . . I have been searching for many years to make the right connection.'

'Who is speaking please,' Mrs Wood said firmly.

'My name . . .' The girl coughed again. 'My name is Tandy.'

'Tandy!' said the table at once and the rest of the room broke into whispers.

Tandy? *Tandy?* What happened to Mona?

'Tandy . . .' The girl repeated. 'Tandy Starr. I . . . I come from the . . . sea.'

'From the sea?' cried Hepzhi and Sheba at the same time.

'She has the same surname as your spirit guide,' said Alexandra. 'Do you think . . .'

'No,' said Mrs Wood, but 'Tandy' continued . . .

'Is my voice heard?' Tandy croaked. 'A girl called Mona came to find me. She told me that her time with Miss Finch is over . . .' She coughed. 'That Miss Finch no longer requires a child guide.' The girl's head rolled. 'Emmeline is now a woman to us in the spirit world,' she said.

'How lovely,' whispered Sheba.

'Well,' said Mrs Wood, scrabbling to keep control. '*Tandy*. You are most welcome. I am delighted to have been a part of Miss Finch's education.'

'How lucky we should feel,' said Mrs Green. 'For Tandy to choose our table to reveal herself.'

'There is someone here,' Tandy continued. 'In the shadows. I can't see her properly. She's . . .' She coughed, and the girl's chin gave a jerk. 'I see . . . Hello? Are you here for Miss Finch . . . Oh! Oh, she's rude.'

The table laughed, hesitantly. Mrs Wood's jaw gave a little pop.

'I know you,' Tandy said. 'Emmeline knows you. You've been . . . you were here before . . .'

'Who is it?' shouted Sheba, before yelping, '*You didn't need to pinch me.*'

'. . . Who are . . .' Miss Finch's head moved fitfully. 'Who are you . . . Who . . . what are you saying . . . what did you *say* . . .'

An electric silence. And then:

'*Vi? Thee there, gal?*'

'Enough!' Mrs Wood snapped. She had told the girl that these kinds of performances were unwelcome at her patrons' tables, just as she had told her that there were to be no more damned Thirzas!

'Who is it?' gasped Hepzhi.

'*I said, is thee there, Vi?*'

'Mrs Wood.' Mrs Green sounded unsettled. 'Violet. Is she . . . is she talking about you?'

'No,' Mrs Wood said, firmly. 'That's not my name.'

'*How can thee forget me, Vi?*'

'Enough!' Mrs Wood said, but her voice was drowned beneath the excited whispers of the sisters.

And then. '*How could thee ever forget me, Vi? How could thee ever forget thou Thirza!*'

'Stop!' said Miss Newman, clutching Mrs Wood's arm to keep her steady.

'*My name is Thirza!*'

'That's enough, I said!' shouted Mrs Wood, and she slammed her hand down on the table so hard that the glass cases on the walls sang. The table was suddenly silent, all eyes on her in horror. 'We've had this nasty soul come through Miss Finch before. She is not welcome.' She raised her voice. 'You are not welcome here, Spirit.'

Miss Finch coughed, her head rolling, her shoulders jittering. Then she fell still. 'She has gone but she has weakened Emmeline,' said Tandy, her voice feeble. She coughed again and her voice broke into a croak. '. . . I have so enjoyed talking with such accomplished ladies. I hope I can see you again soon.'

The girl exhaled and her body dropped into her chair.

'A light!' called Alexandra.

'A drink!' called Mrs Green.

The table erupted as the girl surfaced, pressing a hand to her brow and stifling a yawn.

'Let her come to,' Clore was saying, moving protectively to her side to block the younger sisters who were trying to get to the girl.

The room was suddenly blindingly bright and Mrs Wood squinted up to see Miss Newman standing beside the gas jets switch. She held her eyes, but Miss Newman, again, shook her head.

'Did something happen?' the girl asked, confusion crossing her face like clouds. 'Has something happened?'

'Oh Miss Finch!' said Mrs Green. 'You were magnificent. Magnificent! But who was that horrible spirit . . . ?'

'Mother,' warned Alexandra as Cressida shoved a glass of sherry into her hand. Then she turned to Miss Finch. 'You were very good, but you must be exhausted. Drink something to restore yourself.'

'Mona?' she asked, giving the sherry a look of complete bafflement. 'Did Mona come?'

'No,' said Mrs Logan, the eldest Green daughter. 'Not Mona. You have a new guide, Miss Finch,' she took a moment. '*Tandy*.'

'What about the . . . ?' said Sheba, but Alexandra silenced her with a look.

'Tandy?' said the girl, blinking.

'Oh, she's a *find*, Mrs Wood,' said Mrs Green over the girl. 'I can't understand why you've kept her hidden for so long. Don't you think, Mr Clore? Don't you think she's a breath of fresh air?'

Clore's eyes were dancing over the girl. 'You are quite fascinating,' he said, and his hand slipped to the girl's shoulder.

And then the girl looked at Mrs Wood and the light she saw in her eyes made her recoil.

My God, she thought with yawning realisation.

What a *fool* she had been.

CHAPTER 23

She gathered herself, piece by piece, back into Mrs Wood, but when she spoke, it was as though her words were coming from the bottom of a well. Somehow, with the useful excuse of post-séance exhaustion and the arm of Miss Newman, she navigated the walk from the séance room to the drawing room, where she took a glass of champagne that felt like sand in her mouth, before moving back through the hall and into the waiting cab.

All the while her eyes were fixed on the girl, incredulous at her lack of judgement. Her utter blindness to the truth when being able to see everything was what she had built her life on.

There was no *talent* there.

The girl hadn't coincidentally landed on Thirza through skill or chance. She understood that now. Somehow the girl had found it out. Somehow she had found the whole, dirty mess of Mrs Wood's past. She knew her *birthday*, for God's sake. How ridiculous could she have been to think that anyone could've simply *read* that in her?

There was a reason why Mrs Wood had hidden her truth. Why she had kept Thirza so deeply buried that not even Mr Wood or Miss Newman knew: if anyone should discover her close connection to Thirza, a Medium so famously fraudulent, she would suffer a ruin so absolute there would be no question of recovery. She would lose her patrons, her friends, her life.

But now, the worst kind of person had discovered it. The kind of filthy fraud who found the dirt before they found their mark. She had met a few in Hull, but she had never believed that she might ever be taken by one.

From the moment Mrs Wood had stepped off the train at Kings Cross in 1859, her talent had been the only thing that remained of her life before. She had removed her accent, changed the length of her stride, how she wore her hair, her name, her story.

Everything but her skill.

Over the years she had grown secure, never complacent, but secure that the secret would stay just as it should: hidden. How could it not? No one alive knew her truth, she had been so certain of that.

But she had been wrong.

She could hear Miss Newman and Miss Finch talking around her in the cab, but their words were so meaningless they might have been a pair of twittering birds.

The cab began to slow and she came to, looking out onto the dark street, recognising that they were almost at the junction with Westbourne Grove, where ordinarily they would continue on along Hereford Road towards Miss Finch's.

But not tonight.

She banged on the roof and Miss Newman jumped.

'Are you all right?' she asked as the cab pulled up with a jolt.

'Miss Finch,' she said. 'Could I have a few moments with you at Chepstow Villas?'

'Violet. We're all exhausted,' said Miss Newman. 'Can't it wait?'

'No, it's all right,' said the girl. 'Of course, I don't mind.'

Mrs Wood dropped the window. 'Chepstow Villas, driver,' she called.

'Right y'are,' the driver's voice came from above and the cab rocked and rolled as he clicked the horses back into motion.

She pushed the window up and returned her gaze to the empty seat before her, holding onto the smooth, leather strap that dangled from the ceiling as the cab swept around the corner onto the Grove so that she didn't fall indecently into anyone's lap.

Miss Newman hesitated in the hall as they put their hats and cloaks into a yawning Eliza's hands.

'Is something the matter?' she whispered while Miss Finch noisily unwrapped her cloak and handed it to a begrudging Eliza.

'I'd just like to go over the new spirit guide,' Mrs Wood said, unable to meet her eyes. Had Miss Newman guessed? Had she become so lax that she had been giving herself away to them all?

'Did I do something wrong?' Miss Finch appeared beside her, the wide eyes and simpering tone turning Mrs Wood's stomach.

She tried to smile. 'Why would you think that?' she said.

'Are you cross?'

'Do you need me?' Eliza said, her voice cutting through the hall. They turned to look at her, laden with the summer cloaks and bonnets. 'Only I was about to close up.'

'No,' she said. 'You go up once you've disposed of those.' Miss Newman stifled a yawn. 'You too, dearest. Please. We shan't be long.'

Miss Newman gave her one final curious look, to which Mrs Wood brightened her smile. 'Really,' she said, and made a light shooing motion which took almost every ounce of the energy she had left.

Miss Newman turned to the girl. 'Don't keep Mrs Wood late,' she said. 'We have a busy day tomorrow.'

'When don't you!' said Miss Finch.

'Go on, Eliza,' Mrs Wood continued. 'I'll lock the door after Miss Finch.'

'If you're sure?' said Eliza. 'There's ham in the larder if you're hungry. I could make you some cocoa . . .'

'Really,' said Mrs Wood. 'We'll manage ourselves.'

Eliza gave one last glare of suspicion before turning to follow Miss Newman up the stairs.

Mrs Wood watched them go, remaining still until she had heard the distant click of first Miss Newman's door and then Eliza begin the flight to the attic.

Then she turned to the girl, her stomach giving a little when Miss Finch lit up with her usual smile: bright, hopeful. Expectant.

She looked away. 'Shall we?' she said as she walked towards the back parlour, hearing the girlish scuttle as Miss Finch rushed to catch up.

Her whole body was thrumming with fury and she lit the lamp on the mantel with shaking fingers, turning it up to full so that she could see the girl's face as they talked. Then she poured them both a deep glass of sherry, passing one to the girl before taking up her own.

'Sit,' she said, her hand firm on her stomach to steady herself. When the girl didn't move, she indicated firmly with her eyes. 'Sit.'

And the girl sat, smoothing her skirt as she took a sip of her sherry. 'What a treat,' she said.

Mrs Wood ignored her, staring instead at the trembling flame of the lamp until she heard the girl give a little laugh. 'Is everything all right, dearest?'

Mrs Wood took a breath and turned.

'Tell me about Thirza.'

The girl looked up, her expression a cartoonish vision of virtue in the bright lamplight. 'Who?'

'Thirza,' said Mrs Wood.

The girl shook her head. 'I don't . . .' Then she stopped. 'Do you mean that awful old lady who's come through a few times?'

Mrs Wood held her gaze steady. 'You know who I'm talking about.'

The girl gave a dismissive laugh. 'Who am I to know what spirits . . .'

'Enough.'

'I mean, all I do is what you've taught me. I just open myself up and . . .'

'Enough!'

The room rang with Mrs Wood's voice and the girl sat back as though she'd been slapped.

'Mrs Wood, please. Are you unwell? Shall I fetch Miss Newman? Why won't you sit . . . ?'

'I am perfectly well.' Her voice was tight around her teeth.

Miss Finch stared up at her. 'Mrs Wood . . .' The girl's voice trembled, her eyes glittered with tears, one falling like a perfect diamond as she dropped her stare to her lap.

Mrs Wood's heart pounded in her throat, the girl's behaviour driving anger over the fear. She was ready. She had to know. 'You tell me what you know,' she said. 'And then we can talk about what you want.'

The girl sat for a moment, another tear falling into her lap, before she gave a sudden inhalation and looked up. Mrs Wood started: instead of one of Miss Finch's saccharine expressions of tortured emotion, the girl's face had transformed into something Mrs Wood hardly recognised: there was no girl there; no innocence. The eyes that met hers were, though still damp with earlier tears, staring brazenly right back at her with the confidence of an equal.

'All right,' she said, her mouth curling at one corner into a sardonic smile. 'What story would you like? That Thirza was a brandy-soaked old fraud who never shut up about how rich she could've been?'

Mrs Wood reached for the back of her chair.

'Or,' Miss Finch continued. 'This one's probably a bit more of what you're looking for: that Thirza, the brandy-soaked old fraud who never shut up about her failures, was actually your very own brandy-soaked old fraud of a mother. How about that?'

Mrs Wood's knees buckled and she sat heavily, everything focused on maintaining her facade while the girl's leering smile reared up in her vision and she braced herself for the whole, hideous truth to spill out everywhere.

'How?' she asked, but her voice was feeble and barely made it beyond her lips. She cleared her throat and took a moment for a second chance. 'What makes you so sure of what you're saying?' She swallowed. 'My mother is—'

'Obviously I'm not talking about the one you made up who lives in the nice house outside Hull with the nice doctor husband. I'm talking about the Great Thirza Thwaite – the notable Medium, fraud and drunk.'

Mrs Wood reached for her glass and took a large mouthful, forcing it down and coughing at the heat. 'I think you have me mistaken.'

Miss Finch dipped her chin, rolled her head suddenly, and there was that grotesque voice again. 'Don't deny me, child! Do you forget the fun we had?'

'That's enough!'

The girl looked up and laughed. 'I know, Vi. I know everything. The filthy little rooms,' she said. 'The scratching around for pennies to fill your mother's pot. The time you were discovered beneath the table at Bury.'

How could she know? How could she? No one knew.

No one but Thirza.

A clarity shone inside, like a ray of sunlight. That phrase. The one the girl had said that had pricked her ears. *Illusion is everything.* How had she been so deaf? That was Thirza's phrase. That was what the woman lived by.

And then, of course, the horror story of her birthday.

The girl had been dangling it before her the whole time and she hadn't even noticed.

What a fool she had made of herself. How hilarious she must've appeared to the girl. How pathetic.

Another shock gripped her chest. Was this part of a bigger plan between the girl and her mother? Was Thirza outside now, waiting to finally take it all away from her?

'Where is she?'

The girl smiled happily back, clearly enjoying herself. 'You mean Thirza?'

'Yes, Emmie. Thirza. Where is she?'

'Thirza's dead, Vi,' she said.

She sat back, the wind taken from her in an instant.

She had assumed it, but knowing for sure . . . Thirza was dead.

'You didn't know,' said the girl.

Of course, she hadn't had it confirmed before. She'd always assumed that had to have been the answer to her silence: there was no way that Thirza could still be alive and leave her alone. Not for this long. But now, hearing it; knowing for sure. Dead? She had been so vast to her: so powerful in her work and strong with her fists. Until the Dentist, Thirza hadn't just been her mother: she had ruled her, trained her, owned her. Her world had been only Thirza.

It seemed impossible that someone so omnipotent should do something so pedestrian as die.

'I'm sorry,' said the girl, sounding genuine, and Mrs Wood looked up.

'When?'

'About this time last year.'

Last year? She had been alive all that time and she hadn't hunted her down and demanded her piece. Thirza had actually let her go when she disappeared. An ache filled her chest and she had a sudden vision of her, wizened and shattered by drink and poverty, a fetid figure dying down some back alley, picked over by strangers with no idea that she had once been the Great Thirza Thwaite.

Oh, Mam.

'When she wasn't in drink, she was kind,' the girl said. 'She taught me everything she knew. About Mediumship, about life and about you.'

But the girl was from Chatham. And she had left Thirza in Hull. 'How on earth did you even meet her?'

The girl shrugged. 'She'd been in Chatham a while before I met her. I think there had been a man involved.' Of course. 'She was living in a room with a grate that hadn't seen a fire in months,' the girl continued. 'We took her in, me and my mother. We did what you should've.'

'It's not as simple as that,' she said.

'Isn't it, though? You couldn't be associated with a woman like that once you were a woman like this.'

'She didn't tell you, did she. What she did, I mean. She didn't tell you that.'

'If you're talking about her ruin, then yes, she did. She used it to teach me the importance of details.'

'No,' she said. 'I meant that she didn't tell you about what she did to me. Her daughter.'

The girl raised an eyebrow. 'Other than giving you everything she had.'

Mrs Wood couldn't help the laugh despite herself. 'No,' she said. 'No, that's not what I meant.' She settled forward, holding the girl's eyes in hers. 'Would you like to know the truth?'

The girl mirrored her, planting her elbows on her knees. 'Yes, please.'

'When I was sixteen, the Great Thirza Thwaite sold me to a stranger. A dentist she met in a London public house. He had contacts who wanted Mediums, and she wanted money. So, she sold me. And then they took whatever I earned between them while he showed me around the country as his granddaughter, the aspiring Medium Violet Bell. No one asked why we shared a room wherever we went. I suppose they assumed it was economy. He was so charming and respectable – why would they think anything else?'

A flicker of revulsion had passed across the girl's face, but she held Mrs Wood's eyes. 'And Thirza knew everything. Of course she did.'

The girl gathered herself. 'Still, you did all right out of it.'

'This isn't Thirza,' she said, gesturing to the room. 'Thirza may have given me the foundations of Mediumship, but I am Mrs Wood through my own hard work. She was a reader, a good one, but she couldn't apport like I can. I learned to do that when I was free of her. I earned everything you see. All of it.'

'But without her introducing you to that man, wouldn't you still be stuck in Hull?'

'I worked for her from the moment I could make a noise on cue until that man died. She had taken everything I earned, everything I was until that point. I owed her nothing.'

The girl was about to speak, her face pinched in sarcasm, but Mrs Wood interrupted her.

'You know for all of her mistakes, she was a brilliant Medium,' she said. 'She could read people like that—' She snapped her fingers, and the sound echoed in the silent room. 'The way she was exposed . . . a woman of her calibre deserved better. If she were to be sunk, she deserved to be sunk in glory. But even in her ruin, she failed. Her foot tangling in a skirt at a society table. How ridiculous is that? She kept telling me it could've happened to anyone. Anyone inebriated, of course. Anyone complacent and careless enough with a false sense of one's own abilities.'

'You didn't have to stop supporting her, though. Who would have known?'

'Thirza sold me, Miss Finch. Do you understand what that means? She was my mother. But, to her, I was just another means to make money. When that dentist died, the transaction was complete, and I could finally shut the door on her. After everything, I earned that right.'

The girl gave a sad shake of her head. 'She talked of you all the time.'

'I'm sure she did.'

'Cried, often. You were her only child. She worried for you. Missed you.'

'Missed the money she had clawed from my back.'

The girl shrugged. 'Perhaps. But she was good to me.' The girl's tone had shifted, and Mrs Wood looked at her. 'My mother . . . she struggles. Thirza was our neighbour, and she helped me when Ma was poorly.'

In her whole life, she had never known Thirza to have an ounce of altruism and, for a moment, she allowed herself to wonder if she had mellowed in those final years.

'She even moved in with us when things were really bad. Then, stayed on when Ma was better.'

Perhaps not. 'Of course she did.'

The girl shook her head angrily. 'It wasn't like that. She was kind. She looked after me while Ma was working. Made sure I stayed on at school until I was ready, then she taught me all she knew. I was doing séances for money before I was thirteen. I was able to put food on the table and coal in the grate because of her.'

'You were able to feed her, Miss Finch. You stoked the fire that kept her warm. And I'm sure the odd tot of brandy.'

'And then she told me about you.'

She felt herself instinctively brace.

'She'd get in her boots and start talking on and on about this wealthy daughter she had. A real success, she said. The best Medium in London. At first, I thought she was making it up. I mean, she was kind, but she was in a bad way by then. I couldn't believe that her daughter would be living it up in town. I mean, what kind of person would you have to be to have wads of cash but leave your own mother homeless?

'But then she showed me a cutting, this fancy lady with all this hair and jewellery. A proper lady. No one would've put you two together, but I could see the family resemblance in the picture of you.' She swiped her finger in the air, pointing at her eyebrows. 'You are the spit across there.

'Then she started telling me that she could introduce us. "She owes me everything she's got," she told me. "If I ask her, she'll take you on. She'll make you as rich as she is.'"

'I'm sorry she did that.'

'She kept saying she'd write to you, but nothing ever happened...'

'Miss Finch, I've not heard from Thirza in years.'

'...In the end, I got tired of asking, so I came to London instead. I found anyone who would talk about you, tried to find where you lived, thinking that as soon as I told you who I was, who I had been taught by, you'd welcome me in with open arms. But then someone told me the other story. The one where you're this fancy girl from a rich family. You weren't the daughter of some ruined old Medium; you were the daughter of a doctor.'

Mrs Wood sank a little; how humiliating to have her own lie repeated back to her.

'So, I went back to Thirza. You're a liar, I said, and she started wailing, saying you were ashamed of her. That you changed your name and changed your story because you didn't want to have anything to do with her. So, I told her: You write to your girl and introduce me, or I'll tell the whole world what you've just told me. I'll ruin her too.'

The girl's face had become harder, her eyes smaller.

'I was so ready,' said the girl. 'I could feel it. I knew that if you met me, you'd see that too. And I'd have the future I know I deserve. But then ...' she gave a humourless laugh. 'The old baggage died before she could write the bloody letter, didn't she.'

She smiled. For all her posturing, the girl had no idea. Thirza would never have written that letter. Not in a million years. As soon as she had made good on the promise of connecting her little friend to someone more interesting, more powerful, she would've lost her bargaining chip. The whole time she needed warmth and food and drink, she would keep the promise alive. Of course, she would.

But now, because of Thirza, the girl was here and the threat was worse.

225

'What do you want?' she said.

'You know what it's like to grow up with nothing. To have to make a candle last a month or make fires from scraps of street coal and horseshit. To not know if you're going to eat that day. Thirza promised me that you would get me out. She promised me.'

'But I took you in without knowing any of this. You didn't need Thirza to become my pupil,' said Mrs Wood. 'So why are you bringing her up at all?'

'You're not so very different from your mother: you would never have taken me in if there hadn't been anything in it for you.'

'I liked you. I thought you had potential.'

'For yourself,' she said lightly. 'You thought I had the potential to help you.'

'Why does that surprise you? Why wouldn't there be something in it for me? I've invested so much time in you. Of course, I would expect a little something back.'

'But what?' she said with exaggerated confusion. 'What could I, a pretty young inexperienced Medium, ever do for you, the Great Mrs Wood?'

She stared back.

'Except perhaps keep you interesting?'

She gave a snort of indignance. 'I lost a client because of your inexperience. That's not the sort of interest I need.' She took another inhalation. 'What do you want?'

The girl smoothed her skirts. 'I want you to endorse me. To all of your patrons.'

'For what . . .'

'You're going to tell them that you've decided I'm ready to go it alone. And that they simply have to be one of the first to sit at my table.'

Mrs Wood couldn't help the laughter bubble in her throat. 'I'm not going to tell them any such thing, Miss Finch. Given half the chance, I shall be telling them entirely the opposite!'

'But . . . ' the girl blinked, a picture of innocence. 'Mrs Wood. I'm your pupil. You took me in. Introduced me to everyone. I've been into some of your most important patrons' homes. Imagine what they should say if we were to fall out.'

'They have known me too long . . .'

'Oh, I know, but imagine what they should say if, after all this time, they were told who you really are? Daughter of the Great Thirza Thwaite! Medium, Drunk, *Fraud*. I'm sure they'll remember her, and if they don't perhaps Mr Clore would be able to remind them all.' She paused. 'I wonder what happens to Mediums associated with frauds. What happens to their big old houses, all their fancy dress and all this nice, nice stuff? Their patrons?' She pulled a face. 'I mean, that would be bad enough.' She leaned forward. 'But could anyone ever trust a Medium again who wasn't only associated with a fraud but the *daughter* of one?'

'That's enough, Miss Finch.'

'Imagine the scandal: the Great Mrs Wood revealed to be nothing but a street Medium and daughter of the shameful Thirza Thwaite. My goodness! What would your patrons *do* if they were to discover the truth!'

'Enough!' Mrs Wood stood, her mind in chaos as she placed a hand on the mantel to disguise her furious trembling. She took a breath; her heart was steadying. She took another. She turned. 'How much will make you go away?'

The girl stopped and appeared to be considering it.

'How much do you think I'm worth, Vi?'

She blinked. 'You must have an idea,' she said, but the girl laughed and shook her head.

'Keep your money, Vi,' she said.

She looked at her. 'Surely we could come to a figure that . . .'

'I want your reputation, Vi,' she said firmly. 'I want everything you have.'

'And you could, Miss Finch,' she said in confusion. 'You're good.

227

You know that. Work hard. Remain unimpeachable. Prove your-self . . .' she trailed off as she saw Miss Finch flapping her hand dismissively.

'I don't want to wait years. I don't want to sit at lowly tables or put up with dull, penny-pinching widows before I get what I deserve.'

'I worked for all of this.'

'Of course you did.'

Mrs Wood set her jaw. The girl didn't know everything. She cleared her throat, concentrating on pulling herself together as she settled herself stiffly back into her chair. 'I've always admired your ambition,' she said evenly. 'I admired the passion you said you had for helping others. I thought that you saw it the way I did. I always assumed that you cared as much as I about the comfort Mediums can provide for those in—'

'All I'm asking is that you open doors for me, Mrs Wood. Just like you're already doing. But more. Sooner. I want to be on every-one's lips. I want them all to come and see me, Mrs Wood.'

Mrs Wood couldn't keep the laugh from erupting. 'You want me to do that for you? After all this?'

'It's hardly a stretch. I mean, you're already doing it,' she said with a sweet smile. 'I just want you to do more of it.'

'And if I don't?'

The girl stopped as though surprised by the question. 'What is there stopping me from telling everyone your truth?'

Mrs Wood steadied her hands in her skirts as her mind whirled. 'I have done everything right by you, Miss Finch,' she said as evenly as she could manage.

'You have. And I'm asking that you continue to do so. But at a greater pace now that we're being open with each other.' She leaned forward and patted Mrs Wood's knee. 'In some ways you must be grateful. Surely, after all these years, you've been considering with-drawing. Wouldn't I be the best choice to take your place?'

At that Mrs Wood gave a sharp laugh. 'I'm not withdrawing, Miss Finch. I couldn't, even if I wanted to . . .'

'Then I'll have no choice but to save your patrons from any future embarrassment. The truth will be better coming from me. I'll make sure that Mr Clore isn't too vicious towards you in the *Spiritual Times*. Perhaps you might be able to find a bit of work somewhere else. Up north, perhaps. Where they're less . . . discerning.'

'But why would they believe you? You're my pupil. Why wouldn't they just abandon you too?'

'Because I'll be the one who exposed the Great Mrs Wood for the cheat and the liar she is. I'll be the one who pulled the wool from their eyes and showed them that you're no better than your drunken fraud of a mother.'

The girl assumed a sudden expression of devastation, her eyes already swimming with tears. 'I never knew,' she whispered. 'Of course, I wondered when I was her pupil why she did not share the visions and visitations I had, but she was so . . . strict with me I dared not mention for fear of another thrashing.' Her voice gave a sad quiver as a tear slid, on cue, down her cheek.

'They wouldn't believe you over me,' Mrs Wood said finally, but she was shocked by the lack of conviction even she could hear in her own voice.

'It's up to you,' the girl said brightly, wiping the tear away with her little white hand. 'Do you want to go out as the Great Mrs Wood, or would you prefer to be remembered as a heartbroken fraud?'

Mrs Wood looked at her hands; her fingers had been working unknowingly on the skin around her thumbnails, and now red beads of blood leaked into her black skirts. She swallowed. 'If I do this, I don't want to hear Thirza's name again,' she said.

'As long as you stick to your side of the bargain, you won't.'

The girl's face had returned to sweet girlishness and she closed her eyes.

She had been so blinded by the girl's potential to reposition her own career, so distracted by her excitement around the girl's talent that she had forgotten to pay attention to everything else. She was a woman whose whole life had been spent reading even the most unconscious tells and yet she had missed all of this.

She had a sudden memory of Mr Larson, leaning in and asking, 'I mean, Mrs Wood, who is this girl?'

It transpired that the girl was a cuckoo. A viper.

Her downfall.

She looked up and gave a single, curt nod.

Mrs Wood had been felled by her own feckless fear.

CHAPTER 24

In the days that followed, a sense of paralysis spread over her like a fever, filling her ears and making her joints ache.

She was undone, broken.

And yet no one could know. She had to get up each day, put one foot before the other and curate séances, read clients and make the unthinkable real while being jolly and bright and clever and completely, completely normal.

The strain was immense, and she began to feel as though she were splitting into two distinct halves: one who continued to charm and delight, the other standing dumbly in its shadows like one of her spirits.

Miss Newman could see that something was wrong, but she had grown so busy with her society that when Mrs Wood – the charming, delightful half of her – simply smiled and insisted everything was fine, she couldn't press for long enough to get through the toughening facade.

Gradually, though, a new way of existing began to dawn on her. On the surface, nothing was changing. And she thought: as long as she smiled and agreed that the girl was good, she could simply carry on working without impediment. How was that any different to how she had been working before?

Illusion was, after all, her forte.

Mrs Wood rallied.

Her work could continue. She could survive.

'Yes,' she said to Mr Yurick when he enquired about a private consultation with the girl. 'I'm sure you would enjoy that. I'm actually offering these at my home on her behalf. Let me see what date suits you.'

'Oh, not to worry yourself, Mrs Wood. She gave me her details last week,' he said, pulling out a cream-coloured calling card with Miss Finch's name in a scrolling script on one side.

'Oh,' she said. 'How nice.'

'It says here: Mrs Wood's famous pupil.' He looked up. 'That's nice for you, isn't it?'

She smiled tightly. 'Then, of course, feel free to contact her.'

Her tables evolved but continued seamlessly; no one but the most attentive, or concerned, would notice: the shift in the balance between the two Mediums wavering imperceptibly until Tandy and Jack Starr were wreaking havoc in relatively equal doses. Mrs Wood might enter her patrons' homes first, but it was Miss Finch who would be the first to ask questions about their host's health and family.

A slow, inching move towards uninvited equality. Perhaps, Mrs Wood found herself thinking one quiet afternoon, this was what Miss Newman's work was doing on behalf of all womankind: creeping up on the patriarchy moment by moment, gesture by gesture so as not to raise a single red flag.

But she was still working, she reminded herself. She still had her stipends, and she was still the Great Mrs Wood. That was all she could care about until the girl disappeared again.

'It's good for you to share the pressure,' Miss Newman said after a session at the Countess's, where Miss Finch had delivered a successful close reading of one of the Countess's relatives which resulted in the relative asking for Miss Finch to see her privately. 'You can't be the Medium to everyone, Violet,' she said, which made Mrs Wood want to stamp her foot and tell her *of course I can!*

And then Mr Yurick cancelled his private consultations alto-gether, saying it was easier for him to get to Miss Finch's, what with his hip, and Mrs Wood had to stop herself from writing back and saying that she would miss neither him nor his wretched breath.

With Mr Yurick's regular consultations went his regular gifts.

And then Miss Cram wrote and said that Miss Finch had invited her to her home for a private consultation and she was very excited because she wondered what the girl could do out of Mrs Wood's shadow. 'I'd be more than happy to arrange this for you,' Mrs Wood wrote back, but no reply came and after that Miss Cram and her enthusiastic dogs dropped out of Mrs Wood's monthly schedule without any further word.

Despite her optimism, these were blows. Significant ones. The edge of panic began to permeate her set facade.

She had endorsed the girl, as she had promised. And then she had relied on her history with these people. She had thought that her reputation and years of proven experience would mean more to them than a flibbertigibbet.

The loss of Mr Yurick and Miss Cram reduced her.

She increased her conversations with Mr Larson. Why had she told him that she was able to support herself in the absence of Mr Wood's investments? Why had she been so pleased with herself – a woman who created her own income! – that she couldn't foresee what might happen if that income dried up? But when she intimated that a swift return would be preferable, he'd simply looked worried and told her that if she ever needed *help*, she need only ask. Which, of course, she could not.

Instead, she instructed Cook to purchase a single joint of meat a week from the Kensal Green butcher and to make it last, telling her that she wanted to reduce her waistline, and this was the method the Dowager used. She shut up the attic, moving Eliza and Cook to the back rooms on the first floor and changed the brand of sherry in the decanters.

With another Grand Séance coming up she sold an armoire from her dressing room that had belonged to Mr Wood's mother.

'I shan't miss cleaning that thing,' Eliza said as the men lugged it down the stairs. 'All them barley twists.' Mrs Wood touched her arm gratefully.

And Mrs Wood had looked around the dressing room with a bright smile and said, 'It feels so much larger in here now, don't you think?'

All was not lost, she repeated over and over and over to herself in the grimmest periods of the summer. Her most generous patrons remained by her side. The Dowager and her family. The Countess. Mrs Pepperdine. The Colonel and his wife. And the Greens, for whom she had been hosting tables almost as long as she had been in London. She continued to see them all regularly, as if nothing had happened. Sometimes, although rarely, even without the girl.

As summer slid away, her table séances continued but the girl took up so much space she found herself almost embarrassed by her own desperation to be heard.

At some point in September, Mrs Jupp had the gall to write after she had joined a Circle séance with Mr Larson, asking for Miss Finch's address. 'I can easily arrange a séance for you two if you would like,' she had responded, but she heard nothing back and then Miss Finch kept dropping into their conversations how lovely Mrs Jupp's home was. She had to swallow hard when Mrs Pepperdine – *Mrs Pepperdine* – told her that she was going to take her niece to see Miss Finch when she was in town: they were the same age and she felt that they would get along famously.

And then Colonel Phillips sent a letter splattered with port, letting her know that his wife was going to start seeing Miss Finch for her private consultations instead, as she reminded her of their lost daughter. 'Of course,' she had written back. 'Would you like me to be there to support her?' But apparently, they did not, because all she received in return from him was a birthday card addressed to someone else.

As summer gave way to autumn and the leaves in her garden

began to curl and yellow at the edges, with no other choice, she became a reformed optimist: wasn't it nice to have more time in the afternoons and evenings away from the dark. Her daybook *had* been very full for the previous years. Perhaps she had needed to shed a few lesser clients, she thought. After all, she could now enjoy the little things, such as watching the leaves change colour and quiet moments of reflection. And without needing to host all the time, those adjustments she'd been making had become hardly noticeable to her. So she had lost those few patrons. Mrs Pepperdine was a dull widow who would run out of money before she ran out of life. Mr Yurick was a half-wit. And Mrs Phillips . . . poor Mrs Phillips had always been a good client. But things move on.

It was all manageable, she thought as the nights grew longer, and she brought her woollen gloves out of the drawer; she had forgotten how cold the house became in the evenings when there was no one else there. But with Miss Newman barely stopping for supper these days before disappearing off to one of her society events, she was able to indulge herself in the rare silence. It was good for her, she thought as she sat alone, watching a meagre fire crackle and spit in the back parlour most evenings. Listening to the clock in the hall. Hearing carriages continue on past the front of the house. After all these years of hard work, she realised that perhaps she did need the odd afternoon and evening's rest. A period to restore herself so that she could come back, more vital than ever, once the girl's appeal had diminished and everything returned to normal.

Besides, it wasn't as though she didn't have anything to do: she still had her Circle. They kept her busy at least once a week. And she could rely on the loyalty of her closest patrons: the Dowager and Lady Harrington and Mrs Farnham and the Countess and the entire, wonderful household of Mrs Green.

Mrs Eileen Green
5 Orme Square

28th September 1873

My dear Mrs Wood,
Thank you so much for writing to offer a séance for Sheba's
birthday. I certainly do remember each table you've given us for our
girls' eighteenth birthdays – I laughed at your reminder of
Alexandra's where we had that visit from that funny old knight!

I have no idea why I have not let you know this before, an
oversight on my behalf that is unforgivable. However, and I am sure
you'll be relieved to know with all the other demands on your time,
we shall not need you for Sheba.

You know that Sheba and Miss Finch have become friends since
you introduced them all the way back in May. They are so near in
age it feels a little inevitable but, as I'm sure you're aware, it has
been cemented through the care and attention Miss Finch has given
her this summer: Sheba has suffered from nightmares for the past
few years (old hags, of all things) and Miss Finch has been a
tremendous help in managing those through private consultations.
She has been quite changed.

For that reason, Sheba asked if Miss Finch might host her
coming of age séance, and her father and I have agreed. The girls
feel so much calmer with Miss Finch in the room. I don't know if
you've noticed that. You must be very proud that it was you who
introduced her to us. We are very grateful that you did. She is
almost like family now.

Of course, you and Miss Newman are more than welcome to
come too. It will be held at our house on the 1st November at eight
o'clock. Do let Rhodes know if you are able to join us so that we
can ensure there are enough seats at the table.

We are now away in Lancashire visiting my husband's mother until the end of the month, but you must come for tea when I return, certainly before Christmas.

On this note, and I appreciate that it is rather delicate, I am sure you understand that I will need to place a hold on further gifts while we are not actually sitting together. We shall have no chance to see you for such a long time and Mr Green will not approve if I should keep it running. Going forward, I think a more ad-hoc arrangement would suit us better.

With greatest respect,

Eileen

CHAPTER 25

The loss of Mrs Green was something she could not ignore.

She wrote to Mr Larson with a very brief overview of her reduced income. He wrote back, telling her again that the ships would be here soon and that the best thing she could do was to stop supporting the girl. To which she lied and told him that she already had. She had wanted to, of course, but provoking Miss Finch with such conversation felt unjustifiably dangerous by that point.

The world was growing cold, but with hardly any visitors, she instructed that the grates remain empty in Chepstow Villas, convincing Eliza that it was another part of the Dowager's fashionable health ritual.

The Circle, along with Miss Finch, continued to come each week and, while she hated every second the viper was in her home, she did enjoy seeing her friends; with her more interesting patrons choosing private consultations with the girl, she'd been left with a sparse herd of dour widows and widowers for her consults who were far from fun.

But there was no avoiding the reality in the space around those moments when the gaps in her usefulness stretched wider and wider. And as September slid into October, she found her carefully cultivated optimism waning: the quiet evenings began to feel like prisons rather than holidays. Mrs Reynolds had given her an embroidery hoop when she had mentioned she wanted to take up a new hobby, but she had the fingers of a clown and the white linen was so dotted with blood she threw it in the fire after two long, painful afternoons trying to cross-stitch a daffodil for Miss Newman's Christmas present.

Instead, she sat alone, trying to read beyond the first line of a novel or stabbing out a tune on the piano or going through her linen cupboard. And all the while, no matter how hard she tried, her mind would drift to Miss Finch's own dark séance room. She imagined a single candle picking out the delighted faces of Mrs Green, Mrs Pepperdine, Colonel Phillips and other shadowy jewel-drenched sitters, all holding hands around the table she had bought the girl. She could almost smell the hot wax of the candle on the mantel, hear the sound of their captivated sighs and gasps as the girl manifested bouncing lights or apples or the voice of Miss Cram's mother, and it all felt so real she had to glance around to make sure she was alone.

What fun they would be having without her, she thought with acid growing in her stomach. What fun around the table she had purchased for the girl, in the chairs she had selected for her, their treacherous rumps settled on the blue jacquard seat cushions she had commissioned. What fun as they laughed their way home and wrote to all of their friends about how much they *admired* the girl. What a *talent* she was.

Couldn't they see how different the girl was to her? Couldn't they see that she had no moral fibre, no care and consideration for the people she worked with? Couldn't they see that she was hungry for one thing and one thing only?

Sometimes, when she had been left alone to think for too long, she would find angry little half-moons across the pads of her palms where her fists had balled so tightly to stop her from screaming at the injustice of it.

One evening, a week after a lack-lustre October Grand Séance where Tandy was rather too much, she spent a busy few hours driving herself mad. Somehow, she convinced herself that the reason why the Dowager hadn't responded immediately to her letter suggesting she visit for a séance with her family was due to her being, almost certainly, shifting to Miss Finch. The vision of them all sitting together without her became so colourfully real, that when Miss Newman still hadn't returned by the time Eliza shut up the house, she forced herself from the back parlour and onto the occasional chair in the hall to wait for her.

She couldn't go on like this.

She had to do something.

At just after ten, she sent Eliza to bed and sat in the shadows, waiting. At half past, she heard voices on the street outside. Miss Newman and a man. Through the side window, she saw her withdraw her arm from his and he tipped his hat, waiting as she climbed the steps and slid her key into the lock.

She started when she saw Mrs Wood, sitting in the dark on the chair where they usually kept packages and glanced over her shoulder. 'Good night!' she called to the figure on the street, and shut the door quickly, turning the key in the lock and dropping it into the china bowl on the console as she said, with forced jollity, 'Well, what a surprise!'

'Did you have a pleasant evening?' Mrs Wood asked.

'Yes, well . . . no. We were stuffing envelopes but it was worthwhile,' she said, tugging her gloves off and leaning to light the lamp that sat beside the china bowl on the console. 'It's very dark. Has Eliza gone to bed?' The lamp flared quickly, throwing a brash, chemical light onto the near vicinity and she looked startled anew when she looked at Mrs Wood. 'Is everything all right?'

'Was that your gentleman friend?' she nodded towards the street and Miss Newman flushed, turning away to remove her hat and hang it on the stand in the corner.

'He's a friend of the cause, Violet,' she said defensively, and shook the cloak from her shoulders. 'He lives on Blenheim Crescent so on the occasions we are at the society together he will walk me home. Don't go getting any ideas.'

'Was there anything else?' Miss Newman asked in the silence and Mrs Wood smiled.

'I was wondering,' she said, and Miss Newman narrowed her eyes, clearly readying herself for another volley of the kind she'd been receiving recently. 'I'm worried about our Grand Séances . . .'

Miss Newman looked taken aback. 'What do you mean?'

'I'm . . .' She paused, gathering herself. 'I feel as though they don't belong to us anymore.'

'But they're in your home.' She looked at her and Miss Newman finally gave a resigned nod. 'I can see why you'd think that.'

'We don't even have planning sessions on our own anymore . . .'

'With the girl . . .'

'Exactly. The girl.'

Miss Newman settled against the console. 'Things have changed,' she said. 'It was always going to happen when you invited her to join the Circle. I thought that's what you wanted.'

'It was,' she said. 'I assumed that once she had gained enough skill she would use her talent . . . elsewhere.'

Miss Newman laughed. 'I never took you for being naive, Violet.'

'I'm not!' she said.

'How could you ever think that once you'd given the girl access to all these people – all this *wealth* – she would simply pack up and go.'

She looked away. Being reminded of what a fool she had been was painful. Even if the girl hadn't turned to blackmail, would she have ever gone back to Chatham? 'I'd like us to plan something fun for the November séance.'

Miss Newman crossed her arms. 'Are you thinking something like the feathers?' she asked.

Mrs Wood gave a snap of a laugh. 'Goodness no!' she said. 'Absolutely nothing like that.' She saw Miss Newman smile. Good, she was thawing. 'I was thinking an apport. Of myself,' she said.

Miss Newman's eyes widened in surprise.

'Not to Holborn, of course. Something more suited to a Grand Séance: unforgettable but modest.'

'Which makes sense with your knee.' They shared a smile that gladdened Mrs Wood. How alone she had felt. How right it was to be with Miss Newman again. 'All right,' said Miss Newman with a nod. 'I'm supposed to be stuffing envelopes again tomorrow morning, but we could put our heads together after lunch? I shall give my apologies for the lecture in the evening. Someone else can put out the chairs for once.'

Mrs Wood leapt to her feet, her knee giving a pop so as not to be forgotten, and she reached for Miss Newman's hand. 'Is he a gentleman?' she said suddenly. 'The one who walks you home.'

Miss Newman dipped her chin in a way she had never seen her do before and gave the tiniest of shrugs, her eyes on the floor. 'He's just a friend,' she said eventually.

'Good,' she said and turned away.

Mrs Wood's Grand Séances had changed since the girl had turned the screws. She still held them on the first Tuesday of every month and the ballot winners continued to sit alongside her patrons. But now she shared the second half with the girl and she had to concede that some of the patrons in her chairs weren't there for her.

But November's Grand Séance was going to be different. November would offer up a little of the old Mrs Wood magic, and the thought cheered her immensely.

If the girl complained, she'd simply remind her that if her recommendation was to mean anything, she needed to remain of interest to the public's critical eye.

This thought had made her laugh: wasn't that why she had invited the girl to join her in the first place?

What she had not counted on, however, when she'd come up with her idea, was how rusted her body had become; it had been a while since she had moved herself quite so vigorously and her joints weren't as responsive as they once had been. Within a week of practice, she'd thrown her knee out twice and acquired a bruise the size of a dinner plate on her rear.

'We'll have to reduce the skirts,' Miss Newman had said late one Saturday night, straining beneath the heel of Mrs Wood's boot.

They had stolen into the garden to practise beneath the cloak of a bone-chilling starless sky, their breath pluming above them as they heaved and panted beneath the round, white moon.

'I keep catching the . . . hem,' said Mrs Wood.

'Precisely,' said Miss Newman, blowing a strand of escaped hair out of her eyes. 'It'll make finding your footing easier.'

'I'm coming down!' Mrs Wood landed awkwardly, and they stopped for a moment to catch their breath. Mrs Wood pressed her hands against the constraints of her stays as she shook out her sore leg. 'Perhaps we should do the magnolia,' she said, nodding towards the twisted trunk close to the house. 'I wonder if the distance is adding to the . . . complexities.'

'That one won't hold,' Miss Newman said with a frown. 'And you breaking your neck isn't quite the impression we want to give.'

They stood back, rubbing their arms and blowing on their finger-tips, as they looked up towards the beech's bough. Mrs Wood pushed the stepladder a few inches to the left with her foot and began another inspection of the trunk to check a new route. 'There's a nook here,' she said, sliding her hand onto a protrusion in the bark. 'If we place something . . .' She took a length of rope from the basket of odds and ends they'd placed on the garden bench, tossing the knotted end up and over so that it looped (after the third attempt) around the bough and secured the ends together. She yanked it tight to test its strength and smiled at Miss Newman. 'Ta-da.'

Miss Newman brought their lantern to the front of the tree and checked the view, returning to give a silent clap of her hands. 'Excellent work,' she said.

She felt good. Activity was good. Her body felt stronger and so did her mind, which was perhaps why she had found herself able to sit with Miss Finch at Lady Harrington's and Mrs Farnham's in the past week without too much irritation.

Because *this* was what she was good at. No. Not good. Brilliant. There was no Medium alive who could apport as well as her and on Tuesday evening she was going to remind everyone of what they had been missing. The feathers were a misstep. This was the *real* Mrs Wood.

CHAPTER 26

The house filled in its usual manner for her Grand Séance that November. She settled herself in *her* chair at the front of *her* séance room and saw all those familiar faces smiling back at *her* from the shadows. While she had to acknowledge that some of them were now there for the girl, there was the Dowager with Solange and Lady Harrington. There was Mrs Farnham beside Colonel and Mrs Phillips. And Mr and Mrs Reynolds, their shoulders pressed together. And the Countess, back from Italy at last. And Mrs Pickering and Mrs Preston in the middle row, heads craning to catch her eye. There was Mr Larson settling himself in beside dull Mrs Jupp after extinguishing the candles, and Mr Clore watching the girl intently from the front row.

This was what she did.

This was Mrs Wood at her finest.

The séance rocketed along. Miss Finch got a bit at the beginning, guided the guests at the table through a series of games and messages, her voice sliding between Tandy and her own. She had added dancing lights to her repertoire but it was frustratingly obvious to Mrs Wood that she remained enough for the room just being sweet, funny, *obnoxiously innocent* Miss Finch.

Still, she thought. They hadn't seen what she had prepared for them yet.

With Miss Finch settling back, some of the Circle chipped in with their visions, Mrs Hart's hand squeezing Mrs Wood's bloodless when Miss Brigham's highwayman popped by, and then Miss Finch had a few moments again and then, with an agreed rap on the table, the baton was passed finally back to Mrs Wood. After she'd delivered leaves and branches, emptying her bodice to make the necessary dashing about that was coming up much easier, a message appeared on a slate saying *beautiful autumn* and the table began to shake enthusiastically.

Mrs Wood gasped, asking for a candle to be lit on the sideboard so that she could look about her.

'Something is brewing within me,' she said breathlessly, surreptitiously sliding her slippers off beneath the table. 'The spirits are feeling playful. They are saying . . . they missed me?' She closed her eyes and her head lolled back as she let out a moan. 'Come,' she said, her chin rolling to rest on her chest, her eyes closed. 'What would you have me do?'

She paused.

The room was silent, everyone holding their breath.

She laughed, eyes still closed but her head upright now, facing the audience. 'I cannot do that! I am an old woman!'

'What?!' called Solange from the horseshoe of chairs. 'What can't you do?'

Mrs Wood stopped and opened her eyes, smiling. 'They want me to go for a run in the garden with them.'

The Colonel laughed loudly.

'You find the idea of such a sight funny, sir,' said Mrs Wood coquettishly.

He huffed and puffed an apology. 'I'm sure you would be perfectly . . .'

'Wait!' She held up her hand. 'No,' she said before listening to the air. 'No, I don't think . . . I've not done such things for a long while. I am out of practice . . .' Her hand remained raised to deter interruptions. Then she stopped and looked to Mr Larson, who was seated across from her at the table. 'They want the light out,' she said. 'They need all of my energy.'

He nodded keenly and snuffed the candle, throwing the room into a dark, twittering excitement.

'Please,' said Miss Newman. 'Mrs Wood requires silence for her energy.'

'No, that's good,' said Mrs Wood. 'These spirits like the noise. They're asking . . .' She hesitated in the expectant silence. 'They need energy. *I* need energy. Come!' She began to rub her feet upon the rug. 'They want us to rub our feet. Rub your feet on the floor!'

At first they rubbed their feet tentatively.

'More!' shouted Mrs Wood. 'It's working!'

The room was filled with the sound of feet whisking backwards and forwards on the rug, accompanied by a few strenuous grunts from the most committed.

And then, suddenly: 'We're doing it!' she called, her voice was rising in the room.

'What was that?' called the Countess. 'Is that . . . it's your skirt! Mrs Wood your skirt touched my cheek!'

'They've carried me up!' said Mrs Wood, her voice falling from the ceiling. There was a loud jangle from the chandelier 'Ouch!' she said. 'I didn't see that.'

As she climbed across the sideboard, she felt the turn of Miss Newman's elbow, ducking to avoid being clunked by the broom handle as it thunked across the ceiling above.

'I feel you moving up there!' said another voice. 'Slow down!'

Another tinkle of the chandelier. Another bump on the ceiling. 'Ouch! *Ouch!* Be careful!' she shouted. More bumps. 'They are so careless with me!'

The feet began to slow through distraction. 'Keep going!' shouted Miss Newman. 'If we lose the energy, she'll fall!'

Laughter, intensified whisking, bumping as Mrs Wood descended gingerly from the sideboard, holding her skirts she slipped towards the door in stocking feet. It was unlocked, as planned, and she waited for another burst of excitement before she wrenched it open, slamming it from the other side with a shocking BANG! that let off an avalanche of excited shrieks and exclamations, loud enough to cover any potential creaks or cracks as she bolted along the dimly lit corridor towards the back doors.

And then she was down the iron garden staircase, shoving her feet into the waiting slippers, the noise of confusion audible through the vast séance room window above, counting down as she pushed herself on towards the tree, the ladder and certain resurrection.

'Help!' she cried, levering herself precariously across the limb, dragging her skirt up as she lifted the aching knee into position. 'Help!'

A slow light began to glow around the edges of the séance room shutters, and the sound of distant confusion carried through the still night.

'Help!' she called again, louder now that she was better settled.

A shutter flew open and a rotund figure who could only have been Colonel Phillips was silhouetted against the room, peering through the glass.

'I'm here!' she shouted, waving her handkerchief from the tree. 'Colonel Phillips! It's me! I'm here!'

With a shout, he saw her and threw back the other shutter, pointing and gesticulating wildly in her direction.

'*She's out there*,' he cried to the gathering crowd behind him. More kerfuffle as her sitters clamoured over one another to see while Colonel Phillips bellowed through the glass. 'Stay there! Don't move!'

'Oh, I will,' she shouted back. 'They got me up here, but they won't get me down!'

'Hold on!' shouted Solange, gathering her skirts then disappearing. Out of view, she heard her shout. 'Unlock the door! Somebody open the door!'

And then, almost as though they were sucked out as a single entity, the séance room emptied and the crowd, led by Miss Newman, appeared at the back doors, throwing them open and clanging down the staircase into the night. Someone called for lanterns, which Eliza duly brought almost as though she had been prepared, and while the men fussed with them, Miss Newman hurried across the grass towards the tree, obscuring the stepladder, pushing it with her hip as she feigned assistance so that it slid away silently into the black shadows.

'Are you all right?' she whispered.

'I am perfect!' Mrs Wood hissed back.

The lanterns bobbed and bumbled down the garden until the crowd were beneath the tree, arms were raised aloft to try and tempt Mrs Wood down, but she stayed there, clamped to the bough as though in absolute fear. Eventually, a ladder was called for and Mr Reynolds found one in the store, staggering back towards the beech beneath its awkward weight.

It took several attempts to secure the ladder, Mr Reynolds innocently underlining that spirits were the only plausible explanation for her flight when he proclaimed: 'It's impossible to make it safe against this trunk!' But finally, the ladder was up and Mr Larson climbed a few rungs with his hand stretched out towards Mrs Wood, which she accepted gratefully.

'Thank you, dearest,' she said, her feet fishing around for the first step while the crowd beneath her broke out into spontaneous applause.

As soon as she was back on earth, the Colonel took charge of her well-being. 'Are you well? Do you require a doctor? Is anything hurt?'

'No, no,' she said, patting herself down. 'I appear to be all present and correct.'

'You went right through the window,' someone said.

'And all the way up into the tree,' said someone else.

'It's a miracle!'

She contained herself, making out she was far more tired than the throbbing adrenaline would ever allow, reaching out to Miss Newman for support. Solange and Mrs Reynolds clustered around and as they gushed with compliments, she threw glances over their shoulders and into the shadows, looking for Mr Clore. There he was, waiting at the back for her. He stepped forward as though he were about to say something, but the Dowager placed herself in her eyeline instead and steered her away.

'Mrs Wood, you are quite magnificent!' she said. 'But your spirits are really too naughty! Next, you'll end up on the moon and how shall we ever get you down from there?'

And then everyone laughed and began to turn back towards the welcoming, yellow light of the house. Mr Clore continued to dawdle and when she came near, he raised his brow towards her. 'What fun,' he said with a small smile. 'Clearly your spirits have learned from their previous error.'

She restrained her delight, excusing herself to wait for Miss Newman to join her.

'Well, that went well,' she said as she slid in beside her, an excited smile lighting her face like Christmas. Mrs Wood squeezed her arm close and then looked back up the garden.

'Let's have some more champagne,' she called after the group and some of them cheered. She looked at Miss Newman. 'Thank you,' she said, her throat suddenly thick with emotion.

Miss Newman squeezed her back. 'Time to celebrate,' she said, and they began to follow everyone towards the house. 'Your knees held up.' And Mrs Wood laughed. 'You know, I'll eat my hat if you're not back on the front page come Thursday morning.'

As they began to climb the staircase that led back into the house, she saw the girl waiting at the top with a flat, humourless smile.

'You go on,' she said to Miss Newman, who hesitated. 'Really. Make sure they've all they need.'

As Miss Newman disappeared, the girl took her arm.

'You didn't think to include me?' she hissed.

'Hush now. You know as well as I that I have no say over what the spirits will do.'

The girl glared. 'Tandy has been bothered by a terrible old lady on the Other Side recently. And she's had some truly shocking things to say.'

Mrs Wood kept her composure. 'This is what I do, Miss Finch,' she said, her voice as light as she could keep it. 'Surely it's in your interest for me to have these moments. Otherwise, what's the point of me?' The girl's eyes didn't shift. 'Come. They'll be wondering where we are,' she said, and extended her elbow towards her. 'Let's close the table and then everyone can go home excited by the work we've done tonight.'

She could sense the girl's hesitation, but a gust of laughing conversation came from inside the house and her face suddenly softened and she was a sweet girl again. She slid her arm into the crook of Mrs Wood's arm and patted it, as though she were an elderly relative. 'Well,' she said loudly as they stepped over the threshold together, 'I do hope those spirits weren't too rough with you. You are far more delicate than you look!'

'They were a touch,' she said, matching the girl in tone and volume. She was rubbing her back with her hand and said, as they entered the séance room: 'I hope they don't do that again for a long time!'

And she smiled as her guests all protested vehemently that they absolutely hoped for the opposite. 'It's like old times,' the Dowager said. 'I had almost forgotten quite how marvellous you were when the spirits take hold of you.'

Before Mrs Wood could say anything, her arm was squeezed by another guest and then the Countess's brooch spiked her chest as she pressed an enthusiastic kiss onto her cheek. She turned and a feather was in her face. Turned again into a cloud of Mr Humboldt's acrid breath.

But there it was: the adoration in all of their eyes.

It had been worth it.

Just as she knew it would.

MEDIUM PREDICTS WE SHALL SEE A FULL SPIRIT IN LONDON BEFORE THE YEAR IS OUT!

Front-page story
Spiritual Times, 6th November 1873

Exciting news has reached our ears directly from the bird's mouth. Miss Finch, that is. Yes, we have it on excellent authority that Miss Finch, London's favourite new Medium who began her public life at the table of one of our longest-serving Mediums, Mrs Wood, has been working closely with her spirit guide, known as Tandy, to bring her forth to a room, *in the flesh*.

You have heard correctly!

Miss Finch has been assured by Tandy that together they will present her to us in the materialisation of a full spirit.

The first this country will ever have seen!

And she has said, with charming and, if we may say so, typical enthusiasm, that she believes this will occur before Big Ben takes us into 1874.

Miss Finch, we remain humbled by your masterful gift.

Anyone wishing to apply for a seat at Miss Finch's table can now also apply directly to her via our dear editor, Magnus Clore. Form an orderly queue, please, ladies and gentlemen!

From The Séance Roundup
pg26, Spiritual Times, 6th November 1873

Mrs Wood conducted her usual monthly Grand Séance (alongside Miss Finch) on Tuesday night, where she was lifted into a tree by some playful spirits. We wish her well in her recovery.

CHAPTER 27

They sat for a while in the silence of the drawing room, the clock ticking in time with Mrs Wood's heart.

The girl, overdressed and late, sat in Miss Newman's chair on the other side of the fireplace, fiddling with an elaborate curl as she blinked and smiled inanely.

'It's true then?' she said eventually, and the girl's smile slid to one side and the dimple in her left cheek deepened.

'What do you mean?' she said, her eyes playful.

'That's what you told him?'

She swiped some unseen dust from her skirt. 'Mrs Wood, I have no idea what you're talking about . . .'

'*Clore*,' she said, her voice a thunderclap and the girl sat up, the smile faltering. 'You really told him you were going to materialise a full spirit?'

'I did.'

'But why?'

The girl rolled her eyes and dropped back impatiently into the chair. 'Because that's what I'm going to do. Why? You think I can't?'

She breathed to control the pounding pulse in her neck, working hard to keep her face unreadable. 'I'm surprised, that's all,' she said.

Well. That wasn't entirely true. She'd been surprised that after all her hard work – after the pain, the bruises and the gash she'd discovered on her shin when she had undressed the evening of the tree apport, she had been surprised that Mr Clore had chosen not to flourish an exaltation of her brilliance across his front page.

Furious, disappointed. Flummoxed, even.

But she had not been surprised that the girl had purposefully trumped her, only that it was with the promise of a full spirit materialisation.

There was something warmly foolish about the suggestion that made her feel almost sorry for the girl.

Almost.

'So, you have until Christmas to bring Tandy out.'

'The New Year,' she said.

'You think, after less than a year of working in London, you're capable of materialising a full spirit? Safely?'

'Yes,' she said slowly, mimicking Mrs Wood's tone. 'I do. And I'm having my own cabinet built as we speak to prove it.'

Mrs Wood put her hands up. 'I cannot be a part of this anymore, Miss Finch,' she said. 'I have not and will not be associated with a Medium who performs such silly spectacles. You will be exposed and that will hurt the people who have come to trust you. I cannot support such behaviour. I cannot be associated with a fraud, you know that, Miss Finch.'

'*Au contraire!*' the girl said, and laughed. 'The Countess de Livigne taught me that,' she said. 'It's French.'

Mrs Wood blinked back.

The girl shrugged. 'It means *on the* contrary.'

'Thank you.'

The girl smiled. 'And I'm saying that because you *have* been associated with a Medium who was exposed as a fraud. Haven't you.' In an instant, the girl closed her eyes and dropped her chin to her chest, rolling it side to side as she growled: '*Vi, love. 'Ow could yer forget meh? I'm 'urt. I'm really 'urt . . .*'

'That's enough, thank you.' But she gripped the arms of her chair to keep herself still, forced herself to calm as the girl opened an eye and smiled.

'So, you do remember your poor old *mam*, then.'

'You're more like her than you even know,' Mrs Wood said finally, and the girl gave a snort.

'Me and Thirza? I'm flattered but . . .' the girl said.

'Did you learn nothing from her? It was ambition that made her careless. Is that what you want too?' She leaned forward, her hands resting on the girl's knees. 'Don't do this,' she said. 'Don't take advantage of your new position. You're good, *Emmeline*.' The girl looked up at the sound of her name. 'You know that. *London* knows that. Remember what you told me? You said that you wanted to help people. You wanted to make a difference to them. You can still do that, you don't need silly gimmicks to be successful.'

'It was gimmicks that furnished this house, though, wasn't it? Or was your big Flight all part of your lifelong need to help? How is a spirit materialisation any different?'

'I cannot in good conscience allow a fellow Medium to take advantage of other people's vulnerability.'

The girl gave another snort. 'Dearest, isn't that what we do?'

The air went from Mrs Wood for a moment. 'Is that what you think *I* do? You think I take advantage of people? I do exactly the opposite. I *help* people, Miss Finch. I ease their suffering. I hold their hands through the darkest days of their lives. Without me, my patrons, my followers, they would have no outlet. No place to go where they felt safe to be vulnerable. I don't take advantage of that. I take it very seriously. Just as a physician cures those who are sick through disease, I cure those who are sickened by grief and loss.'

'So that's what all your flights and feathers do, is it? *Help the vulnerable*.' The girl gave a smile that so incensed her it took all of Mrs Wood's strength to keep from slapping her face.

'Are you a fool?' she said, her jaw rigid. 'They are my evidence. Those events prove to my sitters that I am real. That the spirits trust me. That *they* can trust me. Without spectacle in the light, there would be no belief behind closed doors.'

'Well then,' said the girl, unruffled. 'A full spirit will have to be my evidence.'

'But that's not evidence. That's a performance. The spirits speak through me. They act through me. I am their conduit and everything I do is about fostering that relationship. Dressing up, presenting yourself as a spirit is none of those things. It's about you and you alone. Not your sitters or their grief. You.'

There.

It was out.

The wall between them was gone.

Miss Finch inhaled slowly, her eyes settling lazily on Mrs Wood. 'And yet,' she said. 'It's what people want. Have you lost touch so much that you don't understand that?'

She looked at the girl. The jut of her jaw, the set of her shoulders. Those insolent eyes. What had she done?

'I'm afraid, as you insist on continuing with this ridiculous stunt, I will have to relinquish my financial support.'

'And Thirza will . . .'

'Oh, stop it, Miss Finch. You don't need me anymore. Do you really need my patronage that much? Why risk tarnish through association with a fraud? You're clearly doing very well on your own, aren't you. From what I see in the *Spiritual Times* it appears that way.'

The girl thought for a moment, her hands rubbing on the wooden ends of the armchair. 'Well,' she said eventually. 'I suppose I make ends meet. And if I'm stuck, I can always ask Humboldt. He's very helpful. And there's Magnus . . .' She paused and gave Mrs Wood an amused look. 'I mean Mr Clore, you know.'

'Remember what I've said, Miss Finch. Be careful who you take private patronage from.'

The girl smiled. 'P'raps you wouldn't've needed me quite so much if you'd had the good sense to secure yourself a private patron on Mr Wood's passing.' The girl gathered her skirts and stood, revealing a peek of her soft leather winter boots, different from the ones she had worn to the Grand Séance the previous week. She noticed Mrs Wood looking and turned her ankles. 'My gentleman does like to spoil me,' the girl said.

Mrs Wood busied herself standing and arranging her own skirts.

'I shall see you at Saturday's Circle then,' the girl said.

'Indeed,' Mrs Wood replied, tugging in quick succession on the bell-pull for Eliza to come with the girl's belongings as quickly as possible.

'Lovely,' the girl said as Eliza appeared, breathing hard, practically shoving the cloak, hat and suede mittens onto the girl.

She watched her dress for the steely winds outside, the noise of her mindless chatter a small, winged insect fighting a windowpane.

She had never, even in the worst days, met anyone more repellent in her life.

CHAPTER 28

She was not in the mood for the Circle on Saturday afternoon. The house had been quiet, mostly empty, since Miss Finch had left on Thursday morning and she had found herself losing interest in anything more than stewing, irritated even by the few consultations she still had.

From the moment she woke that morning, she resented the fact that soon her hermitage would be filled with noise and bodies, and she would be forced to entertain.

Miss Newman swept in late from a morning with her society. She rushed to the lunch table, apologising, before grabbing a slice of bread and butter and excusing herself to freshen up ahead of the Circle's arrival at two. Once more alone, Mrs Wood finished her own plate and went into the séance room, taking her time to light the candles, close the shutters and draw the curtains. This had been Miss Newman's responsibility before she became so distracted by her cause, and she felt a stab of resentment with each strike of the match and rearrangement of a chair.

Eliza came in, bustling with hot water and teapots, and she suddenly felt close to her; as though the past fifteen years had never happened and she was as low as she had been born. She imagined herself, stuffed into a maid's uniform, bobbing and scuttling in deference (not that Eliza ever did either of those). She moved next to her, looked at her hands as she set out the teacups and saw how they were worn raw by carbolic and scrubbing brushes. She held her own pale fingers out tentatively. Flexed the joints and imagined them cracked and weeping like Eliza's.

'It's jam tarts,' said Eliza, and Mrs Wood jumped away with a start. 'For tea,' she said. 'Cook's done jam tarts.'

'Oh,' she said, shoving her hands behind her back as though Eliza had any idea of what she was doing. 'I'm sure they'll enjoy them,' she said, then hesitated. 'There's some ointment on my dresser,' she said. 'For your hands. In the green glass pot. Feel free to use it.'

Eliza eyed her. 'What's wrong with my hands?'

She flushed. 'Nothing,' she gabbled. 'I just thought . . . If you ever wanted . . .'

But Eliza was already at the door. 'I'll bring the tarts up. Or would you prefer I keep myself and my revolting hands out of sight?' She left the room oozing disapproval, leaving Mrs Wood alone with her embarrassment.

The room now smelled of hot wax and sweet tea.

A fine thread of web, cluttered with dust, drifted weightlessly across the ceiling, its line thrown in shadowed relief across one corner.

All these little things she had never stopped to notice before.

All the little things that would be obliterated as soon as . . .

The front door rattled loudly.

. . . they arrived.

It was as though she were trapped in a henhouse.

Noise, noise, noise as the ladies, including the girl, shed voluminous winter layers onto poor Eliza; clucking and squawking around the sideboard, crumbs cascading from mouths to bosoms to her carpets, tea slopping in cups, dripping into saucers. Her head felt like wet sand, the voices thudding uselessly against her understanding, a cacophony that she couldn't decipher.

Miss Newman was taking too long to return from her room, and the sisters were looming, their words sounding like a string of pearls, and she raised her hands in submission and said, above the din, 'I just . . . I need to . . .'

As she fought her way from the crowd, her heart was pounding, her mouth dry.

She tried to swallow but her throat was so parched she gagged instead and gave a sudden gasp for air that she couldn't seem to find.

Was she dying?

She found her way into the drawing room, panting as she reached for the back of the duck-egg sofa. Her hands were wet and shaking as she clutched the rough damask linen, tremors racked her body, her knees barely keeping her upright as she fought for each breath.

She was dying.

She had to be.

Was this what it had felt like for Mr Wood? This white-hot terror?

She tried to sob at the horror of it all, but it caught in her throat and made her choke again.

And then she was aware of someone behind her, but she couldn't let go of the sofa.

She gulped, slumped forward. Her heart was a taut, frenetic drum in her throat, her ears, across the surface of her skin.

And then there was a hand. A familiar hand; red, scuffed, reaching for her.

She clutched at it. Watched it turn as white as her own in her grip.

'I can't . . .' she gasped. 'I can't . . .'

'Here,' Eliza said, her voice quiet and calm beside her ear. 'You take a seat here. I'll get you a tot of something.'

But she grabbed for Eliza's arm. 'Don't leave me,' she said. 'I . . . I don't want to . . .'

She gave an easy laugh. 'I'm only going to the sideboard.'

She settled Mrs Wood on the sofa, instructing her to keep breathing, and as the world steadied in her vision, she watched as

Eliza poured out a deep glass of sherry, the crystal decanter's stopper tinkling in the quiet of the room as she replaced it.

And then Eliza's chapped hands were in front of her again, holding the glass. 'Here you go. The sun's over the yardarm, so it's allowed.' She looked up and Eliza winked at her.

She took a sip. And another. With each shaking breath, she sipped, until she found her heart begin to quieten.

She wasn't dead, she realised as the trembling in her arms and legs began to dissipate. She finished the glass in her shaking hands; felt the heat of it in her chest.

'There you go,' Eliza said. She had settled on the coffee table, leaning forward on her arms, the keenness of her eyes the only sign of concern. 'Keep breathing.'

She heard a laugh from beyond the room and jumped, turning too quickly towards the door before dropping back against the sofa in relief. Eliza must have closed it.

'Course,' she said when Mrs Wood looked at her. She smiled. 'A funny spell like that don't need to be shared with friends.'

She breathed again, holding tight to her tears. She was not going to cry in front of Eliza, no matter how surprisingly kind she had been. 'Was that what that was?' she said, shivering as though the room were an icebox. 'A spell?'

Eliza shrugged. 'What my old ma used to call them,' she said. 'But who knows.'

'Do I need a doctor?'

She shrugged again. 'Perhaps,' she said. 'Do you want me to fetch Dr Hamble?'

She thought again of the Circle, blathering away in her séance room, and imagined their faces when that hairy old curmudgeon arrived out of the blue. Imagined the story Miss Finch would tell Mr Clore at one of their increasingly regular suppers. 'No,' she said. 'I feel much better already. Thank you.'

There was a knock on the door, and she was about to call out that she needed a moment, when it clicked open and Miss Newman popped her head around. 'Is everything all right?' she asked. 'The ladies said you were looking for something.' She stopped, her face dropping, closing the door behind her and rushing across the room. 'Good God. Violet? Are you ill? You look dreadful!'

'She's fine,' said Eliza, standing and brushing her skirts. 'Touch of indigestion.'

'I felt a bit dizzy,' she said. 'That's all. I thought it best to sit for a moment.'

Eliza picked up the empty sherry glass. 'I'll take this,' she said, her tone, her movement, everything as bland as if nothing had ever happened.

Miss Newman slid onto the sofa beside her. 'You look awfully pale,' she said. 'And you're shaking.'

'I'm fine,' she said, concentrating on keeping her fingers still. 'Really. I am.'

'Violet, I've been thinking . . .'

A ball appeared in her stomach Miss Newman's tone was so serious, so heavy. So different. 'I'm fine,' she said.

'You need a holiday. Take some time away. I can look after the house. This year has been—'

'No,' she said, shocked at how desperate she felt at the thought of going away, not being in the house. Being truly, truly alone. 'No. Please. I'm perfectly well. It was only a funny spell.'

'Miss Finch can always manage things for you while you're gone. I'm sure she'd be happy—'

'No.' She snapped her skirts. 'Absolutely not!' But her resolution was instantly exhausting, and she wavered standing. 'This is *my* Circle, Sarah,' she said, but she swayed again and when Miss Newman reached out to steady her, she clung to her outstretched arm for a moment before she cleared her throat and walked carefully away. 'Don't fuss,' she said over her shoulder. 'I'm absolutely fine.'

But she wasn't.

She was able to sit with the Circle, smile, engage somewhat, but while she appeared recovered, she was overwhelmed by sudden flashes of memory and she kept her hands in her lap to stop the table from seeing the tremors that shook her every so often like aftershocks.

She tried to move into a trance, but her mind wouldn't stay still long enough to do anything more than follow the voices of the rest of the Circle.

'Thank goodness for Miss Finch,' Miss Newman had whispered when the Circle closed and everyone got up for their cups. 'While you're not feeling quite the ticket, it must be a relief knowing there's another talent nearby to support you.'

'Don't let Mrs Hart hear you say that,' she said, turning her gaze to her Circle, watching as they milled around the fresh tea-things, watched them pour tea for the girl, load her plate with tarts, fill her up with compliments. How could they not see, she thought, watching the girl eat the attention up. How could they not see her for what she was?

Her knees felt soft and unreliable. 'Ladies,' she called. 'Could someone make me a tea?'

'Of course,' said Mrs Reynolds, reaching across the group of ladies to commandeer the pot.

'What's wrong with you?' asked Miss Brigham.

'I've had a very busy week.' The lie was easy and she smiled lightly as Mrs Reynolds fluttered to her side, carefully placing a cup of tea before her, a pink wafer finger in its saucer. 'Thank you, dearest,' she said, looking up, and Mrs Reynolds flushed and sat in the chair beside her, sliding her own cup over from her seat across the table.

'You seemed quiet today,' she said. 'I was going to ask . . .'

'Honestly,' she said, patting her hand, which she had rested on her forearm. 'I'm quite well. I promise.' She sensed the sisters hovering nearby and turned to look up at them. 'Yes?'

The sisters shared a glance. 'Well,' said Laetitia, sitting quickly in the vacant chair on the other side of Mrs Wood while her sister had to make do with the one further along. 'Well, Hyacinth and I have been talking—'

'It's just a thought—' interjected Hyacinth, bobbing about, frustrated by having to sit, obscured.

'And we had that conversation, didn't we?' Mrs Wood saw Laetitia look at Miss Finch, who remained at the sideboard, and noticed the smile flicker in her eyes.

'We did?' she said.

'Yes, don't you remember? About . . .' she looked at her sister, then at Mrs Wood. 'We were wondering if perhaps, with it being so cold and everything, we could hold some of the Circles at Emmeline's.'

She fixed her face in a half-smile. 'Miss Finch's?' she said, blinking.

'Yes,' said Hyacinth. 'We know that we've always come to yours, but . . .'

'That's not a bad idea,' said Miss Brigham. 'Especially when it gets icy.'

'That's what we were thinking,' said Hyacinth. 'For us, and for you, Miss Brigham, it's but five minutes' walk to Emmeline's home rather than—'

'But what of me?' said Mrs Reynolds. 'And Mrs Wood and Miss Newman? We shall have to travel . . .'

'Your sort can afford to take cabs,' Miss Brigham said, without a hint of embarrassment.

'But we've always held our Circles here,' Mrs Reynolds continued, her gentle voice rising an octave. 'It wouldn't be the same if we—'

'Makes no odds to me,' said Mrs Hart. 'If it did, we'd be holding them at mine. My home is much larger, and you have no idea how hard it is to get away some days—'

'Miss Finch?' Mrs Wood's eyes were on the girl. 'Do you have any thoughts?'

The girl smiled sweetly. 'Laetitia and Hyacinth mentioned it to me the other day, but I told them that I wouldn't consider it without your blessing. This is your Circle, Mrs Wood. I have no hope of hosting to your standard, nor do I have any desire to remove your wonderful friends from this wonderful room.'

'Of course you don't,' she said.

'It's such a nice place, too,' said Laetitia. 'She's made it very cosy.' Was that a slight? From an *Adams* sister? She had been trying so hard to keep up appearances with a fire in the séance room when the Circle came, but perhaps it was no longer enough to chase the toughest chills away now that winter was near.

'I'm so glad you find it agreeable,' she said, biting back her anxiety.

'Oh yes,' she said. 'She's got such nice taste. We're regulars now, aren't we Emmeline!'

She continued to smile as magnanimously as possible. 'It sounds as though this is something you all want,' she said.

Miss Brigham gave a shrug, and Mrs Hart said, 'If we're offering rooms, you could consider my second drawing room. It's much bigger . . .'

'Don't you think it would be fun?' Hyacinth said, glancing between Miss Finch and Mrs Wood.

'I won't do it unless you agree,' said the girl. 'I told the ladies that I would not hear of making any changes without your permission.'

Of course she did. Mrs Wood held the smile as firmly as possible. 'If you feel that this would work better for you, then you should go ahead.'

'We could alternate,' said Hyacinth. 'One week Emmeline's, one week yours.'

'Yes!' said Laetitia. 'It would be a shame not to come to your home anymore,' she said. 'I would miss your cakes far too much!' And she gave a merry trill of a laugh, rousing the rest of the room so that Mrs Wood had to join in or expose herself.

'Well,' she said, her voice settling the Circle. 'I suppose that's agreed then. Miss Finch?'

'It sounds like a very good plan. I know I shall enjoy hosting, but please don't expect such treats as you receive here – I have no cook!' she gave a little sideways glance. 'Yet!' And the sisters laughed again.

The only thing she wanted now was them all out.

'Ladies,' she announced, 'I am sorry, but I have a consultation coming this evening, and I really must prepare.' Another easy lie that no one would, of course, even begin to question.

As the Circle slowly peeled away, pressing kisses onto her cheek and warm squeezes to her hands, she felt like a cypher, so faint and insignificant that even the slightest breath would turn her into dust.

CHAPTER 29

'I hear you're ill,' said Mr Larson, standing in the hall with his hat in his hand, Fox wriggling at his feet.

Mrs Wood had come from the back parlour, where she had been reading the same first line of a Braddon novel over and over again, just as he arrived with Fox in tow. The surprise of seeing someone made her flustered, and she was suddenly acutely aware, and mortified, that he had stumbled upon her wrapped in two old woollen shawls with a knitted hat perched on her head like a tea cosy.

'Who told you that?' she said, snatching the hat off. 'There's nothing wrong with me.' She fluffed her hair briskly with her fingers.

'That's what I said. I've never known you to be anything but hearty with health.'

She gave a curt nod. 'Thank you,' she said, but he didn't move and she felt a pulse of panic. 'Is there a problem with the investments?'

'No. No. All is progressing. Not as quickly as you would like, I know. But as I've said we must . . . Are you sure you're all right, dearest? You do look a bit . . .' He squinted at her as though she were being appraised for sale.

'Mr Larson?'

'You need some fresh air,' he said, finally.

'I have things to do about the house.'

'The air is quite warm, warmer than in here anyway. And you're looking almost grey, Violet. A walk is what you need.'

She waved her hand dismissively, but he persisted, lurching down the hall towards her, Fox straining to remain as close to the door and the promise of a walk as possible.

'Get your things. We'll walk up to Kensington Gardens and back.'

He was in front of her now and she felt a sudden, awkward heat. It wasn't that she'd been avoiding Mr Larson, but here he was, his shoulders a straight line against the light from the windows beside the front door. His long, pale face scrutinised her, so close that she could see the delicate creases that spread from the corners of his eyes like a sunrise and some forgotten bristles near his left ear. She swallowed and turned away. She had been lonely, but this was Mr Larson, she reminded herself. There were limits.

'I can see you won't be deterred,' she said.

'I promised Mr Wood I would keep you well. I cannot allow you to wither away in here, Mrs Wood,' he said. 'Human beings need fresh air. Lots of it.'

They walked in silence for a while, Mr Larson taking great, unperturbed strides while she turned talking points over in her head that wouldn't find their way to her tongue. Every so often Fox would sniff at something, perk up his ears unexpectedly, bark at a bird, but apart from acknowledging the strangeness of the dog, they walked on in silence.

Westbourne Grove was busy beneath the white sky. Carriages, carts and cabs rattling around lumbering omnibuses and street sweepers and costermongers with death wishes; the tinkling call of the shop bells, determined shoppers hurrying past the gold-lettered window of the Italian barber, the jewel-coloured display of Maison Nouvelles, the overwhelmingly-cluttered window of the ironmonger and the florist with buckets and buckets of blooms. Ahead, the clock on Whiteley's department store read twenty past two. Had it really grown that late? What had she been doing all day?

'Let's get off this madness,' Mr Larson said suddenly and took her elbow, turning her from the thrum of commerce into the welcome peace of Garway Road, where the stationer's on the corner gave way to grand, porticoed homes and birdsong and a smart pavement planted with flimsy plane trees.

Their feet tap-tapped in the cool air as they walked towards the looming spire of St Matthew's and Kensington Gardens.

'I heard something else,' he said, as though they had been in the middle of a conversation all along. 'About the girl.'

'You mean Miss Finch,' she said with a sagging sensation. Wasn't there ever anything else to talk about?

'Of course,' he said. 'I haven't been able to find the right time . . .'

She smiled. 'So, you had an ulterior motive for this walk?' And he gave an uncharacteristic laugh.

'It's always a pleasure to walk with you, dearest,' he said, and she couldn't help her heart turning a little.

She watched her toes pop from beneath her skirts as she walked. 'I'm gathering you've heard that the Circle will be going to Miss Finch's every so often.'

He nodded. 'I did,' he said. 'Aside from the fact that I was not told in person, I was also surprised that you had agreed.'

She gave a smile. How she envied his innocence.

'I don't believe we have ever met, the Circle, I mean – anywhere but at yours.'

'We haven't,' she said, her eyes ahead.

'So, what's prompted the change?'

'Oh, you know,' she said. One foot in front of the other. 'The Adams sisters and Miss Brigham, of course, they thought it might be more convenient.'

'*Convenient?*' he said. 'This isn't a public outing.'

'They live near the girl, Mr Larson. It's not unreasonable . . .'

'But it's your Circle, dear. Of course it's unreasonable.'

She couldn't resist patting his arm. 'Things change, dearest,' she said. 'And I don't feel I have the energy to fight them at the moment.'

Fox was suddenly immovable, sniffing around a stone balustrade before settling into a squat. They politely turned their backs, and while he was looking at her, she kept her eyes trained on the steeple ahead. 'There's something between the two of you, isn't there,' he said, frowning. 'I can't work out any other explanation for you to willingly allow Miss Finch to become so dominant amongst your own people.'

'Don't be silly,' she said with a forced laugh. 'You're being dramatic.'

'This isn't like you. Private séances, I understand, but to even contemplate sharing your public table with an unknown seemed out of character from the start. But now, to almost give it up—'

'I haven't given it up!' she said. 'That's not what's happening at all.'

'What does this girl have over you?' he said, and her eyes flew to him.

'What are you talking about?' *What have you heard?*

He held up his free hand. 'Forgive me. I don't mean to be so familiar,' he said. 'But . . .' Fox had finished, and Mr Larson paused to kick the mess into the gutter. He flicked the lead and they began to walk on. 'It has made me wonder.'

What would happen if she told him?

'I'm sorry if I offended . . .'

'I'm doing a good deed,' she said. 'That's all. And it's helping me out too. I've been so busy since Mr Wood passed on. I feel as though I haven't had a moment to myself.'

She could feel him looking at her, sensing his mistrust of her words. What did he want? She couldn't help an instinctive smile twitching the corner of her mouth. What would he say if he knew? What would he say if he knew that the thing Miss Finch had over her was the truth? She stole a glance at him. His head was tilted, his eyes sharp with concern. She imagined how he might look at her when he realised she was lower than Miss Finch; that the Great Mrs Wood was the daughter of a charlatan and a fraud. That everything he thought he knew about her was a lie.

She looked away. 'It will work itself out,' she said, forced to raise her voice as they drew closer to the noise of Bayswater Road. 'You'll see.'

'I hope so,' he said, taking her elbow as they came out of the side road, gently protecting her from the chaos of traffic before them. 'It's your table I want to sit at. No one else's.' He stopped, squinted across the road. 'Isn't that . . .' He craned around a gig, trotting at snail's pace. 'It's . . . *Mrs Hart!*' he shouted. 'Mrs Hart!'

She peered in the direction of his gaze and he was right. Mrs Hart, in a long purple coat and huge purple feathered hat, hesitated – she was turning into the Coburg Gate with a stooped woman dressed in grey and black, clutching a small boy and a white dog no bigger than a cat. She joined Mr Larson's wave.

Mrs Hart met their eyes and raised her hand. She turned to her small menagerie, saying something to the stooped woman, who tugged the boy's arm, making him jolt, and took him and the ridiculously small dog on while Mrs Hart waited for them to make the perilous journey across the road.

Bayswater Road had been so challenging to cross that by the time they entered onto the Broad Walk, Master Hart and his elderly nanny with the cat-dog were nowhere to be seen.

'He'll be down at the pond,' Mrs Hart said with a sniff. 'He's positively obsessed with boats at the moment. Mr Hart wants to get him one, but he'll only break it and that will be worse.'

'Are you well, dear?' she asked. 'What a nice surprise to see you.'

'Yes.' There was something in her tone that made her skin prickle.

'Are you well?' she asked again, and Mrs Hart gave a pronounced sigh.

Mr Larson, walking on the other side of Mrs Wood, said: 'Your boy is growing,' as though Mrs Wood hadn't spoken at all.

'Isn't he,' said Mrs Hart. 'We're at the tailor almost weekly these days.'

'Such a fine boy,' said Mrs Wood, a touch disingenuously: she had never shown a moment's interest in Mrs Hart's obnoxious offspring. But she was testing her. 'So like you.' Surely she would prick at that blatant lie?

'Not at all,' she replied brusquely. 'Unless you consider my hair to be white?'

Mrs Wood laughed awkwardly. She hesitated, the gravel crunching beneath their slow feet. 'I'm glad we've run into each other,' she said, and when Mrs Hart didn't say anything, she continued: 'We haven't hosted a table together in such a while, I was hoping . . .'

Mrs Hart gave a bark of a laugh and stopped. 'Is this a serious question?' she said.

'Well . . . yes. Isn't that what we've always done . . .'

'When was the last time you and I hosted together. The two of us?'

She felt a heat crawl into her cheeks, hoping that none of those people walking past either recognised her or overheard Mrs Hart's tone. 'I'm not sure what you're—'

'It was *February*, Violet. Almost a *year*.'

'Come,' she said, attempting to loop her hand into Mrs Hart's arm so that she could draw her into the privacy of the wooded path. Desperate for this to happen without Mr Larson *right there*. 'Let's—' But Mrs Hart yanked her arm free and glared at her.

'And now Miss Finch doesn't need you anymore, you're suddenly asking if we can work together again.'

'That's not how—'

'Of course it is!' she said, her voice snapping through the air. She could feel eyes turning to them.

'Fenella, please. There are people watching.'

Mrs Hart glared about her, and she was sure that she was about to say that she didn't care, when Mr Larson stepped in and said: 'Mrs Wood's right. This air is too strong. It's making you behave in a most out-of-character way. Come.' And instead of resisting, she allowed him to take her elbow and walk her ahead into the seclusion of the holly-lined path that led off the wide walk. Mrs Wood followed, humiliated and humbled by Mrs Hart's anger, collecting her thoughts as she scurried to meet them. She had got it all wrong. Couldn't she see *why* she may have prioritised Miss Finch?

'Fenella,' she said, coming close, and Mrs Hart turned but wouldn't look at her. 'Please. I'm sorry if I've appeared anything other than your friend in the past few months.'

'It's not about friendship,' she said sharply. 'You and I have sat at tables together for years. I would go somewhere and people would say *and how is dear Mrs Wood* and I would say *she's very well* or whatever because I knew. Or they wouldn't even have to ask because you'd be there and we'd be doing a séance. But now. When they ask, I have to say . . . *to be honest, dears. I don't know.'*

'Well, that's not true,' she said, unable to hide her indignation. 'Just because we've not held a mutual table for a while, it doesn't mean that you and I haven't spent time communing together.'

'With the girl!' she snapped. 'You're always introducing her to everyone. She even shares your Grand Séances, for God's sake—' She stopped to apologise to Mr Larson and then continued: 'Were you ever planning to allow me to do that?'

'If it concerned you so much, why haven't you said anything before?'

'Why should I?'

'I am many things, dear friend. But I am not a mind reader.'

The implication hung between them as they glared at one another, and Mr Larson began feebly.

'Ladies. Please—'

'And now, the girl's getting all the attention, I'm once more of interest. You didn't think that perhaps I had established my own practice with someone else in all that time? That I was sitting around waiting for you to return and everything would be . . .'

'I was being polite!' she blurted, irritated and angry. 'That's all, Fenella. I thought you might like it.'

Mrs Hart's nostrils flared and she felt Mr Larson's hand on her arm.

'You really think I haven't invited you to share a séance with me because I'm busy with Miss Finch?' she continued. 'You're so bloated with self-importance that you wouldn't even consider that I haven't invited you because you're not good enough?'

Mrs Hart's cheeks shone as though she'd been slapped, and she narrowed her eyes. 'Well,' she said, adjusting the front of her jacket. 'You shall find me at Miss Finch's table in the future.' She turned to Mr Larson and gave him a curt nod. 'I hope to see you there too. I think we're all beginning to see the true character of this woman.'

She stood, reeling in the wake of Mrs Hart's fury, watching as she disappeared around a turn in the path. She reached out for the steadying influence of Mr Larson's arm, her mind spinning. Why had she said that? She hadn't meant any of it. Mrs Hart was a difficult woman, tough to like, but she was a good Medium and she had always enjoyed sharing séances with her in the past: she was gifted and confident and she was of her age.

It didn't matter that Mrs Hart had been so prickly; she, herself, shouldn't have said what she had. They were in society together; they should be championing one another.

'That was very unfair, Violet,' Mr Larson said.

'Thank you, Mr Larson,' she said, and turned away, pushing her hands deep into her muff and heading back to Broad Walk.

Mrs Hart was her ally. *Why had she done that?*

She heard Mr Larson pounding on the path behind her, the

rough panting of Fox thinking it was a game. She stopped, turned. 'She's wrong,' she said. 'I didn't know she felt like that.'

But instead of offering comfort, Mr Larson held her eye. 'I think the only person who's wrong here is you.' And she had to gather all her strength not to strike him.

'You don't understand,' she said. 'None of you do.'

He grabbed her as she tried to turn away. 'Then tell me,' he said. 'I made a promise that I would always be there for you. But how do you expect me to help if you won't tell me what's wrong?'

She looked at him for a moment, her jaw clenched tight, and she thought again what he would do if she told him the truth. Imagined the horror spreading across his face, the loosening of his grip, the whip of the wind as he disappeared from her life. She pulled away. 'Mrs Hart's always been difficult,' she said eventually. 'I'm sure my life will be far simpler without her in it.'

Miss Emmeline Finch
12b Leamington Road Villas

12th November 1873

My Dearest Miss Newman,

Is Mrs Wood well? I received a letter from Mrs Green a few days after our last séance saying that she was concerned for her. She said that she's seemed distracted and not at all like herself the last few times she's seen her. She did look rather pale after her escapades at the Grand Séance last week too. Didn't you think? I hate for Mrs Wood to be seen as anything but great to her patrons, but perhaps this is a sign that she needs to rest.

I wonder if we should talk with her about taking a proper rest. Perhaps she should go to the sea for a few months. I'm sure the fresh air will make her feel better.

You know that she must not worry about her patrons. I have told her that I am here to help her whenever she needs, but, while she's clearly not herself, you might consider sending them to me. I'm sure she'd be grateful for the break.

Anyway. My datebook is getting very full over the next few months. Nothing like Mrs Wood's, I know, but since moving to Leamington Road Villas, I've found that nearly all of my neighbours are in need of spiritual contact. Especially when they discover whose table I learned at!

You would not believe how many letters I receive each week now asking for my time. I am really quite worn out. Thank goodness I have youth on my side.

Miss Brigham and the Adams sisters came this weekend for a little séance around my nice new table and it was such a fun afternoon. You would have loved it, Miss Newman. It's my turn for the Circle next week, but perhaps you'd come when they come at the weekend too? Perhaps with Mrs Reynolds? Three o'clock on Saturday. I'll order cakes in from Cathcart's as I did last time – they went down a treat.

And Mrs Hart is coming for a séance tomorrow, which will be fun. Did you hear what Mrs Wood said to her? Do you suppose that's all part of this mental erosion? She isn't always as nice as she should be to you either, Miss Newman. She can be so rude about your work towards Women's Rights, which I am wholeheartedly in support of and am grateful as anything that you are out there fighting for all of us ladies.

If I weren't so busy, I'd spend more time with her. She has been like a mother to me, and I don't want her to think that I'm abandoning her. Especially now my dear own mother is staying with me. Do you think she's feeling hurt by that?

On nicer things, you must come at the weekend with the sisters and give yourself a well-earned break from her home, you are always welcome here in mine. I don't believe you have visited since I took my new rooms. They are so much bigger and smarter than my old one on Tavistock Crescent: even my meagre furniture seems to look nicer in them. Do come soon!

I await your response with much anticipation.

Eternally yours,

Emmeline

CHAPTER 30

Once she had read the letter, Mrs Wood wondered if perhaps Miss Newman had left it sandwiched between her notebooks on her nightstand in her bedroom, the edge peeking out so seductively that should Mrs Wood happen to be in there for some other reason, she would find it.

She sat heavily on the bed, the thick, cream stock paper balanced between her fingers, Miss Finch's childlike scrawl covering it like knitting.

She read that first line again . . . *Is Mrs Wood well?*

How long had they been writing to one another like this?

How long had Miss Newman been entertaining the gibberish of this girl while she watched Mrs Wood flounder?

The front door slammed downstairs and she fumbled the letter in surprise, scrabbling to catch it as it fluttered to the floor.

'Violet?' Miss Newman's voice echoed around the house and she swooped the letter back up and, without thinking, shoved it into her pocket.

Downstairs, Miss Newman opened the door to the back parlour, and she took the opportunity to tiptoe to her own bedroom, slamming the door shut from the landing for maximum effect.

'Is that you? Violet?'

'Up here,' she called back, slipping easily into the now habitual facade that everything was fine.

'Are you all right?'

'Of course,' she said, leaning over the banister and seeing Miss Newman looking back up at her from the hall holding something

278

in her hand. The duplicity turned her stomach and she forced herself to smile. 'What's that?'

Miss Newman held up an off-white pamphlet and waved it in her direction. 'It's here!' she said.

'What's here?'

'My pamphlet!' she called. 'Come and see!'

Mrs Wood stepped back and settled herself, smoothing her dress, the letter strangely reassuring against her leg as she made her way to the stairs. 'What pamphlet do you mean, dear?' she called, seeing the swish of Miss Newman's skirt disappear into the drawing room.

'Don't tease,' she called, and Mrs Wood grimaced. She had clearly forgotten something important.

Miss Newman was waiting for her on the window seat, a fat carpetbag at her feet from which poked a wad of, she assumed, the same pamphlet she was holding in her hand.

'Well,' she said as she settled opposite. 'That looks very interesting.'

'Look,' she said, holding it out. 'Read it. Look . . .' She leaned forward, pointing out her name on the front of the pamphlet she held.

'*The Time Is Now* by Miss Sarah Newman,' read Mrs Wood, turning it around in her hand with an approving nod. 'And Mr George Sandford.' She stopped and looked up. Miss Newman pressed her lips together and looked away with the hint of a blush. 'Is that . . . ?'

'My friend, yes,' she said, recovering herself. 'He has some excellent points, and is terribly articulate. For a man.'

Mrs Wood raised an eyebrow and flicked through the pamphlet to see ten pages of dense close-set type. 'Oh,' she said, turning to the back page. 'The Central Committee of the National Society for Women's Suffrage. Is that what your society is called?'

'You really haven't listened to a thing I've said about my work away from here, have you.'

'But it's such a mouthful,' she said. 'You can hardly expect me to remember the committee of central women's . . . What is it again?'

'The name of the society isn't important,' Miss Newman said, a sudden chill in her voice.

Mrs Wood buckled back. 'Of course, it's not.' She opened the pamphlet again, scanned through the first page and smiled. 'It's very good.'

'Thank you,' she said. 'We worked so hard on it. Does the urgency come through? Did you get to the part where I remind this nation of the fact that women are dying because of inequality?'

She dropped her eyes back to the words. 'Oh yes,' she said. 'There it is . . .' She squinted, as if that would help the sentence make sense. 'You make a very good point.'

Miss Newman sat back. 'You should come to one of our meetings one day.'

'I should,' said Mrs Wood vaguely.

'You would be such a good advocate. Imagine. A woman who makes her own money, in our society.'

Mrs Wood flushed. 'That's not something I would ever discuss in public, Sarah.'

'You would inspire a whole generation of women.'

'All I have ever done is what I love. That's hardly inspiration.'

Miss Newman gave a sigh. 'You promise me that you'll read it, won't you? That's all you have to do. Read it.'

Mrs Wood held the pamphlet to her chest, forgetting everything in that moment. 'I absolutely promise,' she said. 'What an achieve-ment, Sarah. You must be very proud.'

'I am,' said Miss Newman. Then she reached to gather the bag, heaving it onto her lap.

The letter felt unrelenting in her pocket. Should she say some-thing? Should she interrupt Miss Newman's obvious delight with this? 'Are you leaving again?'

'Got to get these out,' she said. 'But I shall be home later. And we can discuss your thoughts on what I propose.'

'Excellent,' she said with a smile, watching Miss Newman stand

and heft the bag into the hallway. She couldn't let this hang between them. Their friendship meant too much. 'Sarah.' Even as she began to talk, she couldn't believe that the words were coming out. 'Sarah, can you explain this?' And she pulled the letter from her pocket.

At first, she was confused. 'What is . . . ?' She stepped forward, squinting to see what Mrs Wood was holding before stopping, the colour leeching from her face. 'You went into my room,' she said. 'Why did you do that?'

'I was looking for something.'

'In my private space? I would never have expected such a thing from you, Violet.'

'Why is that girl writing to you? About me. Why is she asking you to look out for me? Visit her home to work without me?'

'Who knows?' she said, with a laugh. 'I didn't ask her to write to me, but there's nothing of concern in her letter, is there? She's worried about you being tired – and I'm inclined to agree with her.'

'There's more to it than that. She's suggesting that you send my patrons to her.'

'She doesn't mean—'

'It's right there!' Mrs Wood said, flapping the letter. 'What else have you two been planning?'

Miss Newman flinched in surprise. 'What is wrong with you? Why would you even think we'd be planning something? Unless you found my notebook listing all of the ways we're working against you.'

Mrs Wood started. 'What?'

'I'm being sarcastic, Violet. I'm suggesting that you're being unfair for even thinking that I'm colluding with Emmeline. You brought her into our lives. You made her part of our Circle, took her to your patrons' homes. You're the only reason that I know the girl. Why on earth would I be conspiring with her to hurt you?'

'But what am I to think?'

'What am *I* to think? I thought we were supporting her. I thought we were proud of the fact that she was making a success of her life. Wasn't that part of why you brought her in? To give her that opportunity.'

'I brought her in because I believed she had talent.'

'And you don't anymore? Because, from what I can see, the girl is incredibly talented and she's using it to her advantage. The same as you.'

She's nothing like me! she wanted to scream. She imagined the change in Miss Newman's face as she told her what a filthy little blackmailer the girl really was. But then she would need to reveal her own truth and she would lose Miss Newman, just as she would lose everyone else should it come out. Miss Newman would never understand why she hadn't told her. And she would never continue to work with someone so steeped in lies.

She was trapped. Exactly as the girl had engineered.

'You have to let whatever you have built up against the girl go,' Miss Newman said, placing the bag of pamphlets on the floor, her voice calm, as though she were soothing a child lost in a tantrum. 'It's not healthy and it's unwarranted. She is hard-working, dedicated—'

'Then go and work for her!' Mrs Wood's words rattled around the drawing room, bouncing off crystal and vases. The force of them shocked her.

'Now you're being ridiculous.'

'Am I? You're barely here anymore as it is. What difference would it make to me?'

Miss Newman sat back as though she had been struck. 'What difference would it make? What are you talking about?'

Mrs Wood gave a snort.

'Miss Finch is right,' Miss Newman said, and Mrs Wood looked up, startled. 'You aren't yourself. I've tried to look beyond it but you've been . . . unusual for a while now.'

'That's the girl's poison talking,' she said, vindicated. 'And look how easily you fell for it.'

'I'm talking about you, Violet. And what I'm seeing with my own eyes.'

'There is nothing wrong with me!' That voice. The shrill, panicked voice she would read on anyone else as the sign of an unsettled mind. She cleared her throat. 'There is nothing wrong with me, Sarah,' she repeated, calmer, more precisely. 'I'm just disappointed with you.'

Miss Newman gave a sigh. 'I mean, would a holiday really hurt?'

She blinked at her. 'You *are* colluding with her, aren't you.'

'Violet, stop this.'

'You know this is part of her plan. She wants me out of London so she can take the last of all I have.'

'Violet! You are sounding like a lunatic!'

But she couldn't stop now, even if she tried. It was as though the real Violet had left her body and all she could do was watch in silent horror as the fury and the fear of the past few months unleashed themselves in a chaos of irrationality. 'It's what you've been planning all along isn't it!'

Miss Newman sat quickly beside her, reaching for her hands, searching out her eyes. 'Violet, please. You're talking absolute nonsense. You can't believe that . . . Violet . . . We're a team. Let's not . . .'

With the public's interest fading, it would only be a matter of time before Miss Newman tired of her. And if she didn't succumb to the excitement of the girl, she would flee to the bosom of her women's society. And then she would be alone. The thought was a knife.

'I think perhaps it's time you left.' The words sounded so far away that there was still hope that they hadn't been said at all.

Miss Newman sat up in confusion. 'Leave?' she said.

'It will happen before we know it anyway,' Mrs Wood continued, her eyes remaining steady on Miss Newman's. 'You're hardly here anymore as it is.'

Miss Newman sat back, blinking. 'I was suggesting a holiday from the work,' she said. 'For you. That's all.'

'But perhaps—' She swallowed. 'What I need is a holiday from *you*.'

She waited for Miss Newman to disagree, to tell her she was being ridiculous; to laugh, to dismiss it. To tell her that she would never leave her, not in a million years. But nothing came, and in the silence that enveloped them she swallowed the last of her hope. 'Perhaps we have run our course.'

'You can't be serious,' Miss Newman said.

'All I ever wanted from you was loyalty,' she said. 'How can I trust you now?'

'When have I ever given you reason to distrust me, Violet? After all these years, why would I turn my back on you now?'

'You can stay in a hotel if you need, I shall cover the first few nights but after that I suggest you make your own arrangements.'

The house tick-ticked around them.

'You really want me to go, don't you.' She could hear her breathing beside her, hoping that she would say something that would undo everything. But instead, when she spoke again, Mrs Wood knew that it was done. 'Save your money,' she said quietly. 'You have no need to worry about me.'

She kept her eyes firmly on the street beyond the window as she heard Miss Newman climbing the stairs, knowing that if she were to look up her resolution would fail. This was for the best. Miss Newman would leave her eventually, didn't everyone?

She spent the rest of the day in the back parlour listening to the whispers and footsteps around her, taking softening sips of sherry.

At half past two, she heard the bumping of trunks on the stairs, the creak of the door and then the quiet click as it closed behind her closest friend in the world.

CHAPTER 31

A holiday from Miss Newman!

How naive had she been.

Dismissing Miss Newman hadn't made anything better.

It had simply thrown her deeper into the rut.

Not only was she now alone in the house, rattling from dawn to dusk with no one to break up the day, she was entirely incapacitated in her work.

Her focus had always been on the delivery, and it was with regretful frustration that she realised how little she actually knew about the technical side. Before Miss Newman, she had been a predominantly trance-based Medium, and before that, with Thirza, she had been the one hidden beneath tables or galloping about in the dark. She had never done both, and after an attempt at her first Circle without Miss Newman, it was clear that, at her age, learning how was going to be impossible.

And so it became gnawingly obvious: without Miss Newman, there could be no escapades and japes and only the bare minimum of the apporting that had made her name.

She had never learned that side of their double-act – there had never been any need to. Where did she start when faced with sourcing a pineapple in December ahead of a séance with a group of spinsters in Hammersmith (the sort of table she would never have had to consider but a few months before)? Even getting dressed had become an entirely limited affair: she couldn't contort herself enough to safely stuff her skirts properly, and no matter how hard she tried, she couldn't extend her arms far enough to get anything down that narrow channel in her corset.

And where did she keep the tea set before it was apported so that it emerged without a tinkle? Where did she keep anything larger than an acorn before it appeared, come to that?

The two séances she delivered in the week after Miss Newman walked from the house – one for the Dowager and a rather shaky Circle – were vanilla at best. Nothing crashing in, nothing appearing from her person. She remained an excellent trance worker, but she knew that people didn't come for that and, she had to be honest, she was a little rusty on all the details. Trances relied on a stream of words, but she'd forgotten most of the Bible passages in her repertoire and, when she tried to revise them in the evenings, they wouldn't stay in. She began to worry that she would use the same passage twice and someone would notice.

Without Miss Newman, she had been forced to cancel the Grand Séance for December, placing a notice in the *Spiritual Times* with the excuse that the season was too busy and she would see them all in January.

January! Who was she fooling? If she couldn't do a séance to a bunch of old ladies without Miss Newman, how would she ever be able to perform the showstopping feats required of a Grand Séance?

And it transpired that Miss Newman had taken her dismissal seriously. Even if she wanted to crawl back to her on her hands and knees with desperate apologies, she couldn't: for the first time since they had met, she had no idea where she was. Discreet questions to the Circle had yielded no intelligence and so she had simply told them loudly that Miss Newman had been called to care for a sick friend. She daren't risk asking anyone else.

When Mrs Reynolds said that she had bumped into her while walking in Hampstead Heath, it was all she could do not to leap on her and ask how Miss Newman had looked. Did she look as broken as Mrs Wood felt? Did she clamour for information as much as Mrs Wood wished she could?

But she didn't. She just smiled and said that, of course, that was very close to where the sick friend lived.

One desperate afternoon, after a lunchtime sherry or two, she went to the hall she knew the society used, but she was told that they had moved to one near Paddington, and that felt too far from home at that moment. Besides, as she'd made her way she'd become less and less confident that confronting her former aide amongst radical women was the best approach.

But it wasn't the void at her séances that worried her the most. It was the empty seat in her house.

She had thought her world was growing smaller with the diminished call on her time for séances and consultations, but Miss Newman's comings and goings had been glimmers in otherwise serge-grey days. Sometimes she would go upstairs and sit in the chair in Miss Newman's room, the little sampler pillow she had left behind on her lap, trying to pretend that she was simply out running an errand or in another room.

She had betrayed her, that wasn't in question, but she was also her closest friend and now she was gone the days yawned and she lurched from lonely meal to lonely meal, bolstered by sweet sherry, the occasional funny spell and endless dreams of the complete and utter destruction of Miss Finch.

AT LAST: ENGLAND'S FIRST SPIRIT HAS BEEN SEEN!

By Magnus Clore
Front-page story
Spiritual Times, 11th December 1873

Sitters at Miss Emmeline Finch's séance last night couldn't believe their eyes when one of the most masterful, and prettiest, Mediums working in England last night delivered the nation's very first full spirit materialisation!

We all gathered at Wornington Road Mission Hall, as instructed, and then at a quarter past nine, Miss Finch entered her cabinet and went into a trance. Within minutes, the cabinet door began to tentatively open, and a slim, white arm was revealed. Then, as though materialising before our very eyes, the spirit emerged from the darkness: a beautiful, soft and feminine sight with a flowing spirit shroud and surprisingly bright eyes shining from a smooth white face.

She announced herself as Tandy, daughter of the famous pirate, Jack Starr (many of you will already know from Mrs Wood's séances of days gone by) and proceeded to speak for herself and for other spirits from the Other Side. She moved very slowly upon the stage, leaving no sound from her feet as though she bore no weight at all.

The door to the cabinet was opened by Tandy at one point, and the Medium herself could be plainly seen sitting inside, exactly as we had left her.

Tandy seemed as delighted and shocked as the entire audience – featuring Lady Morgan and Mrs Pepperdine, who are becoming ardent patrons of this young Medium, and the cream of spiritualist society including Mrs Green and Colonel and Mrs Phillips. The spirit sang a song about the sea, which was entrancing and bewitching, before a coughing was heard from the cabinet and she complained of weakness before drifting back towards her Medium.

As the cabinet closed behind her, there was a great amount of coughing that could be heard, enough to cause a wave of consternation amongst the crowd, but then, almost as soon as the spirit had disappeared, the cabinet door opened and Miss Finch was revealed in the shadows, slumped in exhaustion. So depleted, in fact, that she was helped to her feet for her farewell by yours truly, who then assisted her towards her private rooms.

An unforgettable evening, indeed, and one that has changed the course of scientific discovery before our very eyes. I defy anyone to come to one of Miss Finch's séances and perceive anything but truth and honesty. She is surely the best Medium operating in the land today.

As Tandy disappeared behind the veil, she promised to return. I know I speak for us all when I say that we cannot wait to see her again.

CHAPTER 32

She had never missed Miss Newman more than when she sat alone at the breakfast table that morning with yet another copy of the *Spiritual Times* and yet another knife in her back.

The girl had done it. She had thrown all of Mrs Wood's concerns away and performed her ridiculous stunt anyway. Which, of course, was no surprise. Not really.

The girl had presented the world's first full spirit. She had done the thing that society everywhere had been desperate to see and now everything had changed.

So. What now?

Mrs Wood was never going to follow suit. She was never going to be the one who leapt out of cabinets or sang shanties in a shroud. Not simply because she couldn't, but because her principles would not allow. And now, nothing she did would come close to the work she had done before. Now that they had all seen the spirit, no matter what happened, no matter how gross and unprincipled it was, a flight across the garden would always come up short.

The injustice was bitter in her throat.

What would society get from their newfound favourite? What would she give them other than a production? Where would they find their solace? Where would they find their peace? The girl's audience was made up predominantly of people Mrs Wood had once considered her own patrons, followers, *friends,* and while their disloyalty continued to smart, the thought of their disappointment when they realised that Miss Finch was not what she said she was, was almost visceral.

Yes, they had abandoned her but after the hours she had devoted to all those who had sat in her parlour or table, she couldn't help but care.

Her disgust at the whole thing curdled with the sherry from the night before and her head throbbed as she tried to make sense of it all. Miss Newman would know what to do, she thought, pushing away the toast and eyeing the decanter on the sideboard. Miss Newman would say exactly the right thing:

Oh pish, she'd say. *That girl is nothing but a circus.*

'But a full spirit, Sarah,' she would reply. 'They were all there!'

What does that matter? The girl will be revealed and everything will return to normal.

Would Miss Newman say that? Would she understand?

Of course I understand. I know why you feel the way that you do. I have been by your side throughout.

'Then what would you do?' she asked the gathering form. 'How would you stop this girl before she ruins everything?'

She felt Miss Newman thinking, could hear her fingertips tapping on the table and then, suddenly they stopped. She had it.

I would expose her, dearest.

Mrs Wood sat back as the shape of her closest friend blinked out and smiled at its memory.

Of course that was what Miss Newman would do. She was clever and practical. Miss Newman would remove the girl before she humiliated society and restore herself to their affections in the process.

It was so refreshing when they thought alike.

'Thank you, dearest,' she said to the empty room before pushing her chair back and dipping her finger into the butter dish, sucking it as she headed for the back parlour, bumping directly into Eliza, who was standing in the hall.

'You all right, madam?' she said, her face a mix of curiosity and casual disapproval.

'Yes!' said Mrs Wood. 'Perfectly.' Then she stopped. 'Eliza. Do you know where one might buy a pineapple?'

⁓

When one is considering ways in which to ruin a Medium, Mrs Wood realised, one must talk to a Medium who has been ruined.

Before she had been exposed in January, Mrs Trimble was a quiet fixture in London's spiritual society. She had been a good Medium: reliable, not flashy, with a list of patrons slightly lower down the social scale than Mrs Wood. During their time in Miss Quinn's Circle, she had respected her effective, if somewhat plain, work. And she admired that she was cut from the same cloth as her: dedicated to improving people's lives rather than the acquisition of nice dresses and fancy homes. She was sweet, kind and, when she had last seen her, grandmotherly. That Mrs Trimble had been ruined at all shocked her; another painful reminder of what might happen to even the most earnest Medium when one was not concentrating.

There but for the grace of God.

Mrs Trimble's new address was difficult to find: those who had once been part of her Circle had severed all ties following her humiliation and refused to say even a word to Mrs Wood. But eventually, she found someone who was so flattered to be asked by Mrs Wood that she eschewed convention and the address arrived a few days later.

And now.

Here she was.

Poor Mrs Trimble.

Instead of a suite of rooms in St John's Wood with a view and a quiet servant girl, Mrs Trimble now lived above a second-hand clothes shop on the other side of the railway bridge in Shepherd's Bush. Mrs Wood used her handkerchief to wipe off the worst of the filth on the battered and patched front door, and as Mrs Trimble led the way up to her room, the stairs she climbed were bare and broken.

Her room was on the top floor, at the rear – all eaves and crannies, ice-cold and smelling of mushrooms. In one corner was a daybed, heaped with cushions that spoke of a much, much better time. In the other a small stove and a basin, with a neat stack of crockery on the shelf above. Framed prints hung one over the other like a gallery all over the walls.

In the eaves, a small barred window looked out onto the railway line and a paltry, gnarled garden, overrun with brambles. The glass was soot-stained from the engines and one pane was broken and stuffed with a rag. On the table set before it was a chipped sewing machine and piles of fabric heaped beside neatly folded garments.

Mrs Trimble fiddled with a beaded antimacassar that shone in the bleak landscape like a pearl, a vestige of a better time, draped on the back of one of the two chairs that had been wedged into the remaining space before the fire. 'I wasn't expecting company,' she said, smoothing her hair. 'It's only temporary, you understand. It's not exactly . . .' she tried to smile but her face gave up.

'It's very nice,' said Mrs Wood. 'I was meaning to write but . . .'

Mrs Trimble waved her hand dismissively and pinned on a smile. 'There's no need to explain,' she said. 'It was all very . . . Would you like some tea?' She put her hand on the handle of the kettle.

'No,' she said, noticing an elaborate map of mould rising from the skirting board behind the stove. 'Thank you. No, I'm afraid I can't stay.'

'If you're sure? I heard about your pupil Miss Finch? With her full materialisation.'

'Yes,' said Mrs Wood.

'You must be very proud.'

She smiled tightly. 'You look well,' she said, and Mrs Trimble blushed at the lie. She pointed at the piles of fabric to change the subject. 'Looks like you're keeping busy too.'

293

'The shop downstairs has plenty of work for me. We have an arrangement for the rent.'

'Good,' she said. 'I'm glad. And how is your daughter?'

The kettle rattled in Mrs Trimble's hand and she took a moment to steady herself. 'She's in service,' she said brightly. 'A nice family. Very understanding.'

'Well, that's something,' she said. She looked about for somewhere to put her bag, but seeing nowhere clear or clean, she pulled it in close. 'Now, Mrs Trimble. This is a somewhat indelicate question which I hope you won't find upsetting.'

Mrs Trimble's shoulders sagged and she dropped onto the arm of the chair. 'You can say what you like, Violet,' she said. 'It won't be anything I've not heard before.'

'I'm sure,' she said, and finding no chair at her disposal, she settled on the edge of the day bed. 'You must have had a terrible time,' she said.

The woman gave a trembling smile. 'People have been very cruel,' she said and pressed the back of her hand to her mouth, taking a steadying breath. Her fingers were red and sore-looking, the nails clipped short. She remembered holding those hands in hers at so many of Miss Quinn's séances all those years before. They had been soft; as gentle and unworked as a child's.

'What happened?' she asked abruptly, and Mrs Trimble gave a laugh.

'Is that a serious question? Have you been living beneath a rock?'

'I don't mean what happened here,' she said, raising her hands to the room. 'I know that, of course.'

'Then what are you asking?'

'*How?*' she said.

Mrs Trimble frowned. 'I've just told you . . .'

'Exactly how, though. I mean: what was the mistake you made?'

She narrowed her eyes. 'What do you want?'

'I'm curious,' she said, nonchalantly as possible. 'I'm curious how someone as talented as you has ended up . . .'

'. . . Here,' she finished and smiled sadly. 'I was worried. It's silly now I think about it. I was growing . . . older and . . . I was flattered when he asked for a seat at my table. It had been a while since I had attracted someone new.'

The familiarity stung, but she continued on without missing a beat. 'What were you doing? How did they . . . ?'

Mrs Trimble gave her a long stare that reminded Mrs Wood she had not lost the art of the read. 'What are you up to, Violet?' she said.

'I'm simply curious,' she said again.

Mrs Trimble seemed to be thinking about her words, her mouth twitching. She sighed. 'Someone struck a match,' she said, eventually. 'I was midway through a piece and someone struck a match and there I was.'

'That's all,' she said. 'No warning? Just a match and that was it.'

'Of course, I insisted that I was mid-apport, that the spirits were hoisting me around but . . . There was no denying. The harmonica was in my mouth and I was most certainly not in my seat where I was supposed to be.'

She nodded and thought for a moment. 'Who struck the match?'

'Some little brute,' she said. 'I took him for a student – someone interested in the Other Side. Turns out he was a friend of some researcher or other.'

They shared a moment of derision before Mrs Trimble continued with a shake of her head. 'I was charmed by his interest. I should've seen . . .'

'But it was a match, that's all.' How easy that must have been. 'One flash of light and your reputation . . .'

'I kept some clients going for a while, I was surprised how loyal some of them were, but . . .' she looked pointedly about the shabby room. 'In the end, I was too ashamed of myself to do anything of note and eventually they lost interest. I was no longer the Medium they wanted me to be.'

The room was suddenly too close. 'I really must . . .' Mrs Wood said quickly, and stood, gathering herself. 'It's been very nice to see you, but I really must . . .'

'It's like you always said, Violet,' said Mrs Trimble, her red, cracked fingers running across the beautiful, beaded antimacassar. 'Illusion is everything. Once the belief in you has gone, there's nothing anyone can do.'

11th December 1873

Dear Mr Clore,

*I am but a humble follower of the spiritualist movement compelled
to write and speak out against the obvious hoodwinking by a
fraudulent Medium within your very pages. These people are such a
scourge, bringing the good names of those with whom they associate
into helpless disrepute.*

*I refer, of course, to the young, inexperienced Medium, Miss
Emmie Finch, who has recently appeared in London from a small
backwater with no prospects and taken in by the celebrated
Medium, Mrs Violet Wood, with no financial compensation
whatsoever. As a great supporter of Mrs Wood, known for her
unprecedented gift and the levels of care and compassion she shows
her many, many influential friends, it causes me inordinate levels of
distress to see that Miss Finch is not using a single ounce of the
respectability she must have learned during their time together and
is, instead, relying on sensation and gimmick.*

*As an ardent student of spiritualism, I cannot believe that a
spirit may be manifested into flesh. Which, therefore, leads me to
conclude that this girl is a fraud and a charlatan if she is
suggesting that she is making this happen.*

*I feel it is only right to let readers of the Spiritual Times know
that this is both a terrible untruth and a dreadful hoax by a young
girl who, unfortunately, does not know any better, no matter how
much her tutor tried.*

With the very best of intentions,
A N Onymous

Magnus Clore
Editor
Spiritual Times ~ 2 Red Lion Court ~ London

12th December 1873

Dear Mrs Wood,
I return your letter with but one request: do not reduce yourself, my
dear. It is unbecoming.
  Magnus Clore

CHAPTER 33

The days had become so long, despite the drawing in of nights.

One late afternoon, she sat bundled beside the small fire in the back parlour that failed to cut through the ice in the house. The only thing that was warm was her stomach, lit up by the cheapest sherry it was respectable to buy.

'Soon,' Mr Larson had replied when she had written requesting an update on the ships. 'I expect to hear an arrival date any day soon.' But any day soon felt a day too long.

She had had no clients at all that week and none scheduled for the week after. No tables. No patrons.

No income.

The Dowager was the only one of her patrons who was continuing her stipend, but she hadn't requested her company in weeks and she was certain that she was only keeping it up out of pity.

Still, even if she had the energy to host something, she would struggle to present the house in any way that resembled the polish people such as the Dowager would expect. Burning the candles to nubs, as she now did as a matter of course, led them to splutter wax stains like stars over her linens and surfaces, and she had sent a heap of coal across the séance room rug in the process of divvying out what remained in the scuttle, the cloud of coal dust now a huge smudge which she couldn't afford to have cleaned.

The fire hissing disappointedly in the grate was the first she had lit in two weeks.

Oh, the irony. The holiday that Miss Newman and the girl had conspired to enforce had come to her anyway, in exactly the manner she had feared.

This was not fair, she thought again, staring at the feeble red embers. She didn't deserve this.

She had forgotten to replace the fireguard after the fire had been lit and, with a sudden pop, a spark shot like a meteor towards the hearthrug where it landed, red hot, smoking as it burrowed into the pile. She dropped awkwardly to her knees, reaching without thinking to tamp it out with her hand. The spark still held heat, though, and as soon as she placed her hand on it, she yelped and jumped back. The danger was out but there was a hot mark across the pads of her middle and ring finger of her right hand.

With an irritated sigh, she pushed herself to her feet, sucking on the worst of it, readying herself to call for Eliza and some butter. This was all she needed. She looked at her injury, which was already beginning to blister, and instinctively her mind went to her diary – worried that restricted use of her hand might impact on . . .

She stopped.

Impact on what? Raising a sherry glass? Staring at a wall?

She stopped again, her uninjured hand on the bell-pull.

An impediment. That was all that was needed to restrain a Medium.

She blinked. Something was uncoiling in her mind.

She yanked on the bell but opened the door anyway and called through the house. 'Eliza? *Eliza!*'

Eliza stomped up the stairs from the kitchen. 'I heard the bell the first time,' she grumbled, then stopped when she saw Mrs Wood sucking on her hand. 'What've you done?'

'Nothing,' she said, her mind on what was forming. *She couldn't do it herself. She wouldn't be able to get near her.* 'I need my cloak.'

'Let me see. How've you done that?'

'It's fine. Really.'

'I'll get some butter.' She turned, gathering her skirts as she started to irritably stomp down the stairs before Mrs Wood stopped her.

'It's fine. Please. Don't fuss. I need to go out.'

'Are you mad. It's almost dark.'

'I know. But . . . it's important. Where's my cloak?'

'Madam! What are you doing?'

Mrs Wood turned at Eliza's abrupt voice. 'Don't fuss! I shall wrap up. I just need to . . . Where's my cloak?'

'It's on the stand, madam. Where it always is.' Eliza gave an irritated snort but went to fetch it anyway, heaving it over her arm along with Mrs Wood's bonnet. 'What's so urgent that can't wait until . . .'

Mrs Wood put her arm out. 'My cloak.'

'I suppose I'll have to come with you,' she said begrudgingly, wrapping Mrs Wood's cloak over her shoulders. 'Stop you getting murdered and all that.'

'I'm perfectly fine on my own,' she said, and stuffed the bonnet onto her head. 'You can look after me when I get home.'

Eliza crossed her arms and looked pointedly at her. 'Stick to the lighted roads,' she said, taking the ribbons of Mrs Wood's bonnet and looping them below her chin. 'And don't look at no one.'

'I shall be a ghost,' Mrs Wood said and slammed the door behind her.

After leaving the chemist on the corner of Hereford Road, she walked the entire length of Westbourne Grove as though in a trance, arriving at Porchester Road with absolutely no idea of how she had got there. Eliza was right: it was indeed getting dark; the shadows had grown long and deep about her and all that was left of the day was a thin, blue line.

She pressed on in the twilight, seeing the railway bridge ahead, rolling the plan in her head, smoothing its edges so that by the time she arrived it would be perfect, gleaming.

At Westbourne Park Villas, she quickened her pace past the soot-stained terraces, heartened to see that there was a lamp blazing over his front door.

The girl would be stopped, she thought, her finger on the bell. And she would be stopped for good.

She rang the bell again and saw a figure through the etched glass panel in the door, tall and dark against the gaslight.

'Mr Larson,' she said, as the door opened. 'Mr Larson, I need your help.'

Mr Larson had inherited the house on Westbourne Park Villas from his aunt, and clearly hadn't had the inclination or the interest to usurp a single piece of her antiquated decoration and furniture.

He sat opposite Mrs Wood in the cluttered parlour, his hand on a crocheted antimacassar, a large figurine of a Siamese cat on the table beside him, its ceramic coat gleaming orange and yellow in the firelight.

She had never been in this house before and as she drank in the chaos of dark paintings hanging from the burgundy walls, the rows of ornaments featuring a density of sad dogs and crying children, the tapestry cushions and swagged drapes, she was struck by how strange it was that he, this sparse, precise man, lived in such a tumultuous wreck. How little we really know people, she thought.

'This is a pleasant surprise,' Mr Larson said, turning his teacup in its saucer. 'I'm afraid I don't have an update beyond what we discussed last week on the investments—'

'It's not that,' she said, and took a breath, placing her own cup and saucer onto a pile of books beside her. Fox, who had collapsed into instant sleep at her feet the moment she had sat, gave off contented snores in the silence as she allowed the perfectly formed marble of her idea to roll into her hands.

She looked at Mr Larson. 'You once told me that you would do anything for me.'

He put his teacup down. 'Is something wrong?'

'Do you remember when you said that? That you would do anything for me?'

'Well,' he said. 'Of course. I promised Mr Wood that I—'

'Did you mean that? When you said that, did you mean it?'

He cleared his throat. 'What's wrong, Violet?'

'The girl . . .' she began, but she heard him sigh and she looked up sharply. 'Why does everyone do that?'

'Miss Newman said you had developed something unpleasant toward the girl,' he said.

'Miss Newman is no longer part of my Circle,' she said, and he raised his eyebrows.

'What? *When?*'

She waved her hand dismissively. 'Did you mean it?' she said, the weight of the idea overriding everything. She needed to tell him what he had to do before she lost her confidence. 'Did you mean it when you said you would do anything?'

'Well,' he said. 'Yes. But, Violet—'

'I need you to do something,' she said. 'I've never asked anything from you before. But now, I need you to do something.'

She could hear the air whistling in his nose. 'What is it?' he said, eventually.

'This girl—'

'Violet—'

'*This girl,*' she continued. 'She worries me. She should worry us *all*. This full spirit materialisation is a problem.'

'You surprise me,' he said, and she stopped.

'What do you mean?'

303

'I thought you would be excited by this. I thought you would be proud that your pupil had been the first to achieve such a feat.'

She looked at him. 'You believe her?'

He disappeared into thought for a moment, shaking his head, the line between his eyebrows a crevice. 'I don't know,' he said finally. 'I – we – . . . full spirit materialisation . . . it's always been something we have dismissed,' he said. 'But when . . .' He gave a sorrowful sigh. 'I'm so confused.'

'It's hard, dearest. I understand.'

'You've never doubted her gift, Violet. You have always spoken of her as a talented Medium—'

'—and she is!' she said.

'So why would this not be real?'

She sat back in her chair. 'I won't be the only person to doubt her,' she said. 'Now that she's making a name for herself with such spectacle, they'll all come sniffing around: the scientists, the cynics. The *gossips*. Not everyone has her best interests at heart. Not everyone is like us.'

He frowned at Fox, who shifted onto his back with a satisfied sigh.

'She is seen as my pupil,' she continued as she watched him process each of her words. 'The more she presents this fraud, the more of a charlatan she will be considered and her inevitable exposure will reflect upon me. You know that. If we nip this in the bud now, it can be put down to childish enthusiasm. But the longer she is permitted to hoodwink society, the greater the impact on my reputation. After all I have done, Mr Larson. Can you bear for me to be so unnecessarily affected?'

He sat for a moment, breath whistling faintly in his nose.

'After all I've done for her, dearest,' she repeated. 'She is a viper in our nest, Mr Larson. All the Circle's hard work, tainted by the foolishness of a child.'

'And you're sure it's not true?'

He dropped his elbows onto his knees, his eyes returning to Fox's pink belly at his feet. His nose was a straight line, the fire lighting one side of his long face with a soft, orange glow.

She leaned even closer, placed her hands on his wrists. 'The longer the girl continues to perform her lies before all of these people, the more catastrophic the outcome. For everyone.'

Their faces were closer than they had ever been. She saw every careless blemish, every missed whisker. His lips were dry, a tiny scar she'd never noticed before denting the right corner.

'Please,' she said, her words a whisper, travelling the inches between her mouth and his. 'Help me to help her.'

He swallowed, looked away and then back, his eyes sad and serious.

'Tell me what you want me to do.'

She waited a moment then put her hand in her pocket and passed him the brown paper package she had purchased in the Hereford Road chemist. So innocuous, so small.

He stopped as a tiny brown bottle slid into his hands. His cheeks paled.

'Just a drop, that's all.'

He said nothing as he examined the vial, turning it in his hand; his long fingers dwarfed it, made it look even smaller, even more innocuous. His eyes watched the viscous liquid rolling inside, from one end to the other. Then he nodded abruptly, closing his hand over the bottle with a speed that made her jump. 'Careful!' she said . . .

'It's all right,' he assured her. 'The glass is strong.' He sighed. 'It needs to be.'

His torment was so obvious that she instinctively reached out. 'If I could do it myself, you know that I would,' she said. 'But I cannot be there. She would be too suspicious, for a start, and . . . I cannot be associated with it. It would be worse than . . . In the dark, no one will know,' she said. 'In the dark it could be any of those people she invites into her circus.' She put her hand on his wrist. His heart beat like a torrent beneath her fingertips.

'What do I do if someone sees me?'

'Act as though they haven't,' she said.

'And if I pass her the water immediately afterwards . . .'

'. . . It will minimise the impact.' She leaned forward. 'This is the only way,' she said. 'It's the only way we can get her to stop making a mockery of everything we stand for as Mediums. She will not listen to reason. You know that.'

'And the water will soothe her. I can't bear the thought of hurting anyone . . .' It took all she had to not shake him.

'It will. I promise.' She remembered the man who had suffered a far more brutal attack outside the Hamburgh Inn when she was small, hearing his screams as pails and pails of water were turned over his arm before Thirza had pulled her away. *The water will help him*, she'd said. He'd lost the use of that arm but he hadn't died, which meant that Thirza had been right.

'Only a tiny, tiny drop of the stuff on the hands, Mr Larson,' she said encouragingly. 'She'll barely feel it, but it will force her to stop and think about what she's doing. A materialised spirit with the same scars on her hands as her Medium will be sure to raise suspicion.'

A thin line of sweat beaded across his upper lip.

'It's for her benefit too, Mr Larson. We don't want to see her ruined, do we?'

He dropped his head. 'I feel like a wicked person,' he said. 'Don't *you*? She's a girl. Wouldn't talking to her be a wiser solution? Get her to see that she's behaving—'

'Don't you think I've tried that? The girl won't see reason. I've told her again and again how important reputation is, how foolish it is to go beyond one's gifts in search of position. Her refusal to listen is leaving her vulnerable to vultures like Humboldt. Imagine what a man like him would cajole her into for money.' She stopped, suddenly and acutely aware of how close she had come to revealing knowledge of life that she should never have known.

Mr Larson rubbed his face. 'Perhaps if I were to—'

'Mr Larson. The girl will listen to no one but herself. We will snap her out of that folly, make her realise the great mistakes that lie ahead by returning her to sensible discourse.' She leaned forward. 'We are protecting her when no one else will. We are doing this for her own good.'

He took a moment before he finally raised his head and nodded. 'If it will help the girl in the long run,' he said. 'I will do it.'

Her body sagged with relief. 'So, your invitation is for Wednesday?'

He nodded again. 'At five o'clock. According to Miss Finch, the first dark of the day is good for materialisations. It'll be at the Wornington Mission Hall again,' he said. 'Just like the first time.'

'Sit in the front row,' she said. 'And the moment she comes out of that cabinet, do it.'

'Are you certain that it won't be a spirit?' he said.

Mrs Wood started to laugh, but seeing the earnest expression on his face she softened. 'Well,' she said. 'I suppose you'll find out either way, won't you.'

CHAPTER 34

After everything had been agreed, she left Mr Larson's home lighter than she had felt in a long time. She settled herself into the cab Mr Larson insisted on paying for and trotted happily home. It was a good plan. One that would ensure that things would return to normal, smoothly and with no serious ramifications. With her hand disfigured, the girl would be forced to drop her fraud, and return to simpler, less interesting activities.

And everything would go back to the way it had been. When everything had been good.

But then she woke to a grey, bleak Tuesday filled with nothing but the ticking clock and the memory of when her daybook had been so full its spine would fall apart. At first, the thought of how that would soon be returning to her was a poultice on her sore soul, but . . . she couldn't get the thought of that man outside the pub in Hull out of her mind. The victim of the acid attack. She could hear his screams, a terrible bovine cry, howling down the tunnel from the past.

Would the girl scream like that? Surely a dab of the stuff wouldn't do so much damage? Surely it was the amount the attacker had used that burned that old drunk's body so badly that – had she imagined this? – it steamed beneath the sloshing buckets.

She thought of the girl, her petite, childlike hands. Steaming.

She had another sherry and ate some coffee cake.

The girl needs to be stopped, she repeated.

She wondered about Mr Larson. He had seemed almost despondent when she had waved cheerio to him the night before, standing on the pavement before his house raising his hand once and staring blankly after her.

She imagined him now in his dead aunt's house, watched by his strange village of figurines, drinking tea and eating toast from flowered china. The pharmacist's bottle a bare bump in the pocket of his jacket.

She saw his eyes, rimmed with lashes more fitting for a child. Registered that confused, hurt look he had given her when she had asked him for this one act of loyalty. Saw him understand that he could not say no.

Could he?

Should he?

She took up her sherry again and the day drifted back into a reassuring muddy haze.

And then it was Wednesday and she woke with another grinding head and a stomach full of eels.

What was she doing?

Mr Larson would not have agreed if he had thought it was wrong.

Would he?

I can't bear the thought of hurting anyone, he had said, and now the words caught her middle like a knife and she had to call Eliza to top up the decanter, insisting pointedly that *someone* had been helping themselves, not caring how little impact that had when it was simply Eliza and herself and Cook, who moved like a ghost, in the house.

The day grew muddy again, and in the afternoon she went for a nap, waking with a desperate thirst, stumbling painfully to the back parlour with the expectation of Mr Larson sitting there waiting to inform her that he could not go through with the plan.

Expecting that he would see sense.

Hoping that, of all the people who knew her, he would be the one who would not judge her for what this most certainly was.

Madness.

Absolute, resolute, dreadful, *dreadful* madness.

She swallowed the rising bile and squinted at the clock.

It was after four.

The girl's séance began at five.

And he had neither come nor sent a message.

There was still time, she thought. He could simply be on his way.

She rang for water and bicarbonate of soda and Eliza brought up two fizzing tumblers, standing over her as she drank first one salty glass then the other. She hiccupped quietly into her hand and gave a feeble smile of thank you.

'Are you all right, ma'am?' Eliza said, and Mrs Wood waved her hand dismissively. 'You don't seem yourself.'

Mrs Wood squinted at her. 'I don't?' She gave a cold laugh.

'It don't seem right,' Eliza said suddenly. 'You've done a lot of good in your time, madam. I'd hate for you to forget that.' Mrs Wood's gaze slid back to the fire and she heard the more familiar sound of Eliza sighing. 'Just so you know, there's no more sherry until tomorrow, now,' she said. 'That person who's been helping themselves finished the last bottle and it's too cold out there to go and get any more.'

Mrs Wood looked away again. 'Dreadful behaviour,' she muttered, clearing her throat and holding her hand to her forehead to still the thudding. 'Are you sure there's nothing from Mr Larson?'

Eliza hesitated at the door. 'Are you expecting something?'

She gave a resigned shake of the head. 'No,' she said. 'Not really.' The man was loyal. *Beyond* loyal, if that were possible. He was a Labrador. She had asked him to do something unspeakable and, naturally, he had agreed.

She sat up.

What was she doing?

Of course, he wouldn't tell her that he couldn't do what she asked. It wasn't in his being: he had agreed and he would follow through.

What a position to put a good friend such as him into. What she'd done was unforgivable.

She remembered him on Monday night, his head in his hands. *I am wicked*, he'd said, and she'd thought him dramatic.

But he was right.

There was wickedry at play. Grotesque, disgusting, repulsive wickedry. But it wasn't him. It wasn't poor, loyal Mr Larson who had promised to look after his closest friend's wife, no matter what.

It was her.

She was the wicked one.

She was the one full of wickedry.

The Great Mrs Wood. Wicked criminal.

She looked at the clock. It was almost five.

There was still time. She could get to Wornington Road in a cab within ten minutes; the girl would barely have begun.

'A cab,' she said, stumbling to her feet.

Eliza gave a fractious tut. 'I'll go and get you a bloody bottle if you're that desperate.'

'No! No, no, not that . . .' she waved her hands in irritation. 'Just . . . just get me a cab.'

Eliza rolled her eyes. 'All right,' she said, going to the door. 'But make sure you wrap up. It's death out there tonight.'

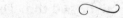

It took her far too long to get to the Mission Hall. She could see the Board School's clock on the corner showing half past five as the only cab she had been able to attract trundled around the corner of Wornington Road, its wheels scraping on the wet cobbles.

The girl would be well into her performance.

Had he already done it?

She craned from the window, searching out the hall in the blue shadows, starting when she saw it lit up like Christmas with light streaming from the wide-open front doors, silhouetting a small crowd, grappling on the top steps.

Oh no.

The cab slowed, and she could see that one of the shapes was Mr Larson – hatless – and her stomach tightened as another man turned in the light. Humboldt. Furious, scant hair awry, grasping the back of Mr Larson's jacket as though he planned to throw him down the stairs.

Before she had time to think, she had opened the door of the cab and stumbled onto the puddled pavement, calling out. 'Mr Humboldt! Stop! Please! It's not his fault . . .' She reached the bottom of the steps, panting back at the chaos of five men, hatless, askew, outraged, who had paused in their tussle to stare at her.

'Violet?' said Mr Larson.

'Mrs Wood?' said Humboldt.

'Please. Leave him alone. He didn't—'

'Are you part of this?' said Humboldt, his lip curling. But he had loosened his clutch on Mr Larson in surprise, and, sensing an opportunity, he slipped quickly away.

'This has nothing to do with her,' he said as he started down the steps.

'That's not true,' she said, but he caught her arm and pulled her along the road with him.

'It has *nothing* to do with you,' he said through his teeth.

'Don't think you'll get away with this, Larson!' shouted one of the men, raising his fist in their direction. 'We shall tell the whole town what a devil you are!'

'I'm so sorry,' she said. 'What have I done . . . ?'

'Keep walking,' he said, yanking her alongside him so quickly that she couldn't speak until they had rounded the corner onto Acklam Road, where, a few strides later, he stopped. She leaned against a railing, catching her breath while Mr Larson stood before her as though trying to assimilate what he had just done.

And then she saw how damaged he was. His hair was crumpled, his collar torn and a patch of his right sideburn was missing. She stopped, raised her hand towards his face, but he pulled his face away with an anger she had never seen from him before.

'I should never have asked you to do it,' she said. There were welts across his cheek that shone raw in the streetlamp. She pressed her hand to her mouth. 'What have I done?'

'I didn't do it,' he said.

She looked at him. 'You didn't?'

'I don't know what nonsense is playing in your mind, but did you really think that I would hurt a young girl simply because you asked me to?'

The wind disappeared from her – that he hadn't done it, that he was angry. That he had been as disgusted by her as she had been.

'I'm sorry, I should never . . .' she said again, feeling the uselessness of the words.

'You absolutely shouldn't,' he said. 'How could you even come up with something so appalling? I don't know what's happened to you, Mrs Wood, but I would never have expected you to suggest something so—'

'But something happened?'

His jaw flexed, and he looked away. 'I grabbed her,' he said.

'You grabbed her? You mean, you grabbed Miss Finch?'

'I grabbed the *spirit*,' he said. 'It came out of her cabinet, and I grabbed it.'

Despite it all, her curiosity could not be contained. 'What did it feel like?'

'Warm,' he said after a moment, staring at his boots. 'Flesh-like.'

'Do you think it was a . . .'

'No,' he said, and she realised again how thin the line was that she walked; and how little weight she had given to Mr Larson's own beliefs. 'It was not as I imagined a spirit to be. It was so very . . .'

'Human?'

He thought for a moment. 'I don't know,' he said. 'I don't even know what I grabbed. I don't even know if it was Miss Finch or—'

'Thank you,' she said, as a swell of relief rose to absorb her: the girl was unharmed, but Mr Larson – dear, clever Mr Larson – had exposed her fraudulence anyway. 'Thank you for helping me,' she tried to reach his eyes. 'You showed her for what she is. We can all—'

'Is that what you think I've done?'

'Well . . . yes,' she said. 'You grabbed her. Surely people saw—'

'They saw me grab a *spirit*. They saw the *spirit* flee to the cabinet shrieking that I was breaking the bond and killing her host.' He blinked and shook his head, clearly reliving the whole incident. 'And then I was sent to the floor by a host of boots and hands.' He pointed at the hole in his sideburn. 'This was an elderly lady's work,' he said. 'Humboldt actually saved me from the worst of it, if you can believe that.'

'But you helped me. I'm eternally grateful,' she said, and he gave a sharp, mirthless laugh.

'I didn't do it for you,' he said.

'But—'

'Whatever feud you have with that girl is nothing to do with me.'

'Then why would you do that?'

'For *me*!' he shouted, his voice echoing around the rows of narrow terraced houses and two young women walking on the opposite pavement clutched one another with a giggle. He ducked his head close to her. 'I did it for me,' he continued. 'Lies matter to me too, Mrs Wood. The integrity of spiritualism *matters* to me.' She thought of his dead twin, remembered the sobs he gave up when she first brought him through.

'Of course. I—'

'I needed to know if she was true or not. *I* needed to know if the girl really had materialised a spirit. Had that honestly not occurred to you?'

She felt the heat in her cheeks. She had been so caught up in her own anxiety that she hadn't thought for one minute that Mr Larson might also have an interest. Her stomach rolled again, the momentary delight of his actions warped by the reality of his intent.

'Your silence says everything,' he said, and she tried to respond, sensing the precipice she was on, but the words would not come. 'You are changed, Mrs Wood. And no matter what I promised your husband, I can no longer be around you. It is too painful to see the woman you have become.'

'Mr Larson. I know that I asked something terrible of you. I know that . . .'

But he had turned away, raising his arm towards an oncoming cab. 'I shall arrange for your investment portfolio to be passed to a colleague.' He stopped and looked at her. 'You'll be relieved to know that one of your ships is due to dock on the thirteenth of January. I have no more duties to perform.'

'Mr Larson, please. I don't care about that. You are my friend. I can't imagine—'

'I shall see you home,' he said, over his shoulder, still not looking at her. 'And then we shall continue our lives separately. I do not doubt that you will survive perfectly well without me.'

CHAPTER 35

The end of 1873 loomed in dark days passed in a haze of sherry and humiliation. She coddled herself in the back parlour, wrapping up against the slithering fingers of winter, warming herself from the inside out.

In the gloom, she sat lost in memories of a better life: when all she had worried about was her looming fortieth birthday. Last Christmas she had been surrounded by friends, her home had been full of joy with fires blazing and the tree in the hall, decorated with candles and cards and ribbons. There had been festive séances at her patrons' homes: Mrs Green's tree larger than the one at Buckingham Palace, while the Dowager had slipped her a small package containing a diamond pin as she left. And on Christmas Day, she had invited Mr Larson to join her for lunch with Miss Newman, and they had spent all afternoon settled around the dining table, indulging in roast duck and plum pudding.

It seemed impossible that everything should have changed so irrevocably in the space of a few months. And yet, it had. Since she had made the stupid mistake of inviting that snake into her world, everything had soured until now, only a few weeks from Christmas, she was alone, in a house with no paper chains, no trees, no joy.

When the doorbell rang one long afternoon, she had cowered in her back parlour, waiting for Eliza to come up from the kitchen.

'Who is it?' she had hissed through a crack in the door.

Eliza moved discreetly down the hall, craning to see through the hall window. She stopped and looked back at Mrs Wood. 'It's the Dowager.'

The Dowager! 'Tell her I'm away,' she said frantically, the image of her current state of dishevelment rearing in her mind's eye. 'I cannot see her. Tell her I am away!' She slammed the back parlour door, pressing her ear to the wood to hear the Dowager's voice, expecting her to tell Eliza that Mrs Wood's services were no longer needed.

But she didn't. She simply said that she had been passing and wanted to extend Mrs Wood Christmas greetings in person. Was she well?

'Yes, my lady,' said Eliza, and she felt a flood of gratitude towards her. 'Well and busy.'

'I see,' the Dowager said. 'Will you tell her I came to see her? I would like us to talk should she have a few moments soon.'

Her heart sank as she returned to her chair. Of course, the Dowager would relinquish their relationship in person. She was honourable to the end.

She stopped opening her letters, unable to bear the vague apologies or excuses from former friends and clients. She had no private consultations booked in. She only glanced at the front page of the *Spiritual Times* before throwing it onto the kindling pile for a future fire, not risking a longer look in case she should see her own name. The scandal for Christmas was, of course, Mr Larson's attempt at exposing Miss Finch and how it had failed.

Poor Mr Larson. What had she done to him?

It is too painful to see the woman you have become.

He had been right. She hardly recognised herself anymore. Her eyes had grown puffy and the whites were pink at the corners, her skin was waxen, and new lines cut like stitches into the edges of her lips as though she were a hundred. How lucky he was that he could avoid seeing what she had become. There was no escape for her, she was stuck with that dreadful Caliban staring back at her.

She hadn't dared to even formulate the notion of what Mr Wood would think, the truth enough to make her walk out into the cold and never return. When she allowed herself to pry around its edges, she felt his shame like the pain of the very vitriol she had thought would save the scraps of her life.

How could she have ever considered maiming the girl just to be rid of her?

How could she have drawn poor Mr Larson into a plan of such atrocity?

The shame, the disgust. No matter how many sherries she drank, neither abated. They rose with her in the morning and faded out when she succumbed to the night.

And beneath it all bubbled the realisation that without her even having to whisper about Thirza, the girl had broken her.

The girl had won.

There were five letters on the console waiting for her when she came down on Christmas Eve morning. The one on top was in the Dowager's handwriting. She put them all in the drawer of the console, unopened. She couldn't bear any more rejection. Not today.

She moved unsteadily towards the back parlour, where she remained for six hours, watching the room grow blue with the dying day and blurry until, while the rest of Chepstow Villas final-ised their plans for Christmas Day luncheon, she made her way back upstairs, foggy and alone.

The house was cold and dark, Eliza having been given a rare night away at her sister's in Nunhead, Cook in the kitchen waiting until she could slip out to Midnight Mass.

Eliza had left the bones of a fire in her grate, but she lacked the spirit to light it, deciding to save it until she couldn't feel her toes. She touched her faltering candle to the stub on her nightstand and sat heavily on the edge of her bed, staring at nothing but the flickering walls. Undressing felt too great an effort, especially with no one to help. She thought for a moment of simply lying down as she was, but a second thought of her dying in the night and being found in such a state of disrepair roused her enough to force her to her feet.

If she were to die tonight, she would do so in a fresh nightgown.

She carried the gown over to the dressing table, draping it over the door of her armoire and was about to *finally* pick up a brush when her eye was caught by a movement inside the cabinet that started her heart. A mouse? Oh God. Eliza dealt with mice – what was she supposed to do without her here to dispose of it?

She tentatively reached for the door, peering around the edge into the darkness.

Another flurry of movement and she was forced to duck as an enormous moth launched itself from her dresses, a dusty wing catching her forehead as it bounced across the room and out into the landing. She sat on the floor, a hand pressed to her throat, willing her heart to steady as she pushed the armoire door closed. But as she did, she paused.

Her heavy, black séance dress hung in the shadows like a criminal.

The silk was cool beneath her fingers, stiff in places where moisture from some piece of séance collateral had seeped through, or a drop of champagne had been left unwiped. She pushed her hands into the skirts, searching out the pockets and openings, everything feeling strange and foreign from this angle. As she explored inside one little hidey-hole, she felt something small and hard against her fingertips, stuck tight in a narrow corner.

She worked her fingers to prise it out, rolling it up the lining until it popped free into her palm.

A stone. Smooth and pale.

She turned it over, and blinked, sitting back on her heels. There, scratched white on the grey surface were the initials SN.

S. N.

Sarah Newman.

Miss Newman.

She ran her fingernail over the marks, turning the stone, wondering if perhaps she was reading something that wasn't actually there.

Was it a sign?

After a moment, she closed her fingers and turned her eyes to the heavens.

Yes, she decided. Finding a stone like that, when they were usually so meticulous in unpacking her after a séance, and that stone being carved with Miss Newman's initials.

It was absolutely a sign.

Mrs Reynolds had been bewildered and then concerned when Mrs Wood arrived at her door while she and Mr Reynolds were enjoying a quiet Christmas Day breakfast.

She had managed to tame her hair that morning, but without Eliza, she'd been forced to ask Cook to help her dress, and in her confusion at being above stairs and inexperience at dressing a lady she had ended up leaving the house with a loose corset and a dress that hadn't been completely buttoned. Still, it was nothing a large shawl couldn't hide, and she struck out before the clock struck ten after a sherry-free breakfast with a long-overdue Christmas card and hope.

As she strode along the wet pavements, the resolve felt as strong as any substance, and she carried the little stone with Miss Newman's initials in her pocket, her fingers instinctively touching it as she passed beneath the gaze of the increasingly grand terraces towards Pembridge Square.

'You must join us,' said Mrs Reynolds, coming to meet her at the door. 'We're having smoked trout and eggs.'

'I won't, dearest,' she said, remembering to smile. 'It's very kind of you, but I promise that I've eaten already.'

'Then a drink. A festive glass?'

'That would be lovely . . .' she said, swallowing hard. 'But I really must keep to my word. It's so silly that I misplaced her address!'

'Oh, these things happen,' Mrs Reynolds said with a sweet smile. 'I'm sure she'll be absolutely delighted to see you. Now. I just need to remember where I put it . . .' She drifted into the drawing room.

She was suddenly aware of Mr Reynolds' eyes from the breakfast room and threw him a bright smile.

'Merry Christmas, dearest!' she said. 'Sorry to interrupt!'

'We're always happy to see you,' he said, raising his glass with a cheery smile. 'It's been far too long.'

'It has. You must come for supper in the new year,' she said, surprising herself with how much she meant it. She put her hand in her pocket. The stone was warm.

She could hear Mrs Reynolds rooting through papers, followed by a sudden 'ah-ha!' And then she was rushing back into the hall, flapping a scrap of paper in her hand. 'It's a bit of a scribble, but . . .' she passed the scrap to Mrs Wood, squinting at the scrawl of ink. 'I think that's an "r",' she said, pointing. 'Yes. It's *Thur*low Road. She said it was near the Smallpox Hospital.' She grimaced. 'Rather her than me.'

'Thank you,' she said, staring at the address: *35 Thurlow Road*.

'And you won't take the carriage?' Mrs Reynolds said. 'Morton could have it ready in no time, I promise.'

'There's an omnibus that goes to Hampstead.'

Mrs Reynolds pressed her hand to her mouth in horror. 'On your own? On Christmas Day? I won't hear of it. You will take our carriage and that's that.' And she bustled her through to the dining room, calling out to her girl to fetch the groom and ready the horses.

With all of her strength, she declined the champagne, accepting instead some hot drop scones with apricot jam while she waited for the carriage to appear, listening to Mrs Reynolds' delightfully inconsequential news of a mutual acquaintance becoming a great-grandmother. Oh! How she had missed inconsequential news.

And when the carriage finally pulled up before the house and Mrs Reynolds walked her to the door, she realised how long it had been since she had visited anyone other than for Medium business. She turned, clutched Mrs Reynolds' hand. How soft it was. How pliable and warm. And she thought for a moment of how Miss Finch's 'spirit' hand would have felt when Mr Larson had grabbed her.

Enough. No more. She touched the stone in her pocket.

Today was about reconciliation.

'Will you send her our festive wishes?' Mrs Reynolds asked as she helped Mrs Wood into the carriage. 'Will you tell her that we miss her?'

She smiled as she settled her skirts. 'I will,' she said, and the carriage rolled away from the kerb before Mrs Reynolds could say anything in response.

She looked at the address in her hand, the ink blurring slightly beneath the heat of her fingertips.

A distant flurry of nerves began in her stomach and she pressed her hand around the stone.

It's a sign, she said.

Everything was going to be all right.

CHAPTER 36

Thurlow Road was part of a new development near Hampstead Ponds. A curving, elegant street dotted with saplings and lined by large yellow-brick houses bright with fresh pointing and gleaming window frames.

Number thirty-five had drawn blinds at all of its windows, but she could see the glimmer of light around the edges of the first-floor window and so, asking Mrs Reynolds' groom to wait, she clambered down to the pristine pavement and made her way up the black-and-white tiled path to the front door.

The house was crisp with newness, smart and expensive looking. What kind of person was Miss Newman staying with? Did the women of her society really have incomes that would afford them homes like this? Perhaps she had misjudged things . . .

Her finger hovered over the modern doorbell, its white dome a tiny moon in the shadows of the porch.

What would she say if Miss Newman wasn't there?

She swallowed the bubble of panic.

Ring the bell.

Ring the bell and make amends.

She took a breath and rang the bell.

After a moment, she heard someone coming down a flight of stairs and then a short, middle-aged woman in a purple dress opened the door, startling her.

'Can I help you?' the woman asked, her voice clipped but not unfriendly.

She hesitated. Was this informality what passed for staff in this quarter? 'Is Miss Newman at home?' she asked eventually, and the woman turned her head.

'Sarah!' she shouted into the house. 'Sarah: there's someone at the door for you.' She turned back and smiled. 'Merry Christmas,' she said.

'Yes, of course!' she replied, remembering herself. 'Merry Christmas to you too.' There was a pause, during which she felt the woman's eyes measuring her. 'I'm sorry to interrupt . . .' she said.

'Do you support suffrage for women?' the woman in purple asked, and she looked at her.

'Do I . . . ?'

'Don't waste your time, Marge,' said a familiar voice from the stairs. 'She's a lost cause.'

She looked beyond the woman – *Marge* – and watched Miss Newman emerge, hem-first, until she saw her face – fresher, wider than she remembered – and the relief she felt at finally seeing her was so overwhelming that it took all she had to restrain herself from pushing past poor Marge and embracing her.

'Violet,' said Miss Newman, standing out of reach. Her voice was remarkably, painfully flat. 'What are you doing here?'

She held the stone in her pocket, trying to feel the strength it had given her when she'd found it.

'I should . . .' said Marge, pointing up the stairs. 'Eloise Trotter brought over a little magic lantern show this morning,' she said to Mrs Wood. 'A group of us gals are enjoying a stroll down this year's highlights. You're welcome to join—'

'I think we'll go for a walk,' Miss Newman said quickly, patting Marge's arm with a warmth that stung Mrs Wood's heart. 'I'll bring up some mulled wine when I'm home.'

Marge glanced between the two of them and gave a breezy smile. 'Well. You're always welcome,' she said to Mrs Wood. 'A friend of Sarah's is a friend of mine. And I always enjoy changing people's minds!'

They waited until they heard Marge return to the room upstairs, the opening and closing of the door releasing a bubble of delighted female voices.

'She seems pleasant,' said Mrs Wood.

'Margery Land heads the North West London branch of the society,' she said. 'She's more than *pleasant*. She's an inspiration to thousands.' She reached up to the stand beside the door, extracting her old black cloak, tying it around her neck before collecting her bonnet. 'Shall we?' she said, knotting the ribbon beneath her chin.

Mrs Wood stepped back to allow Miss Newman to walk out onto the street. 'The Ponds are the other side of the high road,' she said. 'We shall make a circuit. I can't be long. I'm expected.'

The tension between them was unbearable as they walked towards the busy road, Mrs Wood turning the stone over and over in her fingers, feeling its initials with her fingernail.

It had been a sign. Hadn't it?

Now here, with the friend she had banished from her life, bristling beside her, jaw flexing as they waited to cross the teeming high road, it felt silly. It was nothing more than a leftover stone, that was all. And the initials were probably meaningless.

And still they hadn't spoken.

Not even when a dray cart had nearly caught the back of Mrs Wood's skirt.

Finally across the high road, she followed Miss Newman down a side street where houses gave way to wild, bare-branched trees and unruly bushes. Miss Newman suddenly veered left and strode between a riot of gorse and over a muddy hillock, turning onto the Heath with a confidence that awed Mrs Wood. She knew this world that was so alien to her.

She had read about the Ponds, seen pieces that spoke of people swimming in them, and so she was intrigued to see them in person, imagining a tranquil expanse of glittering water. The flat, brown pond rimmed by tangles of weeds and bushes that greeted her, therefore, was a disappointment, and the sheer number of ducks and swans cruising its surface made her wonder at the sanity of anyone who chose to dive within.

'Shall we?' Miss Newman said, and Mrs Wood realised she was indicating a bench just off the path. She nodded and followed her over nubs of grass to settle on the wooden seat, putting her hand in her pocket as Miss Newman sat beside her, staring out across the depressing water.

'I found this,' she said, opening her palm and showing her the stone, the SN less bright after being rolled in her fingers for so long. 'It made me realise what I had done.'

Miss Newman glanced and snorted. 'It took a stone.'

'Your initials,' she said. 'Look. Your initials are on it.'

She glanced again. 'Turn it around,' she said. 'That's not an SN. It's NS. Nathanial Sharpe. From October's Grand Séance? The one with the dead father. The one you missed out altogether because you were too distracted by Miss Finch.'

She blinked and turned the stone.

NS.

Of course.

He had been at the table, but she had forgotten him entirely. She thought of him now, sitting in the gladdening light at the end, blinking, the confusion that no one had come for him written large across his face. And all that she had done was ignore her mistake and squeeze his arm and tell him that sometimes this was what happened with the spirit world. *Our power was too strong for the weaker spirits.*

What a fool she had been. Then and now. In so, so many ways.

She closed her hand and dropped the stone onto the grass at her feet.

'I need to tell you something,' she said. 'It won't excuse my behaviour, but maybe you'll understand why I did . . . what I did. You deserve to know the truth.'

She felt Miss Newman shift. 'If it's about the girl—'

'It's not,' she said. 'It's about me,' she said. 'It's about who I am.'

For the first time in her adult life she told the truth. She told Miss Newman how she hadn't come from a wealthy doctor but an unknown sailor and had grown up damp with poverty and sold by Thirza to keep her in drink. She told her about Thirza's ruin, how hard she had worked to hide it.

Then she told her how the girl had found out, and what the girl had done. The blackmail, the slow creep over her patrons.

The truth flowed from her.

Every last drop.

And as she spoke, she watched Miss Newman's face, waiting for the disgust, for the disappointment and the repulsion.

But it didn't come.

None of it.

When she had finished, her body trembling with the flush of adrenaline and fear, Miss Newman remained still. She watched her eyes flickering as she replayed what she had just heard, waiting for the change.

But it didn't come.

Her heart pounded in her throat. 'Sarah?'

Miss Newman kept her eyes on the pond. 'Why didn't you tell me?'

'How could I? By the time we met, I was established; the *lie* was established. If I told you, it would've changed everything.'

'Not that,' she said. 'I don't care about your past. I mean about what the girl did to you.' She shook her head. 'I allied myself to that little vixen. I thought you were being cruel to her. I thought you were jealous and ill-tempered and . . .' She threw her hands up in the air . 'Oh, I'm so *angry*, Violet.'

Mrs Wood looked at her hands. 'I'm sorry. I should—'

'Not at you, you dolt. At *me*! I've been such a fool. I didn't trust your judgement—'

'She's very good at what she does, Sarah.'

'Yes. She is. But so am I.'

Mrs Wood gave her a half-smile. 'Yes, you are.'

'I wish you had told me.'

'How could I?' she said. 'I would have had to tell you everything. And I couldn't. Not then. I felt so certain you were going to leave me too. I've lost so much, Sarah. I couldn't bear the thought of you turning your back on me too.'

'And so you hurt me instead!'

She looked away, blinking hard at the embarrassment.

'Suggesting I couldn't be trusted was the worst thing you could ever have said to me,' Miss Newman said.

'I know,' she said. 'I'm so sorry. After being dropped by so many of my patrons . . . when I found the letter I didn't know what to think. I just assumed . . .' She stopped. 'I know that I was wrong. I'm sorry.'

Miss Newman was quiet. A pair of swans took off from the surface of the pond, their wings snapping like applause in the cold air. 'So why now?' she asked eventually. 'Why didn't you come after me the moment I left?'

'The house is so quiet without you, Sarah. I've had plenty of time to consider my appalling behaviour.'

Miss Newman looked at her for a moment. 'I read about Mr Larson and Miss Finch,' she said.

She bit her lip and looked away. 'I've not been myself, Sarah,' she said.

'This is what happens when you're left to your own devices,' she said before exhaling crossly. 'How did I not see what that girl was doing?' she said.

'Because being ruthless doesn't mean she's not excellent at what she does, Sarah,' she said. 'I was drawn in by her, as much as anyone.'

'Violet,' she said. 'It's my job to look for the flaws.'

'And she's been trained to hide them.'

328

A young family appeared on the path, two small boys bowling ahead with handfuls of bread for the birds on the pond while the parents strolled behind, arm in arm. They watched in silence as the boys threw whole chunks of bread at the ducks clamouring suddenly at their feet.

'I read your pamphlet last night,' she said.

Miss Newman shifted on the bench. 'You took your time,' she said. Then, after a moment: 'What did you think?'

'It was very interesting,' she said, as earnestly as she could muster. 'I liked the bit about women needing access to employment that matches their intellect. I don't think that will go down well with men.'

'It won't,' said Miss Newman with a satisfied smile. 'An awful lot of them anyway.'

Mrs Wood paused before she asked, tentatively: 'How is your friend?'

She felt Miss Newman sit up taller. 'He's . . . ah. He's very well.'

She smiled as she looked at her, her cheeks had pinked. 'What's his name?'

'George,' she said. 'It was in the pamphlet you said you read.'

'Oh yes,' she said quickly, and Miss Newman smiled.

'George wasn't planned, Violet. The last thing I expected when I joined the society was to fall in love.'

Love. It hit her like a stone. 'Of course not,' she said, feeling her face flush at the intimacy of the idea. They had never spoken about *romantic love*. Apart from Mr Larson, there had never been any talk of men in that way at all. She had simply assumed that, at her age, Miss Newman was looking forward to life as a treasured friend and assistant. Before all the mess with Miss Finch, she had always appeared content with her lot. Hadn't she? 'I . . .' Mrs Wood began, stumbling to find the most suitable words. 'I . . . I suppose . . . I never really thought that you would . . .'

'Be loved?'

She looked at her lap. 'No,' she said quietly. 'Not that.'

'When you made the decision to remain a widow, Violet, did you assume that I had elected to remain a spinster too?'

She tried to laugh the comment off, but it stuck in her throat. 'I didn't really . . .' she began before giving up. 'I assumed that you and I would grow old together. Like the Adams sisters. But more sensible.'

A smile cracked the corner of Miss Newman's face. 'You forget how much younger than you I am, Violet.'

She flashed a glance, enjoying the ease that had returned so quickly between them.

Miss Newman sighed. 'I know,' she said. 'No one has been more surprised by what's transpired than I,' she said. 'Trust me.'

Mrs Wood patted her arm. 'He's very lucky to have you.'

'Thank you,' said Miss Newman, covering her hand with her own. 'I feel very lucky to have him too.'

They sat together for a moment longer. 'You're sure you won't marry Mr Larson?' she asked, as Mrs Wood removed her hand and pushed it into the warmth of her pocket.

'I'm not that miserable, Sarah,' she said before pausing. 'I'm . . . I'm assuming that this means you won't be coming home,' she said as casually as she could. 'But you know that you could if you wanted.' Her heart thudded in the silence.

'I'm sorry, Violet,' Miss Newman said quietly, and her heart sagged. 'It's not because of this. Or because of what has or hasn't happened before. It's because . . .' She turned to Mrs Wood. 'You've read my work now. You must understand that this is important. I'm needed here, Violet. These women, they're changing the world and I'm actually part of it.'

'You've always been one for grand ideas,' she said, forcing levity.

'I need to do this. For me.'

'And womankind,' she said, and Miss Newman smiled into her lap. 'It won't be the same, Sarah,' she said. 'It can't be.'

'Let's not get all maudlin about this,' said Miss Newman. 'I'll still be around. But . . . my place is here now. With the work.'

She was too late. She knew that now. She had tried to save herself by pushing Miss Newman away, but she had been wrong and now there was nothing to be done to resolve it. Not for her. She took a breath. There was nothing she could do to take her life back to the way it was again. It was over.

Miss Newman took her hand and gave it a squeeze. 'You'll find another assistant,' she said. 'I'll help you.'

A group of ducks began thrashing excitedly around on the pond, their quacks offering a welcome respite from her thoughts.

'There is still one thing I should very much like to do,' Miss Newman said as the ducks settled as quickly as they'd erupted. 'A final hurrah as they say.'

She looked up expectantly.

'I want to make sure that girl gets her comeuppance,' she said. 'After all that viper has done, don't you think that would be fun?'

Miss Emmeline Finch
12 Exhibition Road, Kensington

2nd January 1874

My dear Mrs Wood,
Happy New Year! Did you have a nice Christmas? I had lunch at
Claridge's which was very nice and then a little séance with some of
my patrons. Oh, it was really quite lovely. You should've been there.
Mrs Green was in wonderful spirits.

You will see that I have now moved rooms <u>again</u>. Mr Clore,
who's so nice really, found me a splendid little place in Kensington
that overlooks the park. I say little, it has four rooms so Mother
now has her own bedroom which has made her happy. Magnus has
made it really quite comfortable for me with lots of lovely new
furniture. I gave the stuff I had in Westbourne Park away – it
didn't look right in the new place. I hope you didn't spend too much
on it, it really had become terribly shabby in such a short amount
of time.

I'm sure you heard about what your friend Mr Larson got up to
the other week. It was very naughty of him, but I know he feels loyal
to you so perhaps he couldn't help it. My patrons have been telling
me that it must've been your idea but I tell them they're wrong
because you would never sink so low. Or risk your reputation. Not
after everything we've talked about. That would be silly, wouldn't it.

I can help you, though, because I know how dangerous gossip like
that can be. I could put all those rumours and nasty bits of gossip
to bed by having you as a guest at one of my future
materialisations. I think if the public see that we are not enemies,
perhaps they'll think more fondly of you again. And wouldn't it be
nice to be back together?

January is ever so busy, so shall we say the first Tuesday of

February? I'm assuming you won't be holding your usual Grand Séance. I don't think you're doing those anymore? I've not heard anything about them recently, anyway, and Mrs Green said to me that she thought you were retiring.

Please do confirm. I understand Miss Newman is no longer with you, so don't worry about preparing anything. It will be enough just to have you in my audience.

Yours very truly,

Emmeline

CHAPTER 37

She kept the letter and the plan she had worked up in a new note-book to herself until Thursday morning when Miss Newman had arranged to come to the house for a visit: the first time she had seen her since Christmas Day.

That week, she ate breakfast each morning watching the families up and down Chepstow Villas remove their wreaths and wrestle the bright festive greenery from the lampposts. When everything was gone, the bareness was disappointing, another reminder of what the dark days of December had stolen from her.

But Miss Newman was a jewel on the horizon.

She chased Eliza around the house all that week, making sure that the deepest cobwebs were dispatched, moving potted plants and trinket boxes around to cover the new darns and stains, rotating rugs to hide stubborn dirt and turning the drapes to hide the frayed edges.

And when she arrived on the dot of eleven that Thursday morning, she filled the hall with her glorious presence – all bold voice and fresh air.

'Hello house!' she called, reaching out to touch the fat leaf of a succulent that hid a wax burn on the console. 'I've missed you.'

'I've lit the fire in the parlour,' Mrs Wood said. 'Come. Eliza will bring some tea in a moment. Unless you wanted coffee? She could make you some coffee . . .'

Miss Newman waved her hand. 'Don't be silly. I'll take what comes.' She took a deep, slow breath. 'It's lovely to be back.'

'Your room is still where it was,' she said, and Miss Newman gave a laugh.

'I've not even been here five minutes,' she said.

'You can't blame me for trying,' she said. 'I miss you.'

Miss Newman placed her hand on her arm. It was warm from her gloves. 'And I miss you,' she said. 'This was my home for a long time.'

'It's *always* your home, Sarah.'

'But right now,' she said, heaping her coat and hat onto the cloak stand, 'we have work to do.'

Miss Newman read Miss Finch's letter with active eyebrows, the colour slowly rising in her cheeks until she dropped it with a flourish of disgust onto the side table.

'What a vole,' she said. 'How did I not read what she hides between her lines before?'

'It's shocking, isn't it.' How wonderful it felt to finally be able to release her frustration and anger. And how wonderful to be able to release them upon Miss Newman again!

'Her audacity! And Mrs Green?'

'You know the girl's got some friendship or other with Sheba.'

'But retiring?'

'I doubt she said any such thing. Every word in that letter is a jab of her rapier. Why would that one be any different.'

Miss Newman took up the letter again, holding it to the light of the lamp and squinting at the lines, her mouth moving slightly as she read.

'You know,' she said, turning to Mrs Wood. 'You know, we could make this work in our favour.'

'Yes,' she said. 'I know.'

Miss Newman's eyes widened in delight. 'Oh really?' she said. 'What are you thinking?'

'Why would I ever go to that horrible little hall on Wornington Road,' she said. 'I've not been in such an establishment since I left Hull.' How pleasant it was to be able to say such things without fear. 'And nor shall I ever again in the future.'

'You're suggesting she come here?'

'I'm certainly not suggesting we go to her *splendid new rooms* in Kensington.'

'Perish the thought.'

'I've been thinking: we invite her here, we host her with all her new patrons – and some of my former fickle hearts. We'll look magnanimous in our generosity while she performs one of her full spirit materialisations before far too many people in an unfamiliar environment.'

'What could possibly go wrong?' Miss Newman said.

'What *could* indeed?' she said. 'And wouldn't it be serendipity if we were there to pick up the pieces and send our guests home happy. Apart from Miss Finch, of course.'

'What about the cabinet? Would she even be able to bring it?'

'You remember the Kendall brothers used to tote theirs every-where. You couldn't move for cabinets going in and out of Mediums' homes at one point in the sixties.'

'Ah,' Miss Newman said. 'The heady days of spirit faces.'

'Precisely.'

'But surely a cabinet for a full spirit will be much bigger than one for faces.'

The door swung open and Eliza appeared with tea. They sat back, swallowing their words, as she stomped inelegantly across the room.

'Nice to see you, Miss Newman,' she said, pushing the rattling tray onto the sideboard.

'And you too, Eliza.'

'Cook made your favourite madeleines,' she said, and Miss Newman gave a sigh of pleasure and got up, leaning towards the plate of warm cakes as she reached for the pot.

'She's a treasure,' she said, filling the cups.

Eliza gave an approximation of a smile and wiped her hands on her apron.

'Is everything all right, Eliza?' Mrs Wood asked, accepting a brimming cup of tea from Miss Newman, a yellow madeleine resting in its saucer. 'You're hovering.'

'I weren't earwigging,' she said.

'What are you talking about, Eliza?'

'You know it's not my custom to go around listening at doors, only you was talking when I come in. About cabinets.'

'Why was that of any interest to you?'

'Well,' she said, crossing her arms. 'It's probably nothing, but . . . this girl I know from the grocer's, she's started doing for Wornington Hall.'

Mrs Wood shared a glance with Miss Newman. 'Oh?'

'And, you know, *Miss Finch*' – spoken with true Eliza venom, and Mrs Wood thought that perhaps Eliza should be her yardstick going forward; *she* had never liked the girl – 'keeps *her* cabinet there.'

'How interesting,' she said with careful nonchalance.

'So, you know,' she said. 'When I heard you was talking about cabinets, I thought you might like to know that. P'raps you might find it helpful. I don't suppose it'd be hard to get a look at it.'

Mrs Wood sat back in her chair. 'Eliza,' she said, 'are you suggesting you undertake some . . . research for us?'

She shrugged. 'Whatever you want to call it,' she said.

'It would be useful to know how it worked,' said Miss Newman. 'I have an idea of what she might be using, but . . .'

'And your friend has said that she'll show you?'

'She owes me a favour,' she said.

'And she understands the value of discretion?'

'Who's she going to tell that cares?'

Mrs Wood looked at Eliza's face with its cast of eternal disapproval. Eliza had never been part of her work, she had kept her

337

firmly innocent, there in the background with strong tea and heaped plates, cleaning up the séance debris, beating the stains from her séance dress, sweeping away the burned séance sketches from the fireplaces. That she had done it all without any apparent curiosity was her greatest asset to Mrs Wood.

But now, she was offering something that would bring her into the secret; something that would make her complicit. Could she trust her?

'It's up to you,' Eliza said eventually, turning. 'S'no skin off my nose.'

'If you insist,' she said, and Eliza stopped and looked back. 'It would be interesting to know what it looks like, Eliza. Just so we have an idea of how big it is if the girl decides to bring it here, you understand. And if it comes in pieces. If there are seats within . . .'

'Course,' she said, with a shrug. 'I'll let you know when I'm going. You can give me my instructions then.'

After Eliza closed the door behind her, Mrs Wood looked at Miss Newman.

'An unexpected gift,' Miss Newman said.

'Indeed,' she said. 'It won't hurt to know how that thing works.' She took a mouthful of her tea.

Miss Newman raised her cup and smiled over the rim. 'No,' she said. 'It certainly won't.'

12th January 1874

Dear Mrs Wood,

Thank you for apologising. I do appreciate it. I knew you had your own little worries, but it was nice to hear you were sorry not to have seen the culmination of this past year's work.

I'll be honest: I wasn't sure what to do about the invitation to host a séance at your home. I'm sure you would like Wornington Hall - it's very nice there. They even have hot-water bottles for the elderly, so you'd be more than comfortable.

But returning to Chepstow Villas is too tempting - wouldn't it be nice to present Tandy in the flesh in the very place where I began all those months ago.

So: yes. I'd love to host a séance at your house. And so would Tandy! Shall we say 3rd February? I know that would ordinarily be your Grand Séance day, before you gave them up, so I assume you'll be free.

You're very kind to offer to transport my cabinet, but I shall have it delivered with me. It will fit in your séance room as it fitted easily into Colonel Phillips' the other day and yours is slightly bigger than their little parlour.

On a note of professionalism, I'll need complete privacy once it's been set in the séance room - I am sure you understand how precious a Medium's cabinet is and so I trust you won't be offended when I lock the door.

Thank you too for allowing me to invite my own patrons. I shall send my list through nearer the time, although I'm sure you'll recognise some of them!

I shall see you soon,

The very kindest of regards,

Emmeline

CHAPTER 38

The night of Miss Finch's séance was a night of firsts.

It was the first time Mrs Wood had entertained since the Circle in November. With the income from January's ship cargo filtering through, she had managed to cobble together enough to throw a party without anyone noticing her depreciation.

It was also the first time a séance would be held in her home, and she would not, officially, be part of it.

The thought had always seemed preposterous – besides being a waste of her talent, who would have the courage to think that they might do anything better than the Great Mrs Wood? In the Great Mrs Wood's home!

Of course, that person would be Miss Finch.

So tonight, her skirts were empty. Miss Newman had no notes, and all the preparation they needed was a puff of powder and the selection of appropriate jewellery. She sat before her mirror, Miss Newman finishing off her hair with a diamond comb, feeling lopsided, unfinished, as though she had left something on an omnibus.

It had been a while since her hair had received such care, and with Miss Newman's expert touch it glowed in the light of her candle stub.

'There.' Miss Newman smiled at her in the glass. 'Perfect.' She returned the smile then fluffed another layer of powder over her nose and pinched her cheeks. It didn't remove the years, but at least she looked a little more alive. And she had to acknowledge the sparkle in her eye that had returned with her friend; plotting clearly suited her.

A bang came from downstairs and Miss Newman stared curiously at the floor. 'What do you think she's doing in there?'

Mrs Wood turned in her seat. 'And with whom.' Miss Newman's eyebrow went up.

The girl had arrived at six, entering the house in a riot of crimson silk, riding on a wave of fuss and noise, flapping around the two men who sweated beneath the weight of her cabinet, reminding them repeatedly not to bump it. That it was very expensive. That she'd have their jobs if they left a single mark.

She had stopped to check Eliza's work in the séance room just before the girl arrived and found the room felt already alien and unwelcoming, as if it knew it was taking on the character of someone new.

She had turned the gaslights on for Miss Finch to place the cabinet, the jets sputtering and smelly after months of inactivity, but the sconces and sticks were prepared for later with sleek new candles ready to cast their small pools of light as soon as the mantels were off. As requested, the table had been removed, placed on its side in the back parlour, and spaces left around the rows of chairs, again as requested, so that Tandy could dance around her patrons. And on the sideboard, she'd left a discreet buffet of cordial beside a selection of hors d'oeuvres and a bowl heaped with fruit.

Miss Finch followed her cabinet inside, berating the men again for almost scraping it, and Mrs Wood stood respectfully, strangely in the doorway.

'It's heavier than it bloody looks,' rasped one of the men as they dropped it into position to the left of the window, wiping his forehead with the back of his hand.

'That's why I'm paying you more than you're worth,' said the girl, scouring the wood for any marks. Finally, she stood and turned to the older one of the pair, her finger on the side panel. 'There's a scratch.'

The man shrugged. 'It was probably there before.'

'You and I both know that it wasn't. We looked it over together.'

The man looked at his mate. 'Yeah, but Jim's right,' he said. 'It's heavier than I remember. If we'd known, we would've brung another man.'

'Pish,' the girl said dismissively. 'You're just trying to get more money out of me.' She opened her pocket and pulled out a few silver coins, holding them in her small, gloved fingers. 'This is what we agreed on delivery.' The man looked at them as they landed in his palm and then back at the girl. 'You'll get the rest later tonight when you pick it up.'

He turned back to the coins and shook his head. 'We'll bring Bert,' he said to his mate, patting him on the back as they walked out of the room, tipping his hat towards Mrs Wood. 'Evening,' he said, and she gave a faltering smile as they went by, leaving a trail of sweat and tobacco in their wake.

'No Humboldt tonight?' she asked, turning back to the girl. 'On the list. I noticed his name was absent.'

'Who?' said the girl, distracted with the gleaming brass catch on her cabinet.

'Humboldt,' she repeated. 'I noticed his name wasn't on your list of guests.'

'Oh him,' she said with a laugh. 'God, I don't go around with that dullard anymore.'

Poor Humboldt, finally empty of use, and she smiled when she realised that she felt a sudden and strange affinity with him.

'It's a handsome piece,' she said, nodding towards the cabinet, which was just as Eliza had described: tall, dark wood with elaborate scroll ornamentation. Miss Finch's name had been engraved in looping script across the front door, which was held shut by a brass catch. 'May I see . . . ?' She began to walk into the room, but the girl stepped in front of her.

'I'd rather you didn't poke around, if you don't mind,' she said.

'You know as much as anyone that a Medium's cabinet is her own private affair.'

Mrs Wood laughed. 'We were less protective when we used them,' she said, but the girl wasn't listening; she was looking at the offering on the sideboard.

'Is there no champagne?' Even the girl's voice register had changed: it was deeper, rounder, full of 'h's and 't's that rang in her diction as clear as bells. And when she spoke, she could hear the Green sisters in her intonation, see their mannerisms reflected in the movement of a hand, the toss of her head. 'Can you be a dear and ask Eliza to bring some?'

'Of course.' She watched the girl as she fussed with the drapes and smoothed the edge of the Persian rug with her toe. 'Do you need anything more?'

The girl turned. 'No,' she said. 'Thank you.'

'Well. You know where we are if you do,' she said, and the girl blinked.

'And Eliza'll bring the champagne?' she said.

Mrs Wood gave a quick nod. 'I'll have it sent up straight away,' she said.

The girl walked her from the room, placing her hand on the door handle proprietorially. 'Tell her to knock and leave it outside the door, won't you. I could do without any more interruptions.' She gave a dry smile. 'Full spirit materialisations are exhausting. As I'm sure you can imagine.'

'I'm sure they . . .' she began, but the door was already closed, and her words fell against the hard wood instead.

In the following few hours, while she and Miss Newman got themselves ready, they'd heard very little from the room beyond the occasional bang or curse. The door had remained locked. As she thought of her beavering away inside, she experienced a sudden flash of doubt: the girl had behaved appallingly, but did she deserve what she and Miss Newman had prepared? Was it right to take

343

something from a person who had pulled herself out of the gutter, just as she herself had? Even if she had clambered all over Mrs Wood to do so, stomping her out of society without a backward glance, did she deserve the ultimate punishment a Medium can ever endure?

Miss Newman caught her eye in the mirror. 'Are you ready?'

The girl was young. She would be ruined in London, but she could go elsewhere. She was obviously clever: she could take what she had learned and build something of a career somewhere new. Somewhere far, far away from Mrs Wood and everything she would rebuild when the girl had gone.

She met her own eyes in the mirror. Steady and determined. 'Yes,' she said and pushed herself back from the dressing table. 'I am.'

Maintaining her smile throughout the arrival of her old patrons and friends had been physically painful. Here they were, the people she had taken for loyal patrons until they had disappeared into Miss Finch's parlour as soon as the girl had smiled prettily in their direction. Colonel and Mrs Phillips, greeting her as though they weren't traitors. And Mrs Jupp, fluttering in with Mrs Pepperdine, offering up lies about endless colds keeping her low. The Adams sisters had the decency to look cowed, which was reasonable considering she hadn't seen them for well over a month.

'You look well,' Miss Brigham had said, thumping her on the back. 'This is all fun and games, isn't it!'

Did they have no shame?

Did they not know what they had done?

Only Mrs Hart met her with cold derision, something she felt strange admiration for.

As she circulated, her certainty that someone would say they were sorry for abandoning her began to diminish, hearing nothing but thanks for the champagne and how nice the house looked. The Countess beckoned her to her seat in the drawing-room window.

'Dear thing,' she said. 'I must tell you something . . .'

'Oh?' Mrs Wood said, hoping that finally, someone was about to apologise.

But the Countess pointed at her plate, a long thin finger tapping the top of a glossy-topped puff pastry treat. 'What's in this?'

'Oh,' she said. 'Oh. It's a . . . cheese, I think.'

'Your Cook is the envy of the town, Mrs Wood!'

'What a shame you've not been here to enjoy it more,' she said, testing the water.

But the Countess waved her hand dismissively. 'So busy!' And put the treat in her mouth, turning to her consort to complain that he was breathing too loudly. Mrs Wood smiled and moved on.

The Dowager, hidden in the fireside wingback chair, caught her arm as she passed. 'Violet,' she said, making Mrs Wood jump. 'There you are!'

She thought immediately of the letters from the Dowager she had not opened, the visit she had not returned and forced a smile. 'There are, too!' she said. 'How are you, dear lady?'

'Where have you been?'

'Looking after my guests, dearest . . .'

'I don't mean *tonight*, I mean the past few months.'

She tried to maintain her smile. 'I was . . . Christmas was so busy and . . .'

But the Dowager wasn't angry. She looked hurt. 'I was worried,' she said. 'You disappeared without a word.'

She stooped so that she could speak without the whole room listening in. 'I'm so sorry that I've worried you,' she said, now at eye level with the old aristocrat. 'Between us,' she said. 'Miss Newman had to go away for a while, and I wasn't feeling quite myself without her.'

The Dowager gave a mollified sigh. 'Well,' she said. 'That makes more sense. But you should have written. I always considered you a friend, Mrs Wood.'

'Of course!' she said, flustered by the unexpected kindness.

'Good,' said the Dowager. 'I'm only here tonight for you, you know that, don't you? I have no interest in Miss Finch's silliness.'

'I'm sure there won't be any of that,' she said. 'She was always exemplary at my table.'

'We miss you, Mrs Wood.'

She squeezed the Dowager's small, bony hand. 'Thank you,' she said. 'And I'll be sure to arrange something with you as soon as we can.'

'Make sure that you do. Inactivity is ruinous for one's nerves.'

Someone was tapping a glass, and she patted the Dowager's hand again and stood to find out who.

Magnus Clore stood in the doorway, a knife glinting in the lamplight as he tapped it against one of her best crystal glasses.

As the rest of the room turned to look at him, a satisfied smile spread across his face. 'Ladies and gentlemen. Firstly, thank you so much to dear Mrs Wood for allowing us to see Miss Finch's work in her own home. It is a generous act for a Medium such as you, Mrs Wood,' he said, raising the glass in her direction. 'Perhaps she will inspire you tonight and you will feel able to revive your tables once more.'

There was a smattering of applause, but Mrs Wood was acutely aware of an uncomfortable shifting in the room. 'Now, without further ado . . . Miss Finch is ready.' Clore continued on.

Genuine excitement bubbled through the crowd. Was this what it was like when she was in the back parlour, and her readiness had been announced?

'Let the night begin!'

And he bowed like a ringmaster before beckoning the guests to follow him, which they did in a rush of perfume and anticipation.

It took moments for the room to empty and, when it had, Miss Newman was revealed waiting for her at the door.

'You look rattled,' she said, and Mrs Wood took the glass of champagne Miss Newman held in her hand and drank it.

'Warm,' she said with a grimace then hesitated as Colonel Phillips' voice carried along the hall proclaiming how nice the room looked. 'Are you sure we're doing the right thing?'

Miss Newman looked at her. 'You're having second thoughts.'

'These people,' she nodded towards the detritus the guests had left in her drawing room. 'Do I even care that they're now part of her audience rather than mine?'

Holding her gaze, Miss Newman leaned in. 'This isn't about that, Violet. The girl is ruthless. She's used everything you have worked for as a stepping-stone to fame. She can't get away with it.'

Mrs Wood sighed. 'Can't she?' And Miss Newman stood back, weighing her up.

They stood in silence for a moment until Magnus Clore appeared. 'Are you coming?' he said.

'Don't make any decision now,' Miss Newman murmured, taking her arm. 'If it comes to it and you don't want to, then we won't. It won't make any difference either way. To the séance, I mean.'

She nodded. 'All right,' she said. 'I think that's best. Let's see how it goes . . .'

'Come on, then,' said Miss Newman. 'Aside from the fact that it's that girl doing it, I'm rather intrigued as to what this spirit will actually look like, aren't you?'

Magnus Clore was in his absolute element.

He stood at the front of the room, forehead gleaming with excited perspiration, his hand on Miss Finch's tiny waist. She, in turn, smiled coyly beside him, her gold hair shining in the low light; cheeks fresh, red dress ridiculous.

'As I was saying,' he said as Mrs Wood and Miss Newman slipped into two chairs at the very back of the room that appeared so strange to her from the unusual point of view. 'During this evening's event, we must make sure that all hands and feet are tucked away and that no attempt be made to touch the spirit should one be manifested. Unless you are offered, of course. Tandy may take a liking to you. It has been known.' He gave an unseemly wink, and the guests responded with a flurry of titters. 'But I must warn you all that unsanctioned touching can break the connection between spirit and Medium. Such a thing might kill Miss Finch immediately.' *Gasps.* 'Let's not take any risks.'

He took a micro-step back and tipped his head to Miss Finch. 'Miss Finch, the room is yours.'

'Thank you,' she said and nodded back at him. Then, she turned and swept the room with the same benevolent smile Mrs Wood had used so many times. 'There are no guarantees,' she said. 'I may not have the strength to materialise Tandy as it's been such a busy time, but Mrs Wood insisted, so . . . here we are!'

Then she said: 'Mr Clore?' He stepped beside her, flicking a length of thin, white cord from his pocket. He looped it around her wrists, pulling it tight and knotting it with a flourish. 'Thank you,' she fluttered, and then turned to the rest of the guests. 'I don't suppose anyone could check my binds? We don't want anyone accusing me of trickery!'

Colonel Phillips' hand shot up, but his wife yanked it down again. Mrs Hart's hand remained, and Miss Finch called her over, putting her wrists up to her. 'Can you put your fingers beneath the binding?' she asked, and Mrs Hart began tentatively poking about. 'Is it tight enough, do you think? Does it feel like I could wiggle free?'

'No,' Mrs Hart said, eventually, checking the lengths of the knot.

'It's very tight.' She gave the girl's arm a concerned squeeze. 'Does it hurt?'

'It's all for the greater good,' said the girl. Then she threw an enchanting gaze across the room, eliciting breathless sighs from some of her sitters. 'Without further ado, then, let's begin. I do hope we have some success.' She gave a special smile to Mr Clore. 'If you wouldn't mind, dear friend,' she said, and Clore set about extinguishing the candles in the wall sconces with his snuffer.

As she watched him squeeze and stretch his way around the room, Mrs Wood endured a fresh wave of missing Mr Larson – he would've executed Clore's job with far more elegance and greater speed – followed by a swift kick of guilt. Of course he would not be welcome in Miss Finch's presence after the hullabaloo at Wornington Road. But she was still painfully aware that they had not spoken either since the incident. Of all the things she was putting right, his distress following the girl's séance had been so raw and the thought of how it had all been her fault made her too sick for her to even contemplate an apology. She had gone too far for that.

The last candle went out and the room was ready; darkness pierced by the necessary single candle on the sideboard. It wiffled and warbled as Clore picked his way back to the front, sending ripples of undulating light onto Miss Finch's cabinet.

Miss Finch gave one final dramatic bow, and then Clore helped settle her into the cabinet, straightening the abundant skirts of the ridiculous red dress around her ankles. Then, she gave a last smile and a wave of her bound wrists before Clore closed the door on her, looping the catch firmly into place. As he slid into his seat in the front row, the room descended into anxious anticipation.

CHAPTER 39

After a few moments of silence, moans began to come from inside the cabinet. Then, as their intensity increased, there came the sound of scuffling, the cabinet juddering as though a struggle were occurring inside. Then, after a sudden bang, and a moan that was almost a scream, there came a muffled cry of '*Help!*'

The guests began to look nervously at one another. Was this supposed to be happening?

Another cry and then: BANG! And the door of the cabinet popped open a fraction.

The room rippled with excitement as a pale arm snaked out. The fingers, bright in the gloom, flexed and trilled.

Another moment, and here was a shoulder, draped in something flowing and white.

And then the door opened a little wider, and more white draping emerged.

Gasps erupted around the room, followed by urgent shushes.

The door creaked as the complete form finally emerged from inside, and a figure draped in white stepped forward.

It was here!

A spirit!

In the flesh!

A few guests around Mrs Wood rose in their seats, trying to get a better view as the shape gathered form in the shadows.

It looked about, a white shroud casting a shadow over its face so that only the outline of its features could be made out: shadowed eyes and a thin line of a mouth. And then it began to move with a lightness that was unearthly, drifting to the front row of guests where it stopped, the shroud floating to stillness as it continued to gaze, almost unseeingly, about the room.

No one moved. Apart from Miss Newman, who sat back with a poorly disguised sigh of irritation.

'She's not even trying to disguise her face,' she whispered, but Mrs Wood pressed her finger to her lips, returning her attention to the figure.

'*Hello?*' Even after all this time away from the girl's work, Mrs Wood knew the voice: Tandy had come. 'It's awfully dark,' she said. 'I cannot see you very well.'

'We're here!' called Mr Clore. 'We can see you!'

'Good,' said the figure, the line of her mouth stretching into a smile. 'I am Tandy. I am Miss Finch's guide, and I once was a girl on the high seas, forced into pirate life by my father, that rogue, Jack Starr.' There was a rustle of movement as people remembered where they had heard that name before. 'Father says hello, Violet!' Tandy called, and Mrs Wood raised her hand in awkward acknowledgement.

'Well,' she continued, undaunted. 'It most certainly is a pleasure to be here. Before you. In the *flesh*!' Tandy stretched out her hand and wiggled her fingers. She giggled. 'Look!' she said. 'Fingers!'

The guests laughed too.

Tandy then raised the bottom of the shroud and looked quizzically at her bare feet. She stretched them out. 'Toes!' she said. She pressed her fingers to her face, the tips making soft dents in the plump flesh. 'Oh, I missed this sensation,' she said. 'I miss being tickled!' She ran her fingertips over the inside of her wrists and shivered, and the room gave up a collective sigh.

'Miss Finch is being so generous to me,' she said. 'Giving me her energy so that I can visit properly with you. It's the hardest thing a Medium can do, you know,' she said. 'Of all the spiritual activities, this takes the most from them. I am eternally grateful.'

Another sigh.

'If more Mediums were brave enough to do this, imagine how society would be improved.' She wafted her arms about slowly as she talked, the folds of the shroud drifting dreamily about her. 'I see so many on the Other Side who would dearly love to share their wisdom with you all. If more were willing to give themselves up to the spirit, we wouldn't lose our greatest field marshals to battle; they could sit beside the living instead, guiding and instructing as they did in life. We would not lose our engineers to accidents; they would continue building and designing to superiority. We wouldn't lose our loved ones to disease; they would be with us forever, not just in our hearts but by our sides. We would be *complete*.'

Noises of agreement.

Miss Newman shifted irritably beside Mrs Wood.

'Look for yourself,' said Tandy. 'See what Miss Finch gives of herself to bring me through!' And she drifted back to the cabinet and swung the door wide open.

There, in the dark interior, a bright red dress, exactly like the one Miss Finch had been wearing, could be seen, set off against pale, white skin. Tandy reached across and lifted the single lit candlestick from the sideboard, bringing it close to the open door. It threw sharp shadows across the figure inside, clarifying that that was indeed Miss Finch's dress, lowering the light to show that her wrists were still tied. Then she raised the flame, showing the Medium's chin dropped on her chest, her golden coils falling to obscure the details of her face.

'Thank you,' Tandy said and blew the unconscious girl a kiss. Then she returned the candle to the sideboard and pushed the door closed, obscuring the figure inside once more as she slipped back to the guests. 'I have been so lucky to make a connection with this young woman. If my money had any value now . . .' she paused, patting her hips and laughing, '. . . or if I had any at all, I would give it all to this girl. She is changing the world!'

352

Miss Newman cleared her throat.

The guests had become more confident now, calling to Tandy for her to come near – exclaiming that she smelled of the sea, that her fingers had left damp remembrances on their clothes. 'Your energy is making me stronger!' she cried. 'See!' And she gave a little jig, dandling her fingers and shroud perilously close as she passed between the rows, where guests sat on their hands to avoid any unintentional – and potentially lethal – touching. As she went, she sang songs and passed on a message to Mrs Phillips from her daughter and one from the grandmother of an MP Mrs Wood had not met before.

With every step the spirit made, every sweep of her hand, every laugh from her throat, the room became more and more convinced that Miss Finch had brought before them a full-blooded manifestation of a person from the Other Side.

She had made the unthinkable come true.

And then, as Tandy performed a quick pirouette, a moan came from inside the cabinet, and she stumbled to a standstill.

'Oh,' she said, suddenly unsteady on her feet. 'Oh! My Medium is growing weak. My strength is fading . . .' She began to drift towards the cabinet. 'I must return now, I must return, or I shall drain Miss Finch of all of her energies, and she shall surely pass on.'

Amidst quiet calls of disappointment, Tandy returned in the same manner as she had arrived: disappearing slowly, limb by limb into the cabinet, while singing a verse from 'All Things Bright and Beautiful'. Then, as the final notes hung in the air, the door snapped suddenly closed, and the moans and bangs inside intensified until they abruptly stopped.

After a minute or so of silence, there was a loud rap on the door, and Mr Clore leapt up and, grabbing the candle, whipped the door open.

And there was Miss Finch, blinking in the darkness, her hands tied tightly, her cheeks shining with tears.

The room erupted into raptures, and Miss Finch leaned heavily on Mr Clore as she staggered back into the room. She appeared battered, her hair crumpled around her face, marks visible on her forehead and arms.

'Are you hurt?' someone shouted.

'Only fatigued,' she said, her voice weak but still capable of carrying. 'It looks worse than it feels. When the spirit returns, you get tossed around something rotten.' She stifled a yawn. 'I'm assuming Tandy came, then?'

'Yes!' cried the sitters.

'She was magnificent.'

'She was wonderful.'

'She sings like a bird!'

Mr Clore patted the air to calm the room.

'Thank you, everyone,' he said, putting his arm around Miss Finch's shoulders. 'We are extremely grateful for how well you have received us here in Mrs Wood's home.'

'We are,' said Miss Finch. 'And,' she smoothed her hair, taking a step forward. 'I wanted to say a personal thank you to Mrs Wood for her generosity in hosting me tonight. You will know that I came up through Mrs Wood, and it is an honour to now be leading séances in her presence. Particularly before an audience made up of my newest and most favourite patrons.'

A polite round of applause threaded its way through the room as the girl kept her smiling eyes on Mrs Wood's.

Miss Finch raised a hand to continue speaking. 'Thank you,' she said. 'I'd like to take this opportunity too, to remind you all that Mrs Wood is still very much open for business. After such a wonderful evening, I would be doing her a disservice if I didn't let you all know that she is offering private consultations to anyone who'd like one. Isn't that so, Mrs Wood?'

Mrs Wood's cheeks burned, her jaw rigid as she kept herself under control. She smiled tightly as Miss Newman's fingers dug into her leg.

'You're not retiring quite yet, are you, no matter what people think!'

Mrs Wood choked out a laugh, the eyes of the room suddenly upon her. 'What kind words,' she said as lightly as possible. Miss Newman's fingers were cutting into her now, and she had to shake them free.

'Miss Finch!' Mrs Phillips was on her feet. 'Miss Finch, that was just wonderful!'

Colonel Phillips engulfed his wife in shushing. 'Not now, dear,' he said briskly, tugging on her to return to her seat.

But Mrs Phillips was not to be assuaged. She waved his attentions away, her eyes clinging to Miss Finch. 'Tandy said she has spoken with my daughter. It was almost as though she were here. It was almost as if you brought my daughter to flesh too!'

The girl smiled magnanimously. 'I'm so glad you feel that way,' she said. 'It gives me great pleasure to know that you have been touched by my work.' Then she paused and Mrs Wood watched her, instinctively aware of what she was about to say, willing and hoping that she would not.

'You know, Mrs Phillips,' the girl said, as though the idea was only just coming to her. 'Perhaps it's not impossible that, under the right circumstances, I *could* bring your daughter to flesh.'

Mrs Phillips gave a strangled cry. 'Do you mean that?'

'Miss Finch!' Mrs Wood was standing. 'That's quite enough.' But all eyes were on the girl and she may as well have been shouting in Dutch.

'I don't know for sure if I could, but, in a more private situation, I could certainly try.' She was gathering momentum, bolstered by the excited whispers that passed like a gale through the guests. 'It may not be immediate, but I would do all I could to try and bring the spirit to you, dear lady.'

'Do you mean that?' Mrs Phillips said, her voice breaking with emotion. 'Do you really mean that I might see my daughter again?'

'I would try my hardest,' she said.

The whispers were intensifying to a rumble so that Miss Finch had to raise her voice to slide her bolt home.

'No matter how many private sessions it took, I would keep on trying!'

Fury flared in Mrs Wood. The girl had looked at the naked grief of Mrs Phillips and seen not an opportunity to help but an opportunity for advancement. Miss Finch knew she could not bring Mrs Phillips' daughter to flesh. The most she would do was tease the poor woman with unfulfillable promises. To receive a message from a spirit was one thing; to touch and be in the physical presence of one was a lie that went against everything Mrs Wood, as a Medium, stood for. A lie that showed the truest of the girl's colours. Miss Finch had no interest in helping Mrs Phillips; Miss Finch only wanted to create another lucrative opportunity for Miss Finch.

Mrs Phillips may have had her head turned by the newness of the girl, but Mrs Wood had known her for too long to stand by and allow the woman's grief to be so callously exploited for the sake of *performance*.

She could not allow it.

She would not.

Half the people in the room had already dropped Mrs Wood in favour of this shiny new thing and she knew that standing up to the girl would cost her the reputation she had been so desperate to keep for the remaining loyal few, but she could not let this continue: if she were to be cast out, she would be cast out with honour.

And so, as the guests gasped and clamoured at the girl, calling for her to bring their own lost ones forward, Mrs Wood turned to Miss Newman, who was ready for her with bright eyes.

With the faintest of nods to her beloved friend, she opened her mouth.

'Wait!' Mrs Wood's voice carried like a shot, and the atmosphere changed in a heartbeat, as guests arched and craned to see what was going on.

Miss Finch threw her a look of sharp irritation.

'Wait!' Mrs Wood continued, getting to her feet and squinting about. 'Someone's here,' she said. 'Someone is still here! Miss Finch, if I may? They feel quite persistent.'

Miss Finch glared through her smile, glancing at Mr Clore, who was staring at Mrs Wood in surprise. 'Well,' she said, collecting herself. 'This is your home, after all.'

'I hear a voice. Don't you hear a voice? Someone is singing.'

'I . . . yes,' said Miss Finch cautiously.

'The candle! Blow out the candle!'

Mr Clore duly saw to the candle and the room shifted excitedly in the sudden, absolute darkness.

'Who is it?' She tipped her head back and threw her voice to the air. 'Who are you?'

An electric silence settled around her.

'Who is it?' echoed Miss Finch, and Mrs Wood was pleased to hear the uncertainty in her voice.

There was a rapping, sharp and clear, like a hammer on wood.

'*Who is it?*' repeated Miss Finch.

The rapping became feverish beats, racing around the walls.

'Calm,' said Mrs Wood. 'You must calm yourself, or we shall never understand you.'

The knocks slowed, moving as steady and true as a heartbeat along the far wall.

Bang!

Bang!

Bang!

'Do you want to speak with someone?'

Bang!

Bang!

Bang!

It was over the sideboard now.

'Really,' said Mrs Wood. 'You're being most rude. This isn't my séance, so I don't know why you're being so naughty. Or perhaps that's why you're ignoring me? Miss Finch? Perhaps you can get something out of this one?'

'Hello?' Miss Finch's voice was frayed at its edges. 'Who are you here for?'

The banging intensified.

Bang!

Bang!

Bang!

'See,' said Mrs Wood. 'It's you they want to speak with after all that.' She gave an irritated laugh. 'Why didn't you say that in the first place.'

'What do you want?' Miss Finch's voice was ruffled, uncertain.

The bangs turned to raps turned to rattles on the sideboard, the silver and crystal ringing like a chaos of tiny cymbals.

Then . . .

Silence.

'Hello?' said Miss Finch.

'Oh! Oh, my goodness! What's . . . I thought you wanted to speak with Miss Finch! Oh, my *goodness!*' Mrs Wood's voice came from higher in the room, as though . . .

'What's . . . is that you, old girl?' said Mr Yurick. 'Something just brushed my face. Where are you?'

'Oh, Mr Yurick! I'm up here!' She called from the top of the sideboard, her voice high in the air above their heads. 'They're so naughty,' she said breathlessly.

The room below roiled with excited cries and shouts as Mrs Wood complained with each bump from the ceiling and clatter into the chandelier from Miss Newman's secret broom handle. 'I felt it too!' 'I think I touched your boot!' 'Take my hand!' 'Watch out for spiders!'

358

'This is too much. This really is too much!' Mrs Wood cried.

'Who is it?' Miss Finch was calling desperately over the din. 'Who's doing this?'

Bang!

Bang!

Bang!

The knocks returned with gusto, speeding along the far wall to the darkest corner.

Bang! Bang! Bang! Bang! Bang!

They took on a sudden, hollow sound.

'Be careful!' shouted Miss Finch, realising what it had landed upon. 'The cabinet is new!'

Thump! Thump! Thump!

Mrs Wood smiled to herself as she heard a muffled, frightened cry come from within that was thankfully hidden by the excitement of her own activities. *Not yet.*

'Calm down!' Her voice was still bouncing over the hubbub as she felt her way towards the edge of the sideboard, readying herself for the dismount. 'Please. I don't understand you when you get like this.'

The knocks slowed.

Thump.

Thump.

Thump.

BANG!

When the screams and shouts from the terrified guests subsided, the room was pitch black and silent.

'Mrs Wood?' said Mrs Reynolds.

'Mrs Wood?' said Miss Newman, breathless from her invisible cavorting around the room. 'Violet?' she called, sliding the old broom handle back beneath the sideboard. 'Violet, are you there?'

'Where's she gone?' Miss Finch's voice failed to hide her irritation.

Concerns for how the Medium had disappeared rippled through the room until . . .

More knocks.

Softer, hollow. As though someone was knocking on the . . .

'Help!'

'Mrs Wood?'

'Where am I?'

The guests were climbing over one another in the darkness.

'Light a candle!'

'Someone strike a match, for God's sake!'

'Who's got them?'

'I have some,' Mr Clore called, then there came the sound of him knocking over the candlesticks on the sideboard in his haste to grab one. He struck a match once, twice, thrice. Threw it down. Scrabbled for another one from the box. Struck it once, twice. Finally, the candle flared, and he lifted the stick, raising it to the ceiling where fresh marks could be seen but no Mrs Wood.

The Medium had, indeed, vanished.

'Hello?' Mrs Wood's voice. Indistinct. Hidden.

The room turned to Miss Finch, still standing at the front, her eyes wide and her mouth slack.

'Where is she?' demanded the Dowager.

'I . . .' she said, her mouth flapping awkwardly. 'I don't . . .'

There was a knock on the cabinet. And another.

'She's in the cabinet!' shouted Miss Newman. 'Listen!'

Two knocks. 'Hello?'

Miss Newman clambered through the melee towards the cabinet. 'Sit down, everyone,' she called as she squeezed her way through. 'Please. There's no need for alarm. Mrs Wood is used to such silliness from the spirits.' Guests dropped back, finding their chairs but settling on their edges, clasping their hands and craning to see into the corner of the room. 'More candles, please, Mr Clore! There's a lamp on the bookshelf.' Miss Newman called from beside the cabinet. 'I can't see how this lock . . . Miss Finch, can you help?'

Miss Finch started. 'Of course,' she said, crossing towards her.

'Let me.' She reached towards the catch on the side of the cabinet, taking advantage of her position to throw a furious look at Miss Newman. '*What are you doing?*' she hissed, and Miss Newman shrugged with innocent eyes, taking the glaring lamp that Mr Clore had lit.

The catch came loose in a flash of brass, and the door gave with a click.

Miss Finch stepped back, peering, along with the rest of the room, to see what had happened inside.

'Mrs Wood?' whispered Miss Newman. 'Mrs Wood? Is that you?'

'Oh, Miss *Newman!*' Mrs Wood said, pushing the door wide open to reveal herself inside. The cabinet was indeed as narrow as Eliza had described, and she was wedged into the seat, her body turned slightly to accommodate her shoulders. But she was inside, and it was precisely as she had thought. 'Can you believe how badly I've been treated?'

Gasps, laughs, spontaneous applause burst out across the room.

Mrs Wood looked at their faces from the shadows of the cabinet: Mrs Jupp, Mrs Pepperdine, the Countess de Livigne and her consort, shaking their heads in delighted disbelief. Lady Harrington: her round face shining in delight. Colonel Phillips pounding his hands together. The Dowager, out-clapping Colonel Phillips. And dear Mrs Reynolds clutching at the Adams sisters, with Miss Brigham allowing a rare smile to turn the corner of her mouth.

And Miss Finch, eyes hot and narrow, her sweet mouth bunched up angrily, her breath coming fast and furious, hissing: '*What are you doing?*'

Mrs Wood ignored her, reaching out her hand to Miss Newman and rubbing the side of her head. 'That ceiling's unyielding,' she said. 'I fear I'll have quite an egg there tomorrow.'

She stepped free of the cabinet, smiling benevolently at the room as it erupted into giddy applause. 'Please,' she said, raising her hand in submission. 'It was the spirits. I can't take any credit!' But then she stopped, her shoulder jerking back as though she'd been snagged. 'Ouch!' she said and turned her head. 'I thought you'd had your fun!' She paused. 'No,' she said. 'We've finished. Haven't we?'

Another jerk.

'What do you want?'

Knocks and raps on the cabinet.

The room retook its seats, eyes shining. *There was more to come!*

'Mrs Wood—' Miss Finch began.

'Shh,' said Mrs Pepperdine. 'Don't interrupt her.'

Mrs Wood dropped her chin to her chest. Closed her eyes. 'How can I help?' A resounding 'Mmmmm' rumbled in her throat while Miss Newman held tight to her arms. Then, after a moment, she staggered, and the humming stopped. She looked up. 'They want me to look inside,' she said, turning to the cabinet.

'What? No,' said Miss Finch. 'Why would they suggest that? It's only a cabinet.'

Mrs Wood shook her head. 'I have no idea, but they're insistent. They want me to look inside.'

Miss Finch put her arm across the door and stared fiercely into Mrs Wood's eyes.

Mrs Wood smiled sweetly back. 'It's not me, dearest. It's the spirits.'

'What's the problem?' Mr Clore piped up. 'Let her look, if that's what the spirits are asking.' And Miss Finch took a reluctant step away.

'I've no idea what I'm looking for,' said Mrs Wood, leaning inside. 'Miss Finch is right: it's just a cabinet.' She hesitated, squeezing her body back into the narrow compartment. She paused for a moment then: 'Wait . . . Is this what you wanted to show me?' Another pause. 'Why . . .' She lifted the thick black curtain that hung invisibly behind the chair, creating the hidden compartment Eliza had told her about at the rear of the deep cabinet.

'My goodness . . .' she said. Beyond, in the room, people were already off their seats again.

What has she seen?

'Why! Who on earth is *this*? And what on earth are you doing in here?'

CHAPTER 40

Mrs Wood backed out of the cabinet before reaching inside to take another small hand in hers. A woman hobbled out into the light, blinking and shielding her eyes. She was small, the same height and build as Miss Finch, and she wore a red dress precisely the same as the girl and a golden hairpiece of coils and curls.

'I apported my mother!' Miss Finch said suddenly, and she stepped back with her arms outstretched, awaiting applause that didn't come. Then she reached her hands out towards the woman: 'Mother, dear! Are you well! What a shock. I cannot believe that you're here! I cannot believe how naughty the spirits have been!'

'Why is she dressed as you?' interrupted Miss Brigham, her voice a trombone.

Miss Finch blinked. 'We enjoy dressing alike,' she said. 'I wasn't sure it would work, so I didn't want to say my intentions. I've never done a full apport of—'

'But her hair,' Miss Brigham continued. 'Why's she got that thing on her head?'

'We like to look alike—'

'I've met your mother,' said Mrs Hart. 'And she was certainly dressed nothing like you then.'

'It's a special occasion.'

'But . . . did she know she was to be apported?' asked Mrs Reynolds. She looked at Miss Finch's mother. 'Did you know?'

All eyes turned to the woman, whose mouth fluttered uselessly. She looked at her daughter. 'Yes?' she whispered.

'What were you doing?'

'Reading?' the woman said.

'Where's your book?' asked Mrs Farnham.

'I . . .' she looked about helplessly.

'What were you reading?'

'It's probably still in the cabinet,' said Miss Finch. 'Isn't it.'

Miss Finch's mother's eyes darted about madly.

'Why are you asking all these questions?' the girl snapped. 'Do you doubt my abilities? Do you think apporting my own mother is beyond my capabilities? Aren't I the first Medium in England to materialise a full spirit? You think a little apporting is beyond me?'

Yes,' said the Dowager, the authority of her voice silencing the room as she moved towards the girl. 'I don't believe for a second you apported your mother. The woman is dressed like you and was found in your own cabinet. What a ridiculous idea that we should believe that she hasn't been stashed there all along.'

Miss Finch's face tightened. 'What are you saying?'

Mr Clore stepped forward. 'My lady. With all due respect, Miss Finch is a talented Medium. I am sure that she—'

'Do you think this is what the spirits wanted you to see?' asked Miss Newman. 'Mrs Wood? Do you think they wanted us to see the truth?'

Mrs Wood blinked innocently back as all eyes turned to her expectantly. 'I cannot tell you the spirits' intentions,' she said gently. 'Although I wonder if they perhaps didn't want to help poor Miss Finch's mother. She did look awfully uncomfortable when I found her in there.'

'It was a lie,' said Mrs Phillips, her voice subduing the growing excitement. 'Tandy didn't see my little girl!'

'She did!' said Miss Finch urgently. 'Mrs Phillips. I wouldn't lie to you, I promise!'

'But . . . your mother . . . It was a lie?'

Colonel Phillips ensconced his wife in his broad arms, hurling a look of contempt at Miss Finch. 'You should be ashamed of your-self.'

'Tandy was here!' the girl cried. 'You all saw her, didn't you?'

But the room was suddenly uncertain. 'We saw a figure,' said Mrs Reynolds.

'Her touch was warm,' said a voice. 'I had thought it might be . . . cold.'

'A fraud?' someone else whispered.

'Larson was obviously on to something!' said Miss Brigham.

'Ladies and gentlemen . . .' Mr Clore's voice wasn't quite as sure as before. 'There's clearly been some kind of mix-up.' He glared at Miss Finch. 'I'm sure there is a valid reason for this woman to have been in the cabinet . . .'

'Yes,' said the girl, grabbing his hands. 'Of course. It's nothing . . . perhaps . . .'

But Miss Brigham was pushing her way to the front of the room, her large shoulder budging the girl unceremoniously out of the way as she bore down on Mrs Wood. 'Bravo, Mrs Wood! Bravo!' She thumped her hands together. 'A triumph!' she said.

And then the Dowager had joined her. Then Mrs Farnham and Mrs Pepperdine. Then Mrs Reynolds and the Phillipses. The crowd grew deeper, pushing Miss Finch and her mother further and further towards the edge of the room.

And then, suddenly, a scream rent the air.

The girl had climbed onto a chair, her hand gripping Clore's shoulder as she pointed, like a Fury, at Mrs Wood. 'If you want to see a fraud – look no further than your *host!*'

Mrs Wood froze. Through the milling bodies, she saw Mr Clore remove the girl's hand and whisper something to her, but she pulled herself away, her face wild. 'The woman has been lying to you all for years.'

This was it.

The girl was delivering on her threat.

A shock of cold fear washed down her spine.

People were starting to turn away again, the noise of the girl sparking curiosity.

'Mrs Wood is no more a lady than some beggar on the street,' said the girl, steadying herself now she was gaining attention. She pushed an escaped golden curl from her cheek. 'Mrs Wood is Thirza Thwaite's daughter. Remember her? The great *fraud*.'

'Thirza Thwaite?' Mrs Jupp said, with a gasp.

'Yes,' said Miss Finch eagerly. 'Thirza Thwaite! You remember her, don't you, Mrs Jupp. The liar and the cheat.'

'I knew I'd heard that name when it came up before,' said Mrs Hart, turning to Mrs Wood. 'Do you remember? I said I recognised the name Thirza all those months ago.'

'Thwaite? Oh, that was a dreadful business,' said Mrs Pepperdine to Mrs Jupp, then she looked at Mrs Wood, blinking. 'Is this true?'

But Mrs Wood's eyes were on the Dowager. She, of all people in the room, would remember Thirza Thwaite. She may not have been in her audience, but she had been interested in the spirits since the idea of séances had first arrived in England. She would have heard of Thirza's disgrace. Of everyone here, the Dowager would know what this meant.

But the Dowager was looking at the girl, her face unreadable.

'Mrs Wood has been lying to you all for years!' Gone was the calm professional; the girl's voice had become a shriek. She cast about and saw she had the Dowager's attention and jumped down from the chair, grabbing at the woman's arm.

'You know who I'm talking about, don't you, dear lady,' she said. 'Thirza Thwaite! She's Mrs Wood's mother. Mrs Wood is the daughter of that terrible fraud!'

'That's enough,' said Miss Newman, reaching for the girl.

'She's been lying—'

'That's *enough*!' Miss Newman wrapped her hand firmly around the girl's wrist, but she tugged away.

'Mr Clore. Do you hear? Our beloved Mrs Wood is the daughter of an exposed Medium. What will your readers think about that?' But Mr Clore had gone from her side, standing instead between Colonel Phillips and Mrs Pepperdine, sharing their look of disgust and confusion.

He crossed his arms. 'You've said your piece, Emmeline,' he said.

'No,' said Miss Finch, panicked. 'No. I don't think you understand. Everything you know about Mrs Wood is a *lie*!' Her eyes scanned the crowd with increasing panic. 'Don't you see? She is false! How can you trust anything she says or does, knowing that?'

'The evening is over,' Miss Newman said, holding on tight so that the girl couldn't wrestle away again. She walked her swiftly towards the door, calling over her shoulder: 'If I may ask you all to follow me, we shall arrange for your carriages to be summoned.'

As the room boiled around her, Mrs Wood remained frozen, her eyes fixed on the floor at her feet, hearing nothing, seeing nothing.

And then the room was empty, and she was alone.

It was over.

CHAPTER 41

With nothing left to lose, Mrs Wood slept surprisingly well. She had expected to endure another night of torment, but after Miss Newman had silently put her to bed, slipping her cool cotton nightgown over her head as though she were a child, she had collapsed into a dark, dreamless state that took her through until dawn.

She watched the blue light around her curtains fade slowly to white and listened to Eliza sweeping out the séance room with no care for the skirting boards.

The worst had happened.

When she forced herself back to the night, the only image that remained clear was the Dowager's pale face turned to her, her eyes flickering with confusion as she clearly tried to reconcile the woman she thought she knew with the woman the girl had revealed her to be.

In the chaos, there had been no chance to explain why she had kept her past a secret to anyone. And even if there had been, in the shock of it all, it was unlikely she would have made any sense. She knew she had taken a risk, exposing the girl, but the girl's outrage had gone off like a firework, a fury that had been beyond her anticipation: she had assumed the girl would seek revenge with the stealth in which she had taken over Mrs Wood's life. She hadn't been ready for the assault to have been so immediate.

She filled her basin with water from the jug, splashing it over her face and rubbing sleep from her eyes.

Through the past few months, when her other patrons and

followers had flaked away, the Dowager had remained loyal. She deserved to hear the truth from her, rather than as gossip that was inevitably brewing across town. And the Dowager deserved the opportunity to tell Mrs Wood exactly how disappointed, at the least, she was.

No matter how heartbreaking it would be, if this was the end, she couldn't sit around any longer waiting for it to find her.

How different she felt arriving outside the huge stucco townhouse in South Kensington. Usually, Miss Newman would be beside her, they would be thrumming with excitement about what they had planned, and she would be expected and welcome. But today, aside from feeling a little warm from the walk, her pervading sense was of fear. She had struck out directly after breakfast so as to maintain her nerve, with no time to write and ask for a moment of the Dowager's time. And besides, there was every chance she'd ask her to stay away, and she would have been denied this chance to, if not resolve things, at least allow the truth to be heard on her terms.

The bell clattered through the house, and she felt sick hearing the footsteps beyond, forcing a smile to her face so that she could pretend to the butler that everything was perfectly all right.

'Mrs Wood,' the footman said, with only a hint of recognition on his otherwise blank face. 'M'lady is not expecting you.'

'I know,' she said. 'But I was passing and . . . Would you mind asking if she might see me?'

He looked at her for a moment, then pulled the door wider. 'I shall confer with M'lady.' She stepped over the threshold with a nod.

'Thank you,' she said, settling herself awkwardly into a chair beside the vast display cabinet glittering with treasures, hoping that Solange wouldn't suddenly pass by and see her before she had had a chance to speak with the Dowager. Her fingers turned in her skirts and she took breath after breath to quell her churning stomach.

At last, after what felt like an hour of ticking silence, she heard footsteps ricocheting off the marble floor somewhere in the house; brisk, male footsteps, and the footman returned, his face unreadable.

'M'lady will see you now,' he said. 'Allow me to take your cloak.'

She hesitated, having forgotten that she was even wearing clothes, and unwrapped her cloak quickly, passing it to him in a bundle. 'Thank you,' she said, patting it into his hands, and set off down the corridor. 'She's in the . . .'

'Allow me,' he said, rearranging the cloak into a neat parcel as he stepped before her, taking the lead in the direction of the garden room. 'M'lady,' he said, when they arrived, sweeping the door open. 'Mrs Wood.'

She swallowed, took a breath and stepped into the room. 'My lady,' she began, finding her almost immediately in the window seat, an embroidery hoop resting in her lap. 'I'm sorry to call unannounced . . .'

'Mrs Wood,' she said. 'I trust you have recovered from yesterday evening's exertions.'

The door closed behind her with a click that jangled her nerves, and she took another moment to settle herself.

'Mrs Wood?' the Dowager said. 'Are you recovered?'

'Yes,' she said. 'Yes. Indeed. And you?'

'Me?' said the Dowager. 'Why on earth would I need to recover?'

She paused. 'It was rather an upsetting evening.'

The Dowager waved her hand. 'Oh, that girl,' she said. 'I never trusted her. I said as much to you, didn't I. All show.' She pointed at the cushions on the other side of her window seat. 'Sit,' she said. 'It's lovely in the sun here.'

Mrs Wood moved awkwardly across the room. Where was the disappointment? Where was the anger? 'I was referring,' she said, perching nervously on the edge of the seat. 'I was referring to what Miss Finch said about me.'

'About you, dearest?' The Dowager looked at her, confused.

'Yes,' said Mrs Wood. 'That I am Thirza Thwaite's daughter.'

'Oh, that,' said the Dowager and, to Mrs Wood's surprise, she gave a dismissive laugh. 'Let's not dwell on that silliness.'

'But,' Mrs Wood continued, holding the Dowager's eyes with her own. 'You need to know that it's true,' she said. 'Thirza Thwaite *was* my mother, and you, of all people, must remember who she was.'

The Dowager gave a shrug. 'I'm sure I saw her a few times about town, but I've seen plenty of Mediums, dearest.'

'But she was exposed,' she said. 'She was exposed as a fraud.'

'So many of them are,' said the Dowager. 'I'm sure it was a terrible thing at the time, but . . . It was a long time ago, Mrs Wood. Why should anyone be concerned about that now?'

Mrs Wood turned in her seat, leaning forward in earnest. 'Because I lied to you, dear friend,' she said. 'I kept from you that I was the daughter of a fraudulent Medium because I was terrified that you might think that that fraud extended to me.'

The Dowager gave another laugh. 'But why should I? I've known you for years and you have never been anything but true to me.'

'I hid who my mother was.'

'Dearest, we all have secrets.' She gave a conspiratorial smile. 'With all those you see in private, I think you probably know that more than anyone.'

She looked at her. 'You aren't disappointed?'

'Disappointed?' she said. 'Why should I be? I have never seen anything questionable in the things you do. I believe in you, Mrs Wood. And a less than honourable mother can't shake what you have proven yourself to be in my eyes. You are my Medium, dearest. I believe in you.'

She sat back, unable to speak. Stark spindles of naked wisteria scraped against the glass behind her, and somewhere from the garden she could hear the snip-snip-snip of a gardener at work.

'Now. Mrs Wood.' The Dowager put her hoop to one side and leaned forward, taking one of Mrs Wood's hands in her own. 'Dearest. It's been so long since you've visited me. Would you think it awfully rude if I suggested a little séance now that you're here?'

'You want me to host a table?' she said. 'Now?'

'Solange is around somewhere and I'm sure Lady Harrington will be home before too long. I know they'll be delighted to see you. Your exposure of that girl last night was all they could talk about in the carriage home.'

'You still want me to be your Medium? After everything?'

'Why wouldn't I?' blinked the Dowager. 'I believe you are the best Medium in town, Mrs Wood. That's all I need to know.'

She watched as the Dowager made her way to the door, calling for her staff to ready her séance room and bring tea while they waited, as she sat in the window seat, reeling behind her serene facade.

After everything she had done to keep the secret hidden, everything she had given to the girl to keep the truth out of her patrons' ears, the truth hadn't mattered at all. After everything, they simply didn't care.

And suddenly she heard Thirza's voice, as clear as a bell.

The truth's not important, Vi. If people want to believe, then that's just what they'll do.

Excerpt from the Editor's Column
Magnus Clore
Spiritual Times, 5th February 1874

The scandalous exposure of Miss Emmeline Finch has been addressed elsewhere in this edition. I will, instead, concentrate on more pleasant affairs.

In particular, I would like to express my deepest gratitude to our very dear Mrs Wood. Not only was she a gracious and generous host, as ever, but in the face of Miss Finch's fraudulent tyranny, she continued to deliver extraordinary Mediumship. We all left her exquisite home reminded of why she is considered the best Medium working in London, nay England, today.

I must implore you, dear Mrs Wood: bring back your Grand Séances! I think we all understand why the hiatus at the end of last year, but we trust that you are fully recovered and we shall be entertained, inspired and moved at your tables once again very soon.

I know that I speak on behalf of everyone within the community today when I say: you have been missed!

CHAPTER 42

THE EAST COAST OF AMERICA
1876

The crossing had been unimaginably awful. Absolutely nothing like the White Star posters had promised. Mrs Wood enjoyed no easy ambles along a deck or sumptuous suppers. There was no relaxing on reclining chairs beneath woollen blankets or stargazing from the bridge, and she didn't encounter a single quoit.

Instead, all Mrs Wood saw was the inside of her cabin, with its four oppressive walls growing relentlessly closer as she gripped white-knuckled to the metal sides of her ever-shifting bed.

Eliza, on the other hand, was in her element. Rolling easily with each dip and lurch of the ship as though she were made of ball bearings, describing five-course meals and what larks the other girls in steerage were. She knocked every morning with a jug of fresh drinking water and another laundered nightgown from the ship's service, and after helping Mrs Wood change into it she would ball the soiled old one into a cotton laundry bag, sling it over her shoulder and head off, telling her what she was going to eat for breakfast as she went.

While Eliza had the time of her life, she spent her days staring at the walls, watching the circle of light from the porthole slide from one side to the other, Eliza returning every so often with biscuits or more water or, on one occasion, a green cocktail with an egg yolk bobbing about in it like a great yellow eye that, she said, one of her new friends swore by for biliousness.

It did not have the desired effect and after nine endlessly grim days, the ship finally docked in New York and she had to stymie tears when her foot touched the still-rolling but at least solid ground of Castle Gardens.

Coming to America had been Miss Newman's idea. She had sensed Mrs Wood's listlessness after the exposure of the girl. As the months rolled on, Mrs Wood pretended that everything was fine, but she found it increasingly hard to attend to the worries of those men and women who had forgotten her so easily. She had always assumed that the trust was one way: that society's trust in her was at the heart of her success. But after their abandonment, their swift about-turns felt hollow and she realised that for all her concern about cultivating their trust, they had disabused her of her own. She would look at her host across the table and feel a chilled distance. To them, nothing had changed. There was still the Dowager and her beloved family, of course, but as much as she would have liked she couldn't see them more than once or twice a month for appearances' sake. And so, she had returned to Mrs Pepperdine's home, who was as magnanimous as ever. Mr Yurick turned up for private consultations without missing a maudlin beat. The entire Green family – minus Mr Green, of course – had thrown a party as if nothing had happened.

But it had. As the weeks turned into months and her world began to feel like a chore, she realised that after all they had done, it was she who would never be able to forget.

She wondered too about the girl. If she had recovered somewhere else. After she had been bundled out of the door of her séance room, she was so rarely referenced in public it was as though she had never existed. Did they really not give her a second thought? Was she the only one who twinged each time she recalled what had happened to the girl that night, picturing her saturated in brandy like Thirza, scratching about in some seaside slum? Was she the only one who found it so hard to keep the guilt at bay?

Miss Newman had suggested America over lunch one summer's day in 1875, when Mrs Wood had the start of a cold and had cancelled her work for the whole week.

'A new place will do you good,' she had said over chicken and Jersey royals, her brand-new baby wrapped against her in a way that reminded Mrs Wood of fieldworkers. She had assumed that when Miss Newman and George, the radical writer, married, Miss Newman would have been too old to reproduce, but there she was: Baby Laura. A tiny, helpless thing, as compact as a broad bean with a head like a boiled sweet.

'But what would you do?' Mrs Wood had asked. 'I suppose you could always leave the baby with George. He can get a nurse . . .'

Miss Newman had laughed. 'I wasn't talking about me, Violet. I couldn't leave Laura even if I wanted to.' She patted the lump in the shawl. 'And I have my work.'

'You're going to carry on with all that?' Mrs Wood had said in surprise. 'After . . .' She pointed at the baby with her fork and Miss Newman laughed again.

'*Especially* after . . .' she mimicked the fork pointing at the baby. 'I have her future to fight for now, don't I. Anyway,' she said. 'If anyone should go with you, it should be Eliza. She's proven herself, don't you think?'

Mrs Wood had sat back in her chair. She was right. Eliza had stepped into Miss Newman's shoes after she had retired to first Hampstead and then George. It had seemed a logical move: Eliza knew more than anyone else about what went on in the séance room at 27 Chepstow Villas. She had more than proved her discretion, and she was, it transpired, smart.

As Mrs Wood had grown more selective in the people she worked with, her diary was far from full and so Eliza had time to get to grips with the more sophisticated techniques. She took her into the Circle first, everyone but Mrs Hart welcoming her as though she were a new pet, and she sat quietly in the dark learning cues and routines. The hardest thing Mrs Wood encountered was teaching her how to walk without being heard in Whitechapel and not to tug at her new clothes like a bear in a dress, but while she pretended that she couldn't have cared less about her promotion, Eliza clearly revelled in being admitted into Mrs Wood's world. And excelled.

Mrs Wood felt vindication for enduring her all these years. She had been right to keep her around, after all.

One of the only good consequences of Miss Newman leaving had been the ease on her finances, but with Eliza stepping up she required a larger wage and the pinch had started all over again. The ships were delivering a steady income as they docked one by one over the year, but they did not give her returns at the level of the mine, and they did not come with Mr Larson attached. He visited her only once after that night at the Wornington Mission Hall, surprising her on a bright March morning, but he had not come for her apology; he had come to ask if she might give permission to excuse himself from his promise to Mr Wood and marry Mrs Jupp. She had swelled with emotion – that despite everything, he was still a man of great integrity. But too much had passed between them for their friendship to be rekindled and she pressed a kiss on his cheek along with her agreement, knowing that this would likely be the last time she would see him.

So, when Miss Newman suggested the trip to America, the idea gradually began to take hold. After all, apart from friendship which would be there on her return, what did she have to stay for. Perhaps a tour of America, visiting new homes, meeting new people would help her see a way forward in London.

And suddenly, as though rolling down a steep hill, she was

booking tickets and acquiring a nice family to rent her home; retiring Cook to her nephew's in Essex and selling Mr Wood's library to fund everything. Most of her Circle wept on the last day that they met, pressing tokens into her hand to keep her safe on her travels, apart from Miss Brigham, who gave her a battered old canteen that had been her father's and a thump on the back, and Mrs Hart who asked for Mrs Wood's address book as a gesture of goodwill.

The night before she and Eliza left, 27 Chepstow Villas closed up and, their trunks already on their way to Liverpool, the Dowager threw such a lavish leaving séance for her that Mrs Wood couldn't help but worry that Solange had received one of her premonitions and they were quietly sure that her ship was going to sink.

And then she was vomiting for a week in a small white cube, cursing Miss Newman and her terrible, terrible ideas.

But, eventually, after a millenia, they had sailed into New York and that evening she had looked out of their hotel room onto the hot, teeming streets and felt a strange sense of euphoria.

America loved her. She travelled from home to home, lauded as not just a great Medium but a kind of nobility. She liked that Americans weren't afraid to ask direct questions – 'Tell me about the girl who did the spirit!' was a regular point of interrogation – and that, while they were intrigued by possibilities, what they enjoyed more than anything was a good, old-fashioned séance, especially when the guest of honour spoke in that beautiful regal accent of hers.

Mrs Wood was in her element.

After time in New York with the Dowager's friends, she stayed with the Rosebournes in Boston for Christmas and New Year, thrilled by deeper snow than she had ever seen in her life, while Eliza fell in love with, and then broke the heart of, the son of a nice Catholic family who lived in the tall brownstone across the road.

They performed apports and materialisations of objects. Mrs Wood was hugely active around ceilings and, with spring bursting through while they were in Connecticut, she even made it into a few trees, showering herself and her guests with soft pink blossoms.

Miss Newman had been right. She felt alive for the first time in years.

At the beginning of May, seven months into her trip, she and Eliza caught the train from New York to Philadelphia, where they were to stay with one of Mrs Rosebourne's cousins, Miss Deborah Andrews. They were collected from the station, weary from the journey and ready for a bath and bed, Eliza falling asleep with her mouth open in Miss Andrews' carriage within seconds of settling back on the plush seats.

Mrs Wood looked out of the window at the streets lined with huge buildings, each as elegant as St Paul's. She would never tire of how different the East Coast was. The light was yellower, the days ending more abruptly. Trees grew taller than she had seen in London, and the streets were wider and straighter. She couldn't imagine a day when she wouldn't delight in the rolling accent that purred and curled around each syllable, making familiar words brand new. And she would always remember how friendly they all were. She could smile at a stranger without any fear of repercussion.

Miss Andrews lived in Chestnut Hill, an affluent neighbourhood of mansions and oaks on the edges of the city. As the carriage pulled up outside a house made of gables and shutters, Mrs Wood could see immediately that there would be no early bed: the windows glowed like Christmas and she could see people, lots of people, milling about inside.

She poked Eliza in the ribs. 'Quick! Do something with my hair,' she said as Eliza opened one irritated eye. 'The house is full,' she said, nodding out of the window.

Eliza sat up yawning like a navvy and shook the sleep from her head. 'I'm not sure I can do anything that'll redeem this,' she said,

taking an escaped hank of Mrs Wood's hair between her fingers.
'*I'm* not the miracle worker.'

Miss Andrews was a very different sort of host to the ones they
had grown accustomed to on the East Coast. She owned no pets
(not even a cat), wore straight skirts and talked about suffrage at
every opportunity. After months with kindly matrons and excitable
wives, the wry tongue and impassioned speeches from Miss Andrews
felt so refreshingly familiar that, to Mrs Wood, it was a little like
coming home.

After the shock of the impromptu séance for eight the
previous evening – *Word got out*, Miss Andrews had whispered
over a quivering plate of asparagus in aspic. *They wouldn't take
no, I'm afraid!* – Mrs Wood and Eliza enjoyed a restful night,
then, after breakfast, Miss Andrews proposed a visit to a friend
a few streets away.

'She has been going on and on for days about this surprise she
has for you,' their hostess said, pulling on her hat.

'Is it another séance for eight?' Mrs Wood said, enjoying the
comfort that had grown so quickly between them.

'Twenty, I should imagine,' Miss Andrews said with a wink.

They talked of suffrage most of the way, prompted by Eliza
commenting on a gold ribbon that had been wrapped around the
brim of Miss Andrews' hat which, Miss Andrews explained, was her
nod to the universal suffrage movement.

'You remind me very much of a friend,' Mrs Wood said at one
interval when Miss Andrews paused for breath.

'I do?' Miss Andrews asked.

'Yes,' she said, walking on, her heart warmed at the thought. 'The
very best kind.'

'Good,' said Miss Andrews. 'I hope that means we're set to be friends too.' Mrs Wood gave a quiet smile. She did so like the American way of speaking one's mind. 'Here we are,' her host continued as they turned off the main street onto an avenue lined with budding chestnut trees and great, turreted homes. 'Mrs Bryson's is the third one down.'

Mrs Wood waited a moment before she asked, as lightly as possible, about the surprise Miss Andrews had mentioned earlier in their conversation. Surprises in unfamiliar homes weren't necessarily helpful to her work.

Miss Andrews made as though she were weighing it up. 'Well, all right,' she said, eventually. 'But don't let on I've said anything. She's such a sweetheart,' she said. 'Mrs Bryson, I mean. She's forever collecting all these waifs and strays wherever she goes. And – well – she has one staying with her now. An *English*woman.'

'Ah,' said Mrs Wood. 'I think I can guess what the surprise is now.'

Miss Andrew's gave a sideways smile. 'Apparently she's been a little homesick recently. Mrs Bryson thought you'd cheer her up.'

'So, the surprise is for her guest rather than for me?' she said with hidden relief. Good. One less thing to worry about.

'Oh no,' she said. 'There's a surprise for you too: the guest is another Medium. Imagine!' She gave a conspiratorial smile. '*Two* English Mediums at a table in little old Chestnut Hill. I bet even New York couldn't top that today.'

The *other* English Medium was standing in the shadows of the front parlour, a room made gloomy with drawn shades and too much furniture. But even at a distance, the gold of her hair and the line of her neck as she stooped to stoke the fire – it could be no one else.

Eliza knew it too and she reached for Mrs Wood's arm, her rough fingers tightening as Mrs Bryson squeezed past them and rushed into the parlour.

'Miss Chepstow!' Mrs Bryson said. 'Miss Chepstow, your surprise is here!'

The woman turned and as Mrs Wood moved into the light, the English Medium took a step back and her face flashed with momentary horror. 'Didn't I tell you it would be good!' Mrs Bryson was saying obliviously. She reached out for the woman's elbow. 'Miss Chepstow. This is your surprise. This is Mrs Wood!'

Mrs Wood held the girl's eyes. 'Well,' she said. 'The pleasure is all mine, dear girl.'

'Do you love your surprise?' Mrs Bryson asked.

'I do!' the girl exclaimed, recovering in an instant to become full of girlish glee. 'Mrs Bryson, it *is* a lovely surprise! I am so spoiled!' she said in a voice that had become even more refined. She strode forward, her hands outstretched. 'Are you *the* Mrs Wood? The one I've read about?' She turned to Mrs Bryson as she took Mrs Wood's hand in hers. 'Is this really *the* Mrs Wood?'

The girl's vice-like grip was the only tell that she was feeling anything but joy.

'It is,' said Mrs Wood. 'And you must be Miss . . . ?'

'Chepstow,' said Miss Finch, without a flinch. 'I must say, this is a real treat.' She pulled her hand away, her eyes not moving from Mrs Wood's. 'A real surprise.'

'Isn't it,' said Mrs Wood.

'Chepstow?' said Eliza suddenly, and Miss Finch's eyes flashed as she recognised her.

'This is my assistant,' said Mrs Wood, holding steady. 'Miss Timms: this is Miss Chepstow.'

Miss Finch held her hand out awkwardly. 'It's very nice to meet you . . .' she paused. 'Miss Timms, did you say?'

Eliza stared at her hand before she took it, squeezing it hard so that Miss Finch's fingers turned white. 'Have we met before?' she said.

Miss Finch laughed, retrieving her hand. 'I have one of those faces.'

'She's teasing,' said Mrs Wood, glancing at Eliza. 'You're teasing, aren't you.' She looked back at Miss Finch. 'We had a long day yesterday.'

'They came straight from New York,' said Miss Andrews.

'Did you see the flowers in Central Park?' said Mrs Bryson. 'They're so beautiful in spring.'

'They are,' said Mrs Wood, her eyes on the girl. 'Quite . . . unforgettable.'

They stood for a moment more before a clatter from the back of the house called Mrs Bryson to attention. 'Well,' she said. 'I thought we could have some *elevenses* before the séance to get to know each other.' She smiled brightly. 'That's what you English ladies call it, isn't it? *Elevenses.*' She sighed happily before starting down the corridor. 'Follow me, ladies, I've had it all set up in the garden room.'

'Excellent!' said Miss Andrews. 'Come on, everyone! Let's have some elevenses!' And she turned to follow Mrs Bryson, who had already disappeared into the back of the house, calling: 'What is an elevenses, dearest? Is it a kind of pastry?'

Mrs Wood caught Miss Finch's arm before she could move and they stood like statues, waiting for the sound of Miss Andrews' footsteps to fade away, their eyes locked together. The girl's face was rounder, her waist less girlish. She wore her hair in a simple chignon and her dress was a modest buttoned grey. But she was still Miss Finch in the set of her jaw and the fire in her eyes.

'Chepstow?' Mrs Wood said. 'Original.'

Miss Finch spun around, closing the circle so that only they could hear. 'Don't you dare ruin this,' she hissed. 'Do you know how long it took for me to recover from what you did to me in London?'

She laughed. 'What *I* did?'

'I lost everything, thanks to you.'

'I warned you that trying to run before you could walk was dangerous, Miss Finch. But you wouldn't listen.'

'Was that any reason to ruin me? How is London these days? Are you the toast of the town again, now I'm not around to challenge you?'

'What're you doing here?' Mrs Wood said.

'What I should still be doing in London,' she spat. '*Working*.'

'Is that what this is?'

'It's not what you think. She's a kind woman.' Her face softened a fraction. 'She's been good to me.'

'And what do you get in return?'

'I do tables and readings for her and all her friends, and she lets me live here. I have my own sitting room.' She sensed Mrs Wood's judgement and crossed her arms, ruffled. 'What else was I supposed to do when you had me run out of England?'

'That weren't what happened . . .' said Eliza, and they both started, having forgotten she was there.

Miss Finch glared at her. 'What's *she* doing with you?' she asked. 'Where's Miss Newman?'

'I'm Mrs Wood's assistant now,' said Eliza.

Miss Finch smirked at Mrs Wood. 'Lucky you,' she said.

'She's doing very well,' said Mrs Wood, surprised by a bubble of pride. 'So, you came to America.'

'I couldn't very well stay in England, could I?'

'But your mother?'

'She was no help,' she said. 'All she wants to do is sit around and wait for whatever fella she's set her cap at to come home from the pub. That's no life,' she said. 'Not for me.'

'Well, you've clearly found something better here.'

Miss Finch bristled. 'It wasn't *easy*, Mrs Wood. I didn't walk off the ship and into this house. I had to work the worst kinds of tables before Mrs Bryson found me.'

Mrs Wood didn't doubt her for one moment. She knew this girl.

She knew what she was prepared to do. But despite everything – the shock, the damage the girl had wrought to her financial security, the pain she had delivered by bringing back her mother – all she could feel when she looked at the girl in her nice dress in this nice house with a nice patron, was *relief*. All those fears she had held for the girl had been wrong. Seeing her in this house, clothed, warm, fed, sober . . . she was simply, and overwhelmingly, glad.

She reached out suddenly and took the girl's hand.

'Well done,' she said, while Miss Finch looked back, startled. 'You've survived. I don't know why I ever doubted that you wouldn't,' she said. 'But you have survived.'

The girl blinked. 'Of course, I have,' she said.

'Miss Chepstow?' Mrs Bryson's voice came down the passageway. 'Will you bring Mrs Wood?'

And the girl whipped around, leaning in with sudden urgency. 'You won't tell them, will you? About me. This is all I have,' She gave a panicked swallow, holding onto Mrs Wood's hand as though it were a lifeline. 'Please,' she said. 'Please don't say anything.'

Mrs Wood couldn't help but smile. Here she was on the other side of the world with Miss Finch, of all people, begging for her help again. It had been three years since that chilled February day when they had sat together amidst the doilies of Tilly's Coffee House and the girl had pleaded to become her pupil. Three long years. How much had changed. She herself was rounder, greyer, more inclined to groan when standing, of course, but with a start she realised then how those concerns that had driven her back then were no longer concerns at all. How terrified she had been of the turning tide of popularity, the knife edge she had been forced to teeter upon out of fear of financial ruin.

And the girl was changed by the years too. There were no wide-eyed blinks or dimpled glances: she had sloughed the child-like softness that had so entranced the likes of Humboldt and

Clore and become a woman of angles and hollows and neat, sober attire.

But the ambition was her constant – the unbridled fire of it shone through with as much potency as the day they had met.

And even after everything, Mrs Wood couldn't help but feel that tug of recognition: a connection between one survivor and another.

The girl's hand gripped hers.

'*Please*,' she whispered.

'Miss Finch,' she said finally. 'You know how tightly I hold on to secrets. What sort of Medium would I be if I didn't?'

The girl collected herself. 'Thank you . . .' she began stiffly, but Mrs Wood gave a twinkle of her eyebrows, and she took the girl's arm in hers.

'Let's not keep our hostesses waiting,' she said, leading the girl in the direction Miss Andrews had disappeared, raising her voice as they walked so that it carried through the house. 'Why Miss Chepstow. How funny that we were *both* at the Queen's Garden Party last year! I thought you looked familiar.'

The girl opened her mouth to speak, but Mrs Wood put her finger to her lips.

'Don't tell me you've forgotten what Thirza taught us, dear girl,' she whispered. 'In our world, illusion is everything.' She placed her hand on the door to the garden room and gave one final smile. 'Illusion is *everything*.'

ACKNOWLEDGMENTS

Firstly, to Lucy Morris, my agent and lobster. Lucy, there is no superlative effusive enough to capture how brilliant you are – as an agent and as a human. And to the cool-headed smarts of Andrianna deLone in the US: I am SO glad I've got you on my side.

And my editors, Katie Bowden and Millicent Bennett: crikey, did I luck out with you two absolute powerhouses. Working with you both on Mrs Wood has been the most incredible experience. And to the uber-talented teams at 4th Estate and Harper including Lola Downes, Niriksha Bharadia, Nicola Webb, Emma Pidsley (that cover!), Katy Archer, Anne O'Brien, Tom Hopke, Tracy Locke and Liz Velez. You've all birthed Mrs Wood in such style. THANK YOU!

Thank you to all of the book bloggers and booksellers who have embraced Mrs Wood from the start: your dedication, passion and enthusiasm for books is so important, especially for debuts, and I'm eternally grateful for all the love you have given to this book.

To my English teacher, Marilyn Kellett of Uckfield Community College. You were the catalyst for my writing and my feminism. Thank you.

I have the best writing friends in Frances Quinn and Kate Clark: without Fran there would be no beginning, without Kate there would be no end. Quite literally. Much love and thanks too to my extended circle of Amy Hoskins and Clér Lewis.

Beyond thanks to the Curtis Brown First Novel Award judges, especially Tracy Chevalier: without your faith in Mrs Wood this would be another 20k in the bottom of a drawer. And to the Red

Name Tags, my fellow shortlistees who are, without exception, disgustingly talented and BWF4EVA: Chikodili Emelumadu, Carrie Nelson, Darren J Coles, Debra Hills, Heather Cripps and Dawn Beresford.

To Louise Dean and Tash Barsby at The Novelry: I could never have done this without either of you. Thank you! And to the team at Curtis Brown Creative, especially Anna Davis, Louise Weiner and Rufus Purdy.

I have spent my life surrounded by funny, creative, smart, *brilliant* women and I am *so* grateful for each and every one of them. Special shout-outs to Sarah Jackson, Sarah Graveling, Polly Holmes, Vicky Meadows, Jules Nutland-Frankel and Sophie Johnson. Not forgetting the mums: thank you Maureen Jackson and Sue Graveling for your readerly influence.

Special love and thanks to Nick Tucker, Emily Hayward-Whitlock, Juliet Pickering and Amanda Preston for the inspiration and advice through the years: look what you did.

To my wonderful father-in-law, John Barker, a man of unparalleled kindness. And to Sadie Barker – queen of the hostess trolley, pitch-perfect mum, grandma and mother-in-law, and the best prosecco Friday partner – you are missed every day.

The mightiest of everything to my sherbet mum, Janet Smallwood, who stuck me in front of her old Underwood when I was six and taught me how to type so I could write my stories faster. My warrior sister, Nettie Woodland, who took me to see both Bros and Prince in concert even though she hated every second (weirdo) and is the force of nature everyone wants on their side. And MASSIVE love to my brother-in-law who I forgot to thank at my wedding. You're ace Rich, and we're lucky to have you. To my Auntie Fi and Uncle John Sawyer whose bookshelves have been a lifelong inspiration to me. Thank you for always asking what I'm reading. And to Maureen Byford: thank you for always asking how I am.

Now to you, Rob. My husband, best-friend and feeder. Blimey.

Me getting this book finished was as much a priority for you as it was for me: you always told me to crack on even when it made your life harder. Come What May, Boo. Obligatory thanks to our tiny tyrants, Arlo and Matilda, who are probably, at this very moment, asking if they can have my phone.

And finally: this book is dedicated to my beloved dad, David Smallwood. My dad was only happy when he was telling a story or embarrassing his kids and he excelled at both. He was a brilliantly absurd wordsmith and a born entrepreneur, always coming up with schemes to exploit my talents. Even the ones I didn't have. Pops: I love you and I miss you. This is for you.

AUTHOR'S NOTE

While Mrs Wood and Miss Finch are constructs of my imagination, they were inspired by the rumoured rivalry between two great Victorian Mediums who were stealing the headlines in 1870s London: Mrs Agnes Guppy-Volkmann and Miss Florence Cook.

Agnes Guppy was born in a working-class street in Hull and brought to London in around 1860, when she was about twenty, by a man who presented himself as both her father-in-law and her grandfather, depending on who was asked. (Any real familial connection is uncertain). Agnes's gift and love of fun quickly drew attention from the right sort of people, but it was when the hugely connected Alfred Russell Wallace (Charles Darwin's scientific partner) became one of her supporters that things really took off. She married twice: first to Samuel Guppy who was a friend of Wallace's and gave her unquestionable respectability; and then, after Samuel's death, to another member of the Spiritualist community, William Volkman. Both men had begun as huge admirers of Agnes's talent and continued to be her greatest champions throughout their marriages.

With her standing secured upon her marriage to Samuel, Agnes became a frequent guest at private Circles and rambunctious parties as well as hosting séances of her own. An ambitious and fearless performer she developed an unrivalled ability to apport pretty much any object – the feather snowstorm in this book is based on one of her séances, as well as the more mundane fruit, hair ornaments and tea sets.

It wasn't until 1871, however, that she performed the stunt that would cement her position as London's most audacious Medium.

The result of incredible behind-the-scenes engineering, Agnes was apported over the chimneypots of London from her back parlour in Highbury to land in the middle of a séance taking place in Lamb's Conduit Street, Holborn. Reminiscent of D D Home's levitations (but better), the feat led to Spiritualist newspapers naming her 'The Flying Enchantress'.

Interestingly, 1871 was also the year when Florence Cook, or Florrie as many of her male admirers called her, burst onto the scene. Barely fifteen and working from her parent's front room in Hackney, Florence's charm and talent made quick work of securing wealthy benefactors and within two years she was performing full materialisations of her spirit guide, Katie King, in England and the East Coast of America.

If Agnes, faced with Florence's increasing popularity within the more exclusive layers of society, was put out it was understandable: the threat of female youth to an aging woman reliant on popularity within a patriarchal society is very real. But how far that rivalry went is based on a rather toxic bit of gossip from the famed American Medium, Nelson Holmes. Holmes spent a lot of time in England touring the tables so knew Agnes well. Indeed, they had been friends for a while. But, as seemed to happen quite a lot within the community, there was a falling out which led to Nelson devoting a fair amount of time to spreading malicious gossip about Agnes whenever he could.

And so Nelson must've been delighted when, on 9 December 1873, one of Florence's séances descended into chaos when someone attempted to grab the 'spirit' she had just materialised. That someone happened to be William Volkman, Agnes's good friend and future husband. William had been given a seat at Florence's séance in exchange for a piece of jewellery. When 'Katie' appeared during the séance, William leapt up and attempted to pull her towards a light but was swiftly tackled to the floor by her supporters, losing half his beard in the process.

The scandal was given a shot in the arm when Nelson wrote to another famous Medium, the levitator D D Home, professing that he could hold the secret no more: apparently Agnes had once told him she felt threatened by Florence and that someone needed to throw vitriol in her 'little doll-face' to end her career. Home, possibly as irritated by Agnes's talent as Nelson was, promptly leaked the letter to the Spiritualist newspapers. Something I'm sure Nelson Holmes had no idea would happen ...

Of course, Agnes strenuously denied the allegation and there is absolutely no evidence that she ever said such a thing or even had anything to do with the assault at Florence's séance in 1873. Indeed, William was always adamant that he had been enacting his own experiment and Agnes had nothing to do with it. Perhaps it was the influence of Agnes's well-connected patrons, or the fact she had proven herself to so many of them so many times, that meant that she survived the scandal without any lasting effects. Florence, too, came out unscathed, her supporters seemingly unconcerned by the way the grabbed 'spirit' responded in the confusion. Sadly, though, her fortune wasn't made. By the end of the 1870s Florence had been exposed and abandoned.

When I stumbled across Agnes and Florence's story, it felt like such a rare moment. Here was this incredible, loud and proud sense of rivalry between two women at a time when women had so little agency. Here were two Victorian women who were front-and-centre of their story that was entirely based on their own power and success. My goodness: they were irresistible.

About the Author

LUCY BARKER was the runner-up for the Curtis Brown First Novel Prize with an early partial draft of *The Other Side of Mrs. Wood*. She holds an MA in Victorian studies from Birkbeck, University of London, and has a passion for uncovering the real lives of women from this period. Always a dreamer, Lucy has written stories her whole life and is a Curtis Brown Creative and Novelry alumna. Born in Sussex, she now lives in Bath (by way of London and Winchester) with her husband and two small children.